DRAWN

DRAWN

A ROSE CARVER NOVEL

DAVID ALAN JONES

This book is dedicated to my wife, Deanna, and our children. Without you, I have no words.

1

THE PICKUP

Anna Carver batted the remaining crumbs from table three onto her serving tray with a rag. They fell atop a wadded receipt one of the table's former occupants had used to blot her lips. Crumbs and berry-red skid marks made for a shitty tip, but Anna didn't blame her customers. They had probably planned to leave her a few dollars before they got distracted.

Anna blamed the man at the bar.

People clustered around him, beers forgotten in their limp hands, eyes wide in anticipation of the next climax in his story. He spoke in a rousing voice, one that lilted in just that perfect way to elicit interest from his audience. He smiled and talked and sipped Perrier, reveling in their attention.

The jerk.

Couldn't he see how his antics robbed Anna and her fellow servers of potential tips? Probably not. People like him ignored the help unless the help made a mistake. Then you'd think the world had imploded. Three low-wage waitresses schlepping wings at a sports bar probably meant nothing to this guy. Though every now and again Anna caught him glancing her way.

Later, while running for her life, Anna would kick herself for not

I

pegging him from the start. She should have recognized an incubus when she saw one. But years of slinking from city to city, never once encountering the vaunted boogiemen her father had raised her to fear, had made Anna Rose Carver complacent. She had met her share of succubi and incubi in dive bars and greasy spoon diners. None were operatives of some shadow government bent on ruling her kind. They were just people like her. Nobodies, trying to make it in a down economy.

Anna stopped next to Sherrilyn, the closest thing she had to a real friend these last three months, on her way back from the kitchen. "What are you doing standing around? You've got three tables tonight."

Sherri nodded at two couples next to her without taking her eyes from the man at the bar. "They're tables five and six. Do they look like they're ordering something?"

"What about the guys at seven?"

Sherri glanced over her shoulder. "They look happy enough. Stupid goons didn't order beers after I told them it was buy-one-get-one night. Just steaks and water. Can you believe that?"

Something clicked in Anna's head. She took a longer, more mean-ingful look at the men sitting at table seven. Though handsome, they possessed a manicured plainness that made them forgettable with their close-cropped hair, clean-shaven faces, and identical off-the-rack suits. Matched almost perfectly at average height and build, Anna couldn't distinguish them aside from their hair color: blond and black.

"They didn't order drinks?" she asked.

Sherri shook her head. "Not a damn drop. Must be cops or something."

A tingle of fear coursed down Anna's back. She rubbed her hands on her pants legs, alternately glancing from the suit clones to the guy at the bar. A sea of images floated through her head; all made up, all seeded by her father's paranoia. Men in out-of-the-way places where they didn't belong, watching and waiting. Men with the pungent stink of law about them, but not human law. Society law.

But this couldn't be. Anna chided herself for borrowing fear. Her father had spent most of his life that way, dragging his family across the nation every time a vacuum salesman looked at him funny or a co-worker asked too many personal questions. And here Anna stood, succumbing to the same stupid anxiety. Society didn't care about some waitress in a dive bar in Georgia. So what if she used charm to sweeten her tips every once in a while? Busting her would be like taking down a shoplifter when there were serial killers on the streets.

The couple at table two, whom Anna had hoped would order a few mixed drinks to cap off their meal, stood to join the crowd at the bar, yanking her from her reverie. The guy telling stories seemed to be building to a climax, his audience's laughter coming in more frequent and louder bursts.

"You think he'd go home with me?" Sherrilyn asked.

Anna jumped. "What? Who?"

Sherri rolled her eyes. "The guy at the bar, Matt Snow. I'm gonna ask him before some other girl gets in there."

"What are you talking about?" Anna asked. "You've got a three-year-old at home."

Sherri shrugged. "Aimee will have Tucker down way before I get home. Matt won't even know he's there."

Anna peered at the guy. "He's not even your type. I mean he's, ya know, short. I thought you liked brawny guys."

The look that flashed across Sherrilyn's face could have frozen a glacier. "Either you've gone blind, or you're trying to throw me off. And I know you ain't blind."

The crowd exploded with laughter. Several people nearly fell over, leaning on one another for support, faces red, stomachs hitching, eyes watering. And in the center of it all, Matt's blue eyes found Anna.

He grinned, and a wash of charm rolled over her like hot steam. Her heart raced not from shock or fear as she might have expected, but from a sudden, all-encompassing urge to know this man, to stand in his presence, to never leave his side.

Anna frowned. These were not her feelings. She drew a breath, let it out slowly, and then pulled charm from the only source at her disposal: her family.

Matt's eyes widened. Apparently, he hadn't expected Anna to outcharm him. Did he know her nature? He must have. Why turn his attention on her otherwise?

The fear Anna had earlier shrugged off returned like a thunderclap. Though this Matt Snow wasn't dressed like the guys at table seven—he wore jeans and a collared golf shirt—their appearance together couldn't be a coincidence. Three incubi in a little no-nothing bar in Georgia? Impossible. Her dad had been right.

Time to run.

Anna focused her charm on Sherrilyn. She took her friend by the arms. "Sherri, listen. That guy Matt is trouble. You understand?"

Sherri's eyes glistened, wobbling like orbs of jelly. She nodded.

"You won't remember this in the morning, but he's no good. You understand? Stay the hell away from him."

"Okay."

Matt watched them while bargoers jabbered at him, clapping him on the shoulders, buying him rounds of beers he would never drink. He set his empty Perrier on the bar and started toward Anna.

Anna headed for the back, pulling Sherri along. She stole a glance at table seven. The two plain suits had stood, eyes tracking the women.

Anna dragged Sherri into Pete's office—a tiny, windowless room with a second-hand computer desk, a mini-fridge, and the bar's reinforced back exit. She slammed the office door shut behind them. "I'm not feeling well."

"Sorry." Sherrilyn gazed around as if lost.

"I'm going home early, but I need you to do me a favor first." Anna shot the bolt home on the door, thankful her shaky hands could manage the feat.

"Okay."

Anna spun Sherrilyn to face the back exit. "Drop the bar on the security door the second I'm out. Can you do that?"

Sherrilyn shook her head, frowning. "Pete raises hell when it gets stuck, says the Fire Marshall's gonna fine him."

Someone rattled the office door behind them. Anna ignored it.

"I know, but tonight we need this back door locked down tight." Anna focused more charm on her friend, though she felt horrible doing so, and Sherrilyn nodded.

Something heavy hit the office door. It rattled in its frame but held. Probably the incubi were trying to be discreet. Anna had no doubt any one of them could kick his way inside with little effort, but even with charm, they wouldn't want to draw that much attention to themselves.

Why hadn't they left Matt at the bar? He could have distracted the crowd.

Idiots.

"Sherri?" Anna snapped her fingers before her friend's face.

The older woman looked around from the door, eyes glazed, drunk on charm. "Yeah?"

"The security bar?"

"I'll drop it," Sherrilyn said with a lazy smile. "I hope you get to feeling better."

Anna gave her friend a swift hug. "It was great knowing you." A wash of sadness swept through her. She would probably never see Sherrilyn again.

"Bye, hon."

Anna stepped into a frosty midwinter's night. She hadn't taken time to grab her jacket from the back room, and her bare arms, exposed in her low-cut top, puckered instantly with gooseflesh. Good thing she had worn jeans tonight instead of a skirt.

The security bar screeched into place behind her, and Anna felt a pang of guilt for leaving Sherri with those Society creeps. But they weren't likely to harm a human.

Needing no draw of dexterity, Anna planted a hand on the railing and sailed over it. She landed with a quiet thump that nevertheless echoed in the alleyway.

Had she seriously considered her dad a paranoid fool not twenty minutes ago? The man who had taught her to always wear sensible footwear? She would have to send him something, a thank you, when all this blew over.

Anna considered where to run. Her car? Her tiny apartment that perpetually smelled of kerosene and old cigarettes? Both out of the question. No doubt Society knew about them. She could maybe—

"Anna Rose Carver."

Anna froze, compelled by a sudden flood of charm. It slammed into her like a '78 LTD. Against her will, she turned to find Mr. Popularity, the guy Sherrilyn had called Matt Snow, standing behind her, his face cast in shadow.

The people who had been fawning over this guy in the bar moments ago probably felt like social misfits right now. They believed they knew this man, and wanted to know him better. That desire forged a link strong enough for Matt to steal their charm and turn it against Anna.

"Come with me," he said. "You're in danger."

Anna ground her teeth, drawing charm of her own, battling against his control. "No."

Matt quirked a little half grin. "That's some draw on charm you've got there." He started forward, taking slow, measured steps. "Come with me, and I'll teach you how to get more."

"I don't need more." Anna could feel the limits of Matt's charm. His grip on her weakened every passing second, his influence sloughing away like dead skin.

He drew another step closer, still smiling. "Don't run."

"What do you want? I haven't done anything wrong."

A series of thumps and scraping sounds told Anna that Matt's friends were trying to lift the security bar inside. She had to get away before that happened.

"Did I accuse you of something?" Matt took another step, bringing him close enough to touch her if he wanted.

"Go away," she hissed. Inside her head, she screamed, railing against his control, pushing her charm to its limits.

"Listen to me, Anna," Matt said. His voice quavered. "I'm not part of Society. I'm trying to help you. You're a slinker, so I don't expect you to understand this, but—"

Matt's charm shattered.

Anna attacked.

It had been years since she had sparred with her brother and sister under their dad's watchful eye. He had taught all three of his children, even Anna's older brother Troy, who hadn't inherited the ability to draw, how and when to fight. Though her skills might be a little rusty, Anna figured speed would make up for lost finesse.

She closed the distance between them faster than an Olympic sprinter, intending to land a blistering jab-cross-hook combination. To her surprise, Matt slipped the jab, deflected the cross, and somehow caught her hook, twisting her arm painfully behind her.

"Will you just—" he began.

Before he could finish, Anna drew strength—all she could safely gather—and bent away from his hold on her arm to snag his pants leg and jerk it upward, stealing his balance.

Before Matt even struck the ground, Anna had switched from drawing strength to speed. With perfect timing, she kicked him in the ribs. The blow landed with a sickening crack that sent the incubus hurtling into the brick wall of the Old Siam Restaurant.

Anna froze, one hand clamped over her mouth. Had she killed him? She had forgotten how light incubi could be.

Matt sat up, holding his side. "Ow, dammit. Who taught you to fight dirty like that?" He stood and, leaning to one side, sucked in a deep breath. His ribs slipped back into place with a muffled series of pops.

Anna gaped at him. Had he just healed broken bones in a matter of seconds? Everyone in the bar must be sick as lepers right now unless this Matt Snow had more votaries than the bargoers. A hell of a lot more.

"My dad," she said without meaning to speak.

"Must be a mean son of a bitch."

The sounds of effort behind the security door fell silent. The other two must have given up getting out that way. Anna imagined she could hear them pushing through the crowd to reach the front entrance.

Drawing speed, she spun and dashed along the alleyway onto

Eleventh, which ran straight for a good five blocks before ending at Goldens Foundry. She poured on speed, topping out somewhere around fifty miles-per-hour. The crotch of her jeans started heating up, something they never mentioned in superhero movies. It burned, but she could endure it if it meant her freedom. Or her life.

Anna thought she heard pounding footsteps trailing after her. She couldn't say for certain, with the wind and the sound of her breathing thundering in her ears.

She slowed to make a left-hand turn onto Sixth Avenue, a divided four-lane decorated with trees. At these speeds, course correction became more a matter of leaning into the curve and kicking the ground than simply pointing herself in the direction she wanted to go. And like fighting, it had been years since she had done it.

A squirt of fear raced through Anna's belly. She had misjudged the turn. She barreled across the street—luckily no cross traffic this time of night—nearly losing her footing, and slammed into the back of a Tahoe, crumpling its rear door to the tune of screeching metal and breaking glass. Glancing back, she spotted a figure coming her way: Matt Snow, pelting toward her at highway speeds.

Anna hissed in pain and frustration but kept moving. She limped a few steps before finding her stride, the hurt lessening as she ran, the strident wails of the Tahoe's alarm fading away behind her.

Matt was gaining. She could hear his footfalls clearly now. They grew ever closer despite her draw on speed. She wasn't going to outrun him. She needed a place to hide.

Anna reached the intersection of Sixth and Twelfth and hung a right, this time giving herself plenty of space to slow before making the turn. Twelfth ended at the railway yard behind Goldens Foundry —twenty-five rail lines crowded with freight cars that smelled of diesel fuel, rancid grease, and sawdust.

Perfect.

She raced toward the train cars, sighted one with both sliding doors open, and dove through it. She rolled to her feet on the other side, ever moving, worming her way across couplings and under enormous wheels with preternatural swiftness. She considered jumping atop one of the trains but dismissed the idea. A bright crescent moon hung overhead. Matt and his buddies would have no problem picking out her silhouette against the nighttime sky.

Anna cleared the last of the freight cars and stopped to listen. She could hear someone weaving through the parked trains, but it sounded distant.

Time to hide.

A wooden privacy fence stood to her left. Anna couldn't see what lay beyond it. Good. Drawing speed, she ran at the fence. At the last possible instant, she switched to strength and leaped. She cleared the hurdle by maybe half an inch, and wouldn't have had she not pulled her knees to her chest.

She hit the ground hard and stumbled into the side of a dingy trailer surrounded by heaps of discarded train parts and piles of wooden pallets. She winced at the racket she made, but it couldn't be helped. Hopefully, her pursuers would mistake the direction and wander off.

Anna spun, scanning the near darkness for a likely hiding spot while trying to quell her labored breathing. She started toward a large pile of rusted iron wheels when movement inside the fence caught her eye.

That's when the growling started.

Two Dobermans, full-grown and pissed, advanced on her in the dark, their beady eyes gleaming in the moonlight. Though she desperately needed an infusion of stamina and strength, Anna instead drew all the charm she could muster.

"Hi guys," she said between pants.

Both dogs cocked their heads, ears perking up. Their growls ceased.

"Oh, you're good boys, aren't you?" Anna asked, keeping her voice and her charm high. She leaned against the trailer and slid down to her butt, legs sprawled out before her to catch her breath. The dogs, stubby tails wagging, licked her hands and face.

"Gah, stupid mutts," she whispered, smiling and rubbing their necks.

With the immediate danger passed, Anna drew stamina, replenishing her oxygen-starved muscles, then strength to invigorate her body. Her hands stopped shaking, and she stood, listening hard for her pursuers. The dogs whined and pressed their heads into her hands for petting.

Anna's cell phone rang, and she almost pissed herself. The factory ringtone blared from her back pocket like a vuvuzela amped through a stadium speaker. She fumbled it out with every intention of crushing the thing until she recognized the caller ID.

"Hello," she whispered.

"Anna, what's going on?" Her dad sounded exhausted. "Why do I feel like I've been lifting weights for three days straight? You in trouble?"

"Somebody's chasing me."

"Society?"

"I think so."

"Where are you, hon?"

Anna grew suddenly still. He wasn't supposed to ask her that, not over the phone.

"Wabash County," she said, supplying her end of the coded phrase that meant on the run but safe.

"Stay put," he said, meaning he was in trouble too.

"Is mom okay?" Not part of the code. Anna just had to know.

A long pause. "She's right here with me."

The sound of running footsteps caught Anna's ear. She cut the connection—they had said what needed saying—and gently placed the phone on the ground.

She crouched when she heard the oncoming runner leap toward the fence. Matt Snow appeared silhouetted in moonlight. He landed on his feet, rolled, and came to a stop several yards from Anna and her new pals. He quirked a rather triumphant half smile.

Smarmy bastard.

"Zeus, Apollo," Anna said with more than a little relish. She didn't know the dogs' real names, but these seemed more than adequate. "Attack."

The Dobermans lunged at the incubus, teeth flashing in the night. Matt's eyes went wide, and that smile disappeared.

Anna fled. She had felt Matt's charm back in the alleyway. Though caught by surprise, it wouldn't take him long to subdue the dogs. Best if she wasn't there when that happened.

She sprinted across the enclosure, leaped the other side of the fence, and found herself running along the opposite end of Twelfth Street, headed for Warren Williams Road, her pace faster than any human but slower than before.

Her family couldn't feed her energy demands forever. Surely they were incapacitated by now—too weak to stand, sick from the stamina she had leeched from them, and tired enough to sleep for days. Amazing they had lasted this long.

If they were in trouble, and Anna had taken their strength and speed when they needed it...no, she couldn't dwell on that. If Society had captured her family, that meant she had to save them. They had no one else.

Escape first. Worry about family later.

Anna ran for maybe five minutes, slowing with every step before her draw of speed failed. Maintaining a slow jog, she moved along a poorly repaired blacktop with thick Georgia pines on the left side and an assortment of houses and trailers on the right. Her inner thighs were chaffed to the point of pain. The cold night made her lungs burn and her fingers, nose, and ears ache. She needed to get back to civilization, maybe book a bus or plane, and get the hell out of Georgia.

High beams appeared in the distance behind her. A surge of fear made her heart pound, but she dismissed it. The one guy she had seen chasing her had been on foot, and she had left him miles behind. Catching a ride might be her best means of escape.

She hobbled to the side of the road and stuck out her thumb. She hated hitchhiking. A lot of women disappeared that way, but as a succubus, it posed little threat for Anna. She could charm any pervert out of harming her, and maybe steal a little cash for punishment. The car turned out to be a late model van with government plates. It passed her slowly, then stopped, the driver slewing the mammoth vehicle so that it blocked one side of the road. A sliding door rolled open on the near side, and two men clambered out. They wore black body armor, woolen masks that covered their faces, and helmets with goggles. The first out carried a small machine gun, which he immediately pointed at Anna.

"Anna Carver," said the gun pointer. "You're coming with us."

"What do you want?" Anna's voice shook with fatigue.

"Stand still." The other man held a different sort of rifle. Longer, thinner, and painted neon green, it looked like something out of a sci-fi movie. Anna knew next to nothing about guns, but she stood close enough to see that what he poked into the rifle's chamber was not a bullet, but a dart.

"I haven't done anything," she said. "What's in that? What are you doing? Is that a tranquilizer?"

"Shut up." The guy raised the skinny rifle, sighting on Anna's thighs. She cringed, anticipating a biting sting that never arrived.

Instead, she heard a peculiar series of sounds. First came the distinctive tinkle of breaking glass, followed immediately by a muffled thump like someone smashing a watermelon with a baseball bat. In the next instant, the report of distant gunfire arrived, and the guy with the tranquilizer gun toppled over backward onto the road, a pool of blood, black in the moonlight, spreading below his head.

"Wha—?" was all the second gunman could say before a bullet whizzed past Anna's head, the concussion searing her cheek and buzzing her ears, before biting through his right goggle.

Small bits of glass mixed with something wet and sticky struck Anna as the man fell. Suddenly, she stood alone, two dead men at her feet. She stared at them in horror, mouth agape, hands shaking as the van continued to idle.

Running feet approached. Anna turned to find Matt Snow at her side, gun in hand, a sheen of sweat glistening on his face.

"You all right?"

She nodded stupidly.

"Put the gun down!" said a new voice from the back side of the van. Another black-clad figure stood there. The driver? He held a short rifle leveled on Matt. "Don't think you're faster than me, kid. I've got sixty votaries."

Matt nodded and slowly placed his gun on the tarmac.

"Kick it away."

Matt did so. Then, without moving his lips, whispered, "Distract him."

"What?" Anna asked.

"Don't talk," the man with the gun said. "You." He indicated Matt with the muzzle. "I want your hands on the side of the van. Now."

"Distract him," Matt whispered as he moved to comply.

"I demand to know what's going on," Anna meant to yell, but her voice came out shaky and weak.

"What? Shut up," said the gunman.

"I'm not going anywhere with you." Anna's voice rose as she spoke, gaining conviction. "You're not a policeman. You can't do this."

"Bitch, I don't know who you think you are," the gunman turned so that his rifle sighted on Anna, "but you're about to get—"

Anna never found out what she was about to get. Matt plowed into the guy's knees like an undersized linebacker. The two sprawled against the van's open doorway, Matt raining blows across the gunman's padded chest and goggled face. The guy in black tried to get his gun into position to fire, but Matt simply took the barrel in both hands and bent the chassis. Something cracked inside it.

Matt snapped the gun free and raised it. Moving faster than Anna could follow, he brought it down hard on his opponent's mask. Glass shattered, blood flew, and the guy fell still.

"Is—is he dead?" Anna asked in a small voice.

"No, just out. He'll heal himself when he wakes up. We need to get out of here before then."

"No," Anna said.

Matt tossed the gunman aside like a foam dummy. "I had a feeling you might say that."

"You can't outcharm me," Anna lied. Her family was tapped out, and she knew it. If Matt charmed her now, he would win.

"I know," he said as he bent over one of the bodies. With quick, clever movements, he unstrapped the green tranquilizer gun.

Anna backed away, lifting her hands. "What is this? You just saved me."

"I'm sorry."

Anna tried to flee. If she could dive off the road, maybe put some trees between her and that rifle, she might have a chance at coaxing more speed from her family. Maybe.

Fear like a living thing engulfed Anna. She froze, unable to move, unable to speak. All the world became suddenly bleak and dangerous, full of foul things ready to consume her from the inside out. She tried to scream, to run, to hide within herself. Nothing helped. The fear engulfed her.

Behind her, the tranq gun coughed. Pain blossomed in Anna's right thigh. She stumbled, still reeling with fear, and somehow Matt caught her, lifted her in his arms.

She stared at him, her vision swirling. "What did you do?"

To Anna's surprise, a brief look of shame flashed across the incubus's face. "I couldn't let you run. There will be more of them. We've got to go."

Anna shook her head, her thoughts all sticky like that wax stuff in a lava lamp. She couldn't separate one from another. "No," she whispered. "Not the dart. You made me afraid. You gave me fear."

Matt laid her gently on the van's unyielding floor. It smelled of new plastic and oil and leather. He shook his head.

"I didn't give you fear," he whispered. "I stole your courage."

2

FUGUES AND REVELATIONS

Anna sat upright on a hospital bed in a room that screamed family doctor's office. With its stainless-steel sink, stand-alone wooden closet plastered with neon-colored warning labels, and syringe disposal bag, it rang all the right bells to signal confidence in the medical profession.

Anna hadn't frequented these sorts of rooms much in her life. She could, after all, heal most of her wounds and illnesses by the time she turned eleven. But medical insurance, the golden key to rooms like this, favored stability, a state Anna Carver rarely enjoyed growing up. Still, she recognized the type from TV and movies. It should have made her feel homey and secure. It didn't.

Someone was talking to her. Anna scrunched her forehead, trying to understand the words. She couldn't.

"Water," she croaked.

"Nurse," said a female voice.

Someone pressed a squeeze bottle into Anna's hands. She fumbled a plastic straw to her lips and groaned with relief when the ice-cold liquid hit her throat.

"Anna, my name is Dr. Stanislaw. How are you feeling?" The doctor—a tall blonde dressed in a checkered gingham skirt, silk top, and a white lab coat—peered at Anna with genuine concern. The business end of a stethoscope dangled from one of Stanislaw's overlarge pockets.

"Woozy." Anna shook her head, trying to clear it. Someone had filled it with wool.

"Any idea what was in that dart?" Dr. Stanislaw asked.

"No," Anna said.

"No," said a man in the same instant.

Anna jerked in surprise and twisted around to see who had spoken. She knew that voice. A familiar blond man stood behind the bed. He nodded, and she frowned. She couldn't place his name, or his face for that matter, but a wave of displeasure passed through her at sight of him.

"You shouldn't go shooting women with unknown drugs, Mr. Snow." Dr. Stanislaw's stony expression matched her stern tone.

Snow.

Anna narrowed her eyes at the man—the incubus. He had shot her with a tranquilizer gun. The bastard.

Her anger flared, but just as quickly fizzled out, her emotions cooling faster than they could heat.

Why was she angry? Hadn't Matt rescued her from three Society operatives? Shouldn't she be thankful he had shown up when he did?

"I'm sure you're feeling disoriented, Anna," Dr. Stanislaw said. "But you're recovering quickly. I see no reason to keep you here. Nurse."

The man who had handed Anna the water bottle lowered one of the bed's chrome guardrails and gently positioned her to stand. "Take it slow. If you feel dizzy, sit back on the bed. I won't let you fall."

Anna nodded and stood on wobbling legs. Her head swam. She drew clarity to set it right and came fully awake. Connections she hadn't seen before blossomed in her mind. She felt like someone had stuffed her head with bubble wrap, a feeling she recognized all too well.

"You're charming me." Anna peered at the doctor, then at Matt, and finally even the nurse. "All of you."

"Damn," Dr. Stanislaw said, "you were right, Snow. She is strong."

Matt nodded, a ghost of that half grin playing at his lips.

Anna pulled her arm away from the nurse and drew charm, struggling to overcome the haze in her head.

"Anna," Matt placed a gentle hand on her arm, "you're in no danger here. We're trying to help you."

"Stop charming me," Anna spat through clenched teeth.

"We can't," Dr. Stanislaw said. "I know you're scared. I know you've got questions, and I promise we'll answer every one of them in due time. Right now, though, you need to relax."

"When?" Anna asked.

"When what, dear?"

"When are you going to answer all my questions?"

"Right away." Matt offered her his arm like some lord in a romantic movie, and the charm bashing against Anna's defenses intensified.

Anna grinned at his proffered elbow—absurd gesture, and yet alluring. Slowly, tentatively, she hooked her arm through his. Anna had never dated an incubus; she had never dated anyone really, but Matt seemed like quite a catch. She could get used to taking his arm.

"Get dressed, and we'll go someplace to talk," Matt said.

Anna glanced down, and her cheeks grew hot. She wore a hospital gown that ended mid-thigh, a bra, and a pair of panties. Nothing else. "Where are my clothes?"

"Here." Dr. Stanislaw handed Anna a dark blue polyester tracksuit and a pair of new running shoes.

"What's this?"

"Your regular clothes were ruined," Matt said. "Wear these."

She dressed in a tiny, sterile bathroom while the others waited. She washed her hands and face then stood for a moment staring at her reflection in the mirror, the tips of her dark hair framing her jaw. A voice inside her head demanded she wake up, fight. But she could hardly hear it—a whisper in a gale of charm.

"How are you feeling?" Matt had taken her arm again.

They stood in a wide hallway painted a bland industrial gray. Anna couldn't recall getting here from the hospital restroom.

"I'm sore," she said, "especially this shoulder." She rubbed at a spot high on her right arm and felt a hard nodule there under the skin. It itched.

"Ignore that completely. Forget it," Matt said.

Anna's hand dropped to her side.

Someone, the doctor she hoped, had smeared some sort of goop over Anna's chafed inner thighs. It felt weird but effective. Though the rawness still stung, the salve made it bearable.

Anna drew healing to repair the damage. In seconds, the pain disappeared. Concentrating on her wounds brought back a memory.

Anna frowned at Matt. "You chased me." This mattered. She knew she should feel something right now. Anger maybe? Fear? Charm swept those emotions away, and yet she sometimes caught glimpses of them like rocks just beneath the surface of a churning river.

"You're a real piece of work, aren't you?" Matt gave her a fifty-dollar smile that made her knees go weak. "Relax. Don't think about those things."

They turned corners, lots of corners, and they may have ridden an elevator. Though she felt perfectly lucid at any given moment, time flowed past Anna in fits and spurts, whizzing onward one moment and then slowing to a torpid ebb the next.

She opened her mouth to tell Matt about it, but he wasn't there.

"Do you know where we are?" asked a young woman standing next to her.

Anna jumped. She stood at the back of a large auditorium, the front half filled with chairs, the rear dominated by an enormous buffet table laden with food. Men and women of all ages and races gathered around it. Some ate and chatted, though most stood silent, staring about with baffled expressions.

The girl who had spoken to Anna, a slim redhead who looked seventeen or eighteen, tugged at Anna's sleeve. "Hey. Do you know where we are?"

Anna shook her head.

"I feel really weird," the girl said.

"It's the charm," Anna said, but what did that mean? She tried thinking about charm, but her focus skittered away from the subject like rainwater on a slick windshield.

"My name's Leslie," said the redhead.

"Anna."

"I don't even know how I got here," Leslie said.

"You don't remember?" Anna asked.

"A little. Some guys tried to grab me after class a couple of nights ago. Then that man over there," she pointed at a beefy fellow leaning against the wall, "he brought me here. Well, not here exactly." Leslie trailed off, looking confused.

Anna stared at the man. He stood in a line of at least a dozen others—she couldn't seem to keep a good count—none of whom wore tracksuits like hers and Leslie's. He smiled and nodded before turning back to resume his conversation with the man next to him.

Matt Snow.

Anna tensed. She started forward, intent on confronting Matt. He was doing something to her. She couldn't remember precisely what. Something wrong—an invasion.

She managed two steps and froze. Matt and Leslie's abductor turned their combined gazes upon her. What had she been about to do? It had seemed so important a moment ago.

"You okay?" Leslie asked.

"Yes."

"I keep thinking I should be afraid," Leslie said. "Like, somewhere, you know deep down, I'm scared to death right now."

"Don't be afraid." Anna took Leslie's hand. "I don't think these people are going to hurt us."

"You don't?"

Anna gestured at the table next to them. "You think murderers spring for buffet dinners?"

Leslie's mouth turned up at the corners.

A set of double doors at the back of the hall clicked open, admitting a troop of sixteen men and women dressed in black tracksuits with a sun emblazoned over the left breast. They formed a semicircle around the buffet table. Despite her mental fog, Anna noted the newcomers stood as a wall between her little group and the doors.

An older man, likewise dressed in black, entered. He looked perhaps fifty, which meant, as an incubus, he was likely much older. When he spoke, his voice boomed. "Everyone take a seat."

Anna and Leslie sat together near the front.

Matt and his group filled in the back few rows while the black-suited succubi took up standing positions along the walkway leading to the stage.

"What is all this?" Leslie asked in a hushed whisper. She smiled, her eyes wide with delight. Others in the crowd were asking the same thing, voices rising with anticipation.

Anna felt it too. Crackling excitement. It was like hearing her favorite band tuning up before a concert.

A woman strode into the room, headed for the stage. "That's enough chatter, you lot," she said in a Bostonian accent. "None of you knows enough to do more than spread lies, so stop wagging your tongues."

The room fell silent, everyone's gaze drawn to the newcomer. She wore a pinstriped business suit cut to highlight her sensual figure with a small, silver brooch in the shape of a blazing sun on the left lapel. Though she looked familiar, Anna couldn't place her. A movie starlet? An online content maven? Maybe. She certainly took the stage like a diva, standing poised behind the wooden lectern with perfect aplomb. No microphone graced the podium. She needed none.

"Ladies and gentlemen, my name is Robin Ambrose. I am the de facto leader of Society, or what's left of it anyway. If you don't know what any of that means, you will shortly. We've prepared a short film that will answer many of your questions."

A large projection screen lowered from the ceiling behind the lectern. The lights dimmed, and the image of the older man who had preceded Robin Ambrose appeared.

"Hello," he said with a southern drawl. "I'm retired Master Gunnery Sergeant Roger Earl Lipe. I'm the current head instructor at Camp Den, the facility you find yourself in today. Camp Den masquerades as a military-style weight loss boot camp. In truth, it is an intensive combat readiness course designed for people with unique talents and abilities. In other words, people like you. This may come as a shock to some of you, but if you are within the sound of my voice, you are not, in the strictest sense of the words, a human being."

Lipe's image disappeared, replaced by an aerial view of a compound surrounded by a stone wall at least fifteen feet high. Several steel buildings hemmed in by running tracks, volleyball courts, and other outdoor exercise equipment dotted the landscape. The camera dropped, sinking into a copse of trees, eventually focusing on a group of men and women dressed in blue tracksuits. Rousing music played in the background as they scrambled up ropes, moving so fast Anna at first thought the playback had jumped to double-time. Once they reached the top, which appeared to be several stories high, the group leapt in unison onto a narrow platform maybe four inches wide. Each took up a rifle and fired before they could have possibly taken careful aim.

The image flipped again to show a series of man-sized targets. Bullets ripped through them, piercing crosshairs printed over their hearts. None missed.

Lipe reappeared. "Perhaps you've always had an easy way with people, or you've been particularly gifted when it comes to sports, or you're an incredibly fast healer. You probably thought these were natural traits. They're not. There is a name for our kind—two actually: succubus for the females and incubus for the males. Though, because of historical influence, we are collectively referred to as succubi."

Leslie's eyes had gone wide. She gave Anna a look that asked, *Is this for real?*

Anna nodded.

The image of a young man in a hospital bed replaced Lipe. One of his arms, sliced from biceps to wrist, gushed blood. It ran in rivulets to pool on his bedclothes. Any other time, Anna would have looked away in disgust, she hated horror movies and gross-out videos, but her interest kept her riveted.

"What we do is called drawing," Lipe said.

The injured man held out his arm to the camera. A nurse, standing next to his bed, cleared away some of the blood with gauze, revealing new flesh growing beneath the cut at an impossible rate.

The music gained tempo as a series of short videos flashed by. They showed succubi performing incredible feats like pacing a car traveling nearly a hundred miles an hour, leaping over obstacles far higher than their heads, and lifting weights that should have crushed them.

"Oh my God," Leslie whispered.

The video switched back to a close-up of Lipe's face. "We are not like regular people. Our abilities make us unique, and that makes us targets. Throughout history, our numbers have been few compared to humankind. Secrecy has been our best defense against discovery. That is where Society comes in.

"Unfortunately, a coup occurred three months ago in the highest echelons of Society. Several powerful members of the ruling body seized control and declared their word law. This cadre of traitors calls itself the Indrawn Breath. They believe succubi should rule this world. They have every intention of launching a war against humankind. And they have the might of the United States military at their disposal."

Several people in the crowd began to murmur, but Robin Ambrose shushed them.

"We few gathered in this room are determined to see Society forged anew," Lipe said from the video screen. "It isn't an easy task, but ours to accomplish. And with your help, we can do it."

The image panned out, revealing a bright green lawn with majestic trees behind Lipe. He stared into the camera, and right into Anna's soul. "Welcome to the Order."

3

———

VOLUNTOLD

The lights came up as Lipe's face faded to black.

"Ladies and gentlemen," said Robin Ambrose, who had resumed her position at the lectern, "please separate yourselves by sexes. Men move to the right-hand wall, ladies to the left."

Anna hurried to comply, Leslie at her side.

"Are they going to teach us how to do all that stuff in the video?" Leslie asked as she and Anna joined the growing ranks of women against the wall.

"Looks that way," Anna said.

"This is awesome."

Anna nodded. It was awesome. More than awesome. She couldn't wait.

A couple of women dressed in black tracksuits divided the women into two groups. A raven-haired one, who looked like a supermodel ripped from current tabloid headlines, took charge of Anna's group.

"Follow me," she said in a thick Texan accent. "And no stragglers."

Three more women, likewise dressed in black, chivvied Anna's group out the rear doors into a mild January morning blazing with sunlight.

Everybody groaned, shielding their eyes.

"God, the sun's up already?" Leslie scrunched her face against the sudden brightness.

"No talking." One of the women in black glared at Leslie.

Anna nodded her agreement at Leslie the instant the woman looked away. It felt like the middle of the night to her as well. Where had the hours gone?

They crossed a flat field covered in crabgrass to a dirt running track hemmed in with dogwood trees. Several men and women dressed in blue tracksuits jogged the course, sending up puffs of dust in their wake.

The dark-haired woman leading Anna's group stopped next to the track and turned to face her charges. She smiled, a fetching expression that went nowhere near her stern brown eyes.

"My name is Gloria Torres. I am your head draw sergeant. What does that mean? It means I'm your momma for the next twelve weeks. It's my job to make sure you serve the Order to the utmost of your abilities."

Anna shared a look with Leslie. The younger woman still appeared excited. Anna felt that too, but her enthusiasm had waned. Something strange was happening here.

"Most of you look scared," Torres said. "The rest look pissed. I understand that. I felt scared my first day. Nobody tells you shit, and what they do say makes no sense. You keep thinking, *'I didn't volunteer for this mess.'* And you're right. You didn't."

Anna nodded. She sure as hell hadn't volunteered to join some succubus army. And that's what this was. An army. She hadn't seen it before, but now it was coming clear.

Torres's gaze fell on Anna. "What's your name?"

"Anna Carver."

Torres's eyes narrowed. "That's *Anna Carver, Sergeant.*"

"Anna Carver, Sergeant." Anna met Torres's eyes. She refused to look down.

"I peg you for the pissed group, Carver. Am I right?"

"More scared, Sergeant."

"No." Torres shook her head. "No, you're pissed. You don't want to be here. You don't want to listen to me, or anybody. You don't give two shits who runs Society or the Order so long as they leave you the hell alone. Isn't that right?"

Blood rushed in Anna's ears. She had a sneaking suspicion the sergeant had singled her out as an example for the group. Anna could play that game.

"Yes, Sergeant."

"Good," Torres said. "Being pissed is fine. Shows you got backbone. I like backbone, Carver. That is, I like backbone right up until it makes you stupid—makes you think you can be insubordinate toward me, toward the command. You see, in the military—and believe me, ladies, this is the military—you can either volunteer or be voluntold. You happen to have been voluntold to join our little fight. Some people—maybe even you, Carver—think being voluntold means they're exempt from committing to the cause."

"No, Sergeant, I—"

"Some people think they can ignore orders, slough off, lay around on their bunks and malinger. Is that what you think, Carver? Or are you the type who believes she's too good for the Order? The kind of succubus who uses her charm to get her way in this world. You're the one Matt Snow brought in last night?"

Anna nodded without thinking. Part of her wanted to draw speed and run. It was her natural inclination. But something else, a desire deep within, foreign and yet compelling, wanted nothing more than to please Torres. It left Anna's mind whirling, scrambling for a satisfactory answer while she stood mute.

"Speak when I'm addressing you, female!" Torres shouted.

Anna jerked in surprise, but Torres's outburst at least helped her find her voice. "Yes, Sergeant. Matt Snow brought me here, Sergeant."

Torres flashed her a winsome smile. It made Anna think of toothpaste commercials and piranhas. "Yeah, Snow said you've got a wicked draw on charm—said you overshadowed him when you went one-on-one. That true?"

"Not exactly, Sergeant. I—"

"You want to try your charm on me, Carver? You'd like that, wouldn't you?"

"No. I never—"

Torres stepped forward. She stood two inches taller than Anna but bent so their noses almost touched. Her breath smelled of cheap coffee. "Turn on the charm, Carver. Make me forget my name. Make me give you a foot massage."

One of the other recruits, a svelte blonde with the sort of face and figure that made other women hate her on principle, snickered.

Fine. If Torres wanted a lesson in charm, she would get one.

Anna gathered charm from her family. She got less than usual, which gave her pause. Where were her parents? Her sister? Her brother? The familial link that made her powers possible unfortunately couldn't reveal their location or even their health. But the energy they supplied had weakened, which told a story on its own.

Anna shook her head. Time for that later. Right now, she had a draw sergeant to contend with.

Gathering what charm she could, Anna broadcast it in every direction. A surge of satisfaction passed through her when Torres's smile softened into something slightly warmer than glacial ice.

Anna's fellow recruits succumbed to her charm as well. Their stiff postures relaxed, their folded arms fell to their sides. For one enduring moment, Anna thought she had won. She even had time to briefly contemplate what she should do with the charmed draw sergeant. Maybe a foot massage wasn't such a bad idea.

Then the three other succubi in black moved to stand next to Torres, and the sergeant's smile melted into a scowl. Her eyes narrowed.

Anna stumbled back, but it was too late to escape. Torres snatched a handful of her hair, jerking her head painfully to one side.

"Think you're something special, don't you, Carver?"

"Stop. You're hurting her." Leslie took a step toward Torres, green eyes intense.

The others wore similar expressions of outrage. Several of them appeared ready to pounce on the draw sergeant.

"Drop your charm on them before I get mad." Torres gave Anna's hair a yank.

Anna released her charm. The gaggle of women backed away, looking confused.

"If you ever try that again, I'll put your head through a wall. Understood?" Torres asked.

"But Sergeant, you said—"

"Understood?" Torres's voice blasted from her lips like an air horn. It made Anna's ears buzz.

"Yes, Sergeant."

Torres released her grip on Anna's hair. Expressionless, she turned to the blonde who had laughed at Anna. "You, what's your name?"

The young woman snapped to attention. "Valerie Satterfield, Sergeant."

"You have military experience, Satterfield?"

"I was in the ROTC program at U of U, Sergeant."

"What happened? Couldn't hack it?"

"Three Society bastards tried to kidnap me from the campus a couple of nights ago. An Order operative saved my life."

"Who?"

"Tanner Watts, Sergeant."

"Watts is a good man. Okay, Satterfield, you've got ROTC experience, that makes you squad leader. If I'm the momma around here, you're big sister. You enforce my rules and make sure these ladies work as a team. Got it?"

"Yes, Sergeant."

A group of men led by black-suited male draw sergeants lined up next to Anna's group. They looked as confused and charm-fogged as Anna felt.

Torres spoke with one of her male counterparts for a moment then turned to address the group.

"Every morning you will do calisthenics. You will not draw to increase any aspect of your physicality. If you are caught drawing to enhance your physical training, you will repeat the entire exercise. Is that understood?"

"Yes, Sergeant," said the men and women together.

"Then let's begin."

They started with a mile run. Anna considered asking for an exemption—she had run across most of Columbus, Georgia, last night, after all—but dismissed the idea. Why give Torres another reason to notice her? Besides, she had healed her inner thighs, and a short run would probably do her sore muscles some good.

Anna had been Crossfitting for years. Most towns, even small ones, had a box. It had been one of the few stable things about her life since she had left home. She never used her powers during a workout and prided herself on doing the work as prescribed.

Nonetheless, she ran at the center of the pack to avoid trouble. Others in the group, both men and women, flagged early, some even walking. The walkers got screamed at by every draw sergeant on the field.

After that, they did push-ups and sit-ups in teams of two, one counting while the other did the work—twenty-five of each, no sweat for Anna. She hardly felt it. Still, she took her time, letting others earn the top spots.

Finally, Torres led the group to a set of free-standing pull-up bars on the south side of the field. They were expected to complete five in one minute. Anna did three. She took pride in her acting abilities on the bar, dropping off and struggling to finish another rep several times before giving up.

Torres called everyone to attention on the grass next to the track. It took some screaming from the sergeants, but they eventually managed to stand in something resembling a formation.

Torres stared at them long enough for the silence to grow uncomfortable. "You all saw how pathetic you are. You've lived the average American life, eating crap and swilling crap, which has turned you into crap. And now the Order tells me it's my job to put a shine on you." She shook her head as if overcome with the enormity of her task. "Sergeant Dawson, take these people to the barracks. I don't want to see them for a while."

Dawson, a dark-haired succubus, got the company moving back

toward a set of steel buildings across the track. Anna started to follow, but Torres stopped her.

"Carver, get over here. You too, Satterfield."

Anna and Satterfield stood before the draw sergeant. Satterfield put her arms behind her back. Anna copied her. Two other draw sergeants in black tracksuits remained behind as well. This could not be good.

"Is there something wrong with your body, Carver?" Torres dipped her chin, face serious as if she were genuinely concerned.

"No, Sergeant," Anna said slowly.

Suddenly, Torres was in her face. It took everything Anna had not to flinch. "Then why the hell were you running like a weak bitch on my field?"

"I didn't—"

"You gonna give me excuses? You gonna say you finished with everybody else? If those are the next words out of your mouth, I'll break your jaw."

Anna swallowed. She felt caught out, like a mouse under a swooping owl.

"From this point on, you will give me your all on every exercise we attempt. You will never hold back like this again, or I will personally kick your ass across every square inch of this field. You got that, recruit?"

"Yes, Sergeant," Anna screamed the words, taking a smidge of pleasure from the slight jerk of surprise Torres gave her. What did the woman expect, a fight? Anna wasn't stupid. Did Torres think Anna would say, "Screw you, Sergeant, I'll do what I like?" What would that accomplish? Nothing but trouble. Slinkers didn't survive by being bold or arrogant. They bided their time, hid in the shadows, and ran when their chance came.

"Have you got an excuse for your poor performance today?" Torres asked.

"No, Sergeant. I have no excuse."

Without switching her gaze, Torres said, "Satterfield."

"Yes, Sergeant."

"I'm making Miss Carver your personal project for the next twelve weeks. In addition to all your other duties, you are to make it your number one priority to see that this female works at her highest capacity. Because, if I think Carver is ever giving me less than her best effort, I must assume you're doing the same. And I'm gonna take it out on the both of you."

"Yes, Sergeant," Satterfield said.

"In fact," Torres said, "I think I'll start right now. You see, I know Carver can do more than three pull-ups. She's got at least twenty in her. And if she's got twenty," Torres turned her dark eyes on Satterfield, "you've got twenty."

"Yes, Sergeant," Satterfield said.

"Draw Sergeant Blithe and Draw Sergeant Whidby are staying behind to monitor you, which means you're cutting into their lunch time."

Anna glanced at the two succubi, who glared back in return.

"Now, get to work," Torres said.

4

BESTIES

"This had better not happen again, Carver," Satterfield said as they jogged behind Blithe and Whidby toward the steel barracks.

Anna said nothing, though it pleased her that the beautiful squad leader struggled to keep up. The extra pull-ups had been murder on Satterfield. She had completed them only by having Anna lift her legs, and even then, she had been incapable of doing twenty in one go. She took several rest breaks, during which the draw sergeants screamed at her to get back on that bar, before she finished.

"You ignoring me?" Satterfield tried sounding tough like Torres but failed since her words came out in a wheeze.

"No."

They slowed to a walk as they neared the building.

"Your barracks is through the front door and on the right," Whidby said, pointing. "Don't get lost."

With that, she and Blithe headed for an identical steel building a block away.

Anna toyed with the idea of running. She could draw speed and never look back. Satterfield certainly couldn't catch her, and she saw no black-suited draw sergeants in the area.

But then what? The walls surrounding this place had looked high as a baseball backstop in the video Robin Ambrose had shown them—a backstop a couple of feet thick and made of sheer stone. Anna could never scale them without something to hold onto, and she couldn't hope to leap that high.

Besides, she was safe here. She belonged here.

"No." Anna shook her head against the deluge of charm threatening to drown her. Even without a bevy of draw sergeants crowded around, it felt like a forty-ton weight on her shoulders.

"What?" Satterfield looked annoyed, probably more at her lackluster performance on the pull-up bar than at Anna's outburst.

"Nothing."

The barracks door swung open, and Leslie nearly ran them over. Her green eyes went wide. "You two better get in there. Sergeant Torres asked if you were back four times already. She looks pissed."

"Where are you going?" Satterfield drew herself up, spine straight, like a general inspecting a soldier she finds wanting.

"The platoon's forming up for some kind of training."

Platoon? Anna rolled her eyes. Did Leslie even know what that meant? Anna didn't. "I'm not running another lap."

"We're not. At least I don't think so. Sergeant Torres said we're going to a building called Links. Anyway, all the other girls are done showering. They're getting dressed. I'd catch up if I were you."

"Then get out of our way," Satterfield said, brushing past Leslie.

Leslie sneered at the squad leader's back, gave Anna a quick smile, and headed off to wait on the grass in front of the barracks. Several more women spilled through the door to join her.

Why were they all following along with this insanity? These people couldn't force her to join their army. Kidnapping transgressed human and succubus law. She pulled open the barracks door with every intention of telling Torres where she could shove her orders and her screaming sarcasm. Anna Rose Carver was no soldier.

Yet, somehow, Anna ended up taking a three-minute shower after which Sergeant Torres screamed her into a fresh blue tracksuit and running shoes. It all happened so fast and so organically, Anna couldn't recall when she had given up on having it out with the draw sergeant.

The rest of the platoon—Anna hated using Leslie's word but didn't know a better one—including thirty men from a neighboring building, was already formed up when Anna exited with Draw Sergeant Torres and two of her flunkies. Newly minted squad leader Valerie Satterfield had ordered everyone into perfect rows from shortest to tallest. Surprisingly, she had even left a spot for Anna.

"Good work, Satterfield," Torres said.

"Should I call cadence, Sergeant?" Satterfield asked.

Torres shook her head. "These people wouldn't know how to march if the Saints were leading them. We'll gaggle our way to Links. Follow me, people, and keep up!"

The building called Links turned out to be a sprawling brown brick edifice at the center of camp. It gave off an aura of governmental oppression that made Anna want to run. Recruits milled in and out of its glass maw. Those headed inside looked fresh, but most of the people exiting appeared mentally and physically wrung out.

Leslie, who stood in Anna's row, leaned forward just enough to give Anna a quizzical look. Anna shrugged.

Torres took a position in front of the platoon on the steps leading up to Links. "Listen up. You are about to be put through a battery of tests to determine your drawing aptitude. You are to respect the people conducting these tests. You will give them your full attention and your utmost effort. Should I see you sandbagging, which is to say, being lazy, not trying, I will smoke your ass until tomorrow dawn. Is that clear?"

Anna joined the platoon in chorusing an enthusiastic, "Yes, Draw Sergeant!"

Torres nodded and led them inside. They stood on a high balcony overlooking a warehouse-sized expanse of cement floor some fifteen feet below them. Men and women scattered throughout the place climbed ropes secured to the roof, bounded over obstacles of varying heights, and lifted objects that appeared far too heavy for their slight frames.

"No time for gawking, people," Torres said. "Follow me." She led them down a gently curving staircase.

To Anna's surprise—whether pleasant or sour, she couldn't decide through the charm haze—Matt Snow stood waiting for them. He wore what Anna thought of as a pilot's suit: a one-piece uniform of blue that zipped up the front and clung to his slim body. His sandy hair looked freshly washed. He gave Anna a smile when he caught sight of her.

"People," Sergeant Torres said, "this is Mr. Matt Snow, one of the Order's top operatives. Mr. Snow will be leading you through your tests. Since some of you have little to no experience with your abilities, Mr. Snow will give you a primer. Give him your full attention."

"I'd give him my full attention," breathed Leslie in a whisper so low Anna barely heard it.

Anna whacked her thigh.

"Thank you, Gloria," Matt said. "Good morning. Like the sergeant said, my name is Matt Snow. Right now, I am serving as an acquisition operative for the Order, which means I travel the US and Canada locating succubi and incubi. It's my job to find you before Society does."

Someone in the crowd gave a low groan.

"Who was that?" Sergeant Torres scanned the recruits, eyes intent. "Carver, was that you?"

Anna's heart lurched. "No, Draw Sergeant."

Matt grinned, but otherwise ignored the interruption. "Who here knows what I mean when I say draw?"

Most of the recruits raised a hand, including Anna. Leslie shook her head.

Matt pointed at Anna. "Explain draw."

A flush of charm washed over Anna when Matt's eyes fell on her. It didn't dominate her will—it wasn't that pervasive. It felt like soothing steam tingling her skin. She tried to resist it but failed.

"A draw is a link you have to someone you're familiar with like family or friends." Anna felt befuddled, inarticulate. Was that Matt's charm at work on her? It felt subtle, nuanced, almost nonexistent. She had trouble distinguishing where her feelings stopped and the charm began. "It makes it so you can borrow some of this other person's skills or natural abilities or whatever."

Matt quirked that half grin of his at Anna's rambling, disjointed reply. She had an urge to either blush furiously or punch him in his face.

"Right," he said. "Succubi can borrow abilities from other people. We call a person from whom we draw a votary. Votaries are people who have some emotional link to you. Usually, this means your family and friends—people who think of you often, worry over your wellbeing. But they don't have to be people you even know personally. For example, many movie stars, singers, and professional athletes are succubi and incubi. The more fans they garner, the stronger they become. Most of our kind can draw one thing, charm, and they steal that unwittingly. Several major actors in Hollywood today are succubi and they don't even realize it."

"He's kidding, right?" Leslie whispered.

Anna shrugged. Her dad had always said that, but she hadn't believed him.

"We call succubi who draw charm alone monodraws," Matt said. "They are the most common of our kind—all succubi can draw charm. Polydraws can tap into other attributes like speed, mental acuity, that sort of thing. But we all differ in efficiency. Some might draw enough from one votary to double their speed, while others would need dozens to match that level. Either way, the more, the merrier because drawing from one votary limits your power. Once the votary is tapped out, the succubus loses the draw."

Leslie half raised her hand. "Can we ask questions?" She looked to Sergeant Torres.

"Of course," Matt said.

"These people we're stealing from—"

"Votaries."

"Votaries. Does it hurt them long-term what we're doing?"

"No. They grow weaker in whatever trait you draw while you're drawing, but the effect is short-lived, especially if it's spread across dozens or even hundreds of people."

"Is there any limit to the number we can have?" asked a man in the back.

"None we've found. Some famous succubi have millions of fans, all of whom they use as votaries. But there is a limit to how much you can draw at once."

"What does that mean?" Leslie asked.

"Take me for example," Matt said. "I have dozens of votaries—it's bad manners to ask how many someone has if you didn't already know that. Anyway, it seems logical that I might command the strength of say fifty men, but I assure you I do not. I can bench about fourteen hundred pounds max."

Several in the crowd whistled at that.

"It sounds like a lot, but compared to some members of the Order, that's paltry. No matter how hard I try, I can't draw more than that. It's my limit."

"So, what good is having more votaries?" Satterfield asked.

"Sustainment. I have no control over how I draw from my votaries. The power supplied to me is spread equally across the entire group. So, the more I have, the less each individual must contribute to keep me fully drawn."

"What sorts of things can you draw besides charm and strength?" Leslie asked. The redhead's green eyes shown with interest.

Before Matt could respond, Sergeant Torres said, "We'll cover that later, Phelps. Enough questions. I'm sure Mr. Snow would like to get started."

"The sergeant's right." Matt checked his watch. "We've got about five minutes left, and I still haven't spoken about the two types of polydraws. I'll cover them, and then it's time to start your tests."

Matt glanced around, seeming to search for the thread of what he had been saying. His eyes fell on Anna, and he gave her a tiny grin and nod.

"First, a polydraw is any succubus or incubus with the ability to draw more than mere charm. The skills vary and seem to have no rhyme or reason. A child might draw enhanced eyesight while both parents draw strength. The ability to draw seems to follow bloodlines, not the type.

"The first sort of polydraw, while usually able to access several different traits, summons them one at a time. We call this type 'sings,' for single.

"The second type, a rare breed, are called 'simes,' for simultaneous. These folks draw two, three, even four traits at once. A sime might draw strength, speed, and healing all in one go."

Anna looked a question at Leslie. She had never heard such a thing growing up. Succubi could draw more than one trait at a time? And powers beyond what her father had termed the six pack: strength, stamina, speed, dexterity, clarity, and healing?

"Who knows, one of you might even be a sime." Matt's gaze fell once again on Anna.

Leslie gave her a sly smile, which Anna ignored.

"That's why we're here, people," Torres said. "I'm going to break you into groups of five. A draw sergeant will lead you through various drills, testing your abilities. I will lead one of the groups. But if I hear that one of you disrespected your assigned draw sergeant, I will come down on you like a cattle drive. Is that clear?"

"Yes, Sergeant," sang the platoon.

To her surprise and relief, Anna wound up in a group with Leslie. The young girl, while in no way stupid, displayed utter ignorance when it came to all things succubus. Anna felt sorry for her and, though she knew it wasn't so, responsible. Leslie wasn't much older than Anna's sister, Melody, a senior this year, and a good kid from what she knew of her. It had been four years since Anna had caught up with her family, and she felt estranged from her kid sister. Perhaps that was why she wanted to protect Leslie.

Torres assigned each group to a bevy of sergeants she called up from the training floor. With each name called, Anna's heart sank a little. By the time Torres reached the fifth name, it was clear she intended to lead Anna's group.

"Oh, God," Leslie whispered.

Anna nodded as imperceptibly as she could.

Torres turned to eye Anna's group. "And that leaves me to watch you lot." She locked eyes with Anna. "Satterfield!"

"Yes, Sergeant?" The gorgeous succubus came to attention in front of her group.

"Why are you not in Carver's group?"

"You assigned me to group B, Sergeant."

"Did I not command you to take on the care and feeding of Ms. Anna Carver as your special project this morning?"

"Yes, Sergeant."

"Then get your ass out of group B and join C."

Satterfield sprinted to Anna's group. She held her face expressionless, but her cheeks were rosy, her ears flaming red.

"This just keeps getting better," Leslie said in a low whisper meant only for Anna.

Satterfield glared at Leslie, and the younger woman blanched.

"Get to your stations, people," Torres said to the assembled groups. "Time to see what you can do."

5

———

POLYDRAW

orres and a couple of her black-suited assistants led Anna's group to a small parking lot behind Links, leaving the rest of the platoon inside. She climbed aboard a golf cart parked there while the other two corralled Anna and her fellow recruits into a loose formation.

"Follow me! But no drawing," shouted Torres as she got the cart buzzing down the main road that sliced through the middle of Camp Den.

Anna followed along, but she wanted to stop. Not just the running, this entire succubus boot camp thing. What the hell was she doing here? Why follow these people around like a trained dog? Had she forgotten everything her dad had taught her growing up?

Anna's pace faltered. Where was her family?

"Anna?" Leslie slowed to a walk, head tilted to one side.

Anna stared at the people flooding past them, intent on chasing after Torres. "This isn't right. We're all being duped."

"Keep moving," said one of Torres's assistants. She put a hand on Anna's shoulder, pushing her to resume the jog. A wave of charm accompanied her words. "You need to catch up. You want to do well at this trial."

"No," Anna said, but her body ignored her mouth and started jogging.

"I think this will be fun." Leslie matched Anna's stride.

Anna glanced back at the draw sergeant running behind her, uncertainty clouding her mind. The woman smiled, a pleasant enough expression, but one that brooked zero insubordination.

"I'm sorta excited," Leslie said. "Maybe all this is real."

"It is," Anna said, her voice morose.

They jogged four blocks to a long, steel-framed building. The sign outside read: Indoor Track and Fitness Center.

The building contained a quarter-mile track complete with painted running lanes and long straightaways. A foam pad more than a foot thick covered the wall at the far end of the track. A similar one covered the wall on the entrance side where the track curved sharply. The patchwork of disparate colors—blues, greens, and reds—indicated portions of it needed regular replacement.

"Find a lane and get ready," Torres said. "Your orders are simple. Draw speed and win."

Her two assistants jogged to the end of the track while the group sorted itself out on the lanes.

"Sergeant?" Leslie said.

"What, Phelps?"

"I don't know how to draw."

"You get it, or you don't, Phelps."

Satterfield bumped Anna's shoulder as everyone jockeyed for position. "Stay out of my lane, Carver."

"Ignore her," Leslie whispered.

Anna nodded.

Leslie gave Anna a mischievous grin. "You know, I'm on the track team at school."

"Oh?"

"Yeah. Don't feel bad if you end up watching my ass."

"I'll try to keep up," Anna said, giving in to a smile of her own.

"Get ready!" Torres shouted. She had procured a stainless-steel clipboard and a starter pistol from the cart. She held the gun aloft. "Set."

Anna tensed. Would she be able to draw speed? How would Torres react if Anna failed because her family had nothing left to borrow?

The gun banged. Leslie surged to the front of the pack with a thin, dark-haired incubus. He looked about Leslie's age, maybe nineteen. The two ran with the artless grace of youth, fleet and beautiful.

And slow.

Within five steps, Anna caught and passed them. Speed had always been her most natural draw. She reveled in its power, pleased that it should come so easily at her call. Whatever had befallen her family, they were at least well enough to act as her votaries.

Unfortunately, Satterfield also had a good draw on speed. She, and a man who looked to be in his mid-thirties, matched Anna stride-for-stride. Their turnover rate doubled and then tripled, shoes slapping the asphalt with a sound like tiny thunderclaps.

Anna poured on the speed, pushing herself to still greater effort. The wind lashing at her tracksuit sounded like gunfire. Lungs and legs burning, she pulled ahead of the others as they neared the finish line.

Then her speed slackened. Not all at once, else she would have lost control, but quickly. The others rushed past her, Satterfield in the lead.

Anna crossed the finish line and plunged into the track's foam pad in third place. The rest of the field, Leslie and her young running mate at the fore, arrived several seconds later moving slow enough to stop on their own without the pad.

"Lose your concentration?" panted the older man who had taken second place after Satterfield. He had a friendly smile. "You had me beat till you slowed."

"Lost my draw," Anna said.

"That sucks, 'cause you're fast." He held out a hand. "Garret Timmons."

"Anna Carver."

"Not bad, people," Sergeant Torres said. "About what I expected."

Anna spun in surprise. It seemed Torres had a powerful draw on speed as well.

Torres wasn't looking at Anna, but the way she wasn't looking made Anna's stomach tighten. She hadn't missed Anna's slowdown at the finish line.

"Satterfield, Timmons, and Carver," Torres said, "you're all clearly able to draw speed." She made a notation on her clipboard. "Phelps, Hanks, and Moss, you're fast, but not draw fast. The rest of you are so out of shape you might as well be round. We'll fix that."

Leslie looked disappointed. Moss, the young man who had run beside her, shrugged. Hanks, a thin but hale-looking woman with gray in her otherwise black hair, nodded.

"Everyone fallout back to Links." Torres hooked a thumb at the exit. "We're testing dexterity next."

The recruits started for the door.

"Not you, Carver," Torres said.

Anna inwardly groaned. What now? She barely fended off a frown to keep her face impassive.

Garret gave her a concerned look. "Have fun."

Leslie acted as though she would stay, but Anna waved her off. Moss and she left together.

With the others gone, the building fell silent. For the first time since Matt Snow had shot her with that damned tranq gun, Anna felt almost free. And something else, something even more revelatory, occurred to her.

"You're not charming me," Anna said in a low voice. "No one's charming me."

"I'm dropping my Sergeant Torres face for five minutes. We need to talk."

Anna smelled a trap. "Sergeant, I didn't lose on purpose. My votaries gave out."

"I thought for sure you were going to crash and burn when your speed started to fail," Torres said with a nod.

"You believe me?"

"I was already reaching for my radio to call the medic station when you drew dexterity and righted yourself."

"I—what?"

"You don't know you're a sime," Torres said, marveling.

A sime? Anna hadn't even known what that meant until this morning. They sounded like mythical creatures, something out of a comic book like vampires and unicorns. "Respectfully, Sergeant, I think you're mistaken. I lost my draw on speed and I slowed. I'll admit it was tough to keep my balance, but I didn't draw dexterity with speed. I wouldn't know how."

"Only a sime can run as fast as you, Carver. Without added dexterity, you would run slightly faster than an Olympian. But you, Satterfield, and Timmons were pushing seventy. If you hadn't been drawing dexterity the entire time, we'd be cleaning scraps of you off the track right now. Snow told me you had to be a sime."

"He did?" Anna felt a stupid flush of pleasure at hearing Matt had talked about her and immediately chided herself for it. What was she, thirteen? She couldn't have a crush on the guy who had delivered her to succubus boot camp against her will.

"He said he had a hell of a time catching you, and he's one of the Order's best takers. He thinks you've got amazing natural talent, and I agree."

Anna glanced at her draw sergeant. In the few hours they had known one another, Anna had developed an intense dislike for the woman, but this new side of her was, if not pleasant, at least agreeable.

"Why are you telling me this?"

"I don't have much draw on discernment," Torres said. "Just a twinkle, as my grandmother used to say. But it doesn't take much to tell you're not onboard with the Order. And you're fairly resistant to charm. Those two things make you a flight risk."

Anna said nothing.

Torres grinned. "I'm going to say something I don't want to say, Carver, so listen carefully. Simes like you are valuable. We need you. But here's the rub: you need us just as much. More really. I don't think you get that."

"May I speak freely, Sergeant?"

Torres nodded.

"I'm not here to serve you or your Order. I'm here because one of your people kidnapped me. I don't care about your secret war. It has nothing to do with me."

Torres watched Anna for a long moment, her brown eyes intense. "I get it. Believe it or not, until a few years ago, I was just like you, Carver. My family hid our secret—hid it from everyone, even ourselves. My grandmother tried to keep her children from realizing they were different. When none of her daughters could draw, she assumed the power had died out in our line. Then I came along. I was nine when I started excelling at sports. I broke every track and field record at school—elementary, middle, and high. That includes the ones set by boys. I had my life planned. I would go to the Olympics and win gold in every event I cared to enter, and then spend the rest of my life on Wheaties boxes.

"Then the men in suits showed up. They told my parents I had committed internet fraud, of all things. They tried to take me away. My parents freaked; they were afraid of government types—Hispanic people haven't always had the best relationship with U.S. law enforcement. They didn't want to hand me over, but as far as they knew, I had broken the law. I ran."

"How old were you?"

"Sixteen." Torres's eyes took on a faraway look as if she could draw sight into the past.

"What happened?" Anna asked.

Torres shrugged. "I became a slinker. 'Course I didn't know that word back then. I'm a sime like you. That made stealing an easy career move. I spent several months moving from city-to-city in Texas, lost, alone, and scared to death. Then one day I made the mistake of ditching out of a diner in Waco. A sheriff's deputy chased me. Turned out he was fast too—faster than me. He caught me and had my story inside five minutes. I was so lonely, so surprised to meet someone like me, I told him everything."

"He was with the Order?"

"Yeah, lucky break. He could have just as easily been part of the Indrawn Breath." She glanced at Anna. "But you don't see the difference, do you?"

"One oppressive regime is like any other when you're at the bottom."

Torres grunted, then shrugged as if to drop the subject. "Any idea why your speed failed during the test?"

Anna shook her head.

"Same thing happened when you tried to charm me this morning."

"Yes."

"What have you got? Ten, maybe eleven, votaries. Am I right?"

"Four I know of—my parents, a brother, and a sister. Maybe one or two friends I made on the road, but I doubt it. I've always kept to myself. Things are safer that way."

A look of surprise creased Torres's face. "Four? You nearly outcharmed me with just four votaries? Damn."

Anna shrugged.

"Were they all captured by the Breathers?" Torres asked.

"I don't know. I think maybe, yes."

"I'm about to tell you something—something I'm not supposed to tell you, by-the-by. If, after you hear it, you still want to run, I'll drive you out the gate, give you some lunch money, and wave goodbye."

Anna studied Torres's eyes. The draw sergeant looked sincere. "Okay."

"We've seen this happening with a lot of the recruits. Like you, they don't usually have many votaries. And the ones they do have seem to fatigue easier than they should, leaving our people in the lurch. It's like they're being drawn from by someone else, someone who's running them dry."

"How's that possible? I doubt my family feels close to the people who kidnapped them unless they're being charmed into it. But that kind of thing doesn't last, right?"

"It's not supposed to. You can charm somebody into liking you, but eventually, it fails. No one can force that sort of link for more than a day or so. Even if you're charming the person into liking you, the draw you get from them weakens and eventually dies because the bond isn't real. Whatever Society's doing to create these links, it's making them last."

"So, how's this supposed to make me feel like staying? I need to get my family away from these people."

"Think, Carver. You've got a better chance of finding your family as part of the Order than by going it alone."

"Running and doing pull-ups isn't finding my family."

"And you think being on your own out there will be any better? Where are you going to search, Carver? How about FBI headquarters? CIA? NSA? Because we're talking about Society here—succubi with their fingers all in the U.S. Government. And say you do find them, what then? Do you seriously think you can just save them like that?" Torres snapped her fingers.

"What's the alternative? Stay here, getting shit on every day, and wait for the Order to find them? Are they even looking? I'd be better off alone."

Torres rolled her eyes. "Don't be an idiot. The alternative is learning how to draw—mastering it—and then helping the Order find not just your family, but everyone they've taken. Haven't you noticed how many mass shootings we've had in this country lately? Outbreaks of viruses we thought were beat? Not to mention plain old disappearances. They're all on the rise, Carver. You and your family aren't alone in this. Most of your fellow recruits have lost people too."

Anna stared at the track. "How long has this been going on?"

"At least five years," Torres said. "That I know of. Probably longer."

"What did you call these people who tried to kidnap me?"

"The Indrawn Breath. You know, like the old wives' tale about succubi stealing a person's breath while they sleep."

"So, if these Indrawn Breath people—"

"Breathers."

"—Breathers have found some way to charm people into becoming votaries, then why stop at stealing just succubi?"

"They're not. We've seen them take whole families, though they're careful about that sort of thing. They prefer succubi, but it seems like they'll take what they can get." Torres peered at Anna, understanding making her eyebrows rise. "You got family who can't draw?"

"My brother, Troy." Anna's throat tightened on his name.

Torres nodded but kept silent.

Anna looked at the rec center's main door. An unreasonable feeling of claustrophobia passed over her. "I don't like this military stuff. And the charm you're using on us—it's not right."

That brought a smile to Torres's face. "I hated the military part at first, but it grows on ya. As for the charm? Tough. Deal with it."

Anna wanted to run. That had been her first instinct her entire life —a natural inclination her father had cultivated in her. Fighting it went against her entire upbringing. And yet, Torres's arguments made sense, especially the part about taking on the government. Anna wouldn't stand a chance. Not without draw training. And she wasn't likely to find that outside Camp Den's walls. If she wanted to free her family, she needed the Order.

For now, anyway.

"I'll stay," Anna said.

"Good. Maybe you're not a total idiot after all."

Anna grinned. They headed for the exit together.

"I'm going to be Draw Sergeant Torres when we leave here. You understand that, right?

"Yes."

"Sergeant Torres isn't your friend, Carver. In fact, she doesn't particularly like you."

"Feeling's mutual, Sergeant."

Torres smiled as they emerged into sunlight.

6

———————

DRAWING FROM STRENGTH

Three weeks later, Anna sat in the middle row of an extended van, her forehead pressed against the side window, watching an unbroken corridor of Georgia forest slip past. Recruits—twelve in all—crowded the seats with three draw sergeants along for the charm, Sergeant Torres at the wheel.

Joy.

Two more vans, likewise crewed, followed behind this one.

"No sleeping, Carver," Satterfield said from the front seat.

"I'm not sleeping, Satterfield. I'm enjoying all this freedom."

"I wish we could stop at McDonald's." Leslie, who sat next to Anna, bumped her arm.

"God," said Moss from the seat behind them. "I haven't had a fry in weeks. That crap they serve in the mess does not count."

The thin incubus had attached himself to Leslie's hip after their near synchronous trial run on the first day of training. Since then, Moss took every chance he got to sit near Leslie. Though Anna found him strange, Leslie liked the guy. Maybe she was starved for social interaction. They all were. Or perhaps she liked super nerds. Some women did.

Torres turned onto a narrow drive fronted by a wide, well-manicured lawn. A wooden sign at the corner read: Elmwood Retirement Village.

"Are we on some kind of goodwill tour, Sergeant?" Anna asked.

"Something like that," Torres said.

"Oh, this should be fun," Leslie said. "I love talking to the elderly."

Anna didn't share Leslie's enthusiasm. Her grandparents had died in a car wreck before she was born. She had never spent much time with anyone older than her dad, who was now in his mid-fifties. It sounded boring, but it beat scrubbing floors and toilets, her usual Sunday routine of the last three weeks.

Elmwood was a long, brick building with a covered porch. Scads of senior citizens sat chatting on lawn chairs or scooters in its shade.

Sergeant Torres and her male counterpart, Sergeant Jenkins, got the platoon gathered on the front steps in front of the main building. Anna expected a rousing speech about honoring the old folks, but all Torres said was, "Follow me, people."

They entered a waiting area where the nurse on duty buzzed them through a steel security door a hand span thick, three sliding bolts big around as Anna's forearm nestled inside the frame.

"Tell me that's not odd." Moss eyed the bolts with one eyebrow raised.

"Yeah," Leslie agreed. "They must really want to protect their clientele."

Elmwood reminded Anna of an elementary school with its shiny white floors and wooden doorframes. Yellowed military portraits, old covers of *TIME* magazine, and autographed photos of stars spanning every age of Hollywood festooned the main hall. A glossy print of Greta Garbo hung beside one of some svelte, shirtless guy Anna didn't recognize.

"Ooh, Liam Hemsworth," Leslie said. "He's hot."

Moss made a dismissive noise.

Torres ushered the group into a small cafeteria. "I'll make this quick. The residents of Elmwood are succubi and incubi. All of them served Society in one capacity or another throughout their working lives. Many have volunteered to act as votaries for you lot. Your mission today is to meet as many of these volunteers as possible. They will decide if you're worthy of drawing from them. If so, you will be allowed to interact with them weekly for the next month."

Anna shook her head. Leave it to the Order to make finding friends a military operation.

Sergeant Jenkins opened the cafeteria doors opposite the platoon. Dozens of old people, mostly couples, filed into the room, smiling. Anna swallowed, frozen like the proverbial deer in the proverbial headlights. Just what she needed, social interaction with people so removed from her generation they probably thought computers a fad destined to die out.

Leslie and Moss immediately struck up a conversation with a blue-haired woman while Satterfield chatted with a distinguished old gentleman sporting a wire-thin mustache.

Anna folded her arms. This reminded her of every team sport she had ever played back in elementary school P.E. The perpetual new kid, she had always been the last to be picked, if she was picked at all. Often, a coach or teacher would have to force a team to take her.

"Hi there. What's your name?"

Anna spun to find an elderly woman smiling at her.

"Anna."

"That's a lovely name. I'm Renni, and this is my husband, Lee." Renni, who leaned heavily on a four-footed cane, tilted her head to indicate the wizened man standing next to her.

"Howdy," Lee said.

"This is pretty awkward, isn't it?" Renni asked, grinning.

"Extremely."

"Still, it's not so bad. A little forced, but it works. Would you like to chat a bit? We can get to know one another. We might be a good fit for you."

Anna nodded. "Okay."

They sat in the couple's small living area, Anna on a comfy couch, Lee and Renni ensconced across from her in matching glide rockers with padded footstools. Framed pictures of smiling people, mostly children, hung on every wall. Was it strange they should make Anna more uncomfortable than the elderly couple now eyeing her? She had never lived in a house with pictures. Photos were for wallets and IDs.

"How old are you?" Lee bent forward to eye Anna like a connoisseur inspecting a newfound piece of art.

"You don't ask a woman her age." Renni gave her husband a sour look.

"Twenty-four."

"Oh, Lee, she's just a baby," Renni said. "We have a great, great granddaughter your age."

"Got any children?" Lee asked.

"Uh, no."

"Lee Rolston," Renni said. "You're embarrassing the girl. I'm sorry, Anna, my husband doesn't know the meaning of the word couth."

"I've moved around a lot." Anna shifted in her seat, uncomfortable.

"Slinker, huh?" Lee pursed his weathered lips. "You weren't part of Society growing up?"

Anna laughed. "No. My dad says succubi shouldn't be governed any differently than regular people."

"I've heard that one before. If you believe it, what made you join the Order?"

Anna told them of her last night in Columbus, her mad dash from the Society goons who had come into Pete's, and her subsequent capture by Matt Snow.

"So, you think the Indrawn Breath has your family?" Renni asked.

"Yes." Anna would have said more about her family, but her thoughts kept slipping past them.

"That's horrible." Renni sat forward on her rocker, her aged eyes intense.

"Real Society," Lee said, "the one I served for eighty years, is gone. Those bastards in Washington eroded it."

"Lee Rolston, language."

"Sorry, hon." To Anna, he said, "You grew up hating Society, I get that. Kids follow their parents. But I swear, it wasn't what your father thought. Sure, some shady characters tried to lord it over the little guy. That happens in every government. But the people I worked with were honest and hardworking."

Anna kept her mouth shut. She hadn't come here to argue with some old Society loyalist. But her experiences with the Order made Lee's claims ring false to her ears. So what if the people he worked with a million years ago acted nice? That had nothing to do with the present.

"Lee, the girl doesn't want a history lesson." Renni must have seen something of Anna's thoughts spelled out in her expression. "What are you planning to do after you graduate into the Order, Anna? I've heard you can go free after that."

"Not free exactly," Anna said. "We're like reservists. They can call us up at any time; make us fight if that's what they want."

"You don't want to fight?" Lee asked.

Anna suspected her next words would nix the votary idea for the old incubus. "No, I don't. Honestly, I just wish both sides would leave me alone. They can annihilate one another for all I care. I just want my family back."

"That's why you should fight," Lee said. "Not because you love fighting, but because you've got something to fight for. Don't you agree?"

Anna nodded slowly.

"I don't mean to pry, but have you got many votaries, Anna?" Renni tilted her chin down as if confiding a secret, or perhaps eliciting one.

"No. And it doesn't embarrass me. I've always had my family. That's it."

"Just four then?" Lee asked, silver brows raised.

Anna nodded.

Renni turned to him. "What do you think?"

"I think this girl needs us."

Drawing from Renni and Lee came easily for Anna as if their decision to aid her had opened a floodgate of energy. It coursed through her veins, making her heart race. The longer they chatted, the more intense it became.

"Let's give you a test," Lee said after a couple of hours spent discussing family, politics, and whatever other meandering topics the old couple desired. He rose slowly and motioned for Anna to follow.

Despite her usual reluctance to open up with strangers, or perhaps in defiance of it, Anna had spoken freely with Renni and Lee. She had told them about her upbringing on the run, her life slinking from one state to another, and even her involuntary admittance into the Order. Spilling that way had come as a surprising relief. It was as if she had been holding her breath for years and could now finally exhale.

Maybe she had missed out not having grandparents after all.

Lee opened a small closet off the main room. Woefully outdated suits and sports coats hung inside.

"What am I supposed to do with your clothes, Lee?" Anna asked, grinning.

"Not the clothes. That." Lee pointed to a seventy-five-pound dumbbell resting on the floor. "I got it years ago when I could still draw worth a damn. I haven't been able to work out with it in forever."

Anna drew strength and hoisted the weight in one hand. She laughed in delight. It felt no heavier than a bar of soap.

"Bring it to the living room." Lee made a production of introducing Anna as the strong woman in a traveling circus for Renni's viewing pleasure.

Renni clapped and whistled as Anna first pressed the weight overhead; then, feeling braver, she gave it a couple of light tosses from hand-to-hand.

"I remember when I could do that," Renni said.

Anna set the dumbbell on the floor.

"You've got quite a draw on strength," Lee said.

Anna's eyes went wide. "Oh, God, I didn't take too much, did I? Are you okay?"

They laughed.

"You can't hurt us," Renni said. "We've got dozens of children and grandchildren, not to mention friends. You draw from us; we draw from them."

"Besides, if it's too much strain, we can always clench," Lee said.

"Clench?"

"They haven't shown you how to clench?" Lee sounded scandalized.

"Maybe they don't want recruits knowing how, dear," Renni said.

"Wait," Anna said. "Are you saying I can stop another succubus from drawing from me?" Anna stared back and forth between her nascent adoptive grandparents. If true, this could change everything.

"Of course you can," Lee said. "It's one of the first things they should have taught you. It's an essential skill."

"And not just drawing," Renni said. "A good clench keeps others from charming you, too."

"You're serious?"

"It takes someone with wrecking ball talent to charm you out of a clench," Lee said.

"How do you do it?"

"You just—" Lee began.

"Lee, we're going to get Anna in trouble."

Anna gave Renni a pleading look. They had to teach her this. She needed an edge against the draw sergeants even if she never used it. But how to push Renni into relenting? She turned a spotlight smile on her erstwhile adopted grandfather. Lee knew his wife. He would know what buttons to push.

"If we're sponsoring this girl, that makes her family." Lee gave

Anna a decisive nod. "I want her to have every possible advantage. Don't you?"

"Well, of course I do, but—"

"Let's practice with something safe," Lee said. "Draw eyesight, Anna."

Renni let go an exasperated sigh, her eyes rolled to heaven, but she smiled too and made no more protests. Anna got the feeling she had done that a lot in her marriage to the cantankerous Lee.

Anna drew vision and nearly toppled off the couch. "Whoa. It's like I switched to HD!"

"Now you see it," Lee said, "and now…you…don't."

Instantly, Anna's vision snapped back to normal. She drew harder, focusing on the elderly couple, but nothing happened.

"How?" she asked.

Renni, despite her earlier misgivings, leaned forward. "You draw from yourself, that's the trick. Your charm, your vision, whatever you need. It's that simple. If you know how to draw, you know how to clench. Try it."

Renni winked, and the room went suddenly, catastrophically silent.

Anna jumped in shock, frantic at the sudden hush. Then she saw Lee and Renni watching her, looking supremely pleased with themselves.

Renni mouthed something at her. "Clench."

It took Anna a moment to get a feel for what she wanted. Drawing from herself wasn't something she had ever contemplated. But it was no different than drawing from her family. The energy appeared when she looked. She merely had to grasp it.

Sound returned, rushing in on Anna, dislodging the pall of charm that had engulfed her.

"Good!" Renni said.

Anna staggered back a step. A flood of memories and feelings sluiced into her head as if a dam had broken inside her skull.

Lee caught her arm. "What is it?"

"It's the charm." Renni scooted forward on her rocker to pat

Anna's free hand before sliding backward on the return rock. "Or the lack of it. My guess is she's been drowning in the stuff for weeks."

"They keep making me forget." Anna's voice quavered.

"Let go of the clench," Lee said.

"No. I can't. I'll forget everything." She slapped her free hand to her right shoulder and felt a hard nodule there.

Renni's eyes snapped open after drifting closed. "What is it?"

"They put something in my arm."

"A tracker," Lee said. "It's standard these days."

Anna ground her teeth. Had the Order no limits? First kidnapping and imprisonment, and now tracking devices?

"You can't hold a clench forever, Anna," Renni said, her final words slurring a little. "It's dangerous."

Renni was right. A bead of sweat slid down Anna's forehead. Drawing from herself demanded more energy than drawing from others. If she kept this up, she would pass out.

"You know how to clench now," Lee said. "You can do it anytime you like."

"What if the charm won't let me? What if I forget how the instant I relax?"

"That won't happen," Lee said.

"You're sure?" Anna asked.

Lee looked pained. "No. I'm speculating. But I'm certain if you keep clenching, you'll do yourself a mischief. It plays merry hell with your abilities when you overuse it, and you can't draw from someone else while you're clenching anyway."

"Let it go, Anna." Renni stifled a yawn that turned Anna's name into a soft growl.

"They chipped me!" Tears of outrage stung Anna's eyes.

Lee put a hand over hers. "Please, don't hurt yourself. Let go."

Anna ground her teeth but released the power. A soothing calm immediately blanketed her concern and worry, smothering them in a shared grave.

"I take it you've had no contact with your folks since you got to

Camp Den?" Lee asked. His gaze darted to Renni, who had leaned back in her rocker and was now snoring contentedly.

Anna shook her head, hardly listening. She had been worried about something important a moment ago. She couldn't remember what, but it had distressed her.

"They have to keep security tight on Camp Den. Can't have loose lips on cell phones cluing Society into their whereabouts. But it's a bum deal for you recruits. I tell you what. So long as you don't rat me out, would you like to try your folks on mine?" He pulled a phone from his pocket.

Anna's heart quivered in her chest. "Yes! I mean no. I can't do that. It's against the rules." Her gaze skittered off the phone whenever she tried to look at it.

"Clench," Lee said. "Give them a call."

Anna let go a shuddering breath of relief when the clench worked. "Oh, thank God."

The phone rang ten times before the connection clicked and a ubiquitous female voice told Anna the wireless customer she was trying to reach was not available.

"Dammit." Anna dropped her clench. She handed the phone back to Lee without conscious thought.

"They got email?" Lee asked, holding it out again.

"Oh, yeah! I was so focused on calling, I didn't think. But I can't email my family, Lee. There are camp rules..." Anna clenched again. "Damn. I hate me on charm."

"Hurry," Lee said. "You're shaking."

Anna opened a dropbox website and posted a simple message asking her mom and dad to respond. They usually checked it every week or so in case she or her brother, Nate, had something to say.

Shuddering and sweating, Anna released the clench.

"You okay?" Lee slipped the phone from her trembling fingers.

"I will be." Anna hugged Lee. "Thank you."

The old man patted her back. "You're welcome. I promise things are going to get better."

Anna placed a gentle kiss on the sleeping Renni's papery forehead.

"Don't be afraid to draw on us." Lee led her toward the door, a grandfatherly arm about her shoulders. "We're tougher than you think."

"I won't."

"You're gonna need good votaries before this is through. I can feel it."

Anna smiled. "I think I just got some."

7

———

TALENTS

An electronic horn blasted reveille through the barracks. Several women groaned, Anna among them, but all thirty-five rolled from their narrow bunks as the overhead lights snapped on and four draw sergeants came screaming into the room.

"Up, dressed, beds made, five minutes!" shouted one.

"You've already wasted thirty seconds of my time," screamed another.

A third stood over a recruit who had been dilatory in rising. Though the young girl was now hurriedly folding hospital corners into the woolen blanket on her bunk, the draw sergeant bent to scream imprecations into her ear.

Sergeant Torres remained silent. She stood by the barracks door at parade rest, surveying the mayhem with dark, inscrutable eyes.

Anna clenched, and the charm filling her head evaporated, boiled away by seething anger. Her place in the world tumbled in on her as if she hadn't been conscious of it, of anything, before this instant. She knelt next to her designated cot meticulously folding its scratchy woolen coverlet while strangers screamed at her. Other strangers, nefarious, mysterious, and frightening, held her family hostage while she rotted in this cage, a tracking chip in her arm. Fury did not begin to describe the rage coursing through her blood, her heart. She shot Torres a withering look, one that might have blistered the draw sergeant's skin had she been looking Anna's way.

"You've got to stop that." Leslie stood above Anna, putting the finishing touches on her own bunk.

"Stop what?" Anna froze, suddenly afraid. Did Leslie somehow sense Anna's clench? She trusted her friend implicitly—or would have if not for the draw sergeants' charm drowning Leslie's true thoughts. If she knew Anna's secret, the charm would compel her to rat Anna out.

"Stop baiting Torres."

"You mean stop resisting her mind control?"

Leslie shrugged. She understood charm and its effects, having studied them in-depth over the past five weeks, yet she refused to believe the Order would do such a thing to their own recruits. Why bother when their underlying message served the same purpose and with lasting results?

Military training suited Leslie, a fact that surprised her even more than it did Anna. She had taken to life at Camp Den, embracing it and the subsequent brainwashing that came with it. Not that she saw it as such. Never mind that the draw sergeants had convinced her to lie to her parents, telling them she had, on a whim, decided to quit school and join the Army. Life in the Order necessitated that sort of thing. She saw no charm behind it because she would have made that call regardless.

But not Anna. Leslie's father hadn't been a paranoid doomsayer. Anna's had. And she knew charm when she felt it.

"It isn't right what they're doing." Anna pitched her voice just loud enough for Leslie to hear over the tumult of shouting women and scrambling feet. Her hands shook from maintaining the clench. She held it long enough to cast another steely glance Torres's way before letting it drop.

Satterfield yelled the platoon into formation in front of the draw sergeants on Camp Den's sprawling running track.

Anna drew warmth against the cold weather, though she kept it subtle. Recruits weren't supposed to draw outside of regulated hours. Torres had noticed Anna's skin steaming last week and made the platoon do push-ups until they were a quivering, moaning mess.

"If you're cold, you push!" Torres had shouted as she paced through the ranks.

Torres did not pace today. She stood on a wooden platform generally reserved for whoever was leading PT, hands on hips, scrutinizing her platoon. Her breath came out in sugary puffs. Anna suspected she was drawing warmth too.

"Listen up," Torres said. "There will be no morning calisthenics today."

Someone in the ranks gave a short whoop of joy.

Torres hesitated as if she might call that female out, but then smiled. "Oh, you're happy to hear that? Good. I'm glad you're happy because the head shed has something even better than calisthenics. Today, your names are going up on a leaderboard. It seems someone in HQ has decided that what you females need is competition to fire you up. Which means you're gonna spend the next twelve hours going through draw trials to test what you've learned."

Someone groaned. Anna thought it might have been Leslie but couldn't be sure. Either way, Torres ate it up.

"What's the matter, pumpkin?" Torres asked the platoon. "That doesn't sound like fun? Well, you're right, it ain't fun, but I expect every damn one of you females to give your all. I want Charlie platoon at the top of the board today and every day for the next three weeks of this competition. You will excel, and you will win. Understood?"

"Yes, Sergeant," the platoon roared.

"This isn't going to be the puny tests you've been going through the last month. Those were to find out what you can draw. This competition will push you to your limits. It will test your ability to draw under pressure, even under fire, while simultaneously keeping your goddamn brains screwed in behind your eyes. It will culminate, three weeks from now, with a platoon-level field exercise meant to test not only your abilities to draw, but your unit effectiveness, your willingness to take orders, and your ability to lead when called upon to do so.

"This too, you shall win. Is that understood?"

"Yes, Sergeant!"

Against outrageous odds, not to mention years of slinker indoctrination, Anna managed not to roll her eyes.

"Good. The draw trials begin in twenty-five minutes. Platoon leaders, take charge of this rabble."

A ustin Booker, a lanky incubus with a morose face, long thin fingers, and perpetually moist eyes, looked like a dope. And yet after five hours of competition, Austin's name sat firmly at the top of the pure dexterity leaderboard. Anna shook her head in disbelief as she watched him flick a quarter through a soda machine slot from twenty feet away while skating backward on one Rollerblade.

The crowd of recruits roared their appreciation. Anna could see copious amounts of money exchanging hands as Austin's shot put paid to bets around the training area inside Links. Either the draw sergeants didn't notice—unlikely—or didn't care. They were too busy devising ever more fiendish challenges for the final two contestants: Austin Booker and Leslie Phelps.

"You've got this, girl!" Anna shouted from her place at the front of the gathered crowd. The draw sergeants had at first tried to keep the other competitions going, but as Booker and Leslie's trial grew more heated, they had finally given up, suspending all other trials until the clash of the dextos could be determined.

"Everyone back!" shouted Matt Snow. He had taken charge of this contest thirty minutes ago when the other sergeants had run out of good challenges. "We're bringing out live firearms. If you don't want some piece of you blown off, I suggest you move back!"

The crowd shuffled back a few paces, but they were reluctant to go farther. The lights were bright in Links, the smell of sweat pervasive. Anna didn't mind. It reminded her of a gym—not fear sweat, but the odor of people pushing themselves to their limits.

Leslie skated over to Anna, her face drenched, her eyes wide. "We're gonna have to shoot something?"

"You've never shot a gun?"

"No!"

"It'll be okay," Anna said. "My dad taught us to shoot when we were kids. Just aim and fire, control your breathing, and keep your arms stiff. Don't jostle the sights."

"What?" Leslie folded her arms about her middle like a kid who doesn't know what to do with her hands.

"Just shoot whatever target they put in front of you!"

"Okay!"

At Matt's direction, a couple of draw sergeants wheeled out two metal stands with dartboards affixed to them.

Booker had sat down in the middle of the floor studiously unfastening his single Rollerblade when Matt stopped him.

"Get that skate back on. Both of them." Matt turned to the crowd. "For our next challenge, our master dextos must fire at these targets. Sound too easy? That's just what I was thinking. So, let's add some challenge. Phelps, Booker, you're going to skate from one side of this arena to the other, firing at the numbers I call out. And to make sure I've got your attention, the targets will be spinning!"

On cue, both targets started to spin. Fast. The numbers became a blur to Anna. And though she prided herself on her draw of dexterity almost as much as speed, she knew she would never be so accurate as to hit a target that small, moving that fast.

Leslie looked at Anna, fear in her green eyes.

Anna put on a smile she hoped appeared genuine and gave her young friend two thumbs up.

Matt beckoned the contestants to the targets. He gave Anna that little half-grin of his when he caught her eye, which made her traitorous cheeks flush, then turned back to Leslie and Booker.

What was that about? Anna had caught Matt glancing her way on more than one occasion whenever circumstances of training brought them together. Always on the sly, of course, and he looked away quickly whenever she caught him. But was he checking her out?

Yes.

She had been checked out enough as a waitress to recognize the tells. Anna didn't know how to feel about that. It confused her. Matt Snow had brought her to this godforsaken place. Part of her wanted to brain him with a baseball bat. But what about the other part? The part that felt...what...flattered? Camp Den was filled with succubi. Every one of them a freaking supermodel. But Matt Snow checked her out, not them. Petty? Sure. But it felt good. And the man certainly had charm. Not charm in the incubus sense, but the mundane sort that a draw could mimic but never replace: the kind that made Anna's stomach tingle.

He spoke with Leslie and Booker for a bit, then handed each a small pistol. The draw sergeants yelled for the crowd to move still farther back.

Booker went first. He set a blistering pace, head down, skates slapping the wooden floor with a sound like pool balls colliding. His path described a shallow, perpendicular arc roughly fifty feet from the targets.

"Double twenty!" Matt's voice boomed around Links.

Pop. The pistol must have been low caliber, probably a .22. It made a sound not much louder than a BB gun.

The bullet hit the target, and a few people in the crowd cheered, but Anna couldn't tell if Booker had hit his mark or not.

"Bullseye!" Matt shouted.

Pop.

Just as Booker rolled out of range, his angle to the target surely too acute for even an incubus to make, Matt shouted, "Triple seven."

Pop.

Then it was Leslie's turn. She skated from the opposite side of the building. As with Booker, Matt called out three targets by their dartboard positions.

Anna's stomach churned, and her palms grew sweaty. Mentally, she kicked herself for getting worked up over a manufactured competition run by her kidnappers, but she wanted Leslie to win. Booker had grown up in a succubus family. He had known he could draw charm and dexterity his whole life. That made Leslie, who hadn't even heard of succubi outside mythology classes before a couple of weeks ago, a major underdog.

Matt had the contestants take another pass, this time firing with the opposite hand. When they were through, he relieved them of their pistols and sent them back into the crowd.

Leslie skated over to stand with Anna.

"That was a blast!" she said, grinning.

"I bet." Anna hugged Leslie. "You're amazing! I can't believe how deep your draw has gotten."

"Gina has a lot of grandkids," Leslie said. Gina was Leslie's votary volunteer from the Elmwood retirement home.

Matt and the other draw sergeants, there were twenty of them all told, scrutinized Leslie's and Booker's targets for several minutes. A hush fell over the recruits as they watched with ardent anticipation.

Finally, the judges spread out, Matt at the fore.

Leslie took Anna's hand and squeezed it. The younger woman wore a nervous smile.

"This has been one of the toughest dexterity trials I've ever seen," Matt said. "Before I announce the results, let's give our contenders a big round of applause."

The crowd roared their approval. The people nearest Booker and Leslie slapped their backs and shoulders and offered words of appreciation.

"I'm proud to announce the winner of today's pure dexterity trial, with a perfect score of six hits for six shots, is Leslie Phelps!" shouted Matt, holding Leslie's target aloft.

Another roar from the crowd and suddenly hundreds of succubi and incubi were lining up to shake Leslie's hands or pat her arms or offer her words of encouragement.

Even Gunny Lipe, who must have been hiding in the crowd, came to shake her hand. The recruits parted before him as he swaggered forward in his black tracksuit.

"You were good with that pistol," he said. "Have you ever entered a competition?"

"No, Gunny. I had never held a pistol before today."

Lipe's brown eyes went wide. "You're serious."

"Yes, Gunny."

Lipe grinned like a man whose daughter had just told him she'd been accepted to his alma mater. "Who's your draw sergeant?"

"Sergeant Torres."

"Good. We start general marksmanship training next week, but I'd like to invite you to join our sharpshooting team right away. It's a three-day-a-week class with an eye toward creating elite snipers. If you're interested, I'll send the formal invite through her. She has to approve."

Leslie's eyes widened. "I'd love to!"

"Good," Lipe said. "I'll make the arrangements."

"All right people," Matt shouted, his voice filling the stadium-sized room. "Everyone back to your stations. We have three more cycles to complete before dinnertime!"

A collective groan went up from the recruits, though they hurried to obey, separating into clusters around the draw sergeants assigned to run the trials.

"Help me get these off." Leslie dropped onto her backside and held up one Rollerblade like a little kid. "They're on pretty tight."

Anna unfastened the snaps and began heaving the thing off her friend's foot.

"You still think the Order is manipulating us?" Leslie asked as she waggled her foot back and forth to help loosen the skate.

"I know they are."

"But you have to admit this has been fun. And we're learning a lot. Even you said that last week."

Anna shrugged. "I'll admit they've taught me a few things. And, yeah, this part was fun. I think."

"You think? I'm having the time of my life."

"Maybe that's the charm," Anna said. "And just because something is fun, doesn't make it real."

Leslie grew quiet. All at once her right skate popped off, and Anna started in on the left.

"I've been thinking about that," Leslie said. "What is real, anyway? For all we know, we're just a couple of brains in jars being fed everything we experience, right?"

Anna furrowed her brows. "Where'd you hear that?"

"Moss. We've been talking about your charm theory. He agrees with you, by the way. He says he can feel it too, but he isn't hung up about it. He says it's like when you're a kid and your parents manipulate you into doing something good like eating your vegetables by tricking you or offering you a treat. So what if they're telling you little white lies? The overall goal is good."

Anna pulled off Leslie's second skate and helped her to her feet. "But we're not children."

"Moss says if you're ignorant of something, that makes you like a child on that subject. And I know practically nothing about drawing, even though it's my birthright. So, either I learn from people who know, or I go it alone. And I don't think I'd fare too well outside."

Anna pursed her lips. She was about to retort when Valerie Satterfield took her by the elbow. "We're due at the sime trials, Carver. You'll have time to gab later."

Leslie gave her a grin as Satterfield hauled Anna away.

"What are you grinning at, Carver?" Satterfield asked as they weaved their way through the crowd.

"I think Leslie's going to be okay," Anna said as much to herself as to her squad leader.

"Of course she's okay. Why wouldn't she be?"

"Exactly," Anna said.

8

THE RUNDOWN

Anna found sneaking out of the barracks at night far easier than she expected.

It was all about the now.

Right now, Anna didn't think about escape. That sort of thought would send her back to her bunk with no idea how she got there. Instead, she focused solely on helping a fellow recruit. How could that be wrong?

Melissa Willbrook stood fire guard, which amounted to manning a lectern near the barracks door while the rest of the platoon slept. Unfortunately, Willbrook, a former slinker like Anna, had a monodraw of eyesight, when what she needed at this ungodly hour was alertness. Her eyes were closed when Anna approached.

"Melissa."

Willbrook jumped, nearly toppling the podium. Her flashlight spilled off. Anna drew speed and caught it before it could hit the floor.

"Shit," Willbrook whispered. "You scared me, Carver."

Anna smiled, drawing charm. "Sorry. I just thought you might like a break. I can't sleep, and you look exhausted." All true. Not a whit of lie in that.

Willbrook's eyes fluttered almost shut as the wave of suggestion struck her. "Oh, God yes. You don't have to ask me twice. It's all this draw testing. It's killing me. How are you even awake at this hour?"

Anna slipped an arm around the girl's waist and guided her toward the bunks. No one stirred as they passed. Good. She drew strength, and all but carried Willbrook the last five steps before easing her onto her cot. In a trice, she had Willbrook covered over in her woolen blanket, running shoes and all. With luck, no one would notice her missing from her post before 0600 wake-up call.

Anna drew hearing. She stood still, listening more fiercely than a rabbit. She wasn't planning an escape. Not that. Not *now*. She was simply checking on her bunkmates, something any conscientious guard would do in the long hours of the night. She happened to notice, entirely by accident, that none of the sleeping women's breathing had changed.

Anna clenched.

She wouldn't have long, maybe ten minutes. That was the longest she had managed to hold a clench during classes and training sessions over the last three weeks. It would have to do.

The night held still aside from the see-saw oscillation of crickets and far off warble of frogs. A crescent moon, nothing more than a sliver of white light on the western horizon, provided scant light for Anna's feeble, regular vision. She took her time, scanning for guards, but saw none on the cement pathways surrounding the steel barracks.

Anna headed due south. Though she had never been allowed much freedom to roam the camp, she had noticed fewer buildings in that direction. Did it follow there would be fewer people? She hoped so.

Careful of chuckholes and rocks in the near darkness, she ran at her five-mile pace. She tried not to think about cameras and motion detectors. If Camp Den had them, she was already caught. No use worrying about it. Best to put such things out of her head and keep moving.

The camp wall resolved itself as she drew near: a dark line on the dark horizon. Anna lengthened her stride. Freedom lay beyond that wall. Freedom, and doctors who could remove the chip from her arm.

Her clench faltered. Though she had practiced whenever possible over the last several weeks, Anna hadn't clenched for this long under physical duress. She couldn't take the strain much longer. Her body shook, throwing off her balance, and nearly sending her into a head-long tumble. Time to find out if the charm blast reached the camp wall.

"Here goes everything," Anna whispered.

She dropped her clench and immediately drew speed, dexterity, and intelligence, wrapping them about herself like armor. The camp's pervading charm tried to overwhelm her senses, but at this distance, it could do little more than tug at her desires.

Perfect.

Anna rocketed toward the wall, kicking up plumes of dust in her wake. This would not be easy. She had practiced high jumping every chance she got, but her vertical never quite measured up to the camp walls. But if she could get a hand on the precipice, she knew she could squirm her way over. She had to.

Charging at top speed toward the stone barrier put a flutter of doubt in Anna's chest. This could kill her. Everything hinged on her timing.

She leapt at the last possible instant, hurtling upward, wind lashing her face. The world fell silent for what felt like an hour but was probably half a second. She stretched, using every inch of her short frame. Her fingertips caressed the wall's upper lip followed immediately by the rest of her body. She slammed into the obdurate stone with bone-shattering power that knocked the wind from her lungs. The impact nearly flung her back the way she had come, but she dug in with her fingers, healing her internal injuries even as she scrabbled for purchase with her wet shoes. At last, they caught, and she scrambled up.

Anna rolled onto her back, panting, exultant, thankful for space to lie prone while she caught her breath. Camp Den had taught her some new skills after all, and the votaries she had gained from Renni and Lee had held her in good stead. She lay there for a count of twenty, drawing to recover, then rose to a crouch to scan the surrounding countryside.

Where was she? It had to be somewhere within a night's driving distance of Columbus, Georgia, where Matt Snow had abducted her, but that could be several states. She hadn't even considered the question while under the influence of the camp's charm blast—just another reason why she needed to get the hell away from this place.

Flat treeless land surrounded Camp Den for better than a quarter mile leading up to the wall. Several dark shapes—sheds? small houses? —stood out as darker blobs in a field of black. Shadowy figures boiled out of the nearest one, ten at least, hustling along on pounding feet. Each carried a short-barreled rifle.

Anna's heart squeezed like a fist in her chest.

Someone down there was calling orders. Not shouting but speaking low as if into a mic. With her draw on hearing, Anna caught his words. He had spotted her and was directing his people her way. Five peeled away from the main body, moving at phenomenal speeds.

Anna bolted across the top of the wall, a good ploy for the first few seconds as she put distance between herself and her pursuers. She grinned at her ingenuity. Ironic that the Order had given her all the skills she required to outfox them.

That grin faulted a moment later when she spotted still more troops pouring from additional shacks ahead of her position. Unless something changed, and soon, they would intercept her with ease.

Drawing healing, and giving herself no time for a second guess, Anna leapt. She plummeted like an Acme anvil, struck the ground, and screamed when her ankles snapped with a white-hot flash of pain. She flipped twice and slid to a stop, her legs in agony. The urgent thrum of draw-enhanced footfalls boomed in her ears. She had to move.

She gave her broken ankles a quick five count to mend, then lumbered to her feet. Staggering, she started for the forest, bolts of pain lancing up her shins, into her thighs. Yet, with every step, the pain lessened. Her bones knit; her muscles healed. Within thirty feet she had resumed her normal gait and poured on the speed.

The troops closed on her, but Anna adjusted her angle to outpace them. Several lost their footing in their excitement, somersaulting away with grunts and cries of pain.

One incubus attempted to block her path, brandishing his shotgun, but he underestimated Anna's acceleration. She barreled into him, not even slowing, shoulder checking him with such force he flew backward like a crash dummy.

The trees grew closer. Anna could smell their budding leaves, the almost peppery tang of their bark. These guards weren't going to catch her. No one could. She was too fast. Maybe the fastest succubus in the world.

A woman dressed in black pulled even with Anna. A man did likewise on her opposite side. Wind skirled through the twin barrels of the shotguns they carried.

"Stop!" the female shouted.

Anna struggled to draw more speed and dexterity. Her lungs burned, and her ears rang with the sound of her coursing blood and thrumming heart. She couldn't keep this pace up forever. But she didn't have to. Ahead, perhaps two hundred meters from her current position, stood the outer tree line that marked the beginning of a thick Georgia forest surrounding Camp Den. If she could reach it, she knew she could lose her pursuers. No way more than a couple of them could dodge through the trees at her pace. She just had to beat them there. Concentrating, she pulled a stride ahead, then another. She would make it. Freedom yawned before her with open arms.

Anna's right thigh exploded. She registered the sound of a shotgun blast an instant before she found herself flipping ass over elbow, tearing up the ground in a headlong tumble punctuated by the crackle, snap, pop of bones.

She ground to a halt at the edge of the forest, broken and bleeding and writhing in pain. Her head lay on a gnarled pine root.

"Central, this is patrol lead," said the woman, the shotgun in her hand still smoking. "We got her."

Fifteen minutes later, a mostly healed Anna sat on a leather chair in Master Gunnery Sergeant Lipe's office inside Links, her wrists cuffed behind her back. Surprisingly, her mind felt clear. No obtrusive charm clouded her thoughts. Where had it gone? How was it being so thoroughly blocked? She considered asking her guards—a couple of draw sergeants flanking her on either side— but decided against it. Neither looked particularly talkative. Besides, the female of the duo was the same patrol leader who had ruined Anna's escape with a blast from her shotgun. Anna didn't relish a chat with that one.

A commotion outside caught Anna's attention. Her guards heard it too. They all turned to regard the closed office door.

"Sir, I can't let you go in there." By the sound of things, the guard in the hall had stepped in front of the office door.

"Sergeant, you will stand aside, or I'll set you aside. Those are your choices." Anna knew that voice and the tone of annoyed menace that went with it. Matt Snow didn't need to shout to sound threatening. His words put her hackles up, and he wasn't even talking to her.

"Uh…yes, sir." The hall guard sounded far less self-assured than he had a moment ago.

A shuffling of boots and the door clicked open. Matt strode inside, his face a veritable storm cloud of anger. "Where is she? What did you do—" His eyes lit upon Anna seated between the guards, and he visibly relaxed, exhaling a heavy sigh. "Carver."

Anna sat stunned for a moment. Did she really feel ashamed for trying to escape? What was that? Stockholm syndrome? Did some defeated part of her want to please Matt Snow? To graduate this hell-hole to impress him? She didn't owe him anything, and this stifling embarrassment was pissing her off.

"What the hell are you doing here?" she demanded.

"Why is she cuffed?" The weight of Matt's glare could have crushed Lipe's steel desk. "Get those things off her. Now!"

The female guard—she seemed to be the leader—shook her head, unfazed by Matt's bluster. "No, sir. Standard procedure says we keep escapees on lockdown until they've seen the gunny."

"You can shove your standard procedure—"

"Matt!" Anna drew voice to override his tirade—not all the Order's lessons had been a waste of time—and he turned back to her, his expression melting from angry to worried. That gave her pause, but not for long. Likely, his concern stemmed from losing one of his trophies. What? Did he get a bonus for each successful graduate he kidnapped? "Why are you here? Did you come to chase me down again?"

Matt's face fell. He looked like a kid who had just seen his dog runover in the street. "They told me you were shot."

Anna's anger fizzled under Matt's earnest gaze. It happened so quickly she assumed he or one of the guards must have turned on their charm. But no. She felt not the slightest twinge of interference in her thoughts. By dint of effort, Anna resolutely did not glance at the female guard—she of the smoking shotgun—when she said, "Rubber buckshot. Nothing serious. I got a few bruises, that was all."

So, she lied a bit, better than looking weak to either Matt or the guards.

"Oh. Okay then." Matt seemed suddenly unsure what to do with his hands. He reached toward Anna's cheek as if he might caress it, faltered, and settled for awkwardly patting her shoulder. "I'm glad to see you're not seriously injured."

"Thanks?"

"Well, I had better get back. The gunny will be here soon. Don't want to get in his way." Matt shuffled toward the door and nearly tripped over his feet. Anna had never seen him move with anything less than perfect aplomb. Was he nervous?

"Matthew." His full name felt pleasing on Anna's lips.

He froze in the doorway, his eyes expectant. "Yes, Anna?"

"Thank you. For coming to check on me, I mean."

He quirked that half grin of his and nodded. "Anytime."

Matt left, and the guard in the hall shut the door behind him. Anna turned back to face Gunny Sergeant Lipe's desk, a grin of her own curling her lips despite her growing trepidation and fear. She didn't know what to make of Matt, but she couldn't deny his coming here gave her a warm feeling inside. Maybe he would advocate for her should the Order decide to toss her in some succubus prison for the next twenty-five years on charges of desertion. Or perhaps he would at least visit. Even that silly idea pleased her.

Anna shook her head in an attempt to put Matthew Snow out of mind, though her recalcitrant thoughts kept returning to that stupid grin of his. He confused the shit out of her, and she didn't need that kind of noise right now. She had bigger concerns.

No matter how they couched it with their military-flavored patriotism and us versus them attitude, the Order owned Anna bodily. They might call what they did training, but she knew its real name. Slavery. She couldn't afford to lose her wits to sappy infatuation, especially for the man responsible for kidnapping her in the first place. She had to focus on the here and now.

Anna concentrated on the room around her and what it might say about the man who occupied it. Lipe kept a sparse office. It contained one other chair—twin to Anna's—a steel desk decorated with an old-fashioned ink blotter, and a floor-to-ceiling corner shelf. No computer.

Various medals, coins, photos, and other memorabilia detailing a thirty-year stint in the US Marine Corps covered the shelf. Central to the display, ranking a position of obvious pride, stood a silver tri-fold picture frame, the kind that holds several snapshots of varying sizes. A handsome, dark-haired woman who looked to be in her middle fifties smiled out from the left side. Three young adults, two brawny guys and a gorgeous girl who favored the woman, stared at Anna from the right.

Family photographs on a shelf: that alone shouted the difference between Anna and the man coming to judge her. Lipe represented everything Anna's father had taught her to fear: authority, power, and dominant control. Lipe didn't playact this soldiering business. He had been a marine, and a highly decorated one to judge from the medals on display. No doubt a man like that took abandoning one's post seriously.

Footsteps echoed in the hall outside. Anna could have set an antique watch by their measured gait. Definitely not Matt. The sound put her in mind of Victorian Age drummers signaling the advance on a battlefield. Anna's guards snapped to attention and she, despite herself, likewise surged to her feet, weeks of training getting the better of her.

Lipe swaggered into the office and gave them a dismissive wave. "None of that crap. Zoomies come to attention for an enlisted man." He rounded the desk and took his seat. "Sit down, Carver." He narrowed his eyes. "Wait, get those handcuffs off her."

"Yes, Gunny." The female guard produced a cuff key and released Anna.

"Good," Lipe said. "Now sit, Carver. You two wait outside."

"Gunny," the woman looked askance at her commander, "we aren't supposed to—"

Lipe, who had the prototypical incubus physique, short and spare, save that years of training had imparted to him some girth, nevertheless seemed to grow in his seat. He fixed the guard with a blank stare. The look bore no menace but might as well have been a slap in her face.

The guards left at speed, shutting the door behind them.

"Now, Carver," Lipe said. "Let's talk."

Anna's heart pounded. She fought a nearly insatiable urge to run. That plan had already failed once, and she didn't relish the idea of provoking Lipe's troops into shooting her again. Despite what she had told Matt, those rubber pellets had hurt like hell.

Since Lipe seemed to expect something from her, Anna asked, "What are you going to do with me, Gunny?"

"Reward you, I think, though I'm still debating that."

"What?"

"Why'd you run, Carver? You're halfway through training—you'll be done in no time—you're a sime at the top of her class in nearly every category, and according to Sergeant Torres, you have leadership potential." Lipe leaned back to eye Anna. "So, what's going on?"

Anna hesitated, jaw tight.

"Speak your mind," Lipe said.

"I'm sick of being charmed." Anna leaned forward in her seat. Lipe wanted the truth? She'd give it to him. "I'm sick of being forced to participate in your little war. And I'm sick of this damn chip in my arm."

"Ah, that."

"Yes, Gunny, that. It's intrusive."

"And you don't consider being disappeared by Breathers pretty damn intrusive?"

"I wouldn't know, Gunny. I've only ever been disappeared by the Order."

Lipe narrowed his eyes, and Anna thought she might have gone too far. Then he chuckled. "Torres said you had a mouth. But you also have a point. Look at it from our perspective, Carver. We're fighting what is, for all intents and purposes, the U.S. Government. The Indrawn Breath has its fingers in the NSA, FBI, the Army. What is the Order compared to that? A flea—less than a flea. A microbe. Where the breathers can afford to expend men and material like they're worthless, we have to guard our lowliest troop like they're the last bullet in the foxhole."

"I understand the reasoning—" Anna began.

"It's the implications you fear."

"They scare the shit out of me."

"Because what if you get out into the world and people like me can track you—come find you any time we like."

"Exactly."

"News alert, Carver, because we already did that. And, so did the Breathers. We can find you. They can find you. Who do you want getting there first?"

Anna said nothing. If it meant getting near her kidnapped family, she would take the Breathers over the Order any day. But she couldn't say that.

Lipe's eyes softened, and the ghost of a smile touched his lips. "Did you know I'm a monodraw?"

"What?" Anna scrunched her nose, momentarily thrown by the gunny's non-sequitur.

"I have a pitiful draw on charm. 'Weak as bird's breath' my mama used to say."

"Gunny, I—"

"I discovered my true draw after I joined the Corps. Discernment. I've got that in spades."

Succubus discernment, the ability to predict outcomes based on observation and good old-fashioned intuitive reasoning borrowed from votaries, had never figured much in Anna's life. She hadn't even heard of it before Camp Den. And though she knew some succubi relied on it for their every decision, it seemed a trifling thing to her. She preferred speed. "No offense, Gunny, but why are you telling me this?"

"I have a prediction for you, Carver. You see, I helped set up this camp. Den is designed to instill loyalty and pride in its graduates. And it works for most people because what we're doing here is worthy of those things. Lots of recruits understand that on a gut level. The charm just reinforces those feelings."

"You mean they swallow the Hitler youth propaganda," Anna said. "The enemy is all monsters; we fight for right while they're all sick and depraved."

"Thing is, most of that is true."

"I don't believe that, Gunny."

"I know you don't. You're quite the freethinker. I have a son just like you."

"What's your prediction, Gunny?" Anna did not like being compared to one of Lipe's obstinate children.

He gave her a wintry smile. "Punishment won't work on you. You'll quietly serve the extra duty I dish out until you think it's safe, and then you'll run again. Or you'll wait till you've graduated and get some doctor willing to keep his mouth shut to remove that chip in your arm and immediately disappear."

Anna kept her face expressionless, hands folded in her lap. "What would the Order do then? Hunt me down? Do you really want unwilling soldiers for your cause?"

"We want every troop we can get. But more than that, we want the Breathers deprived of those same troops."

"I'd never join them."

"So you believe," Lipe said. "But if you think Camp Den is brainwashing, I assure you the Indrawn Breath does worse."

"Are we back to the Hitler youth fearmongering, Gunny?"

"Maybe." Lipe rubbed at a spot on his immaculate desk. "You never let me tell you the other part of my prediction."

"Okay."

"There's a mission coming up—an extraction. The Order is looking to reach a young succubus before the Breathers get to her. It's routine stuff. I've told the draw sergeants to provide me with some names of top students we might send along for the experience. I predict, Carver, that if I add your name to that list, you will return here committed to the Order."

"I don't see how, Gunny."

"That's the strange thing about predictions," Lipe said. "Neither do I."

Anna watched Lipe's face, searching for the lie. She found none. "If I go and return feeling the way I do now, do I get to leave sans microchip?"

"You'll go," Lipe said. "And you'll change your mind. But if you don't, I'll buy you a plane ticket to wherever you're going."

"I have your word?"

"Yes."

Anna stuck out her hand, and Lipe shook it. "Gunny, you've got yourself a rookie taker."

9

———

THE ABDUCTION OF EMILY STONE

The drive from Camp Den on the outskirts of Atlanta to the small town of Lucas Falls, South Carolina, took three hours and twenty-five minutes. During that time, Matt had said exactly six words to Anna.

"You still want the heat on?" he had asked about twenty minutes ago.

And because the day was cold, she had nodded. Since then, Matt had kept his gaze on the road and his hands plastered at ten and two on the wheel.

Valerie Satterfield lay on their van's center row seat, sprawled out and snoring, her conservative skirt hiked up around her curled knees. Behind her, Phil Benson, a recruit chosen from Bravo Platoon, sat staring out the side window, AirPods jammed in his ears. Even without drawing, Anna could pick out the tinny buzz of his music over the road noise. She hoped he had a deep draw on hearing. He would need it in his old age.

They had disguised themselves as Mormon missionaries. The guys wore black suits over pure white shirts with nametags pinned to their breast pockets. Snow's read, "Elder Frost." Anna thought it a bad pun.

80

Anna found her ensemble surprisingly comfortable. Her calf-length, seafoam blue skirt afforded her ample room to run and kick. Even better, it contained a hidden pocket below the hip that gave her access to the Kimber Ultra TLE holstered on her thigh. The .45 felt reassuring there.

Her blouse, covered in a busy floral pattern, allowed her to move freely. Too bad she couldn't say the same for the Kevlar vest beneath. Though the weight posed no problem, the arm openings felt tight, rubbing when she moved, and no matter how she adjusted the thing her boobs remained squished. Satterfield hadn't complained, but Anna had a feeling the Order could bury that girl in cement, and she would go down thanking them for the privilege.

They passed a sign that read, "Welcome to Lucas Falls, South Carolina. Population 6,432." Rotary and Lion's Club symbols hung from the bottom.

"Have you ever been here?" Anna asked.

"No," Matt said.

Anna waited for more. None came.

She lowered her voice. "Is there something wrong?"

"Wrong?"

"Do you hate me or something?" Anna threw her hands up. Five days ago, Matt had barged into Lipe's office in search of her. He had threatened a draw sergeant and probably would have turned the man inside out if he had barred the way. Now he acted like Anna didn't exist.

"What?" Matt's voice went up two octaves.

"You heard me. It's not that loud in here."

Matt flicked his gaze to the rearview mirror and then back to the road. "I don't hate you, Carver."

"We've been in this godforsaken van for hours, and that's the most you've said to me since we left. What's your problem?"

Matt glanced at her from the corner of his eye and swore.

"What? Look, if you don't want me on this mission, complain to Lipe. He sent me."

"It's not that."

"Then what is it?"

"Dammit, Carver." Matt ran a hand through his sandy hair and shook his head. "I like you. Okay?"

Anna sat back in her seat, the air gone out of her lungs. "What does that mean?" For a moment, she honestly wondered if she had missed a code phrase in the mission briefing.

"You heard me. It's not that loud in here."

Anna's heart sped up. For the first time in hours, she forgot the mission. Everything suddenly made sense: Matt's sidelong glances at her during training, the way he sometimes met her gaze without realizing it, his mad dash to find her when he heard she had been shot trying to escape. She focused on him. "I don't know what to say."

"Don't say anything."

"I like you, too."

"That's exactly the kind of anything I meant." Matt rechecked the rearview mirror, which made Anna turn.

Satterfield continued to snore. Benson looked like he had dozed as well, music still blaring.

"We like each other. What's wrong with that?" Anna asked. "Does the Order prohibit dating? That wasn't part of our briefings."

"It's inappropriate. I'm an instructor at Den. You're a recruit."

"Not for long. In a few weeks—"

"Stop. Seriously. Let's focus on finding this girl and getting back to camp."

Anna felt her lips compress the way they always did when she grew angry. "Fine."

Matt glanced at her. "Now you're pissed."

Anna popped her knuckles, a nasty habit from her youth. "No, you're right. We have a mission."

"Carver, look, I'm—dammit, I missed my turn." Matt slowed and pulled into the breakdown lane. The van bumped and shuddered across a set of rumble strips.

Satterfield started awake with a little yelp. She shot up, staring around, face damp with sweat. "Everything okay?"

Anna stared at Matt for a long moment. He had done that on purpose. Finally, she turned to Satterfield. "Everything's fine."

They turned off the main road onto a red clay and gravel lane. The van creaked and shimmied its way across ruts and potholes, finally rousing Benson from his music-induced stupor. He moved forward to sit beside Satterfield.

"Is this it?" he asked, peering through the front window at a dilapidated trailer coming into view on the left.

Anna didn't know Benson. She had met him for the first time this morning. He spoke with the speed and heavy accent of a New Yorker, talked incessantly when he wasn't listening to his music, and asked a lot of dumb questions. But he was top of his class in Bravo Platoon, a sime on par with Satterfield, and cool under fire, according to his reputation.

"Yeah," Matt said.

Emily Stone's trailer, a rundown single-wide painted white with brown accents nearly indistinguishable from the rust coating its walls, occupied a grassless lot hemmed in on all sides by similar homes. Much of its lower skirting was bent and warped, or else nonexistent, exposing the black tires underneath.

"No cars in the drive." Matt shut off the van and sat for a moment, scanning the trailer's exterior.

"Think maybe Stone's at work?" Satterfield asked.

"Let's find out."

Matt and Benson mounted the steps, Matt first, leaving Anna and Satterfield to stand in the weeds, sweating. Matt claimed real Mormons did it that way, but Anna figured he didn't want to stand next to her.

Fine. It wasn't as if she had intended to date the guy. But why did he have to admit his feelings if he was going to ignore them?

Focus. Matt Snow didn't matter right now. Freedom alone mattered. She had to find Emily Stone before the Indrawn Breath. Then she could start searching for her family.

Anna tried to ignore the guilt borne by that thought. Gunny Lipe had pitted her freedom against that of Emily Stone. To save herself,

Anna must entrap another in her place. It wasn't fair, but it was trickle-down unfairness, the kind where either you play the game, or you lose.

Anna refused to lose.

No one answered at Matt's knock. He tried again. Anna drew hearing and caught the sound of a television, muffled, playing some commercial about buying gold.

Without hesitation, Matt slammed an open palm against the chintzy door. It banged open as if hit with a shotgun blast.

The place smelled heavily of dog, cigarette smoke, and blood. Anna pulled her Kimber from its holster as the others retrieved their weapons.

The front door opened onto the trailer's cramped living room. The TV Anna had heard outside proved to be a flat screen lying face down on the purple carpet. Next to it lay the inert bodies of three animals: a German Shepherd and two cats. Each had been stabbed repeatedly, throats cut. A long carving knife jutted from the dog's ruined side.

"Holy shit." Benson nearly tripped over Satterfield when he caught sight of the pets.

"Quiet." Matt held his Glock in both hands, pointed down the trailer's short hallway. He motioned for Anna and Satterfield to search the kitchen, a narrow space separated from the living room by one thin wall. Matt headed for the bedrooms, Benson in tow.

Nothing seemed amiss in the kitchen. Besides a crap ton of dirty dishes in the sink and some cat food strewn across the dingy linoleum, the place looked undisturbed.

Anna had made up her mind to follow the boys when Matt and Benson returned empty-handed.

"Nothing," Matt said at the women's inquisitive looks.

"Who killed her pets?" Satterfield asked.

"Breathers," Matt said.

"Why?"

Matt pursed his lips. He scanned the refrigerator, festooned with letters and notes pinned to its metal face with magnets.

"You've seen this kind of thing before, haven't you?" Anna asked.

Matt plucked an envelope off the fridge. It looked like a bill with a pink forwarding sticker on the front. "We need to check this address."

"You didn't answer our question," Anna said. "Why did the Breathers do this?"

Matt stared at his charges, face set, jaw tight.

"Yeah, I've seen this before, that's all I can say. It's Order business. If this is too much for you, stay in the van. Now let's move."

The home of Mr. and Mrs. Paul G. Stone, parents of Emily Stone, was a two-story brick affair with three dormers in the front and a tidy planter full of purple irises next to the broad porch. A large, black SUV stood in the driveway.

The neighborhood looked every bit the upper-middle-class suburb Anna-the-slinker had never lived in, with its chemical green yards and shiny black mailboxes. That was why the scream, emanating from some interior room of the Stone house, chilled Anna to the bone. Muffled and far too weak for human ears to catch, it felt as out of place as a fly in an operating room.

Matt raised a fist, signaling the group to stop. They stood on a narrow cement walk in front of the garage, four missionaries, heads cocked, listening. At another gesture, and with inhuman speed, they drew their weapons.

Matt tried the front door. He shook his head and tried peering through the windows.

"No good," he whispered.

Anna's hands shook. She drew calm to complement the speed and strength already surging through her body.

Matt pointed at her. "Bust the door, then drop. I'll be right behind you. Benson, Satterfield, bring up the rear."

They all nodded. They knew what to do. Small team assault had been the focus of their last two weeks of training.

Anna aimed a draw-enhanced kick at the door, just beside the knob. Though the steel hardly dented, the door's wooden frame splintered with a crack. She dropped to one knee, blocking the door's rebound with her body so that Matt could barrel past her into the main hall.

A man with a crew cut appeared at the opposite end of the hall. He wore a silver Nike jogging suit and carried a SIG P238. Without hesitation, he aimed at Matt and squeezed off a round.

By the time crew cut had decided to shoot, Matt had already darted left down an adjoining hall, leaving Anna a clear lane of fire. Weeks of charm-enforced training took over. Anna lined up her shot and pulled the trigger twice. She expected to see the guy drop.

He didn't.

Faster than Anna could track with her Kimber, crew cut scurried back into the home's living room, putting an interior wall between them. Anna's double tap opened twin holes in the paneling where he had been.

Satterfield and Benson rushed past Anna just as Matt reappeared in the hallway. They followed him into the living room and a grotesque scene of carnage.

A man lay dead on the floor. Blood oozed from his nose and the corners of his lips. He had been beaten to death but showed no signs of puncture or gunshot wounds.

Above him, on a plain brown couch, sat an overweight woman of perhaps forty-five. Her hands were bound at the wrists with nylon cords, her mouth gagged with a neon green ball affixed to a muzzle. And she had no eyes. Where her eyes should have been were two bloody holes, leaking gore onto her face. Her chest rose and fell; she was alive but appeared unconscious.

Two young women sat on a love seat adjacent to the blinded woman. Neither appeared injured. The one with raven hair pressed a small pistol into the blonde's ribs.

The dark-haired one was Anna's little sister.

"Melody?"

"Anna Rose? The hell are you doing here?"

"What am I doing here? Mel, how—"

"Stop," said a man standing over the body on the carpet. In her shock, Anna hadn't noticed him, but at the sound of his voice, her attention skittered away from her sister like metal shavings drawn to a magnet.

Everyone, even Matt, had frozen.

"Matthew Snow." The man drew out Matt's name with exquisite relish, the tone so alluring it made Anna's mouth water. "I had heard you went rogue. I didn't want to believe it. Are these your new team?"

Matt adjusted his grip on his pistol, which he had lined up on the speaker's chest. "Don't make me kill you, Lord."

The other man chuckled as if he weren't in mortal danger. "Put down your weapons," he said. "All of you."

Anna placed her Kimber on the carpet, ashamed at having drawn it in Lord's presence. Benson and Satterfield did likewise.

"No," Matt said without taking his eyes off Lord. "He's charming you. Use your charm. Fight it."

"You too, Matt." Lord turned his full attention onto Anna's team lead. "Put the gun down. You can't clench against me."

Matt stiffened. A tremor ran through his arms, his back, down his legs.

"Stop, Matt," Anna said. "Put your gun down. It's okay."

Matt seemed to deflate. He dropped his gun to his side.

Lord turned to Anna. He wore an expensive suit tailored to fit and accentuate his athletic frame. His dark brown eyes fell on Anna, and she nearly swooned. "Melody, how is it you know this woman?"

"She's my sister, Anna."

Lord smiled, a look of pleased delight that sent tremors of elation down Anna's back. "Sisters? Why, that's marvelous. I see the resemblance. Are you a sime as well, Anna?"

"You're a sime?" Anna gaped at Melody, who beamed and nodded before turning back to Lord. "Yes, I'm a sime."

"That's marvelous, Anna. Tell me, do you work for Matt here?"

"Don't answer him!" Matt struggled to lift his gun. His hand shook with the strain, but the barrel rose no more than an inch. "He's charming us. Draw your own and fight it."

"You haven't taught them to clench?" Lord asked.

Matt shook his head.

"That was shortsighted of you. Not that it would do them much good. Still, foolish on your part."

Trembling, Matt raised his pistol almost to his waist.

Lord nodded at crew cut, who blurred forward to cuff Matt with the back of one meaty hand. Matt spun half around and crashed onto the Stones' coffee table.

Part of Anna wanted to run to Matt—a small part mostly eclipsed by her yearning to impress Lord. She didn't move.

"Do you know these other two, Melody?" Lord caressed Satterfield's chin.

Anna's lips curled as a shiver of jealousy washed through her.

"No," Melody said.

"Pretty." Lord tilted Satterfield's head this way and that, admiring her face.

She gave a demure smile. "Thank you."

With Lord's attention diverted, Anna clenched. She didn't do it to escape his charm. She did it to prove Matt wrong. A suave, trustworthy man like Lord had no need to bamboozle anyone. His charm came naturally, just like his debonair magnetism. The man was a fox. Yes, she had laid down her gun at his request, but why not? He posed no threat to her or anyone. As for his questions, who could fault natural curiosity?

"Do you work for Matt Snow?" Lord whispered to Satterfield.

"Yes. No." She giggled like a little girl, flustered. "We all work for the Order. Matt's our team lead."

"Shut up." Matt had risen to one knee. Crew cut struck him with his SIG. Something cracked inside Matt's face.

Anna's mind cleared as her clench took hold. Her heart trip-hammered in her chest and her breath caught. The reality of the situation sent a spike of fear through her brain.

"What is the Order?" Lord pressed his lips to Satterfield's cheek, speaking the words softly against her lower jaw, intimate, like a lover.

Anna had to act, but how could she without dropping her clench? Crew cut was watching her. She got the feeling he would be happy to slug her with his SIG, given the opportunity. Or maybe shoot her out of hand. Without drawing she couldn't stop him either way.

Time to gamble.

Anna dropped her clench and drew charm. She struggled to focus it on Satterfield and Benson. Though her draw was deep, she had little control of its direction. She hoped her efforts could nudge the others into waking up enough to free themselves, assuming Lord's charm didn't overwhelm her first. In the meantime, she had to fight.

On top of her charm, she drew speed and dexterity, her hands blurring as she clamped down on Lord's wrist, spinning him away from Satterfield. Using their combined momentum, Anna smashed a point just above Lord's elbow with her forearm. It made a satisfying crunch as the joint ripped apart, bending backward at an unnatural angle.

Lord screamed, injured arm tucked to his side.

Satterfield, though rocked by the attack, nevertheless caught her Glock G19 when Anna tossed it from the floor. Benson fumbled his, dropped it.

Anna squeezed off a round at crew cut, but he dodged. She fired twice more, missing both times. The bastard possessed a powerful draw on discernment; he evaded her shots before she could pull the trigger. In a flash, he closed the distance between them, moving faster than she could react. He slammed the knife edge of his palm down on her wrist, and she heard her bones snap like twigs. A bolt of pain shot up her arm. Then, a malicious grin on his face, crew cut jerked her bodily into his outthrust knee. All the air fled Anna's lungs. The pain had hardly registered before he flung her sideways to crash into Matt, who had been lining up for a shot at him.

Satterfield and Benson fared no better. Though they attacked as a team, crew cut evaded their blows with ease. He smashed Satterfield's nose with a savage elbow and then, flowing smoothly from one attack to the next, dove into Benson low at the knees, dropping him to the floor like a wrestler. Two hammer blows later, Benson lay unconscious and bleeding on the carpet.

Lord grimaced as he tried to forcibly jerk his injured arm straight, but the elbow refused to give. It hadn't broken cleanly. He must have possessed a powerful draw on pain tolerance to endure that kind of trauma without much reaction, though beads of sweat did pop out on his forehead.

"Can't heal this till I can get it set properly." His eyes fell on Anna, who lay in a pile of broken coffee table. "You're going to pay for that, woman." He started toward her.

"David, no." For the first time, Melody stood from the couch. She retained her pistol but let it hang at her side.

"No?" He raised a dark eyebrow at her.

"She's my sister. Please, no."

Something in Melody's tone gave Anna pause. She wasn't pleading the way a child might with a parent. She spoke as a lover would. Anna's throat constricted at the thought of her kid sister, just eighteen, in David Lord's arms.

Lord appeared reluctant, but nodded slowly, as if considering a weighty matter. "I'll spare her. This time. Strunk, grab the girl."

Crew cut slung Emily Stone over one shoulder as if she weighed nothing. She made no move to stop him. She didn't even struggle.

Using his uninjured hand, Lord shot Matt three times. One bullet in each knee, and a third in his right bicep.

Matt screamed as did Anna. Blood sprayed across her cheek, leaving spots on her conservative top.

"Good to see you, Snow," Lord said in the sudden, shocking silence. Then he headed out, Melody and Strunk on his heels.

"Melody," Anna said. "Don't go with them."

For a moment, Melody looked strained, confused, then her expression cleared. "I wouldn't follow us if I were you. Lord won't let you go a second time." With that, she turned and left.

Matt groaned, trying to sit up. Anna pressed him back down, ignoring her pain for the moment to check his wounds. "Lie still."

"I think I've got the bleeding stopped," he said. "It's all I can do with the bullets still in there."

The wounds were sealed, but the pink scars appeared inflamed.

"Who was that man? Lord?" Anna asked. "He knew you."

Matt nodded. His gaze flicked briefly to Satterfield and Benson then back to Anna. "David Lord. My mentor."

10

DEBRIEF

The conference room in the Links building smelled of new paint and factory-fresh carpet. Its sterile confines left Anna cold and uncomfortable. She tried to ignore those feelings—they added to her general gloom—as she, Benson, and Satterfield took turns recounting their failed mission to save Emily Stone.

Anna still wore her blood-splattered missionary costume and Kevlar vest. She felt shaky and a little sick. Satterfield, pale and wide-eyed, looked no better. For his part, Benson seemed okay but less talkative than in the morning.

Robin Ambrose paced at the head of the table, one hand pressed to her cheek. It was the first time Anna had met Camp Den's director face-to-face. The woman appeared distraught, though Anna couldn't tell if that arose from the story she was hearing or something else.

Gunny Lipe sat across from the recruits, hands folded on the table. He listened in stolid silence, the grim commander implacable in the face of defeat.

Anna and the others had driven straight here from Lucas Falls. Benson, who had medical training from a stint in the Army, had managed to get the slugs out of Matt's arm using an emergency kit in the back of the van while Anna drove. Matt's knees had been too far gone, the bullets having shattered the upper portion of both tibias and lodged in the joints. Dr. Stanislaw had rushed Matt off to surgery the moment they arrived.

"And then we got here," Satterfield said, finishing the tale.

Robin quit pacing. "You're lucky to be alive. David Lord is a vicious man. His presence there gives me pause. Our information said the Stones were to be investigated by Society, not picked up. And certainly not tortured."

"What was that about anyway, ma'am?" Satterfield asked. "First with the animals, then the girl's parents."

"I'd like to tell you I don't know," Robin said. "I wish what you saw was merely the workings of a deranged man. But we don't think so."

Robin nodded at Lipe.

"What we're about to divulge does not leave this room, understood?" Lipe said. "We've had a hell of a time keeping it under wraps. I'm not ready for the entire camp to hear this when we've got no solid proof for our conjecture."

The recruits nodded.

Lipe adjusted his collar as if it had suddenly grown too tight. "We suspect the Indrawn Breath is constructing, or has constructed, a facility we term a fear factory. They are imprisoning succubi, incubi, and even regular humans in this place where they're forced into vast votary chains constructed on fear."

"I don't get it," Benson said.

"It's a little-known draw," Robin said. "Few succubi can even use it. We associate it with inciting fear in votaries, though in reality, you're stealing their courage. It leaves them vulnerable to unmitigated fear."

Anna stiffened in her seat, her mind's eye flashing back to the night Matt had saved her from those Society takers. She tasted again the inexplicable horror she had felt at the end of the chase and knew for certain Matt had employed fear to stop her.

"I don't see what good that would do." Satterfield shook her head. "This Lord and his man, Strunk, they were more than fearless. They were powerful in ways I've never seen. Charm, speed, strength—they had more depth and breadth than any of us, even Snow."

"The fear draw acts as a link between succubus and votary," Lipe said. "That's its true power. The link."

"When we speak of courage here, it isn't in the classical sense," Robin said. "It's less a measure of one's resistance to fear so much as the ability to keep sane in a world prone to drive the conscious mind batty. There exists between the outside world and our inner thoughts a boundary, a wall of blitheness. Without this, we would fret over every danger we perceive."

"Sorry. I'm still not following you." Benson looked from Robin to Lipe.

Robin made a broad gesture, encompassing the room. "The air here is breathable, yes? But what keeps it so? Who says from one breath to the next the nitrogen-oxygen levels haven't dropped enough to kill you? And what of the sky above us? Do you ever think that there exists nothing between us and the proverbial soul-sucking darkness of space? There's no roof up there, just air and gravity. And what of germs, Benson? Did you know a significant amount of your body mass is bacteria? What are they doing right now? What are they eating? Where are they shitting?"

"Oh." Benson's face had gone slack while Robin spoke. He looked ill.

"These fear-drawn strip their victims of this mental shield. They tear down the wall, exposing them to all the horrors their minds might devise. And when these defenseless people are rife with every horrid thing they've ever been afraid of, the Breathers give them more. They torture them, expose them to terrors we can hardly comprehend sitting here in our cushy chairs. And they make certain, without a doubt, that their victims know them, and know them well."

"And then they become Breather votaries," Anna said in a whisper. Was her family in such a place? Did Melody know? Had she been complicit in putting them there?

"Exactly," Lipe said.

"I never thought for one—" Robin began but cut off when her voice broke. "I never believed they would go so far."

"So, the torture with the animals, the parents," Satterfield said, "that was part of this fear link?"

"Priming the pump," Lipe said. "I'd say they plan to sock Emily away in their fear factory. Torturing those close to her simply initiated the fear link. Lord must have wanted her for himself."

"How long have we known about the fear draw?" Anna asked.

"It's ancient," Robin said. "Where do you think expressions like *take courage* come from? There have always been tales of evil kings and tyrants who locked votaries away in dungeons or towers. But I thought they were cautionary fictions like the Tower of Babel."

"But if there were always people who could use it, what kept them from it?" Benson asked.

Robin gave him a mirthless smile. "Society. This draw requires training, more so than any other. Few began using it naturally. In the past, elders taught it only to select members of our kind, knights of a sort, those who could be trusted to use it with equanimity."

"Not sadistic bastards who enjoy torturing small animals," Lipe said.

"What about my sister?" All the way back to Camp Den, Anna had avoided thinking of Melody, focusing instead on the road, on Matt, and getting to safety. Now she could think of little else.

"Brainwashed, obviously," Robin said. "You felt Lord's charm. I'm sorry, Carver, but she is his creature until we find a way to free her."

Anna remembered the look Melody had given her as she left, following Lord. Was she under that murderer's spell? Or had she some inkling of what she had done?

"They're ramping up to something," Lipe said.

"What do you mean, Gunny?" Benson looked pale, the ramifications of their debrief seeming to finally penetrate his thick skull.

"Like Robin said, the fear draw has been around for ages. And the Indrawn Breath has been exploiting it for some time. But until now, they never took more than a handful of succubi every year. They've increased their take beyond sustainability. There aren't enough succubi in the U.S. for them to keep this up long."

"How do we stop them?" Satterfield asked, her voice low, intense.

"We train," Lipe said. "We act as a team, we strike where we can, and hide when we must."

"The best we can do is continue winning more of our kind to our side," Robin said. "There are hundreds of thousands of succubi in America, millions around the world. We must convince them that the American Society has broken down, that we have to fight to win it back."

Would such an argument have worked on Anna six weeks ago? Hell, a day ago? Short answer: no. The average slinker didn't give two shits what happened to Society—bunch of snooty, holier-than-thou succubi who thought their money and their votaries made them rulers over their fellows with less of both. Talking wouldn't make a bit of difference to the lower class. And Anna had a feeling much of the upper class, those who had positions in Society before the Indrawn Breath took over, and retained them now, were unlikely to give that up for a life of struggle against their peers.

Anna had been shortsighted when she imagined learning all she could at Camp Den only to escape and somehow save her family. More than shortsighted, stupid. But that didn't mean she wanted to fight a losing battle any more than some fat cat Wall Street incubus did. The air smelled about the same on both sides of the Society tracks these days: rotten.

"That won't work," Anna said.

Robin, who had gone on to another topic, stopped mid-sentence to fix Anna with a sterile gaze. "Pardon me, dear?"

"What you said a minute ago about winning succubi to our side," Anna said. "It won't work. Slinkers like me aren't interested in your war. They don't own it, and you can't make them buy it—not without charm—blasting them the way you're doing us. But can you do that to every succubus in America? I mean, is that your plan?"

"Carver," Lipe said in his command voice, his words spiked with all the charm he could likely muster, "you will show Director Ambrose due respect."

"You should calm down." Robin added her charm to the gunny's, urging Anna to relax, to shut her mouth.

Anna clenched. "No."

Robin squared her shoulders, her focus like a magnified sunbeam bent on setting Anna ablaze. "I said calm down. Do you even recall what has you so upset?"

"Stop it." Anna stood, body trembling with the effort of her resistance. "I will not forget. I will not relent. I've had enough of you people clouding my mind. It ends now."

She dropped her clench and drew charm—all she could muster. More than the gunny would ever have. Maybe more than Snow. She had no plan. She drew by reflex and the desire to have her powers at the ready should she need them.

It took several seconds for Anna to realize the others hadn't moved. Though alert, Robin watched her with frozen eyes. The director's mouth hung open as if she wanted to say something, but the words had hit a roadblock in her throat. She blasted Anna with charm in an all-out effort to thwart her control. But failed.

Lipe sat likewise frozen, as did Satterfield and Benson. Their eyes trembled in their sockets.

Anna had snared them. They were in her thrall. The skin on the backs of her thighs tingled with goosebumps at the realization.

She could leave—walk out the door and start running. But no, that had failed the last time. And even if she escaped, even if she managed to remain free for longer than a few days, what then? Camp Den would still be here, as would the Indrawn Breath. Slinkers like her would still be under the cleated boots of these sorts of people.

Anna tightened her hold on Robin, seizing the older woman more fully in a web of charm that kept her immobile without stealing her volition.

"What you're doing here at Den is wrong. It was wrong when Society did it, and it's wrong now." Anna stared into Robin's enraged eyes. "I'm going to let you go in a minute, and you'll probably have me locked away in a cell. But not before you hear me out.

"Until a few weeks ago, I wasn't sure Society even existed. And yet, I was afraid of it. Afraid enough to fear drawing. Afraid enough to fear making close connections with anyone besides my family. No one should live that way, Robin. No one.

"And then you brought me here. You told me that Society had fallen and that now I had to fight to put it back the way it was. Why? So people like you, some elitists I'd never heard of, could lord it over people like me? Don't you see that the succubi you've gathered here, all these slinkers, they're powerful, Robin? More so than you imagined, I bet. We're a resource, a well of allies. One you're wasting by forcing us to your will. That's the same tactic Society has always used. And you're a damned fool for adopting it."

Anna released her charm. She couldn't have held it much longer anyway. Staggering on weakened legs, she narrowly managed to plop back into her chair without sprawling on the carpet.

Robin staggered as well but managed to keep her feet. She planted both hands on the desk before her, panting, a sheen of sweat glistening on her forehead.

"Benson, Satterfield," Lipe said, "restrain Carver."

"No." Robin held up one hand. "Leave her."

Anna met the director's gaze without flinching. She had come too far to back down now.

All fell quiet in the conference room, save for the ubiquitous sound of central air humming through vents.

At last, Robin broke the silence. "You're right, Carver."

"What?" Anna doubted her ears. She sat up straight, trying to decipher just what Robin had said.

Robin heaved a sigh, pulled out her chair, and wilted into it. She looked suddenly older, a woman sagging under burdens unseen. "Matt told me the same thing five years ago when we first laid our plans for this place. He said we needed a fresh start, a break from the past. I feared…"

"You feared what? That you couldn't trust slinkers? That we wouldn't help you unless you enslaved us?"

Robin shook her head, her shoulders slumped, her face all but defeated. "No. I feared you'd give us away to my husband."

11

———

OF GEEKS AND VOTARIES

Anna, Satterfield, and Benson traded looks.

"My *ex*-husband is Senator Jason Kraft." Robin looked like a woman who just discovered mold in her soup.

"Wait," Satterfield said. "That's the guy pushing for us to invade Mexico."

"Yes," Robin said. "He's chairman of the Homeland Security and Governmental Affairs Committee. He's also the leader of the Indrawn Breath."

"Holy shit," Benson said.

"We're fighting your ex?" Anna had never heard of this Kraft guy, which wasn't surprising. She paid little attention to politics.

"We're fighting an organization," Lipe said. "One that views regular humans as nothing but batteries, and slinkers as little better."

"But why the Mexico thing?" Satterfield asked. "All the rhetoric says we need to take out the drug cartels. But if these guys want control over succubi in the U.S., shouldn't they be focused here?"

Robin glanced at Lipe, who nodded.

"Short answer," Robin said. "Vampires."

Anna felt like someone had slapped her face. "You're joking."

"There are vampires in Mexico?" Benson looked as gobsmacked as Anna felt.

"Yes," Lipe said. "They run the drug cartels."

"Wait." Anna held up both hands. "Are you serious? We're talking blood-drinking monsters here? Vampires are a real thing?"

"Yes," Robin said. "As real as you or I. Vampires are a type of succubus—our cousins if you will. We draw through familiarity. They draw through blood ties."

"And your ex wants to attack them?" Satterfield appeared to be taking this revelation in stride.

"It's complex, but yes," Robin said. "Society—at least our version of Society—has a long-standing agreement with the coven kingdoms, the allied vampire clans, that boils down to this: we do not interfere with their business, and in return, they maintain vampire populations under a strict cap within the United States and Canada. It's a unique arrangement unlike anything seen throughout succubus societies around the world. It's kept the peace between us and vampire kind for generations."

"There's more than one Society?" Anna looked from Robin to Lipe and back again, agog.

"Yes," Lipe said. "That's part of the problem. Most nations have their own version of Society. European Society is particularly powerful. They have long striven to keep North American Society in check. And they've succeeded by striking separate bargains with the vampires."

"If our Society begins seizing power on a world stage, the vampires will abandon the treaty," Robin said.

"It's a vampire-succubus cold war," Satterfield said, her eyes wide. "And Kraft wants to launch a preemptive strike by taking out the vampires threatening his southern border."

"Exactly," Robin said. "If the Indrawn Breath mobilizes American forces against them, the vampires will have two choices. They can either fight a limited war, careful to avoid exposure to the humans, or they can back down. Like us, they have strict laws forbidding their kind from divulging their existence to the world at large."

"I hate to admit it," Lipe said, "but the move is brilliant on Kraft's part. He's calling Europe's bluff—if it is a bluff—and using regular humans to do it. And all under the guise of protecting the U.S. from the drug cartels. If he plays this right, he could be President in a couple of years."

"Let's hope it doesn't come to that," Robin said.

A hot wire of fear slid into the pit of Anna's stomach. Not only were there more Societies than the one she had grown up despising, but they were striking bargains with vampires in order to oppress her.

"This is insane," she whispered. "Your kind can't expect slinkers to take this on."

"My kind?" Robin said.

"Society elites. You expect us to fight this war for you, but the odds are too lopsided. Most of us have a handful of votaries at best. I don't think you get that. You might as well toss us into a meat grinder as pit us against the fear-drawn."

"I'm sorry, ma'am, but I'm with Carver," Satterfield said. "Lord and Strunk took us down without breaking a sweat. How do you expect us to compete with that?"

Satterfield gave Anna a curt nod, and Anna thought she might fall out of her chair. Satterfield agreeing with her? Was the sun about to explode?

"We have a plan. It's a bit unorthodox, but if it works for my kind," Robin met Anna's eyes, "then it will surely work for you."

She pressed a button on the desk. "Olivia, send the boys up please." To the gathered recruits, Robin said, "You each know why we chose you for the extraction mission. You are the best Camp Den has to offer: polydraws and simes—rare treasures for the Order. Your run-in with Lord was unfortunate, but it serves to reinforce our reasons for choosing you."

Anna had a feeling Robin meant something more than choosing them for one extraction mission. She started to ask while cracking open the discernment she only just learned to draw thanks to continuing visits with the Rolstons, but the conference room door clicked open.

"Robin!" cried two male voices in perfect unison. They belonged to a set of identical twins dressed in matching lavender suits. They were short men, and blond, with slightly receding hairlines. Their tailored jackets gave them the square-shouldered appearance of athletes—gymnasts maybe. Each gave Robin a faux kiss on either cheek.

"Gentlemen," Robin said, "may I introduce our candidates. This is Philip Benson, Valerie Satterfield, and Anna Carver. Everyone, Brendan and Luke Pruett."

"Fashion experts," said one twin.

"Artists par excellence," said the other.

"Hmm," said the first, "don't forget authors and connoisseurs of all things geek chic."

"Touché. But what would we be without our steampunk sensibilities, and as I so often point out to you, dear brother, steampunk is not geek."

"Gentlemen," Robin said. "We have yet to fully explain the particulars of your plan. Would you be so kind?"

The brothers gave Robin a gracious nod. The one on the right stepped slightly forward. "I'm Brendan," he said. "My brother and I write graphic novels."

"You make porn?" Benson looked perplexed.

Brendan laughed, pressed a hand to his brother's arm. "Couldn't you just eat him up? No, Phil—may I call you Phil?—we do not make pornography."

"Well, not for public consumption anyway," Luke said.

"We produce novel-length comic books."

"Really good comic books."

"For adults."

Phil tilted his head. "So, it is porn."

"Oh, this one's a keeper," said one of the twins. Anna had lost track which was which.

She raised a hand.

"Look, Brendan, she thinks we're in school. Yes, dear, you can have a hall pass, but only if you show the teacher your—"

Robin cleared her throat.

Luke grinned, full lips pressed firmly together. He raised an eyebrow at Anna.

"Are you incubi?" she asked.

"We prefer the term geekubi, but yes."

"The twins are quite well known in certain circles." Robin said "certain circles" the way most people said cat urine.

The twins seemed unfazed.

"We are the artists behind *Hex Kitten*," said Brendan who, Anna realized, wore a red kerchief in his breast pocket, as opposed to Luke's blue.

Blank stares around the room. Satterfield shook her head, though she looked pained at admitting defeat.

"*Goliath's Head?*"

"*A Farewell to Charms?*" Luke said. "*East of Eternity?*"

Now everybody shook their heads except Gunny Lipe, who seemed to have discovered a particularly interesting spot on the wall the moment the twins arrived.

"Those are comic books?" Anna asked.

"Philistines." Brendan curled his upper lip as if he had stepped in something foul.

"No culture whatsoever." Luke put his nose in the air.

"As I said, certain circles." Robin's tone indicated she wanted things back on track. "The point is, Brendan and Luke are plugged into a vast community."

"What community?" Anna asked.

"Geeks," Luke said with obvious pride. "They read our books; they buy our stuff...they know our names."

"You have fans," Satterfield said.

"That's right, sweetie, scads of them all over the world," Luke said.

"Which means votaries," Brendan said. "The more we get, the better we become."

"You can draw art?" Phil asked.

Luke tilted his head at Bravo platoon's top recruit. "You are either the best comedian I've ever met in real life or a complete dupe for happenstance. Draw art. That's genius."

"No, we can't draw art," Brendan said. "We're both monodraws. We draw dexterity. Except, instead of using it to put bullets through the eyes of fleas, we produce the most atheistically pleasing inks since Michelangelo walked the Earth."

"Okay, you're artists." Phil shrugged like a man conceding a point for the sake of argument rather than conviction. "You've got broad votaries. What's this got to do with us?"

"Simple," Brendan said, "our votaries *es su*...uh, votaries. Sorry, I'm shite at Spanish."

"How?" Despite herself, Anna couldn't deny her interest. Gaining Renni and Lee had significantly boosted her power. What would happen if she gained access to thousands more?

"We plan to launch a new series, and we would like to make one of you the main character."

"I'm with Phil here." Satterfield crossed her arms, looking uncharacteristically skeptical. "How does that gain us votaries?"

"We're not talking about simply placing you in a graphic novel," Brendan said. "This isn't Tuckerization. We're proposing a biography. We want a compelling story that documents your struggles against Society, your work to master skills you've long denied or ignored."

"I never denied my draws," Phil said.

"But did you wash them?" Luke asked.

"Huh?"

"Okay," Anna said, "so you make a biography for one of us, and some people read it, and somehow they become emotionally attached to us? Is that what you're thinking?"

"You doubt it?" Luke straightened his already impeccably positioned tie, one eyebrow raised.

"Yeah. How are they going to know us? I can't draw from people I don't know."

"Oh," Luke said. "It's back to school for us, Bren, and now Anna's the teacher. Isn't she precious?"

"Believe us, it works." Brendan rapped his knuckles on the table in time with his words. "And it's not just going to be the graphic novel tying fans to you. You're going to make special appearances all over the place, dressed in your gear, talking your talk, using your name. We'll hit every con east to west. You'll sign a million autographs, you'll shake babies and kiss hands, you'll have raunchy sex with strangers in hotel bathrooms."

"Brendan, honestly." Robin pinched her nose at the spot between her eyes, looking pained.

"Scratch that last part."

"You'll make us stars?" Satterfield sat up straighter, her eyes suddenly aglow. The doubt previously written in her expression had fled.

"What's a con?" Phil asked.

Both twins smiled. Luke pointed at Phil. "Sorry, sweetie, but you're out of the running for protag. Too uninformed. Besides, girls kick ass this last decade. Everybody's using a girl for their main."

"But what about these two?" Brendan leaned a shoulder against his brother's. "Both hot, both sultry succubus material."

"Gentleman," Robin said. "I will not have you leering at or speculating over my recruits this way. I said the final decision rested with you, but if you're going to sexually harass my female candidates—"

"Honestly, my brother would much rather sexually harass your male candidates," Luke said.

"That's just not true," Brendan said. "Wait, what's today?"

"Tuesday."

"Oh, then you're right."

"Robin," Luke hurried over to the older woman, taking her hands, "this isn't meant to embarrass anyone. But the public likes sex appeal, and it just happens that these girls have it. That's all. Dishwashing detergent sells better when it's in a bottle shaped like a well-endowed woman. Why? Because we're all just brains with a moist bit of sex hormones between us and the outer world. You remember that first *Planet of the Apes* remake in the nineties? Abysmal. Don't get me started on the plot holes. But they had one thing right about the cast. They looked at the female lead and said, how can we work her makeup so she looks like a monkey, only doable? And they did it. I would have done that monkey, Robin. So would Phil. So would Lipe if you could wake him from his homo-coma right now. Let us do our job, and I promise we'll make it as painless as possible." He winked at her before relinquishing her hands and turning to nod at his brother.

"Valerie, you grew up where?" Brendan asked before Robin could retort.

"Nashville."

"All your life?"

"Yes."

"And you, Anna?"

Anna shrugged, uncomfortable. "All over. We were slinkers."

"Oh?" Luke glided to the desk and laid across it to look into Anna's eyes. "Romantic."

"Not really. We moved from slum to slum, sometimes lived in cars for months on end. I never went to one school for more than a couple of months."

"You, Valerie?" Brendan asked. "Did you finish high school?"

"I was a junior at Vanderbilt when the Order found me."

"You graduate, Anna?"

"GED."

Luke beamed at her. "She's perfect, Bren. Per-fect."

"Art loves pain," Brendan said. "The more, the better."

"Wait," Anna said. "I didn't say I would agree to do this."

"I will," Satterfield said.

"It's a mission, Carver." Everyone turned at the interruption. Lipe met their eyes with grim determination. "We need you. Your family needs you. I was right in my prediction, wasn't I? You came back ready to stay, to fight."

Anna hesitated. "Yes, Gunny."

"This is your fight."

Anna didn't want to expose herself this way. Being a slinker meant no one knew anything about you unless you told them. And you never did that. "What do I have to do?"

"Nothing," Brendan said.

"Change your name," Luke said in the same instant.

"What? Why?" Brendan spun to face his brother. "I like Anna."

"What's your full name?" Luke bent past Brendan to peer at Anna. "Anna Rose Carver?"

"Rose Carver." Luke sounded awed. His eyes lit up as he turned an unfaltering smile on his brother.

"Oh, that's good," Brendan said.

"Rose Carver, trudging along a bleak dirt road, towering trees on either side of her, sweat trickling down her face in rivulets. She's got an old duffle on her back, filled with stuff, a rifle strapped to it and a pistol at her hip. She's heading into…uh—"

"Dayton, Ohio," Brendan said.

"Dayton, Ohio. The outskirts, though. She's heard an incubus has taken up residence, a Society puke. He's been using charm to hustle the cod fishermen."

"Cod? In Dayton, Ohio?"

"Shit, okay. So, he's been hustling the good farmers and charming the Catholic girls out of their virtues. Rose Carver's come to town to stop him."

"What am I, a cowboy?" Despite her misgivings, Anna couldn't fight the grin turning up the corners of her mouth.

"No. You're a succubus gunslinger," Luke said as if that were obvious.

"Soldier for hire?" Brendan asked.

"I'm certain you can hash out the details later." The look on Robin's face said that while she appreciated the twins, she could stand only so much of them per day.

"Fine, fine, but we'll need access to Rose," Luke said.

"My name isn't Rose."

"Yes, it is." Luke barely turned his head to look at her. "We'll need access to her often, especially during these preliminary days."

"And a generous travel and costume budget," Brendan added.

"Costumes?" Anna felt the situation spinning out of her control. How had she gone from charming the room to starring in a graphic novel?

"Cosplay, honey. You'll get into it, especially with that figure." Luke gave her a quick but thorough up and down with his eyes.

"The hell does that even mean?"

Brendan put a hand on Luke's shoulder, his face serious. "You know what else we need? Body cams."

"Yes! And drones—the ones with auto-follow so Rose can be about her business without distractions. Those don't cost too much, do they?"

"You'll talk budgets with my finance guy." Robin shooed the twins toward the conference room door with due respect, but unrelenting command.

Body cams? Drones? The whole world seemed to be spiraling out of Anna's control, as if it had ever been in her control. "Wait!" She shot to her feet, catching everyone's attention. "What about training? I haven't graduated yet. And missions. Society has my family. I can't go off playing at being a comic book hero when I should be out there searching for them."

"Society has your folks?" Luke sounded giddy at this news. Seeing the look on Anna's face, he backtracked. "Oh, I'm sorry to hear that. Truly. It's just. This could help. I'll shut up now."

"You'll finish training with your platoon," Lipe said. "I promise."

"And you'll go on missions," Robin said. "It's just that some of yours will be dangerous—"

"And others will involve gun battles with Indrawn Breath operatives," Luke said.

"This feels like you're benching me," Anna said, surprised at her own words. But seeing how the Breathers, how David Lord, had treated the Stone family had changed her outlook. Yes, Anna wanted to save her family from torture, but what about everyone else trapped in the fear factory? What about those families yet to be captured? Anna couldn't sit idle with innocent people on the Indrawn Breath's dinner menu. She had to help.

"Quite the contrary," Robin said. "We aim to see you supplied with more breadth of votaries than any soldier in our ranks. If all goes to plan, you will be our premier warrior, Anna."

"Rose," Luke said.

"You will be a match for anything the Breathers throw at us."

"Even David Lord?" Anna asked, her jaw tight with a strange mix of anger and hope.

Robin nodded. "Especially David Lord."

12

OH, CAPTAIN

"So, Rose," Leslie emphasized the name as if she had just learned it, "what's it going to be? A life of lazy, boring freedom? Or all this luxury with me as an Order operative?"

They crouched behind a fallen tree in thick forest shade, the other twenty-two members of Team Blue fanned out around them. They had been in the field—primeval Georgia forest owned by Camp Den—for eleven hours. Per their scouts, they were miles ahead of their nearest enemies. If this kept up, their team might win the final draw competition.

Anna—Rose, she had to start thinking of herself as Rose—swatted a mosquito on the back of her hand. The little suckers were vicious out here. "What choice do I have? My sister's charmed into working with some sick bastard, and the rest of my family is God knows where."

Rose had told Leslie what she could about the failed mission to save Emily Stone. That included Melody's part in the abduction, but nothing about the supposed fear factory. Gunny Lipe had referred to that information as close hold. Rose could respect that.

"Good," Leslie said.

Rose gave her a sour look.

"Not the sister part." Leslie put a companionable hand on Rose's shoulder. "The joining up part." She smiled. "I need you."

Satterfield's voice crackled over Rose's radio earbud. "Carver and Phelps, approach point."

"What's this about?" Rose asked Leslie.

Leslie shrugged.

They made their way to the front of the column, rucksacks bouncing on their shoulders. Not for the first time on this trip, Rose thanked the heavens she had a draw of strength. The prescribed haul for their kits included everything from toiletries to civilian attire. If she possessed human strength alone, like Leslie, she might have started absent-mindedly dropping items along the way rather than lug it through this oppressive heat. Beginning with the two hidden body cams the Pruetts had fit on her. At least the drones were still being programmed, but tech really wanted a field test of the toys they did have.

They found Satterfield squatting behind a boulder. Myra Hanks, a former high school mathematics teacher, sat next to her. Hanks, who possessed an astonishing draw on discernment, had proven herself a near-clairvoyant during the last few weeks of training, making her an indispensable asset for Satterfield. The two poured over aerial footage on a large tablet computer. At first, it appeared to show a small town. Except it had no paved roads leading into it, just a gravel lane that meandered in from the south. The buildings, dominated by a three-story tower crewed by six armed guards on the roof, appeared incomplete. Some were merely painted façades.

"This is it," whispered Satterfield when Rose and Leslie approached. "Hanks says the captains are in that urbanized area."

The older woman didn't look so confident but said nothing to correct her squad leader.

"Are we heading in?" Rose hadn't been pleased when the draw sergeants announced this field exercise. It sounded like a giant game of capture the flag with the bonus that you might get tagged by painful, high-velocity paintballs, the reason the techs fit her with two body cams, in case the paintballs coated one. But now that she was in the thick of the game, she found her pulse quickening. She wanted to win.

Satterfield shook her head. "Not all of us. Not yet. Trees are cleared for at least an eighth of a mile in every direction. There's no way we could make the approach without getting slaughtered."

"You think the captains are in that tower?" Leslie asked.

"I doubt it," Rose said.

Satterfield narrowed her eyes. "Why's that?"

"It doesn't feel right. Why the pretense of a fake town if our prize is inside the most obvious place?"

"Bystanders," Satterfield said. "Lipe or Ambrose, whoever designed this thing, wants our teams spraying innocents while we try to take the tower."

"I'm with Rose on this one," Hanks said. "I doubt the captains are in there."

"Is that a discernment, or just your gut talking?" Satterfield asked.

Hanks cocked her head as if listening to something the others couldn't hear. "Hard to say. I can't see the people we're dealing with."

"That's why I need you two." Satterfield indicated Rose and Leslie. "You've got the most charm in the platoon. I want you to use it to get into the town, figure out where the captains are being held, and clue us in."

"That's a long way to walk without cover," Leslie said. "I could snipe all six of the guards from a tree and save us the trouble."

Satterfield shook her head. "Too risky. Those can't be the only armed resistance."

"You think our charm will reach the tower?" Rose asked. She didn't know how she felt about becoming the team's sacrificial lamb.

"I think you're going to find out."

Fifteen minutes later, having dropped their weapons and exchanged their camo uniforms for jeans and t-shirts, Rose and Leslie strode across the empty expanse between Team Blue's hiding spot and the fake town. Sweat drenched Rose's face. She held her arms up, trying to avoid pit stains. Too late. She cut her eyes at Leslie. "You could at least sweat."

"I am."

"No, you're glistening prettily. Makes me sick."

Leslie laughed.

The previously gravel lane gave way to pavement as it neared the city proper. Without discussing it, Rose and Leslie circled toward the asphalt. A faded sign, its paint chipped and worn, read, "Smash Town."

"Subtle," Rose said.

"Let's hope it's true," Leslie said.

Smash Town consisted of four roads, two running north to south, two east to west. Main Street—there was a sign—bustled with pedestrians while all others stood empty. Men and women dressed in everyday clothes strolled along its narrow sidewalks, chatting on cell phones, jogging, and peering into shop windows.

No one paid Rose or Leslie the least bit of attention. Did that mean Rose's draw of charm obscured their concentration as she intended? Or had Robin and Lipe coached these actors to ignore interlopers? Rose decided to test it.

"Excuse me, sir." She approached a squat man sitting on a wooden bench outside a barbershop.

He didn't look up at first, but when Rose repeated herself, the old guy peered around as if someone had called his name. He looked genuinely confused.

"Guess our charm shield is working," Leslie said. "Now what?"

Rose jogged to the corner of Main and First. There she spun slowly in a circle, observing the town, taking it all in as she added discernment to her draw of charm. While she couldn't hope to match Myra Hanks in that department, Rose had her fair share of insight. Renni and Lee had seen to that.

Of all her powers, Rose considered discernment the strangest, maybe because it wasn't physical like speed or dexterity. Or perhaps the oddness stemmed from what she perceived as a lack of control when it came to this elusive draw. Unlike those others, discernment hinged on the human ability to guess at outcomes. The bulk of this guessing came down to interpreting an adversary's micro-tissue facial expressions—the nearly imperceptible contractions of eye, cheek, or lips. Those, coupled with larger scale body movements, could inform a succubus much about another person's intentions whether she was trying to catch a lie or broker a multi-billion-dollar merger.

But what if these people, these actors, didn't know what she was seeking? What good was discernment when the individuals you could see didn't have the information you wanted? That was when discernment leaped the infinitesimal line between reality and something preternatural. Tiny clues, subtle hints Rose was not aware of on anything approaching a conscious level, stuck out to some dark section of her mind. These could be as minuscule as the way a fake grocer stocked the gum rack outside his store.

Maybe he didn't know where the captains were hidden in this town, but he had seen something—an unusual number of people entering one of the fake buildings, a delivery boy bringing sandwiches to what should be an empty section of town, or perhaps just the way one of the other actors walked. Whatever the trigger, something caused him to place his empty packs of sugar free gum in a certain order concealed even from his own conscious mind. Rose, equally as unaware of that order as the phony grocer, could nonetheless use it to zero in on her target by dint of her draw on intuition.

Or, maybe she was blowing smoke up her imaginary skirt. Either way, she spun in her tracks to point at the Smash Town Credit Union. "There. That's the place."

The bank occupied a small building with a large glass window, cheap red carpets, and one of those rope mazes bank managers set up to keep the tellers from being overwhelmed by customers. Except there were no customers in the Smash Town Credit Union. It contained two teller positions, one empty, the other staffed by a guy dressed in a blue blazer and matching tie. Absorbed in a game on his phone, he didn't notice Rose and Leslie enter.

"Follow my lead." Rose bypassed the line maze to march toward the counter. She maintained her draw on charm until she stood inches from the teller's face. The guy let out a squeak of surprise when she dropped it.

"Hi," Rose said.

"You scared the shi—" the would-be teller began. Then, remembering himself, he straightened his tie, and said, "Welcome to Smash Town Credit Union. How may I help you today?"

Rose gave Leslie a sly smile that the redhead returned in earnest. They drew charm in unison, this time to overwhelm rather than obscure. The teller's face went instantly slack, his glossy eyes riveted on Rose's face.

"Oh, God you're beautiful," he breathed.

Rose gave him her best demure smile. She hadn't much practice with that sort of thing, but by the look on the teller's face, that wouldn't matter. "Thank you. What's your name?"

"Charlie, but I'm not supposed to tell you that."

"It's okay. Can you tell me where they're holding the captains, Charlie?"

His eyes flicked down to the empty counter. A pained look crossed his face as he deliberated. "I don't—I don't think I'm supposed to do that."

Rose glanced at Leslie, who moved closer. "We'd be grateful if you'd help us, Charlie. We really want to find those captains."

Charlie shuddered. "All right. They're in the vault." He hooked a thumb over one shoulder.

Rose came around the counter, tapped on the vault door. "It's real?"

"Oh, yeah. But it's not sealed. The people inside aren't going to suffocate or anything. They have movies and stuff to do."

The steel door had a keypad the size of a notebook computer at its center. Touchscreen buttons glowed on its face.

"Can you open it for us?" Rose asked.

Charlie's face fell. "I can't. Don't know how. But I can get Drakes. He's the maintenance guy for the fake town. He knows how to open it."

"Is he one of the town's actors?"

"No. Just a fix-it guy. You're never supposed to see him."

Rose clicked her tongue. "That won't do."

"I want to help you," Charlie said, his tone piteous. He turned to Leslie. "Both of you at once."

"Yuck." Leslie curled her lips at the besotted Charlie.

Rose keyed her mic. "Blue Ox, this is Bubble."

"Bubble, go ahead," replied Satterfield's tinny voice through the earbud.

"We're Copeland." Rose indicated that they had found the captains but had no way to extract them on their own.

"Roger that, Bubble. We're—" Satterfield cut off.

The next instant brought the report of distant gunfire. Though standard paintball guns—everyone called them markers—made less noise than a well-suppressed rifle, the Order had modified the teams' weapons to sound like regular gunfire. That made it harder for one team to sit in the woods and snipe another from cover.

"Shit," Leslie said.

Rose peered out the window and her throat constricted. Uniformed men and women herded the fake civilians between the two tallest buildings on Main Street. She didn't see many, perhaps seven or eight, but their uniforms were a mix of red and orange tinged camouflage, and that meant trouble.

"Blue Ox, Bubble. You there?"

A static-filled five seconds passed during which several booms rattled the fake bank's plate glass window. Then Satterfield's voice returned.

"Bubble, Blue Ox. We took some fire, but no one was hit. It was a feint. One of the other teams is in the town. What do you see? Over."

"It's two teams, Red and Orange. Looks like they combined forces. Over."

"Dammit."

"Attention, all citizens," said an amplified voice from outside. "Exit your places of business and proceed to the intersection of First and Main for safe haven."

"They're coming," Leslie said. "What now?"

Rose tore the radio from her ear as she raced behind the counter.

She dropped it on the floor. "Charlie, hide. Les, get that thing out of your ear. We're bank tellers."

"But—"

"Do it."

The front door banged open. A big man dressed in orange camo entered with a smaller guy in tow. They looked surprised to see Rose and Leslie.

"Good afternoon, sir. Welcome to Smash Town Credit Union." Rose tried to mimic Leslie's usual chipper tone. Would these guys notice the sheen of sweat on her forehead?

"Did you hear me out there?" the big guy asked. He was way too tall to be an incubus, but genetics wore funny trousers sometimes.

"We can't abandon our posts," Rose said. "Someone might rob the bank."

"Funny." He cocked a thumb over his shoulder. "We've taken the city. The rest of your actor buddies are already out there. My squad leader doesn't want anybody shot that isn't asking for it, but that don't mean I won't tag your ass if it's dragging. Got me, honey?"

"I got you." Rose motioned below the counter for Leslie to follow her lead. She had no intention of leaving the bank without a fight, but attacking these guys unarmed sounded ill-advised. "Come on, Les. Let's go."

Leslie nodded, and they started around the counter headed for the exit.

"Wait," said the smaller guy.

Rose kept walking.

"I know that one. She's Torres's pet sime, the one that keeps winning all the sprint trials."

Before he had even stopped speaking, his partner let loose with a volley of shots. They passed through where Rose had been standing to splatter against the plate glass window with a rhythmic thump-thump-thump, turning instantly into orange slime.

Rose hit the far wall at a dead run, took five steps up it toward the corner, and leapt at the shooter. He twisted to follow her trail but met her foot instead. She pulled the kick—a bit. But the big man toppled sole over crown, taking out his smaller friend in the process.

The little guy remained conscious if disoriented. Leslie swiped his marker and tagged him with it once at point-blank range.

"Geez, that hurt!" He rubbed his chest, spreading finger-sized paint splotches across his uniform.

"Shut up; you're dead." Leslie tossed his gun aside.

"Fine."

She tagged the big guy too, splattering his facemask. She shrugged at Rose's quizzical look. "Don't want him thinking he's still in the game when he comes around."

Rose got back on the radio. "Ox?"

"Bubble."

"We secure?"

"Yes," Satterfield said.

Rose hesitated. "Is this signal secure?"

"They have the town," Satterfield said. "Their forces are already assaulting the tower. Our squad has zero chance of coming in there without taking heavy casualties. I doubt anything you say now is going to compromise us."

"You can't come in force, but could you send one or two people?"

"What for?"

"The king isn't in his castle," Rose hoped Satterfield would take her meaning.

A long pause. "You sure."

Rose glanced at the vault door. "Yeah, but we need Moss down here. Now. We took out a couple of theirs, and I don't know when they're going to be missed."

"Honestly," the little guy said, "I doubt we will. We didn't get put on civie round up because we're super troopers. Bradford there is a sime, but nobody trusts him, and all I've got is a draw on voice."

"Ox, get Moss here quick."

"Roger Wilco."

Gunfire erupted outside. It sounded like the guys in the tower were putting up a hell of a fight. Rose peered out, but all she could see were the civilians. Most sat on the sidewalk or in the street looking bored while their captors stood by smoking cigarettes and chatting, their weapons hanging on straps.

"That's good," Leslie said. "They look complacent."

Twenty minutes passed, thirty. The gunfight never ceased. Twice guards peeled away from the civilian group, jogging toward the tower. Reinforcements.

Rose bit her lip. Their dwindling numbers meant less chance one of them would spot something amiss, but it also meant the opposing commanders hadn't given up. They were hell-bent on taking that tower, but when they did, they would find it empty. Then it would only be a matter of time before she and Leslie were found out.

Game over.

A thumping noise erupted inside the bank's interior wall.

"The hell was that?" Charlie asked, standing up from his hiding place behind the counter, rubbing his eyes. He peered around blearily. "Who are you people? What—"

Rose shot him in the chest, and he yelped.

"Ow, dammit! Was that necessary?"

"Yes."

The thumping continued, growing louder.

"You aren't supposed to shoot the actors," Charlie complained, rubbing his chest and smearing blue goo.

"Shut up."

A crack appeared in the wall, tiny at first, but it spread quickly. The thumping came louder, faster, until a claw hammer burst through, showering bits of drywall onto the red carpet.

"Leslie?" asked a young man's voice.

"Moss!" Leslie ran to the opening.

"Hey, cutie. I heard you two needed the resident genius."

"How'd you know where to find us? I mean you didn't come in the bank part."

"Hanks is with me, and about half the team. Red and Orange are so busy they've pulled in all their point protection. We pretty much walked right in. Hey, back up. This wall's flimsy, but it's still gonna take some work to push through."

A series of booming blows followed by a terrific crack saw the wall crumble outward. Moss, covered in white dust from head to toe, appeared with Hanks and twelve more armed members of Team Blue.

"Carver," Moss said.

Rose stepped forward.

Moss saluted. "Acting Captain Satterfield sends her regards and orders you to take charge of this contingent of Team Blue. She's using the rest to harry the perimeter, make it seem like Red and Orange are under attack."

Rose felt her back stiffen. Satterfield was giving her command of half the team? She didn't know what to say. Almost without thinking, she returned Moss's salute. "Ah, okay."

Moss smiled. "Show me what you wanted me for."

"There's an electronic lock on that safe. Think you can break it?" Rose asked.

"Sure thing, boss."

The big guy, who had been out all this time, groaned.

"You want we should tie these enemies up?" asked Frangle, an incubus with a pronounced Brooklyn accent.

"No." Rose's mind whirled. She never guessed command would throw her like this. Sweat trickled down the center of her back.

She drew a breath. Calm. Be calm. The squad would feed off what they saw in her. Best to look in charge even if she didn't feel it.

Rose drew discernment and mental acuity. Every trait had its limit —she wasn't going to suddenly become Patten or Einstein—but these helped immeasurably. "Okay, people. There's a lot of you for this enclosed space. I want you four back in the tunnel. Secure the entrance you made. The rest of you fan out. I want clear lanes of fire on the door and that opening."

Suddenly, the nearby gunfire ceased. Rose had a fraction of a second to realize this before her radio crackled.

"Bubble, you got incoming. Looks like Red and Orange secured the tower but came up empty. They're doing a house-by-house now, and they're moving in force since they see no resistance."

"You okay, Ox?"

"Fine here but pinned down. They've dispatched at least twenty to take us out. How's the prize?"

"Still wrapped," Rose said. "But Moss is working on it."

"Good. Don't let me down, Carver."

"Roger Wilco."

Rose put her head against the glass to peer down the street. A cadre of at least thirty armed soldiers jogged her way. Divvied up into clearing teams of five to seven, they worked in unison to search every corner of the faked-up town.

"Moss?"

"It's coded," was all he said.

"Yeah, I think I got that. But how long is it going to take for you to break it."

Moss gave her a withering look over one shoulder and got back to work.

"Charlie, does this door lock?" Rose asked.

"Go screw yourself. I'm dead."

Twelve armed succubi turned their eyes on the actor. He shrank back against the wall. "No. It doesn't lock, okay? Damn."

CRACK!

Rose's team turned nervous eyes on her. They all knew that sound from countless tac team drills. Someone had just kicked in the door on the fake restaurant beside the bank.

Rose set her jaw, firming her resolve. "First bastard comes through that door, light 'em up." She pressed her rifle to her shoulder and felt a surge of pride when the others did likewise, their faces grim but determined.

Voices approached, followed by a heavy boot that kicked the bank door off its hinges. A lithe woman wearing red-tinged fatigues charged into the room, greeted by a hailstorm of blue paintballs. They slammed her backward onto her butt. She couldn't suppress a surprised yelp but, playing by the rules, fell immediately still in the doorway.

Nevertheless, her faux death alerted the combined teams outside. A cry of alarm rose, and several of the clearing teams abandoned their assigned tasks to assault the entrance.

After that came chaos.

The gunfire threatened to deafen Rose. She rolled to one side of the counter for cover and clicked the noise dampening button on her earbuds. Then she rolled back and opened fire. Despite her poor angle of attack, she thought she tagged at least three of the enemy in the first five seconds of the assault. The rest of Blue fared better, taking out scads of red and orange enemies as the room began to fill with an inky haze of smoke mixed with paint fumes.

But the numbers were against them. For every red or orange they took out, two more took their place. Myra caught a red pellet in the face shield. A round exploded on Leslie's shoulder. Per the rules, she was out and so had to hotfoot it to a safe corner of the bank. In the next twenty seconds, four more of Rose's remaining defenders fell to enemy fire. No amount of speed or intuition could overcome such a volley.

Someone yelled from inside the tunnel. Rose pulled out an earbud and heard gunfire echo through the gap Moss had opened.

"They're coming in behind us, too!" she screamed, though she doubted anyone could hear over the den of coughing guns and splattering pellets.

"GOT IT!" Moss abandoned the electronic lock. He stood and spun an oversized knob on the bank vault door.

Rose bounded over the bank counter, rolled, and came up in time to see the door inching open. She put her shoulder to it, drawing strength, and it finally gained momentum. The thing must have weighed tons.

Inside the vault stood five draw sergeants dressed in colored fatigues matching their respective teams.

Behind Rose, her last team member fell with a cry. She didn't need to look; she felt it through her discernment. Red and orange soldiers were swarming into the bank, screaming commands, calling for her surrender.

"Sergeant," Rose said to Torres, as an orange pellet struck Moss in the back of the head. "Duck."

Rose drew more speed than she had ever gathered in her life. Unlike intellect, where her limit had been hit and well measured during draw training, she had no idea how fast she could go. Without waiting for Torres to completely drop from view, she painted the other four captains, one blue splatter each. Only then did she flinch, first left then right, avoiding every paintball that came her way, moving faster than her enemies could counter.

She dove backward into the room, gun thrumming in her hand, her body a blaze of speed and dexterity. Moving this fast, she would have thought time slowed. It didn't. Instead, she raced after time, chasing it between jellified blobs of paint, letting not one mar her clothes, her hair, her skin. She crossed the room in seconds, having marked every soldier in her path, kicking off this one, flipping over that one, and putting blue paint on chests and backs, thighs, and arms.

When she landed in the corner, breast heaving, gun raised, she became suddenly aware of Sergeant Torres screaming her name.

"You will stand down, NOW, Carver. Do you understand me?"

Rose stood. "Yes, Sergeant."

People lay groaning on the floor, many of them unable to rise. Rose stared at them in horrified amazement. Had she done all this? The man nearest her nursed a broken wrist, his hand jutting out at a peculiar angle. As her awareness enlarged, taking in those around him, she saw others with similar injuries: broken legs, dislocated shoulders, fingers misaligned from sockets. Realization at what she had done crashed in on Rose like a falling sky. She had cut a path of destruction through the enemy. Though she had intended to tag them, her kicks and pushes, meant to redirect her momentum, had pulverized bones, ripped muscles, and torn ligaments.

"Oh, God. I'm sorry." The marker dropped from her hand.

"No, Carver," Torres said, murder in her eyes. "You're not even close to sorry yet."

13

NO POMP, ALL CIRCUMSTANCE

Five weeks later, Rose and Leslie stood third and fourth in a line of at least fifty recruits inside the main foyer of Links, waiting their turn to declare their intentions with the Order.

Graduation had been a near thing for Rose. Sergeant Torres had fought to recycle her into a junior class, claiming she needed more training after the field exercise incident, but Gunny Lipe had overridden the sergeant. Unfortunately, Lipe hadn't interfered when Torres insisted Rose fill in for all the people she had put in the infirmary. That meant a lot of sleepless nights playing guard and endless evenings spent mopping floors and scrubbing toilets. On top of that, Torres had insisted Rose could not heal herself for the remainder of training, as a reminder not everyone can draw heal. Her hands were still red and tender from all the extra cleaning duty.

Thankfully, graduation had finally arrived, and with it, the big choice: remain with the Order, or return to the real world?

Most trainees had no choice. Now that they had graduated, the Order could no longer afford to feed, clothe, and house them in perpetuity. As monodraws of no significant depth, they had little to offer the Order. A few would return to their old lives with excuses as to their prolonged absences. But the majority would simply go back to slinking—no explanation necessary.

Some monodraws, like Leslie, possessed significant skills. She had graduated top of their class in marksmanship, and second in Camp Den history. If she wanted to hire on with the Order, they would take her, and gladly.

For polydraws, especially simes like Rose, the Order poured on the pressure. First, with guilt. If they chose to leave, it would be a slap in the face to all those who had been taken by the Breathers—a much more horrifying truth for Rose than most others, who knew nothing about the fear factory. Who knew how many innocents a sime might save by joining?

Then came the offers of money. While the Order wasn't immense, it had plenty of cash, owing to several corporations it owned, all of them almost exclusively staffed by succubi. Rose would earn more than six times what she made during her best years waitressing.

The best part? Deciding without the influence of charm. The all-encompassing wave had ceased shortly after the Emily Stone debacle. No one had said anything to Rose about it, but she took pride in having gotten through to Robin on the matter.

"Yeah, what are you going to do, Carver?" Moss held Leslie's hand, no doubt a delicious privilege now that they had graduated.

"Don't you want to be surprised?"

"I just hope we get a dual assignment." Leslie bumped her shoulder against Moss's.

"We will, don't worry."

"Did you do something?" Leslie's eyes narrowed.

"How could I? Camp Den has a closed and completely secure network."

The line moved forward. It was Leslie's turn. She gave her name to the bored-looking sergeant behind a metal desk outfitted with a tablet computer and micro-printer.

With Leslie's attention elsewhere, Moss gave Rose a wink. Though computer skills weren't a draw per se, Moss's deep pull on mental acuity seemed to run that direction, as if intelligence came in different flavors, and his had an extra dose of electronics extract.

"What did you get, hon?" Moss asked when Leslie stepped away with her printed assignment sheet.

Leslie wrinkled her nose. "Team Dog Ears. Sounds butch. I hope it's not a bunch of macho guys flashing their hardware around."

Rose and Moss stared at her, deadpan.

"You two are sick. I meant guns, bozos."

"There's an offer here," the clerk said when Moss gave his name. "You want to hire on?"

"Yes, Sergeant. Team Dog Ears, please."

"It's a random draw, son. Needs of the Order and all."

"I have a good feeling." Moss gave the clerk a million-dollar smile.

The printer spit out a form. The clerk puzzled over it for nearly half a minute, his jaw working in consternation. "That's crazy. You called it. Dog Ears. You must have quite the draw on discernment."

"Been practicing." Moss took the paper, his smile wider than ever.

Rose gave her name, chose to hire on to the cheers of Leslie and Moss, and got her form.

"Son of a bitch," the old clerk said. "I've never seen this thing spit out three of the same team in a row."

"Dog Ears?" Rose asked, amused.

"Yep. That's Lord Snow's outfit."

Rose tilted her head. "Lord Snow?"

"You know, the Night's Watch? Rightful king of Winterfell?" He raised a questioning brow at Leslie and Moss.

"She doesn't nerd," Moss said with a shrug.

Rose checked her form. Team lead for Dog Ears was Matt Snow. A typed message at the bottom invited her to meet him in private at an office in Links at 1730.

He wanted to meet with her? In private? She reread it. Were her cheeks growing warm?

This had to mean something. Matt refused to date recruits, which had seemed like a stupid rule to Rose six weeks ago, back when she wanted nothing more than to escape Camp Den. Now it made sense. A lot of things did.

But Rose had finally graduated, and Matt wanted a private meeting.

They headed for the exit walking side by side, Leslie and Moss chatting animatedly. Rose's mind wandered, harkening back to a hundred illicit smiles and winks she had shared with Matt during her final weeks of training. He hadn't shown up often after their fight with Lord, but he always seemed to have an eye out for Rose whenever he turned up at one exercise or another. She had half convinced herself those stolen glances lived solely in her imagination. Basic training amounted to extended deprivation after all, even for a natural introvert like Rose, which tended to make the stoniest of hearts pine for romance.

Rose read the invitation a third time. No. She hadn't imagined things. He wanted to see her. Alone.

"What time is your appointment with Snow?" Leslie asked with the sort of offhand cruelty dealt by a bitter enemy or an uninformed friend. "I'm seeing him at 1530."

Something deflated inside Rose. The meeting wasn't special. Matt hadn't been waiting for her to graduate so that he could pursue his feelings for her. He wanted to discuss Order business. Of course, he did. What else? Rose felt like a dolt for assuming anything more.

"Rose?" Leslie peered at her, chin dropped, eyebrows raised. "You okay?"

"Yeah. Uh, mine's not till 1730." Why did Rose feel like the whole world had caught fire beneath her? Matt had said he liked her. So what? That had been weeks ago. And what of it? Was he in like with her? What did that even mean? Nothing. Right?

"Great, you want to grab some chow with us, Anna, er, Rose?" Moss shook his head at his mistake, though Rose hardly noticed. "I'm helping Leslie move to Teams Housing after our interview with Snow. We can help you if you like."

"No thanks." Rose kept her voice bright, her face as clear of expression as she could manage. "Everything I've got fits in one backpack."

"Who's your roommate?" Leslie flicked a hand at Rose's orders. "It's printed at the bottom."

Rose scanned her printout, thankful for anything to distract her from thoughts of Matt Snow, at least until she saw the name printed next to hers. "It's Satterfield."

"Ew. Sorry." Leslie made a face like she smelled rotten fish. "Wish we could have roomed together. Maybe they'll let us later, once we've been in Teams for a while."

"Hope so," Rose said, though she had a sneaking suspicion Moss would invite Leslie to move in with him as soon as their probationary period ended.

"Anyway, you should come eat," Leslie said. "Seems like I've hardly seen you these past few days."

"Wish I could, but I've got a medical appointment. I'll catch up with you soon, promise."

Rose did have an appointment, though it wasn't at the infirmary. She crossed the now-familiar main road between Links and Teams Housing, a block of six long, gray buildings that reminded her of World War II-era slums. Each contained forty apartments, two to every shower-toilet combo. Luxury accommodations they were not, but they beat sleeping in barracks rooms filled sixty deep with steel bunk beds.

Rose headed for the apartment at the end of the block. The surrounding rooms stood empty, awaiting new graduates, but not the last one. She heard voices emanating from inside as she drew near, arguing, not heatedly, but with insistence. She knocked, and they fell silent.

Luke Pruett opened the door, his face cracking into a cheesy grin the instant he saw her.

"Rose!" he bellowed, taking her by the hands, dragging her bodily into the room. "Look at you, all rugged chic. You are smoking those jeans, girl." He turned to his brother, a look of shock on his sharp-featured face. "Brendan, would you look at her arms? We've got them all wrong. They're toned, not ripped. That entire second set has got to be redone."

Brendan sat on the bed, a large sketchpad balanced on his knees. "Hi, Rose," he said.

"I got your invitation." Rose held it up, a large sheaf of fine vellum embossed with silver and gold. One side bore her name and the apartment number. The other featured a highly stylized heart, its outer line snaking down to form a curled devil's tail.

"You like the sigil?" Luke pointed at the heart.

"It's beautiful," Rose said.

"It's the motif. I drew it first, just noodling around on a legal pad while trying out concepts for the book. Everything else sprang from that."

"Everything else?" Rose hadn't seen the twins in several days. They had met with her three times immediately following the Emily Stone catastrophe, pumping her for every scrap of information she could remember, both about the mission and her life in general. Then their requests for meetings had ceased until a lower classman delivered Luke's handmade invitation this morning before graduation. The only other contact she had related to this "mission" had been the tech team outfitting her with body cams in her training uniforms. No one questioned any of her coming and going since she had been sent all over the campus running extra duties waiting for people to heal enough to leave the infirmary.

Brendan opened a large portfolio case on the bed. "Have a look."

The first page featured a sketch of Rose lugging a serving tray weighed down with dirty dishes—charcoal on white paper, but exquisitely detailed. Matt Snow sat at the bar, telling an animated story to a crowd of rapt onlookers in the background. Off to one side, two men in suits hunched over platter-sized steaks, their eyes glued to Rose.

"You like it?" For once Luke's voice held no mirth, only honest curiosity. He watched her minutely, his face expectant.

"God," Rose said. "How did you get the bar down so well? I never told you about the Budweiser hoods over the pool tables."

"We went there," Brendan said. "We went everywhere."

Rose stared at him for a moment, speechless. Then she said, "I don't think anybody has ever said this about Pete's, but it's gorgeous. Just gorgeous."

"Thanks," Brendan said. He turned the page.

The next image depicted Rose sitting on her butt in the moonlight, lips spread in a sudden smile, eyes crinkled, two Dobermans licking at her face and hands.

The next showed her standing in the middle of a darkened road, three bodies strewn at her feet, her hands covering her mouth. Somehow, the twins had captured her unspeakable fear at that moment when Matt had stolen her courage.

Every page brought with it memories, feelings she could live again through the twins' artistry. She shuddered when she reached the Stone house.

Melody sat on the couch, pressing a pistol into Emily Stone's ribs while Lord, smirking at Matt, caressed Satterfield's face, Mr. Stone dead at his feet.

Unexpected tears rolled down Rose's cheeks. She brushed them away for fear of marring the charcoals. The twins watched her, smiling, obviously taking pleasure in her reaction.

The last set of sketches were from this morning: graduation, two hundred men and women standing on the training floor in Links. Proud. Triumphant. They had each gone forward to receive a fake certificate stating they had graduated the Camp Den basic training fitness boot camp. But everyone knew what that embossed piece of cardstock really meant.

"I'm glad you like them," Brendan said.

"These are just mockups," Luke said. "The final book will be far better."

"Better than these?" Rose asked.

"Light years."

The final drawing was a quick sketch of Rose's graduation certificate, centered on her name. Beneath this, in stylized script, were the words, *Change is Coming*.

"That's the end of book one," Luke said. "You approve?"

Rose couldn't find her voice. She nodded. She hadn't realized till now what the graduation meant to her. Anna Rose Carver, child of slinkers, had never finished anything like this in her life.

"We have a release for you to sign," Brendan said. "Just legal stuff. Says we're allowed to use your name and likeness and entitles you to residuals."

Rose signed. "Anything else?"

"We go to press in three weeks," Brendan said.

"So soon? Will you be done?"

"We're fast, sweetie. At least, that's what our conquests tell us." Brendan huffed on his manicured fingernails and polished them on his collar.

"And we want to get this thing out in time for the launch party we already scheduled for May," Luke said.

"Party as in music and drinks?" Rose asked.

"Party as in a hundred thousand book and comic fans, fellow artists, influential editors. That sort of thing," Brendan said.

Rose rubbed at the tracking device in her shoulder. "This is something I have to attend?"

"It's called MegaCon." Luke gave her a smile two parts mirth, one part mayhem. "It's one of the biggest geek parties of the year. So yes, you're coming. It's a must."

"Where?" Rose asked, ready to protest it being too far away.

"Florida," Brendan said.

"You're not getting out of this, Rosie," Luke said. "This is just the first of many. We're gonna be making the rounds the next few months. Nothing sells graphic novels like live appearances."

"Plus, Luke and I will be dropping hints about you and *Drawn* everywhere we go the next few weeks." Brendan held up a calendar display on his tablet computer. Every weekend denoted a different event, and each had a special note that read: ***Promote Drawn!***

"Your fans are going to be drooling before you ever set foot at MegaCon!" Luke fairly bounced in place, giddy.

"Don't look that way," Brendan said. "We'll be there with you."

"I'm sewing your costume!" Luke said.

Rose blanched. "Oh, God."

By the time Rose extricated herself from the twins' company, her Fitbit clock read 1734. Careful not to draw speed—no one could use their powers outside approved times on Camp Den for fear of satellite or aerial surveillance—she ran for Links. She hit the front entrance, sweaty and probably smelling of it, at 1742.

She swore.

Matt had reserved an office on the third floor for team interviews. Rose debated waiting for the elevator but ended up bypassing it for the stairs. She took them four at a time, drawing speed along with dexterity to maintain her balance, and bolted through the third-floor doors less than a minute later.

She met Matt in the hall, headed for the elevators. He walked with the aid of a silver cane, something she hadn't noticed when she had seen him from afar at graduation this morning. Seeing him like this brought her up short.

"Never seen a man use a cane before, Carver?" he asked, quirking that half smile of his.

Rose was so surprised to have caught him—she thought for sure he had given up waiting on her and gone home—that she blurted the first thing that hit her tongue. "Not at Camped In."

He huffed. It was something between a laugh and a desultory snort. Camped In was the recruits' name for the place when draw sergeants weren't around.

"I'm sorry," she said. "I thought you would be healed by now."

"I still have bullet fragments entangled in the joint. Every time Dr. Stanislaw thinks she's got them all, there's more."

"How many surgeries have you had?"

"Seven."

"I'm so sorry."

He shrugged. "You're late by the way."

"I'm sorry about that too. I was with the twins." Rose leaned against the wall, self-conscious under his gaze.

"I've seen their sketches. They do good work."

A silence fell between them. They stood next to a large window that showed the main training area on Rose's right and a recessed doorway on her left. She tried the door. It opened.

"Is it too late?" She gestured inside the darkened room. "That is unless you're going to fire me."

"I'm not firing you, Carver. But I want you to know, I had nothing to do with putting you on my team."

"Okay…" Rose raised her eyebrows.

"Left to me, I wouldn't have chosen you for my team."

Rose rocked back on her heels, stung. Had she really raced up here for this? "I'll put in a request for transfer first thing tomorrow."

"No, that's not—"

"Look," Rose said, "you say you like me, but I'm a trainee. Then I graduate, and you complain because I'm on your team. I don't know what the hell you want from me, but—"

Gently, without force, Matt put three fingers to her lips. "That came out wrong. I'm sorry. I would not have put you on my team because then I could do this without feeling like a lecher."

He cupped her face and kissed her.

Rose was no great judge of kisses. She had only ever had one legit kiss in her life. Junior year in high school, in the fourth town her family had moved to in seven months, Brian Greer had taken her to a movie, dinner, and then kissed her in his dad's car outside her parents' apartment. It had been a messy affair, not because Brian came on too strong, but because he had lousy aim. He kissed the bottom of her nose then slid gradually down to pucker against her lips. Despite the awkwardness, it had been sweet. Brian had been sweet.

Her family had moved away a week later when her dad got a job in Kansas.

Matt's kiss was far more pleasant than that one. Though he too was tentative, and not the least bit aggressive, his soft lips pressing against hers ignited a fire in her throat, and strangely enough, her cheeks. She was blushing.

He pulled back. "Was that rude? I don't mean to be. I can't seem to talk when I'm around you. It's like I revert to awkward teenager."

Rose grabbed him by the lapels, pulled him to her. With their lips just touching, she said, "Shut up, Snow."

She fumbled behind her, opened the door, and dragged him inside.

14

———

CONVENTIONAL THINKING

"You're sure about this?" The spandex around Rose's boobs kept bunching underneath. She pulled it straight for the hundredth time.

"What part?" Luke paid her scant attention. He held a mascara mirror to his left eye, checking his eyeliner. The man looked ridiculous. He wore what might have passed for an Egyptian Pharaoh costume, except for everything about it! The high collar reached his pointed prosthetic earlobes. A series of pleats ran down his shoulders almost to the getup's comically dagged sleeves. And as if that alone didn't push him over the cliff of anachronism, he wore his hair in a perfectly coifed bowl cut that made him look like one of the Beatles circa 1965.

"This costume for a start. I feel like you guys should wheel me out there with a stripper pole."

Rose's blue, skin-tight stretch suit left little to the imagination. Thankfully, the twins had sewn in a couple of concealers to keep her more prominent parts from poking through the material. It was supposed to be an assault uniform, the kind she might wear in a firefight against Breathers. And while the overall effect might have been one of toughness and durability with its fake ammo pockets and knee-high leather boots, Rose thought it spoke more of teenage boy fantasies and once in a lifetime honeymoon escapades.

"Stripper pole, huh?" Brendan said. "Not a bad idea. 'Course, that suit wouldn't peel very easily. We might have to oil you up."

Rose swatted his arm in mock outrage.

He grinned.

Rose peeked through the curtain separating her from what looked like roughly one billion people crowded into a conference room. The partitioned waiting area she shared with the twins seemed to grow smaller. She finally understood the *mega* in MegaCon. Mega crowds. Mega excitement. Mega nerves.

Her stomach fluttered. She hadn't known it could do that.

"Don't worry about the crowd," Luke said. "Lots more will show up once we get out there. Those are just the early birds."

"You know," Rose said, "Egyptians didn't wear those sorts of robes."

Luke gave her a withering look. "We're not Egyptians, you Philistine. I'm a Romulan."

"And I'm a Vulcan." Brendan made a show of smoothing his already flat collar. His costume, gold on burgundy with a decidedly floral sense though it contained no flowers whatsoever, favored Luke's. And yet, comparing the two, Rose saw minute differences in the cut and fit that gave each a distinctive flair.

"Is that Star Wars or Star Trek?"

"You are severely undereducated, woman," Luke said.

"So, you have to be a nerd to understand the costumes?" Rose quirked an eyebrow at them.

"Don't even go there." Brendan held up both hands as if stopping an out of control bus. "In a second my brother's going to start a debate about whether it would take a nerd or a geek to recognize proper Star Trek uniforms and aliens."

"A geek." Luke lifted his chin like a priest making a pronouncement on the nature of God.

"Nerds watch Star Trek, Luke. It's well established. Geeks have no utility."

"Both watch, geeks obsess. Fact of life."

"And you're going to tell me nerds don't obsess?" Brendan's fists found his hips, his robes puffing out like an affronted owl.

"Not in the same way. And their obsessions usually lead to lucrative careers in the sciences, whereas geeks can tell you Spock's grandmother's name."

"I still—"

"Guys, please." Rose stole another look through the curtain, and her breath caught. Somehow, even more people had managed to crowd into the conference area. She had never imagined she would yearn for Camp Den, but at the moment, a nice live fire exercise in the back woods sounded lovely.

"Rose…" Luke's expression shifted from outrage to pity in a flash. He took her hands. "Rosie. Look at you, pale and shaking. Are you really that nervous?"

"Yes, dammit."

"You've got nothing to worry about. This is a launch party. These people are here because they love us. Turn on that charm and wow them."

A MegaCon organizer slipped his head through the curtain from the crowd side. "Two minutes, guys."

Rose drew calm and charm.

"See that? You look better already. You've got this." Brendan gave her a reassuring smile.

"Do you know the other reason these people are destined to love us?" Luke asked.

"Why?"

"Because we have plants in the crowd. Robin loaned us a bunch of her newbies. They're all out there charming the hell out of those people."

"You do that at all your launch parties?" Rose looked askance at the twins. That sounded like cheating to her.

"We don't generally have people working the crowd for us; we Pruett boys have more than enough to spare."

"That's something I don't get." Rose smoothed the spandex over her midriff for the thousandth time. The outline of her bellybutton kept showing. "You get these fans through charm, but charm doesn't last. How do you convert them to lasting votaries?"

"Simple," Brendan said. "We give them swag."

Rose arched an eyebrow at him.

Luke peeled a copy of *Drawn* the graphic novel issue one from a stack by the curtain and held it up for display. "Swag as in merchandise. You give a prospective votary something to remember you by, and they're more likely to last. It's a sort of token."

"A talisman." Brendan swiped the comic from his brother and held it aloft in both hands. "A thing of beauty that speaks to them. And even though you give a million of the same token to a million different people, they all cherish the one that belongs to them."

"Athletes do it with jerseys—" Luke began.

"That should be a bumper sticker," Brendan said.

"—musicians with songs, actors with movies and posters."

"And all the great succubus lovers throughout history did it with cheap jewelry and bad poems."

"And Society has never caught on to you doing this? Never came after you?" Rose asked, her anxiety momentarily displaced by fascination. The twins lived in a strange limbo she had never imagined.

Luke shrugged. "We're either so cloaked under spook radar they don't know we exist, or we're too prominent to make disappear. Either way, they don't bother with us."

Rose felt a pang of sudden and surprising guilt. "But if you're seen with me, won't that tip them off you're working with the Order?"

Brendan grinned. "I seriously doubt government spies are watching this lot. We're safe."

"Besides," Luke picked a piece of lint from his otherwise immaculate robe, "I'm far more concerned with talent scouts. I have it on good authority there's an executive from Netflix scoping out this con…since we invited him." He flashed Rose a sinister grin. "If we get that kind of deal, there'll be no end to our votary count."

"Netflix?" Rose scrunched up her nose. "What would a movie site want with my graphic novel?"

"Eggs and baskets, Rose! You think *Drawn*'s our only foray into sharing your story with the world? We've got big plans for you, girl. And that includes the little anime we started drawing the day we met you."

"What's an anime?"

Luke covered his mouth as if scandalized.

An announcer introduced the Pruett twins and their newest star, Rose Carver, before either could answer. The curtain opened to reveal a U-shaped table covered in red cloth with three folding chairs pushed beneath it. Beyond the table stood a legion of giddy fans gathering their collective breaths.

"Tell you later," Brendan said.

He pushed Rose ahead of him through the curtain, and her heart performed an acrobatic move in her chest.

The crowd erupted with an earsplitting roar. Despite protests from the security guards, the first three rows surged toward the table, and Rose took an involuntary step back, instinctively drawing speed and strength. Several of them held up signs with a panoply of hand-drawn figures Rose couldn't identify. Some of the twins' previous comic book heroes?

"It's fine." Luke put a reassuring hand on Rose's back, staying her instinct to fight or run. "They're fans, not enemies."

The twins leaned across the table, shaking hands and chatting as the crowd pressed close. The boys exuded charm, their smiles like chrome in sunlight. Reluctantly, Rose joined the fray, offering her hand to the throng of smiling people. Though she still felt skittish, the crowd's enthusiasm soon overwhelmed her fear. She found herself smiling and greeting total strangers as if welcoming them to her home.

Maybe she had that part backward.

After a couple of minutes, Brendan said, "All right kids, back to your seats. We've got a panel to do here."

Showing little reluctance, those fans who had so eagerly dashed forward with unbridled exuberance a moment before hurried to their seats. And no wonder. Rose could see in their eyes the near drunken euphoria of the good and truly charmed.

Several dozen copies of *Drawn* stood on the table. The cover depicted Rose dressed in a waitressing outfit sprinting down a lonely backwoods road at night, headlights following her in the distance.

Brendan took one of these in hand. "You all know we've got a new book coming out." The crowd tried to cheer, but he held up a palm to forestall them. "This is the story of Rose Carver. She's a succubus. Not a demon, or a vampire, just a woman with some extraordinary abilities. Rose wants nothing more than to live her life like any normal person, but circumstances force her into a high-stakes game of government espionage, murder, and world domination."

"It's a hell of a good read," Luke shouted.

People laughed.

"This," Brendan said, pointing, "is the real Rose Carver. We are ripping off her true story for fun and profit."

Rose smiled. People smiled back, watching her with adoring, lusting, loving eyes. The feeling was intoxicating. No wonder the twins liked cons.

"Feel free to ask any questions you like, except for one," Luke said. "Do not ask us where we get our ideas."

More laughter. Rose didn't get the funny. She would have liked to ask that very thing. Of course, in the case of *Drawn*, she knew the answer.

Hands shot up, and a couple of volunteers with cordless microphones entered the crowd. One handed his to a young woman in the second row dressed as some beast with a uniformly lumpy head and a black leather bustier that lifted her breasts to an alarming, and no doubt uncomfortable, degree.

"Okay," she said, "first, I love Rose."

The crowd applauded.

"Uh, thank you," Rose said.

"What I need to know is will she get more votaries while she's training at Camp Den? I know she already got Renni and Lee, but it just doesn't seem like they're going to be enough, ya know?"

"Oh, an advance reader," Brendan said. "Glad to have you—glad you're enjoying the online preview. Thank you for supporting our Kickstarter."

"As for your question," Luke said, "what do you think we're doing right now? This is all about getting votaries for our Rose."

"We get to be her votaries?" The girl looked star struck.

Rose very deliberately did not squirm in her seat.

"Hell yes. Next time you wake up feeling like you've got a hangover, just figure Rose is out there kicking ass."

Everyone laughed.

A somewhat hefty guy with glasses and curly black hair asked, "Aren't you guys worried about writing yourselves into a corner? Once the Order takes out Society, won't they have to become what they hate?"

"What's that guy doing in our crowd?" Brendan asked. "Shouldn't you be over in the novels section working your panel?"

"Don't try to weasel out of the question," said the guy, grinning. "You're going to face a real conundrum in a few months. How are you going to handle it?"

Luke smirked. "As one of your buddies always says, you novelists have the luxury of rewriting before you go to press. But we comic artists rely on something you don't have."

"Which is?" asked the man with a lilt in his voice.

"A king's wit, my friend."

That brought more and louder laughter from the crowd, most of whom seemed to know the mystery questioner.

Rose felt at sea. Was that guy famous? Someone she should know on sight?

Everything these people said confused her. They spoke English, she understood every word, but the parlance made no sense. And yet, the atmosphere was intoxicating. She felt a kind of acceptance she had never experienced. A bringing-in sort of feeling, a homecoming. And mixed with it came something more, something electric. She could feel the breadth of her votaries expanding.

"My question is for Rose," said a middle-aged woman in the front row dressed as a nineteenth-century Victorian aristocrat. A vampire stake on a hempen rope dangled between her breasts.

"Go ahead," Rose said.

"Are you able to feel each votary—maybe take strength from a few and save the rest?"

Rose felt her cheeks flush. She had never spoken with anyone outside her family and fellow succubi about drawing. "No. I can't draw from just one person. I draw from them all equally."

A young girl, probably fourteen, her face red, her friends giggling, asked, "Where's Matt Snow?"

"Too busy to be with us," Brendan said. "You like Matt?"

The girl looked too embarrassed to answer, but one of her friends yelled, "He's hot."

"You're telling us," Luke said.

"Speaking of hot," Brendan said. "We thought we would have our Rosie put on a little show for you. Would you all like that?"

The crowd cheered.

Rose blanched.

"No one said anything about a show," she hissed in Luke's ear.

"Yeah. It's more exciting this way."

A couple of the event volunteers wheeled out four oversized kettlebells. The men strained to move the things despite the dollies they used. Rose had never seen the like. The smallest kettlebell, its weight indelibly marked on the side, read one hundred twenty-five pounds. The other three weighed one hundred fifty, one hundred seventy-five, and two hundred pounds respectively.

Luke made a big show of calling for volunteers to try lifting any one of the weights. Several people, including a well-muscled guy dressed as He-Man, gave it a go. He-Man managed to deadlift them but begged off performing any swings with the things. He didn't want to throw his back out.

"You know," Brendan whispered to Rose while Luke called for more volunteers, "it occurs to me now we never asked how much you can lift in one go."

"I don't think this is a good idea," Rose said. "It's going to draw attention."

"This kind of attention is good. Nobody in the real world cares what we geeks do at these cons. Not unless we trash our hotel rooms or, well, that's about it. They don't give a shit."

"Now our lovely Rose will take a turn," Luke said, motioning toward her like a model showing off a new car.

The security detail pushed the crowd back, and Rose took her place before the weights. She drew strength and lifted the first kettle-bell over her head where she held it without faltering.

The crowd exploded with cheers.

It was surprisingly easy, Rose found, to maintain her draw. Even with her old votaries, her family, this would have been a manageable weight, but she couldn't have held it so long.

Emboldened by her initial success, and still holding the small weight, Rose grasped the second one and hoisted it overhead too.

He-Man cursed, but he clapped louder than anyone. The women especially cheered, as if Rose represented them in some triumph of womanhood.

Slowly, she lowered the two smaller weights and, ignoring the middle one, moved to the heaviest. She made a pretense of shaking out her arms though they felt fine. The strength she drew just from this crowd put her in good stead. Still, she wouldn't want the twins accusing her of putting on a bad show. Closing her eyes, she took several deep breaths, then took hold of the two-hundred-pound monstrosity and tossed it into the air.

The crowd gasped. A few lifted their arms in that spasmodic, involuntary way people do when threatened by speeding baseballs or oncoming bridge pylons.

The weight flew perhaps two feet above Rose's head, reached its apex, and began accelerating back toward the floor. She caught it in her off hand, slowing its descent so that it swung between her legs, her arm pinioned by its weight against her thigh. Then she threw it back into the air. This time she caught it two-handed and lowered it slowly, quietly to the floor.

The crowd burst into applause. Whistles and shouts of astonishment filled the conference center. He-Man looked like someone had clubbed him.

Luke took Rose by the arm and guided her back to the table. "That was perfect," he said in a stage whisper. "I knew we picked the right girl."

Despite herself, Rose's chest swelled with pride. Did she actually like cons?

The staff chivvied the crowd into a line. It snaked out the conference room door and down the adjoining corridor.

"Is it always like this?" Rose asked.

"Like what?" Brendan asked as he signed a much-abused comic for a gangly kid in glasses.

"Crowded. Loud," Rose said. "Exciting."

Luke grinned at her. "Addictive, ain't it?"

Rose nodded. The kid had shoved his comic, which had nothing to do with her, in front of Rose.

"Would you sign it too, ma'am?" he asked. His voice cracked.

"Uh, sure." Rose smiled at him and scrawled her new moniker under the brothers' signatures.

"I'll have a copy of yours at the next convention," the kid said, before hurrying off.

"Did you guys hear what's happening in Mexico?" asked the next man in line.

Luke shook his head as he took the guy's copy of *Drawn* to sign.

"We're invading." The guy looked shaken. "Tanks rolled over the border thirty minutes ago. It's insane."

"What?" Rose and Luke asked at the same time.

"The president is set to speak about it at noon. But we all know what she's gonna say—it's about controlling the drug cartels. Yeah, right. She just wants to get her hands on their oil. Anyway, you gonna put that in *Drawn?*"

"Of course we will." Luke remained chipper though the color had drained from his face. He took the man's comic, signed, and passed it to Rose.

She signed fast and shoved the book back to the delighted fan. Once he was gone, she leaned close to Luke. "Does this mean we're at war with the vampires?"

"No," Luke said. "It means we're at war with everybody."

15

GUADALUPE VICTORIA

It was six p.m. when the convoy arrived at Guadalupe Victoria, a tiny village in northern Mexico. The sun hung low on the horizon, coloring the clouds in reds and pinks.

Despite the state of war, crossing the border had been easy. Given the amount of concentrated charm held by the thirty men and women of their company, they probably could have told the guards at the military checkpoint they were transporting the Pope to the front lines and still gotten permission to proceed.

"You sure this is the place?" Matt asked from the driver's seat of their blacked-out Suburban.

"As sure as I can be," Myra Hanks said.

Per Robin Ambrose's sources inside the Indrawn Breath, special teams of takers had been dispatched immediately after the invasion with a mandate to track down and capture succubi in Mexico. Working autonomously, these teams were difficult to track, unless you had a near-clairvoyant former math teacher to lead the way.

Rose stared out the window at the town. Its single road, a pitted and pot-holed dirt affair, made their truck shudder, its suspension groaning in protest. Like many tiny pueblos she had seen on the drive in, this one contained a handful of stone buildings at its center surrounded by a few outlying shacks too small to be called houses. Unlike the others, however, its cobblestoned square featured a large, burbling fountain and a parish church. The church's façade, painted a dusty pink trimmed in red, put Rose in mind of old western movies. A bell tower jutted from it, the highest point for miles.

Several of the village's citizens appeared from their stucco homes to watch the newcomers. A woman stood hugging her son to her side in the lee of a weather-beaten building. An older couple riding a pair of matching rockers in front of what looked like a butcher's shop watched them with obvious distrust. And still more faces, solemn and stoic, appeared at windows, watching in silent interest.

Matt's voice buzzed over the team's main communications channel. "Contact crew, assemble next to that fountain. Everyone else remain in the vans. These people have got no reason to trust a bunch of American invaders, especially if they're slinkers looking to avoid the government."

Rose checked the tiny camera affixed to her body armor. Still there. Wearing the thing made her self-conscious, but the Pruett twins insisted, as did Robin and Matt. The boys claimed watching firsthand video put them in the now, whatever that meant. Rose hoped it wouldn't capture her doing something stupid.

A hot May wind whispered through the square as Rose and the other contact team members climbed from the van. Even with evening coming on, the heat was stifling, the air dry and full of blowing dust. Rose wanted to peel off her body armor. The stuff felt like top-grade insulation. But the op order specified all team members had to remain buttoned up. No one knew what to expect from the locals.

Rose stood between Matt's deputy, Tanner Watts, and her old draw sergeant, Gloria Torres, who had brought three members of her team along. Myra Hanks and Garrett Timmons stood opposite them.

Without preamble, Matt said, "We need to find whoever's in charge around here. I figure that will be a constable or mayor. What do you think, Gloria?"

Torres nodded. "Whoever it is, I'm sure he's already seen us. Let's talk to some locals. I figure they'll lie to us, but Carver can charm them."

"That's why she's here." Matt almost grinned.

They approached the old couple on the rockers. They hadn't moved but watched the team with wary expressions. Torres said something to them in Spanish. Rose wished she had paid more attention to her language studies back in high school. She didn't understand a word of it.

The old man answered in a raspy near-whisper, shaking his head no as he spoke.

Rose didn't need to understand the words to interpret the meaning. He wasn't about to cooperate with a bunch of rich Americans.

She turned on her charm.

The old guy's eyes dilated; his focus, along with that of the woman beside him, turned to Rose.

"Ask him again," she said.

"No need," said a voice from inside the butcher's shop. A plump woman wearing a red and green knit skirt stepped from the shadows. "You're looking for me."

Matt regarded her, his expression kind, but guarded. "Are you the mayor?"

"I am. My name is Glenda Rodriguez. Who are you? What do you want?" Though accented, the mayor's English sounded flawless.

"Is there somewhere we could speak privately?" Matt raised his chin, indicating the nearest storefront.

"No."

"It's a delicate matter, Ms. Rodriguez. You might not want your people to hear what I have to say."

"I'm sure I don't. But that isn't going to stop you, is it, Mr. Snow?"

"Please, Mayor, I—"

Rodriguez held up a hand. "Let me save you some time, Mr. American incubus. You know what we are here." She glanced at the six black Suburbans and five vans parked in her town square, so incongruous with the pastoral setting. "And I know what you are. You think because Mexico has no Society that you can come south during war and take us away for God knows what reason? We've heard of this from other villages—the men with their guns stealing away the gifted among them. Americans like you. Scum." Rodriguez spit next to Matt's combat boots.

Matt kept his gaze fixed on the mayor. "Ma'am, I assure you, no one on my team wants to take you from your home. We're not the ones you've heard about. We're here to protect you."

Rodriguez gave a contemptuous grunt. Suddenly, a wash of charm exuded from her, thick and insistent. "Get back in your fancy cars and go home, Americano. You hear me?"

"No," Matt said. "I don't think so."

Rodriguez's eyes widened. Her charm was deep, and Rose could tell the woman was accustomed to being obeyed whenever she leveled it on someone. But it was no match for even Matt's draw of the same.

Thanks to the success of the graphic novel, all those closest to Rose had benefited from her new fans. Though their depth and breadth of votaries couldn't rival Rose's own, Matt, Leslie, Satterfield, and even Torres had gained strength over the past weeks as the twins beat the advertising drum by sending out prerelease goodies like early proof samples and other teasers. When the graphic novel finally hit the shelves two days ago, their votary counts had exploded.

"You won't take us from our homes without a fight," Rodriguez said. "We live here in peace. We break no laws with our gifts. And we have protection."

"You don't have protection against what's coming," Matt said. "The men you fear are on their way now. We've come to give you warning. You should flee. Now. Come back when things have settled."

"Settled? Are you loco? There's a war going on. We're safer here than roaming the desert. Anyway, I told you, we are protected. If you want to help us, then leave. You shouldn't be here after dark."

A sudden voice crackled in Rose's earbud. "Sir, we've got trucks inbound." It was Phillips, a female op, and leader of the Dog Ears' perimeter defense.

Matt keyed his throat mic. "How many?"

A pause. "I count fourteen JLTVs. Several of them are category B. They've also got eight utility vans. The big kind."

JLTVs, or Joint Light Tactical Vehicles, were the U.S. Army's answer to the all-purpose, all-terrain assault transport for the twenty-first century. Armored enough to enter a hot zone and yet light enough to maneuver quickly, the powerful trucks could deliver troops to the front lines of an assault with minimum chance of interdiction barring anything besides serious firepower on the opposing side.

The Order possessed no such firepower.

"Category B," Watts said, his face grim. "That means they're outfitted for troop transport. We're looking at probably seventy-five, maybe up to ninety personnel."

Matt nodded. "Mayor Rodriguez, the people you've heard about, the Americans who kidnap succubi, they are here. You need to get your people out of this village. Now."

"No," Rodriguez said, hands on her ample hips. "You're not going to scare us into a trap, Americano. You think we can't fight, but you're wrong. And tonight, you will pay for your stupidity."

A distant, heavy thrum echoed from the northwest along the town's single meandering road. A static-filled curse blasted over the radio, and then Phillips's voice returned. "Captain Snow, we've been made. I don't know how they saw us, but five of the vehicles have broken off. We have enemy converging on our position. They're polydraws, sir."

"Can you fall back—get to the village?"

"No, sir. We're cut off."

More gunfire erupted. The steady *clack-clack-clack* of automatic rifles was punctuated every few seconds by the sternum-shaking boom of something much higher caliber.

Rose's stomach twisted. Live fire exercises at Camp Den couldn't compare to the real thing. Sure, the thundering booms felt familiar, but Rose's instructors had never shot at her with deadly intent. The people discharging these weapons possessed no other objective. They fought to kill, and that difference sent a cold shiver of fear down her spine, not just for herself, but for her team.

A column of dust rose in the distance. Faintly, Rose could hear approaching engines. She drew hearing and made out the individual vehicles, nine of them—chugging diesel power plants running at top speed.

"Everybody out of the vans," shouted Matt into his radio. "I need shooters positioned on the road and around the plaza. Watts, take care of that. Keep the firing lanes clear and the civilians off the streets."

"You got it, boss."

"Phelps."

"Yes, sir," Leslie said. The young sharpshooter kept pace with Matt as he strode across the square. She carried her favorite rifle strapped over one shoulder.

"I need you in that bell tower." He pointed at it with two fingers. "I'm pulling our forces inside the village, so if you see something moving outside the perimeter, shoot it." He turned to Rose. "Get the drones in the air."

She considered arguing. Rolling death rushed toward them in the form of armed Breathers. Was now the time to worry about the succubi twin's demands? But one look at Matt's face shut her up quick. "On it!"

Watts had organized a pass line at the back of one van, handing out guns and equipment with phenomenal speed and efficiency. He gave her a nod when Rose stepped forward. "Drones?"

"Yes, sir." Rose fought down her embarrassment and kept her eyes on Matt's exec. Everyone else in line had received a weapon of war to defend the team and the village. Watts would issue those to her as well, but not before the hard-plastic case he handed her now.

It contained six jet-black quadcopters no larger than Rose's hand, fully charged and programmed to follow her every movement. Connected to a satellite feed and backed up to secure hard drives in three of the team's vans, the tiny voyeurs couldn't fail to capture Rose in exquisite detail. She hated them. They made her feel like a prima donna. And she couldn't escape the subtle, and the not-so-subtle, stares she got when the drones buzzed into the air to float forty feet above her head, each positioned to catch a different angle.

"It'll be worth it," Watts said, giving her a sympathetic look and a slick, black rifle. "I've been collecting Pruett comics for years. They'll make something amazing out of all this."

"I guess."

"Gringo!" Mayor Rodriguez stormed toward Matt until she stood almost in his face. "You're going to fight them? In my village?"

"If we don't, they'll capture you," Matt said over the tumult of running feet, shouted orders, and distant gunfire.

"And what happens then?" Rodriguez put her hands on her hips and bared her teeth.

"Then you'll wish you had listened to me."

16

OVERRUN AND OVERWROUGHT

Rose pressed her armored back against an adobe wall, her sub gun held muzzle up before her. The sounds of automatic rifles echoed strangely through Guadalupe Victoria, masking their origins, but the strident *pock-pock-pock* of bullets striking the other side of the wall left no doubt. The Indrawn Breath held the road.

"How are you doing up there, Phelps?" Matt asked over the shared channel. He, along with Valerie Satterfield, crouched next to Rose, pinned down by heavy fire.

"Good, sir," came the sniper's terse response. An instant later her M40A5 coughed from overhead—a distinct crack and hiss that cut through the din.

Rose couldn't see Leslie's target, but considering the girl's skill with firearms, she assumed the shot found its mark.

The Breathers sent a storm of bullets flying back in response to Leslie's shot, striking the tower, sending puffs of smoke into the air and showers of ancient adobe clattering to the cobblestones. One bullet hit the bell. Its peal echoed low and dull through the village.

"Dammit, people," Matt shouted into his radio. "Keep up the

suppression fire. We're outgunned, and Phelps is the only one keeping us alive right now! Phelps, you okay?"

Leslie didn't answer, but her rifle barked three times in rapid succession. A man screamed on the second shot. He fell silent on the third.

"That girl's good," Satterfield said, nodding.

"Yeah, but she needs help," Matt said. "We've been at this too long. The Breathers are getting antsy. I can feel it. They're not going to mess around with us much longer. With our forces split, there's nothing stopping them from launching a frontal assault. They probably haven't so far because they don't know how many people we've got in the village."

"You think they're waiting for full dark?" Rose asked.

"Definitely."

Though the sun had already dipped below the horizon and the first stars twinkled overhead, a dusky glow persisted. It cast Guadalupe Victoria in a fading red light as ominous to Rose as the encroaching gunfire.

"We can't let them seize the initiative." Rose lowered the infrared monocle attached to her helmet, her one solace against the oncoming night. "They'll slaughter us in the dark. They've got the numbers and the equipment advantage. Our best chance is to strike first."

Matt stared at Rose. She saw fear beneath his stony expression. Not fear of combat, or even death, but rather the sort of fear experienced by a parent whose child is in danger, or a military commander who realizes he has led his soldiers into a no-win situation.

"I'm sorry," she said.

He shook his head, fingered the mic at his throat, but hesitated.

Suddenly the gunfire outside Guadalupe intensified. Rose's draw-enhanced ears picked out the sound of running feet. "They're charging."

Watts's voice rang over the common channel. "We've got at least fifty enemy incoming. Assault rifles, body armor, night vision goggles."

An explosion rocked the east side of town, sending a plume of dust and heavier soil skyward. The scent of freshly turned earth mixed with the already acrid odor of spent gunpowder.

Matt stared at Rose, his face ashen. "Proximity bomb."

The Indrawn Breath's forces had reached the city. They both knew her duty. She had been chosen for this. For a moment, he looked as if he might say more, but she shook her head.

"Reserve, counter on my mark," Matt said, using channel two on his radio. He got his feet under him, ready to rise. Rose and Satterfield followed suit. "Three, two, one. Mark!"

Order ops boiled from the surrounding buildings. Rose dashed from her hiding spot to join their number at a dead run, leaving Matt and Satterfield behind. She assumed her place at the fore, spearheading the Dog Ears' counterattack meant to slow, perhaps even stop, the Breather offensive. Her heart twanged in her breast as she surged forward, outpacing even the fastest of her fellow ops. She screamed defiance, vaguely aware of the buzzing cadre of drones jockeying for position above her.

A tide of black-clad, masked figures charged into the plaza. The Breathers wore full night vision goggles, not the monocle style favored by the Order, making it easy for Rose to distinguish between friend and foe as she caught them out in her single-eye display.

She let her sub gun hang on its strap as she ran, preferring her less cumbersome Kimber in this sort of close-corridor fight. Drawing dexterity, sight, speed, and discernment, Rose rushed the oncoming horde, placing shots with preternatural precision. From ten yards away, she put a bullet in the gap between one Breather's face mask and the Kevlar at his collar. Another she dropped with a shot under his arm as he aimed at one of her teammates.

Bullets whizzed past her like streaking comets. Moving without conscious thought, she jigged and juked, stepping out of harm's way milliseconds before hurtling death could take her. Dust and gun smoke filled the air, turning the narrow corridor between buildings into a miasma of twisting shadows and recursive echoes.

Rose sprang from the murk in a swirl of blazing gunfire. With a deft twist, she executed a spinning layout, bullets missing her by inches, and took one incredibly long, silent moment to drop the spent magazine from her Kimber and reload on the fly. Literally.

She landed atop a Breather. The woman never knew what hit her. Rose pummeled her to the ground, rolled, and leapt again, lower this time, angling her trajectory toward a weathered wall. She kicked off it, bullets razing the spot nearly the instant she moved. She landed amid the enemy.

The main comms channel buzzed in Rose's ear. Matt was still alive —still giving orders—though he sounded winded, harassed.

The Breathers nearest her turned Rose's way, but they seemed so slow in reacting. Evading them was a trifle—the barest of a dodge here, a blocked blow there. These were not the fear-drawn foes she had expected. With an efficiency that would have astonished her only weeks ago, Rose set about dismantling the Breathers' front ranks.

She holstered the Kimber, lifted the nearest Breather by the weapons harness on his body armor, and spun him around in a circle like a pool noodle. A swath of bodies went flying. Rather than let the man go, Rose allowed his weight and momentum to spin her about so that she momentarily resembled a discus thrower. With a savage yell, she flung him further into Breather ranks, clearing a lane for the Dog Ears to fill.

Several bullets scored on her chest, arms, and helmet as she performed this maneuver. The concussions were powerful, the impacts staggering. Though her Kevlar kept the projectiles from penetrating her flesh, pain blossomed in her temples, up her right arm, in her left knee.

Rose shrugged these off, exchanging for a moment her draw of stamina for one of healing. The hurts faded, the stiffness disappeared. She drew her Kimber and dove toward the next wave of foes.

For several minutes the world dissolved into a staccato series of precisely timed punches, kicks, and trigger squeezes. Matt's reserve force had caught up to her. They engaged the Breathers in the narrow alleyway between a grocer's brick store and what smelled like an herbalist's shop.

Rose lost herself in a blanket of discernment. She felt like a robot, acting out a predetermined series of commands that kept her just ahead of danger while doling out mayhem on every side. As she moved, she could feel Leslie's precisely timed shots backing her progress. They worked in fluid concert, Rose dancing between her enemies as Leslie cleared the way.

Rose ducked, allowing her friend's wickedly accurate sniper round to take out the incubi before her. Then she jumped high into the air and Leslie's rifle coughed five times in a row, surgically removing a commiserate number of the enemy.

Unfortunately, the Breathers' numbers were too great to sustain this forward progress. For every one Breather Rose and Leslie dropped, two more took the one's place. And though Rose had yet to reach the limits of her vast votaries, already her fellow Dog Ears were slowing. Two went down on her left, victims of fatigue as Breathers bowled over them, guns blazing. Rose surged that direction, covering the sudden gap in the Order's lines, and unintentionally opened another since the ops she thought were behind her had already been overrun.

"Fall back," came Matt's voice over the radio. "You can't hold that line alone."

Rose reversed course toward the plaza. She felt deafened by gunfire, her lungs burned from the acrid smoke, and her uncovered eye leaked tears like rainwater down one cheek. Yet, despite it all, Rose Carver felt more alive, more vibrantly necessary to the workings of the vast universe than she had in all her life. Her heart sang with the melody of battle.

Was this what it meant to be a succubus? Was she not obligated to defend those who gave her power even if they would never realize their danger? What was a votary save an innocent willing to lend her strength, vitality, speed, and all the rest so that she might fight where they could not?

"ALCON!" shouted a frantic voice over the radio, drawing Rose from her near trance-like state. "Cure is gray! Rally point at the fountain."

Rose's footsteps faltered. A bullet struck the thin Kevlar at her throat. She gagged, reeling back, pain a raw current centered on her trachea and spreading out like jagged hooks into her head and down her spine.

Someone tackled her to the ground, a large man with enhanced strength and speed. A knife materialized in the Breather's hand. Rose flinched aside in time to avoid taking its point through her uncovered eye. It skittered off the cobbles with the flinty sound of steel on stone.

"Hold still, bitch," her assailant grunted, as he pitted his strength against hers.

Cure is gray. The words rebounded through Rose's mind, their meaning teetering on the cusp of her understanding. But she didn't want to understand them. Cure for this mission was Matt Snow. Gray meant compromised.

Matt was either dead or at least incapacitated. Either way, Rose needed to reach him.

All at once her mind snapped into sharp focus. Her thoughts narrowed in on the man lying atop her, endeavoring to take her life.

He was in her way.

Rose drew. She drew it all. Every attribute at her disposal suddenly blossomed into white-hot intensity. Her mind blazed with mental acuity, her body surged with strength, and her limbs blurred with speed.

With little effort, Rose sat up, lifting her assailant over her head as she did so. With a growl, he swung the knife at Rose's upraised arm. Bolstered by his draw-enhanced strength, the blade bit through Rose's armor, piercing deep into her flesh where it lodged between the radius and the ulna.

The pain registered as an ache in her forearm. Rose flung the man to one side, sending him hurtling into a gaggle of Breathers harassing the Order's retreat.

She did not later remember sprinting to the plaza's fountain. She must have done it while avoiding both aimed and stray bullets because inside ten seconds Rose was crouched over Matt Snow, her heart in her throat.

"What happened?" she demanded. She saw no blood—no signs of

entry or exit wounds. But Matt's face was pale, his hands cold as winter night, and he was unconscious.

"I didn't see," Satterfield said. "One minute he was giving orders, the next he was on the ground. I dragged him out of the fight and called the team to rally. Where's Watts?"

"Dunno." Rose pulled the knife from her arm and dropped it, bloodstained and sticky, on the cobbles next to Matt.

"We don't have time for triage," Satterfield said. "You've got to fight, Rose. We need you."

"I'm not leaving him."

Satterfield's face darkened, taking on an expression Rose hadn't seen since basic training at Camp Den. "You get off your ass and take it to these sons of bitches or you'll be staying with him in a fear factory! I don't have time to argue. You make your choice."

With that, the buxom succubus took up her sub gun and joined the last vestiges of the Dog Ears in trading fire with the oncoming Breather forces.

Rallied together like this, the Order had managed to slow the enemy's progress, stopping them just inside the village proper.

"Really, it's quite incredible what you've done with so few defenders," said a deep voice over Rose's shoulder.

Gooseflesh dimpled her arms and neck. She spun, still crouched, to find David Lord smiling down at her.

17

———

SISTER, SISTER

"Hello, beautiful," Lord said. "How's Snow doing? Funny how Kevlar can stop a bullet, but it's shit at softening a good hard kick, especially one that could dent a tank." Lord waggled one of his steel-toed boots.

Rose tried to swing her sub gun to her shoulder, but Lord saw it coming. He caught the automatic by its chassis and wrenched it from her grasp with surprising grace.

Drawing speed, Rose grabbed the knife next to Matt and sank it into Lord's thigh.

He screamed.

She had moved faster than he expected.

Good.

"Leslie!" Rose shouted. "Shoot him!" Rose dove forward, her natural urge to press Lord back away from Matt. She took the Breather low at the knees. His head hit the cobblestones with a satisfying crunch when he fell.

"Move, Carver!" shouted Satterfield, her weapon shouldered. "I can't get a clear shot with you in the way."

Rose tried to spin free, but Lord rolled her atop him like a shield. He plucked the knife from his leg and pressed it to Rose's throat, the

160

tip puckering a spot just below her chin.

Four Dog Ears led by Satterfield surrounded Lord and Rose, their laser sights jittering around the man.

"Let her go," Satterfield said.

"I think not." Lord exuded charm like an open spigot.

Rose countered it with her own, protecting her friends. If they clenched now, they were dead.

"You don't think we're good enough to take the shot?" Satterfield asked.

"I'm sure you are," Lord said. "But I'm good enough to evade, and then we're right where we started. Instead, I propose an alternative."

"What's that?"

"I let Rose's sister kill you."

A sword point suddenly blossomed from the chest of the man next to Satterfield. He screamed, the sound liquid and burbling.

Before anyone could react, Melody had taken his place, a smile playing on her lips, a blood-soaked katana in her hand. Without looking, she flicked her blade to one side, striking Satterfield in the throat. The beautiful succubus crumpled to the ground in a spray of dark blood. Melody ducked under a cloud of bullets to plunge her sword deep into the thigh of the next nearest op, a succubus named Katherine. Melody took Katherine's head as the woman fell.

Rose screamed, struggling against Lord's grip. This brought the attention of more Order ops who, without direction, spun to attack the new threat at their rear, dividing their line of defense.

"No!" Rose shouted. "Turn back. Defend the village." But it was no use. The Order's line had broken.

The resulting crossfire missed Melody, who had flattened herself to the cobbles. Instead, it engulfed the remaining Order op who had joined Satterfield in rescuing Rose. His armor soaked up most of the barrage, but a bullet caught him high on the cheekbone. He crumpled.

The battle was lost. A vanishing number of Order ops still fired, but Breathers quickly overran them. Rose squeezed her eyes shut, shock and revulsion battling for dominance inside her head. If she had remained with the defenders instead of abandoning them to help

Matt, they would still be holding the line, and she wouldn't have witnessed her little sister's wanton murder spree.

You're not dead, are you?

The voice in Rose's head sounded so like Matt that for an instant she thought it real. But no, this was her voice, her determination to fight, to win. It berated her without taunting, without malice, but with a quiet, simple question.

No, she was not dead.

Rose drew speed and strength in equal measures. Energy from her votaries filled her senses. Her blood sang with power.

With all the force she could muster, she smashed Lord's face with the back of her helmet. His head bounced off the cobbles with a crack like fireworks. In a flash, she was up, standing over him as he rolled away, his movements sluggish for one of the fear-drawn. He had left a bloody spot on the plaza stones.

Rose was vaguely aware of Melody cutting a swath through the Order ops who had broken away to deal with her. Despite their superior firepower, not one marked her as she spun and leapt and dove amongst them, her sword flashing in the scant light of stars. Order ops screamed as she progressed, a lithe minion of death incarnate, striking them down faster than any human eye could have followed.

Rose stared in horrified fascination, her conscious thoughts momentarily subverted from the battle by sudden alarm bells going off in her head. No succubus moved like that without an inordinate number of votaries. Rose did, but only because the Pruett twins had transformed her into a comic book heroine. Lord did because he relied on the fear draw.

"She's one of them," Rose breathed to the night. Melody was fear-drawn.

Hands shaking, breath short in her chest, Rose raised her Kimber. "Melody!"

Melody spun to face her, simultaneously stabbing back with her sword, catching an Order op in the gut. He dropped like a sack of wrenches. Melody smiled.

"Why?" Rose asked in a voice only the drawn could hear.

"Are you seriously asking me that in the middle of a war zone?"

"Why, Melody?" Rose circled toward the few Dog Ears still attempting to lay down suppression fire against the Breathers' line. She wanted to put herself between Melody and Matt, who still lay unconscious by the fountain.

Melody moved with her, matching Rose step for step, sword raised. "It's your fault I'm with them. You know that, right?"

Rose stopped. "What?"

"The night they took us—Mom, Dad, Troy—we tried to run, but you were drawing from us. We couldn't move—we couldn't fight."

"I didn't know."

"You didn't care," Melody hissed between clenched teeth. "They took us, and you never came. You never tried to find out what happened. Instead, you joined this scum." Melody gestured at the Order ops with her bloodied sword.

"I had no choice, Mel. I—"

"I don't care," Melody said. "Save your excuses. What's done is done."

"But you're drawing from people through fear. Why?"

Melody frowned, eyes narrowing to points of dark hatred. "So I can do this!"

She leapt with such speed, the air boomed ahead of her. The sword flashed down, swinging in a supersonic arch.

Though her heightened perceptions had warned Rose of the impending danger, she barely moved in time to evade the strike. Melody's blade glanced off the Kimber, striking sparks.

Melody rolled, righted herself, and spun to resume her attack, a manic growl parting her lips.

Rose spared a glance for Lord, who had risen but seemed slow to get his bearings. The back of his head was dark with blood, and he appeared shaky.

In the instant it took Rose to make this assessment, Melody had closed the distance between them. She screamed, striking out with the katana.

Without conscious thought, Rose brought her Kimber up to meet the blade, catching it on the chamber side. Steel rang on steel as a jolt of impact-induced pain shot up Rose's arm. Ignoring it, and the fear and horror trying to overwhelm her senses, she darted closer to Melody, stepping inside the blade's reach. Pressing her free hand to Melody's back, Rose drew her sister into an embrace, the .45 snugged against her solar plexus.

The moment spooled out, time a lengthening tendril stretching into the past like hot taffy. Rose felt her finger tightening on the trigger, squeezing it toward the breaking point. This close on, even if the shot didn't penetrate, it might well deal enough damage to knock Melody unconscious. Since she wouldn't be able to heal, the damage could kill her. It would be like taking a hammer blow to the sternum for a regular person—as likely a death sentence as not.

Rose hesitated. Lips brushing Melody's ear, she whispered, "Stop. Please, Mel, stop this. Come home with me."

Melody tensed, her back gone rigid, spine straight. "I—"

A wail split the night. It sent a prickling tingle of fear coursing from Rose's hindbrain across her scalp. She gasped.

Melody jerked in her arms, her body shaking. A little yelp escaped her lips.

The gunfire, which had become nothing more than background noise to Rose, ceased. In the silence, the opposing sides crouched in their respective hiding spots, eyes darting, searching for the source of the phantom shriek.

A door clicked open on one of the adobe buildings facing the square, and Mayor Glenda Rodriguez appeared. She looked shaken, her face pale, and yet she carried herself with dignity.

"Where is Matt Snow?" she asked, her accent more pronounced than earlier—probably due to stress.

"I'm here, Mayor." Matt waved from the ground where he still lay.

Relief flooded Rose. Though Matt looked weak, he was able to sit up.

"I told you to go, *si*? Told you we be okay. No *problemo* with the *policia Americana*. But you no listen. You try to be heroes. Now you make me do the same for you."

"I don't understand," Matt grunted through obvious agony, having just awoken and not yet healed himself.

Another wail reverberated through the village. Succubi on both sides screamed. A few put down their weapons to cover their ears. Rose could hear her faithful drones in the silence that followed.

"You want to live, *gringo?*" The mayor, too, winced at the wailing but seemed less affected by it. "You get your people around the fountain and stay put. Don't shoot unless you want to die."

When Matt hesitated, Mayor Rodriguez screamed, "Do it!"

Gunfire erupted as if to punctuate the mayor's words. Rose tensed, and the rest of the Dog Ears spun to face the road, but the bullets weren't aimed at them. Muzzle flashes flared strobe-like in the dark. It looked as if the Breathers were attacking one another.

"What the hell?" Rose whispered. She had released Melody, who stood beside her watching the firefight with equal awe.

Matt rose to his feet, Rodriguez at Matt's elbow, screaming something Rose couldn't make out. When he came on the common channel, she could hear the little mayor yammering in the background.

"This is Cure. All Ears rally at the fountain. Do not fire your weapons—safeties on if you've got them. Otherwise, blaze the earth. I want all muzzles down. Anyone fires a shot, they answer to me."

"Come with me, Melody." Rose had meant it as a command, but it came out more a question.

For the barest of an instant, Mel's face softened. She started to say something but stopped. Her gaze flicked behind Rose.

David Lord stood there. He held Rose's knife in one bloodied hand.

When Melody looked back, her eyes smoldered with hatred. "When the Indrawn Breath came, they didn't even have to subdue Dad. The wranglers just picked us up and carried us out of the house like luggage. All because you sucked us dry."

"Mel, I was in danger. I had to draw from you."

Screams broke Rose's concentration. These were not the banshee wails of a moment before, but the guttural calls of men and women dying in extreme pain.

Moving with preternatural speed, Lord darted to Melody's side. "We're leaving."

"What's going on?" Melody asked.

"Slaughter." With that, he took Melody's hand and drew her away, the two of them running at top speed opposite the firefight.

"Rose," Matt said over the comm, "get over here."

Rose stared after her sister's retreating form for a moment. She wanted to go after her but knew better. The Dog Ears needed her. She joined what remained of them at the village's single fountain. Too many lay dead or dying on Guadalupe Victoria's dusty streets.

"Where's Satterfield?" Matt asked as Rose took up position next to him.

Rose shook her head, heart in her throat. "My sister—"

"I'm here." Satterfield pushed through the crowd to reach them, her weapons dangling from their tactical straps. Blood stained her tac vest below her throat, a deeper black in the darkness, but the wound looked healed.

"Oh, thank God." Rose hugged Satterfield without thinking. "I thought Melody killed you."

Her former squad leader stiffened, but then returned the embrace. "What's happening?"

"I don't know," Rose said, drawing back. "Maybe Leslie got a look. Have you seen her?"

Satterfield shook her head as she searched the crowd. "I never saw her come down from the bell tower."

A bolt of panic coursed through Rose's stomach. She keyed her throat mic for the shared channel. "Leslie, you read me?"

No reply.

Rose scanned the tower, drawing sight. No movement up there.

"What's wrong?" Matt asked.

"I think Leslie's still in the tower," Rose said. "She might be hurt."

"You no want to go up there, *hermana*," Rodriguez said.

The sounds of gunfire and screaming had grown closer. Rose could see figures moving in starlight just outside the town. The

Breathers were in retreat; only they weren't heading away from the village, but toward it.

"I'm going," Rose said.

"No." Matt shook his head. "You need to stay with us."

"I cannot protect you up there," Rodriguez said. "You stay near the fountain, you'll be safe."

"I can't leave her." Rose drew speed, spun, and ran for the tower. Matt cursed but made no move to stop her. He knew Rose too well to bother.

A wrought iron spiral staircase lined the bell tower's interior. Rose surged up it three steps at a time, letting her votaries supercharge her senses.

She smelled blood.

A heavy wooden door, locked and probably barred from the inside, topped the stairs— standard operating procedure for an Order sniper. Rose kicked it in with one solid blow from her combat boot. It struck the wall so hard the oak wood split down the center.

Rose dashed inside, heart thumping, dread filling her world.

Leslie's body lay in a heap under the tower's single bell. The wooden planks beneath her, otherwise gray with age, ran black with blood. Her head rested several feet away in the dust.

Shaking, crying, mind reeling with a storm of denial, anger, and guilt, Rose stumbled to the balcony's edge and emptied her stomach on the cobbles below.

Impossible. Leslie knew her job. She had locked the door. How had someone come up here to do this? They would have needed to climb the outside of the tower, but surely someone in the Dog Ears would have seen that.

"Not," Rose whispered to the stars, her head swimming in a whirlpool of horrified realization, "if someone distracted them."

Melody and Lord hadn't come into the village without a purpose. Their target had been the sniper raining destruction on their forces. Lord's attack had been the distraction.

Rose turned to face the body, stomach roiling. "And Melody was the culprit."

"What do you see?" Matt asked over the comm.

"She's dead." Rose stood where she could see him in the crowd below her. He turned to the bell tower.

"I'm so sorry." Matt sounded grim. "We'll see to her, I promise. But right now, you need to get back down here. We need you."

Before Rose could respond, a squad of twenty Breathers backed into the village square from the road. They worked well as a team, laying down suppression fire without spraying it in confusion or fear, but Rose noted a hint of anxiety in the way they moved.

"Ears, this is Cure," Matt said on the common channel, "keep the fountain between you and the Breathers. Do not mix ranks."

The Order ops did as they were told, backing away from the retreating Breather force.

For their part, the Breathers paid no attention to the Order. They were too focused on whatever was coming down the darkened street.

Rose squinted into the distance, drawing every ounce of sight her eyes could handle. Her heart gave a kick.

A dozen thin, lithe forms surged into the alleyway between the grocery store and the cantina. They looked human. Most were nude save for one or two who wore ragged pants, the legs torn, the cuffs frayed. The emaciated wraiths drove forward in orderly ranks, their pale skin glowing in the moonlight. Unlike succubi, who danced between bullets, these creatures soaked up the oncoming barrage, their chests and arms pock-marked with entry wounds that did not bleed but closed even as Rose watched.

A babble of curses and exclamations broke out over the channel. Several of the Dog Ears raised their weapons, screaming about vampires.

"Halt!" Matt said. "If you want to survive the next two minutes, you will stand down. Everyone. Those are not vampires. They're wights. They do not think. They kill. Get in their way and you will die."

As if Matt's words had been their cue, the wights suddenly broke ranks, dashing forward like a pack of runners sprinting for the finish line. They plowed into the Breathers' ranks, limbs flailing, eyes gleaming, teeth gnashing.

Rose cringed as she watched a wight sink its teeth into the neck of a fleeing Breather. The man's screams morphed into a fluid-marred burbling as he struggled to flee, but the monster held on, bearing its victim to the ground.

It was over in seconds. The Breathers beat a retreat, most zipping into the dark on draw-enhanced legs. Those who did not escape lay in haphazard rows all about the fountain.

Their job done, the wights fell still, so much so they seemed to become statues—grisly scarecrows meant not to frighten away magpies but people.

A figure strode into the village, his cowboy boots clicking with the precision of a metronome. Tall and pale, though not as pale as the wights, a shock of wavy black hair covered his head.

Mayor Rodriguez, weaving her way between the now inert wights, approached the newcomer.

They stopped in front of one another, and he bent to kiss both her cheeks in rapid succession.

"*Hola*, Mama," he said. "Who are all the *gringos?*"

18

MY ENEMY'S ENEMY

The night had grown cool in the thirty minutes since the vampire arrived. Rose and Matt huddled together, their fingers entwined; the remaining Dog Ears, a paltry sixteen of the thirty who had volunteered for this mission, surrounded them in a protective circle near the village fountain.

Rose couldn't seem to stop her hands from shaking. Matt squeezed, offering silent reassurance, but nothing could console her. Melody had killed Leslie. The thought kept swirling about Rose's head, immune to her attempts at banishing it. The utter shock came again and again in waves as if she were discovering the crime afresh moment by moment.

Rose clamped her jaw shut and shook her head. Matt had the right of it. She had to focus on the here and now. The Dog Ears, the Order in general, needed her. With an effort, she dragged her thoughts away from the gruesome scene in the bell tower and back to the present.

The vampire had divested them of their weapons, which lay in a heap in front of the butcher's shop. The townsfolk, having abandoned their hiding places to crowd the street, watched in silence, their eyes roaming again and again to the pile of firearms.

Mayor Rodriguez, standing toe-to-toe with the vampire, spewed a torrent of Spanish in his face. Her hands danced as she spoke, gesturing often at Matt and the team.

Draw Sergeant Torres stood near Matt, translating the diminutive mayor's words in a low whisper. "...and I'm telling you, Clemente will want to speak with them. If you kill these Americans, he will rip out your liver. They may be stupid *gringos*, but they helped us when we needed it."

The vampire, whom the Mayor called Rubio, seemed unperturbed by the woman's harangue. Like the wights, he stood unnaturally still, eyes half-lidded, watching her without a flicker of expression.

Gradually, the mayor stopped yelling. A long moment passed during which Rubio remained as he was. Then he drew a slow breath, and replied, "Okay, Mama."

Rodriguez nodded. "Good. Should I tell them?"

When Rubio made no reply, not even the barest of nods, the plump woman turned to Matt and his gathered team, a broad, disingenuous smile on her lips.

"Good news," she said in English. "You go to the *hacienda*; you meet Clemente. Okay?"

Rose didn't need a draw on perception to see the woman's fear and nervousness. Rodriguez's accent had grown thicker, her expressions and gestures self-conscious and overacted. She kept rubbing her hands on her skirt as if brushing away something unclean. And the looks she gave Rubio—a troubled mix of anxious foreboding and what Rose took for defeated resignation—only added to Rose's sense of unease.

"Who is Clemente?" Matt kept a calm demeanor, but Rose could feel his trepidation radiating through his hands.

"My husband."

"Couldn't we just go?" Matt asked. "We accomplished our mission here, but we've taken heavy losses. I'd like to collect our dead and honor them."

Rubio turned his head Matt's direction, his eyes two limpid pools of black. They did not reflect the moonlight. "No."

"We don't want any trouble with the coven kingdoms," Matt said slowly, evenly. "We came here—"

The twelve wights, who hadn't moved since routing the Breathers, stirred. Their collective gazes fell upon Matt. The skin between Rose's shoulder blades prickled with gooseflesh, and her pulse raced.

"Doesn't matter why you came, *gringo.*" Though his expression remained flat, his voice monotone, Rubio exuded a palpable menace. "You're on my father's lands. You answer to him."

Matt started to speak, seemed to think better of it, and nodded.

"What about our dead?" Rose whispered. Her throat threatened to close on the lump forming there. "Leslie's in the tower. I won't leave her here. She deserves a proper burial. Her family needs to know what happened to her."

"We take care of her," Mayor Rodriguez said. "There is a morgue in Sabinas. I call them first thing. Promise."

"Thank you," Matt said.

"No. We can't let strangers take her to some godforsaken little city in Mexico." Rose's cheeks burned with sudden anger as she turned to meet Matt's eyes.

"We can accept gracious hospitality when it's offered." He met her gaze with resolve, unflinching; the consummate team lead uninterested in having his orders countermanded. "We're in no position to argue."

"But—"

"No, Carver." Matt withdrew his hand from hers, his voice low, meant for her ears alone. "Open your eyes. We're unarmed and outnumbered. Leslie's dead. We can't do anything for her. Not yet. And I refuse to risk any more lives for a moral point. We don't have that luxury."

Rose ground her teeth but said nothing. Part of her could see Matt's point. Rubio had all the leverage. But that realization did nothing to slake her rage. The mere thought of leaving Leslie's desecrated body lying on the bell tower floor rent her soul in two. She would see her friend given a proper burial, and woe to anyone—human, succubus, or vampire—who stood in her way.

Rose dipped her chin in the barest of a nod.

Matt turned back to the mayor. "*Gracias,*" he said. "When do we meet your husband?"

It took three uncomfortable, silent hours to reach the small city of Guerrero near Mexico's northern border with Texas. Rubio drove the van with Mayor Rodriguez riding shotgun. Though he appeared nearly catatonic, just as he had in Guadalupe's cobbled square, the vampire handled the vehicle with inhuman precision, minding every stop sign, using his signals for every turn, every lane change. It was creepy.

Matt, Rose, and Satterfield sat on the second seat with six more ops filling the back two rows. Behind their van, rounding out their little convoy, came four of the Order's Suburbans loaded down with the remaining ops and Rubio's wights.

How much control did Rubio have over the creatures? They seemed to obey his thoughts, and were perfectly willing to climb into the cars at his behest, but would they launch into a feeding frenzy if he got too far away from them? Rose shuddered at the thought.

The van shook as they tooled along a gravel drive surrounded by forest. The sky above the trees glowed the way it might above an outdoor arena, the clouds limed in soft white brilliance. A ten-foot stone wall crowned with razor wire appeared on their left, spooling out behind them.

Rubio slowed the van as he approached a gate where steel doors on reinforced hinges split the wall. Eight armed guards dressed in military fatigues stood before the gate. They bore a mix of weapons, mostly AK-47 rifles on straps, .45s at their hips, and an assortment of grenades, knives, and machetes attached to their body armor.

Rubio rolled down his window. A guard took one look at him and started yelling over his shoulder in Spanish. The fortified doors swung open, and they drove inside.

The *hacienda* sat atop a hill surrounded by manicured gardens, spreading oaks, and armed men. Rose was no historian, but the place looked old. She could imagine Jesuit priests tending the gardens as parishioners milled up and down the mansion's stone steps, seeking forgiveness and enlightenment. Except now those parishioners had been replaced by militiamen watching the convoy with wary eyes.

Arc sodium lights—the kind used to brighten high school football games—spilled white radiance upon the *hacienda*'s walls and front drive. Rubio pulled the van up to an expansive porch, socked it into park, and hopped out. He rounded the vehicle and opened the mayor's door faster than Rose could have managed on her best day.

With a few rapid-fire orders, he had the Dog Ears out of the cars and surrounded by guards and half-naked wights.

"I am taking you inside now," Rubio said. "You will be guests in my father's house. I expect you to act accordingly. If one of you makes trouble, your leader dies." Rubio pointed a long, minatory finger at Matt. Then he spun on his heels to open the *hacienda*'s double doors.

He led them into a darkened hall, his snakeskin boots clicking on the burnished wood. Expensive works of hand-made art in pewter and brass lined the walls illuminated by strategically placed lights. Though the place appeared meticulously clean, the air smelled musty and close, likely owing to the house's lack of windows. Discolored arches in the stucco evidenced their past existence.

Rubio flung open a second set of double doors at the far end of the house, revealing an elaborately decorated room. It reminded Rose of pictures she had seen of Buckingham Palace, with its gold-on-red carpets and lavishly decorated walls. A dining table large enough to seat twenty dominated the center of the room. A dozen vampires, their pale faces set aglow by wavering candlelight, gathered around it. Heaps of untouched bloody steak dished up on fine china lay before each of them. As if choreographed, they turned in unison from their interrupted meal to stare at the newcomers.

"*Padre*," Rubio called, facing a fat vampire who sat at the head of the long table.

When the one Rubio called Padre spoke, only his mouth moved, reminding Rose absurdly of an animatronic bear. "*Que pasa, hijo?*"

Mayor Rodriguez stepped forward. *"Hola, mi amor."*

The fat vampire's face came suddenly alive. His eyes brightened, opening wide. He smiled, revealing a set of perfectly white, perfectly straight teeth. They seemed normal enough to Rose—no fangs.

"Glenda?" Rising with incredible speed for his bulk, the fat vampire crossed the room in an eye blink. He put his arms around the mayor and hugged and kissed her several times before holding her at arm's length, whispering to her, his eyes ranging about her face with hungry intent.

Matt and Rose shared a look. He shrugged and shook his head. By his expression, Rose knew he had never seen a vampire-succubus relationship like this.

Rodriguez launched into a torrent of Spanish. When she had finished, she turned to Matt and the others and said, "This is Clemente. He is my husband."

For a long moment, no one said a word. The dozen vampires at the table sat like statues watching the succubi. Clemente and Rubio did likewise while the Order ops shifted uncomfortably under their combined gazes. Then Matt cleared his throat as if remembering where and who he was. "It is a pleasure to meet you, sir."

The fat vampire tilted his head, a slow grin spreading across his face. "Is it, incubus?"

Despite the room's elegant décor, Clemente wore an inexpensive collared t-shirt, gray and black in alternating stripes, which stretched considerably over his ample belly. This he paired with ordinary chinos and black New Balance running shoes. He did not look like a threat, but something in his eyes spoke of pure menace backed by a titanic capacity for destruction.

Without warning, the vampires at the table rose to their feet in utter silence.

The Dog Ears stirred. Rose drew strength, speed, and stamina, dexterity, vision, and discernment. She adjusted her feet, readying for a fight. Around her, the others did likewise.

Mayor Rodriguez put a restraining hand on Clemente's belly.

Though Rose doubted the mayor could physically stop her husband should he decide to act, the vampire froze.

"They saved my life," she said in English. "The entire village. They are not *Sociedad Americana*."

"No? Then what are they?"

"Rebels." Matt was breathing hard. A bead of sweat coursed down his forehead. "We fight against Society."

Clemente pointed at Rose. "My wife says that one moves like a seasoned vampire—like the secret *policia* you Americans are sending into our country. They are doing something—something to increase their power, yes? You doing that too, *chica*?"

Rose glanced at Matt. He nodded.

"I have more votaries than most, but I didn't get them the way they did, the *policia* as you call them."

"Then how?"

"That's complicated. I mean, it's because some friends of mine put me in a comic book. I know that sounds stupid, but I'm serious. I—"

Clemente held up a hand, forestalling Rose's stammered reply. He tilted his head, eyes narrowed. "Rose Carver?"

19

———

THE COLLECTION

"And this—this is my pride and joy," Clemente said, grinning so wide he might have been speaking of a favorite child. He lifted a plastic guard on the wall that housed a keypad, punched in a code with lightning efficiency, and stood back as a steel door swung outward to the sound of rushing air.

Rose stood next to Matt, taking comfort from his presence. Once Clemente realized Rose's identity, he had insisted she follow him alone into the bowels of his mansion, dismissing the rest of the Dog Ears into the care of Rubio. A tense moment had passed when Rose refused to go alone, until Matt convinced the vampire to let him accompany her.

Mayor Rodriguez had come along. She stood next to Clemente, a beatific smile on her face. Was she somehow under the creature's charm? If so, Clemente hid it well.

Lights flickered on inside the room, and Clemente stepped inside.

Rose glanced at Matt. Did he feel as nervous as she about following a vampire into this space with its bank vault door?

For her part, Rose couldn't seem to make her hands stop shaking. She tried drawing calm, but it was no use. She felt like a kid walking through her first haunted house at the fairgrounds.

"It's shock," Matt whispered. He squeezed her fingers reassuringly. "It'll pass."

She nodded. Probably he was right. But though she could see that, understand it even, she could do nothing to lessen it. Leslie was dead, and Melody had killed her. Those facts kept exploding in Rose's mind as sharp and painful as the instant she discovered them.

"Come!" called the vampire from within the brightly lit room.

Rodriguez smiled at her fellow succubi. "It's okay. I promise you're safe. My husband won't harm you."

Matt released Rose's hand to precede her into the room. Rose followed, drawing speed in preparation for an ambush. If the vampire wanted them dead, jumping them as they came through the door would be an excellent way to go about it.

Rose was prepared for just about any contingency except the one she found.

She stood inside the largest comic book collection she had ever seen. It was the size of a small grocery store. Racks of colorful magazines, graphic novels, and, yes, regular comics, divided the room into ten aisles. Glossy plastic covers enshrined most of the issues, though several hundred lined what looked like moisture-controlled display cases along one wall.

Rose didn't know much about comic books. But she had picked up a bit of the culture having spent time with the twins. She knew enough to at least recognize the most highly prized items in the comic universe. Brendan and Luke had pointed out a fair share in the ludicrously well-stocked dealers' room at MegaCon.

"You have a Batman number one," she whispered, peering into a glass case.

"I even have Detective Comics number twenty-seven." The vampire pointed farther down the row. "But that is not what I brought you here for, Rose Carver. I have something special to show you. Follow."

On the far wall, under a bank of track lights, stood a silver display rack festooned with comics. By the looks of them, this set was newer than those at the front of the collection but no less cherished. In fact, extra copies of the same issues ran up the wall outside the rack, many in different languages. Rose could see French, German, Spanish, and even what looked like Japanese versions.

"They're all by the Pruett twins," Rose said.

"*Si!*" Clemente beamed like a little boy, his former reserve suddenly forgotten. "I have everything the brothers ever created. But this," he pulled a thick book from the rack to lay it reverently on the display case, "this is their best work to date."

Rose's breath caught. "That's one of the twin's proof copies."

"It is! If you look closely, you'll see it's not yet sealed. One of them even smeared the charcoal on page six."

The cover, which looked more like a photograph than a hand-drawn portrait, depicted Rose's harrowing leap the night she had tried to escape Camp Den. Luke and Brendan had captured her desperation, her fear, her longing to win free, condensing them into an expression of agonized yearning on her face.

"This is weeks ahead of even the online issues. How'd you get it?" Rose stared at the thing in awe.

"Top Kickstarter reward." Clemente managed to look smug without changing his expression. "A mere twenty-five thousand for the proof copy. I count that a bargain. It came with the ten-thousand-dollar reward, dinner with the twins, but I had to give that up when your government closed the border."

Matt whistled at the figures. Rose couldn't imagine spending that kind of money for a comic book, especially one based on her life. The very idea made reason stare.

"It's all true, isn't it?" Clemente asked.

Rose looked to Matt, uncertain what she should reveal.

He nodded.

"Most of it," she said.

A broad grin spread across the vampire's lips. Unlike in the movies and novels, he had no fangs, just very white, very straight teeth. "I knew it. I told Glenda, we know succubi are real, and we know something is wrong with your American Society. I can't believe none of them have noticed *Drawn*." He gestured at the comic.

"Maybe they have." Matt hadn't left Rose's side. He stood shoulder to shoulder with her, not the least bit distracted by the comics, his eyes fixed on Clemente, though now and again he spared a look for Rodriguez. "But what can Society do about it? Arrest the twins? For what? And how would it look if the FBI put Rose Carver, superhero, on its most wanted list?"

"Clever," Clemente said. "Genius. But I've always said that about the twins, haven't I, Glenda?"

"*Si*," said the mayor.

Clemente turned his grin on Rose. "So, that is why you came here, Rose Carver? You are running ahead of your American Society, trying to save the succubi of Mexico, yes?"

"Exactly."

The vampire fell still, watching her. He tilted his head to one side so slowly it was hard to catch the movement.

Rose glanced at Glenda, who shrugged. "You haven't been around vampires much?"

"Never," Rose said.

"They stand still when they think deep. It's how they hunt. But that don't mean they forget you."

"How many are in the Order?" Clemente asked, moving only his mouth.

Matt said nothing.

"Too few to take on American Society, I think," Clemente chuckled. "No, that much I learned from reading *Drawn*. You are few, and most of you are weak as well. Monodraws. Rose is the strongest among you."

"Don't believe everything you read," Matt said.

"Now that I've met you, given your people a place of refuge from your enemies, I'm going to be in the novel, *si*?"

Rose shrugged. "I don't know. I don't write it."

"And if I do you a good turn, I will be a hero," the vampire continued, ignoring her.

"Yes," Matt said, suddenly eager. "You will."

Rose started to argue, but Matt waved her off.

Clemente took the copy of *Drawn* from Rose and stood staring at it for a long, silent minute.

These frozen moments of vampire time sent shivers of unease parading up and down Rose's back. She sidled closer to Matt and took his hand. Though he obviously wanted them free in case something happened, he entwined his fingers with hers without protest.

Matt turned to Rodriguez. "Can I speak to him when he's like that?"

"*Si*, he hears us just fine."

"May I call you Clemente?" Matt asked.

The vampire nodded once, slowly.

"Clemente, Rose needs your help. We all do. You know this attack on Mexico by the U.S. is not over drugs or oil or any other lie the politicians can gin up, right?"

"*Si*. And I know it's not all about succubi either."

"No. It's about power. Society wants to rule this hemisphere—probably the world. And they're willing to kill a lot of innocent people to do it."

"They cannot defeat the coven kingdoms." Clemente met Matt's eyes.

"Are you so certain? You know about the succubi with immense votaries. Your wife saw some of them tonight."

"It's true," Rodriguez said. "I saw two. They were fast as Rubio. And strong, Clemente. Strong as you, I think. If Rubio hadn't had the wights with him, we might have been in trouble."

"So," Clemente said, "this means the fear factory is real, no? The one in *Drawn*."

"Yes," Rose said.

"And your parents? They are trapped inside it?"

Rose nodded, unable to speak.

"Clemente," Rodriguez clucked her tongue at the vampire. "What a thing to ask? You hurt her feelings."

"*Lo siento, senorita*." An expression of sincere regret creased Clemente's face.

"We need your help to destroy the fear factory," Matt said.

Clemente regarded him. He didn't seem surprised at the request. "You've found it then?"

Matt shook his head. "No, but we have some leads. If we could free the people inside, break Society's hold on them, we could weaken our enemies into ineffectiveness."

"And I could be in *Drawn*, no?"

"Of course," Matt said.

Stillness crept back into the vampire's limbs. He stood frozen far longer this time than before, the copy of *Drawn* balanced in his pale hands.

Rose drew strength and dexterity without thinking. Every time Clemente did that, she got the feeling he was about to pounce.

At last, he became animated, his eyes gleaming as he spoke. "I will do it."

"Excellent. Thank you." Matt visibly relaxed, some of the rigidness fleeing his otherwise stiff back.

"But," Clemente held up one finger, "I cannot make this type of decision on my own. Just as you succubi have your Society, I must answer to my coven. Sometimes they are slow about such things. You will stay with me here in the *hacienda* until they answer, *si?*"

Rose wanted to say no, but Matt spoke first. "We would be honored."

Rose gave his hand a hard squeeze. He ignored her.

"*Excelente!*" said the vampire. "I'll make some calls. If the old ones are too slow for you, maybe some of my younger contacts can help. In the meantime, I'll have Rubio put you in the finest rooms we have. Oh, and Rose?"

"Yes?"

"Do you have as deep a draw on charm as the twins portray in *Drawn?*"

Rose shrugged.

"She has nearly the strongest draw on charm I've ever seen," Matt said.

"Good. Good!" said the vampire. This was the most animated Rose had seen him. "That may come in handy."

"Why?" Rose asked.

"One of my people caught a Society operative prowling our gardens not an hour before you arrived. We've tried everything to make her talk, but so far, it's been useless. Maybe you can get something out of her."

A horrible feeling crept over Rose—a sick intuition that made her stomach roil. "Did she tell you her name?"

"*Si*, she did. It's your sister, Melody Carver."

20

————

THORN

A slim, rakish vampire led Rose to a private room. It was large enough to swallow two of her old apartments back in Columbus. A four-poster bed the size of a Cadillac dominated the stucco and wood space. Cool night air rustled the windows, carrying with it the scent of lilacs.

"You like it?" The vampire moved only his lips when he spoke.

Rose nodded.

"If you need anything, let one of us know. You are Clemente's special guest." With that, the vampire slipped down the hall like a shadow, gone in silence.

Matt, who had his room a few doors down, had come with Rose. She hadn't released his hand since they'd left Clemente's vault.

"Are you okay?" he asked.

"No." Rose pulled him inside and shut the heavy oaken door.

"I'm so sorry," he whispered. "About Leslie. And your sister."

Rose kicked off her boots, turned back the covers, and lay in the bed, pulling Matt with her. She pressed her face to his chest. He smelled of sweat and gun smoke. She didn't care. He held her while she shuddered with silent sobs.

"I think my sister killed Leslie," Rose said when she could trust her voice again.

"It isn't her fault if she's under Lord's charm," Matt said. "She isn't responsible."

Rose nodded, but knowing that and believing it were two separate things.

"Clemente wants you to interview her so he can listen in," Matt said. "You shouldn't do it."

"I want to know she's safe." Rose didn't add that she wanted to hear Melody's version of what had transpired in that bell tower.

A sudden, horrible realization struck Rose. "Do you think they've bitten her? Would they change her into one of them?"

From what Rose had learned at Camp Den, vampire venom altered a victim's mind, rendering them pliant, a willing thrall.

"They wouldn't turn her," Matt said. "Fledgling vampires tend to lose memories. They forget most, if not all, of their previous lives. Clemente doesn't strike me as the sort who would risk losing an advantage."

"But you think they've bitten her?"

"I'm certain they have."

Rose stiffened at the image of fat Clemente nipping at her sister's throat. Disgusting. She burrowed closer to Matt, hugging him tight, eager for the comfort of his presence. Drawing insight and intelligence, she pushed herself to separate her emotions from the cold facts.

"Maybe the venom will make her more susceptible to my charm," she said. "That's a reason to interrogate her now. I might be able to break Lord's hold on her if her defenses are down."

"Maybe," Matt whispered, "but we don't know that. And we don't know what the vampires want either. We need their help, but that doesn't mean I trust them."

Rose nodded. "All right, but I want to see her at least. She's my sister, Matt."

"I know."

A fter waiting the entire day, the vampires made her wait most of the next night as well before they brought Rose to Melody's basement holding cell two hours before dawn. The little room, only four doors down from Clemente's comic book archive, stank of sweat, blood, and mildew. A single line of spotlights illuminated the place, their beams focused on Melody, who sat in a dentist's chair, her limbs strapped down with leather bonds.

Rubio smiled when he saw the look of pain and worry flash across Rose's face. "Your *hermana*," he said in a smooth steely voice. "She's tough. You want we should take out the gag?"

Rose clenched her jaw and nodded.

Rubio motioned toward Melody with his chin, and a couple of his flunky vamps hurried to remove the rubber ball gag from her mouth. Blood speckled its white surface.

Several bite marks, lurid red and purple, marred Melody's neck.

Rose turned to Rubio. "Will you let us talk alone?"

"*Claro, Senorita,*" he said with an insincere little half bow. "Just do not release the straps, no?"

Rose nodded. She remained silent until the steel door vacuum sealed behind her.

"They wouldn't leave us alone if they weren't listening," Melody said.

Rose frowned. Her sister sounded muzzy, perhaps a bit confused. The dark circles under her eyes spoke of too little sleep; the burst capillaries around her mouth and neck said other things.

None of that mattered now.

"There was a girl in the tower," Rose said through a jaw so tight it felt bound in copper. "Did you kill her?"

Melody furrowed her brow. "What girl?"

"The tower sniper: red hair, beautiful, young." Rose's voice broke on the last word.

Melody shook her head. She looked concerned, almost empathetic. "I didn't kill any girl in a tower."

"You had that sword. You slaughtered our people."

"Only because they attacked me." Sudden tears glistened in Melody's eyes. "Do you think I like what I've been doing? You do. You think I'm one of them."

"You're not?"

"Of course not," Melody said. "It was Lord. He charmed me. He charms everybody. Do you really think I would do those kinds of things?"

"You swear you didn't kill her? You swear it?"

"I didn't kill her. I'm not a monster, Anna. Not like your new friends." Melody jerked her chin at the door.

"The vampires aren't my friends," Rose said.

"Not the vampires."

"The Order?"

"You don't even realize what's happened to you?" Melody asked, incredulous.

"What are you talking about?"

"Anna, wake the hell up. I'm not the only one who's been manipulated."

"That's not true."

"Let's see," Melody said, "when did you ever dream of shooting a submachine gun? How many times when we were kids did you ever say, 'I'm going to be an assassin for Society when I grow up?' Anna, you've been charmed off your ass, and you don't even realize it. This isn't you, just like it isn't me. Dad didn't raise us to be robots for our succubus betters. Did he?"

Rose rocked back on her heels, heart hammering, brows knit. Despite drawing discernment, she felt no lie from her sister. The girl was telling the truth, at least a truth she believed.

"They used charm on us in the beginning, sure," Rose said. "But that was to get us over our initial fears. If I was being charmed right now, I would know it."

Melody grinned slowly. "Would you, Sis? I mean, you know, boil a frog slowly and all. Maybe you've just gotten used to it. And who told you that you weren't being charmed? Matt Snow? His mother? Don't you think—"

"His mother?"

Melody tilted her head. "You didn't know Robin Ambrose is Matt Snow's mother?"

Rose said nothing, could say nothing. Her face burned.

"Guess that means you didn't know his father is Jason Kraft?" Melody's look of triumph was too much.

"You're lying," Rose said, though discernment told her otherwise.

"Do you know what I was doing the night Lord came for us? Chemistry homework. Stupid, fourth period chem lab shit. And then suddenly I was so weak I couldn't move. I threw up on my bed. My insides hurt like I had run three marathons. And that's when Lord blew in the front of our house, Anna. Me, Dad, Mom, Troy, we were weak as kittens when he came, all because you drew first. I guess if Lord had come a little sooner, you might have been the one lying on the floor unable to move or even talk. But that wasn't how things played out."

"I didn't know." Rose had come in here so full of indignation, so bent on discovering the truth. But not this truth.

"Yeah, I know," Melody said. The grin had slid from her face, just as much of the energy and animation had steamed from her speech.

"Where are they?"

Melody shrugged. "In a fear factory somewhere, I guess."

"There's more than one?"

"I don't know."

"But you've got to know where they are," Rose said. "Haven't you kept your eyes open?"

"My eyes are clouded when I'm around Lord. And I'm always around him. I haven't thought about Mom and Dad in months."

"Christ, I thought you would know."

"No. But I can find out."

Rose stared at her sister for a long, silent moment. "How?"

"I know people inside the Indrawn Breath. You and me, we can get to them together, find out where the factories are hidden."

"We can't do it alone," Rose said.

"Who says? The people who have been lying to you from the start? Did they politely ask you to join their rebellion, or did some wrangler kidnap you?"

"It was Matt."

Melody nodded. "Makes sense. He's the best next to Lord."

"At kidnapping?"

"It's called wrangle-mangle. Means if you can't force someone to come along the easy way, you mess 'em up. Matt's call sign, Snow, he got that because everyone says he comes on like a blizzard. A total whiteout. Somebody resisted, got physical with him, he put 'em down quick."

"You mean he killed them?"

Melody shrugged. "Sometimes. But that's not the real goal. I mean what good is a corpse in a fear factory?"

Where before Rose's face had flushed, infused with heat, now the blood drained from it, from her whole body, leaving her cold. Was this why Matt had tried to dissuade her from interrogating Melody?

"He put people in the fear factory?" Rose asked.

"It was his job, Anna. He was Lord's top wrangler."

"How long?"

"How should I know? Years, I guess."

Rose's vision swam. She drew wakefulness, strength, and calm, but nothing could smooth away the hurt and anger welling inside her. "I'm going to get you out of here."

"I'm not joining the rebels," Melody said. "No more of this brain-washing bullshit. If you get me out, I'm leaving on my own."

"No, you're not."

"How do you figure that?" Melody asked.

"Because I'm going with you."

21

BREAKING TRUST

Rubio and two of his human cronies escorted a fuming Rose back to her room. She wanted to walk alone, but they wouldn't hear of it.

Muffled gunfire like distant thunder echoed in the east.

"What was that?" Rose asked.

"Your *Americano* army moved last night. The fighting's close. A few miles from here."

"Is Clemente worried?"

"No." Rubio was doing that vampire stillness thing again: walking without swinging his arms, barely moving his lips when he spoke. It made Rose's skin crawl.

"Speaking of Clemente," she said, "is he available? I need to talk with him."

"No."

They had reached her door.

"Is there a good time to reach him?" Rose asked.

"No." The vampire turned as if on bearings and sped away, his pets in tow.

Rose stared after him, lips twisted in irritation. She was beginning to despise vampires.

Steeling herself, trying in vain to slake the anger broiling inside, Rose pulled open her door. Discernment told her she would find Matt there.

He sat at a small desk watching a news report on a tablet computer. When he saw her, he stood, a look of concern tugging down the corners of his mouth. "What is it?"

"You were a wrangler for the Indrawn Breath. You put innocent people in the fear factory."

Matt stiffened. "She told you."

"Why didn't you tell me?" Rose shut the door behind her.

Matt started her way, his hand out. "Rose, I—"

"Don't touch me." She pulled away from him to press her back against the oaken door.

He dropped his hand. "You feel betrayed."

"You're damned right I feel betrayed. How could you keep this from me? Why would you?" Her words echoed around the empty room, seeming to bellow back at her from its shadowy corners.

Matt's face dropped. He stared at her boots. "What was I supposed to say? Let's have dinner, and oh, I used to do horrible things for the organization we're fighting against?"

"Do you know where the fear factory is?"

"Of course not. What are you trying to say? Why would I hide something like that?"

"If you put people in there, then you must know how to find it." Rose searched Matt's face. He looked like a man whose lifeline has snapped, spilling him over a precipice.

"It wasn't like that."

Rose folded her arms. "How was it? Did you kidnap strangers and hand them off to David Lord?"

"I didn't know what was happening. The people I took—"

"Wrangled or mangled, right?"

Matt blinked once slowly. "I was told they were dissidents, traitors. It was my job to see they couldn't harm anyone or expose our kind to the world."

"You never questioned them?"

"Not in the beginning." Matt put a hand on the table as if to steady himself. "I followed orders."

"Lord's orders."

"Yes. Lord's orders."

"Where did you take them, Matt?"

"FBI field offices, mostly. None of them was the fear factory. You must believe me. If I had known then what was happening, I—"

"How long before you questioned? How many people did you hand over to Society before you bothered to think what might be happening to them?" Gunfire sounded in the distance as if to punctuate Rose's words, sharp and accusing.

"Rose, you've got to—"

"I don't have to do anything. How long?"

"Eight years."

Rose shook her head. "You weren't going to tell me any of this."

"Don't you think I'm ashamed of what I did?" Self-derision filled Matt's voice, though Rose doubted its sincerity. She doubted a good many things now. "I can't take it back. All I can do is go forward, try somehow to make amends."

"But you aren't making amends, Matt. You're lying. You weren't going to tell me any of this because you didn't have to, not while you had me charm-blasted."

"What are you talking about?" He took his hand from the table to stand straight, his back erect.

"What the hell am I doing here with you, with the Dog Ears? I'm no soldier. You coaxed me into all this. It's not me."

"Nobody's charming you," Matt said.

"Not anymore."

"Not for months. You're the one who put a stop to it. You would feel it if it was still going on."

"Would I? I learned a lot of things I never knew at Camp Den. Maybe secret charm is something you held back from us slinkers."

Matt's face flushed, and his nostrils flared. "If I'm charming you, I'm doing a shitty job of it."

"I'm leaving," Rose said. "And I'm taking Melody with me."

"Wait, please. Let's talk about this."

"So you can charm me into seeing things your way? I don't think so."

"Think about what you're doing," Matt said. "We're in the middle of a godforsaken war zone in a house full of vampires. Do you think for one second you can just traipse out of here with your sister in tow? Clemente isn't going to let that happen, and you know it."

A concussive thrum much louder than the preceding gunfire shook the room.

"Stay out of my way, Matt," Rose said, pulling the door open. "I don't want to hurt you the way you've hurt me."

Matt winced as if she had socked him in the gut.

She slammed the door on her way out.

Clemente's *hacienda* was laid out in three above-ground floors, one directly atop the other. His suite took up most of the third. What else? Vampires loved their things. That included houses, cars, and minions. Especially minions. Rose had learned in the last two days that Rubio was Clemente's only true child, his blood son. The others serving here were just sycophants, hangers-on from various clans of the coven kingdoms who had attached themselves to a powerful lord.

Rose ascended a set of parquet steps, real hand-tooled hardwood carved into a series of interlocking chevrons, not the cheap laminate stuff she had experienced all her life. She expected to find armed guards at the top, but the hallway stood empty. Did that have something to do with American forces swinging this direction? Perhaps Clemente had ordered his guards to the roof or outer perimeter to keep an eye on the battlefront. Did Clemente plan to fight or run? Probably the latter. He took his orders from older vamps, and they seemed reluctant to reveal themselves, thank goodness.

A set of solid steel doors stood at the top of the stairs. They were locked. Rose banged on them with the flat of one hand.

"Clemente," she called, "I need to speak with you."

No answer.

Rose drew hearing and discernment. She thought she could make out a muffled voice, but it was hard to hear over the now constant gunfire outside, which sounded closer than before.

She knocked again but froze before the second strike. A familiar scent filled her nose. Blood. And from the smell, a lot of it. Unbidden images of Leslie's desecrated body shot through Rose's mind. With them, like bosom companions, came rage and heartache, one as strong as the other. Her vision went red. She drew strength and kicked the doors off their hinges with an earsplitting screech of tortured metal.

What lay beyond brought her up short.

Clemente sat at the head of a dining table, dressed in military fatigues that only served to accentuate his girth. A young girl sat on his lap, her forehead resting against the vampire's shoulder.

At the sudden sound of the doors breaking, Clemente stood, blood-speckled teeth bared, and the girl dropped from his grasp, limp as a marionette. Her body made a piteous clatter when it hit the wooden floor.

Despite her discernment, which gave her a near instant understanding of the scene and its ramifications, Rose could not move. Her wide eyes took in the torn flesh of the girl's neck, the glistening sparkle of life's blood on Clemente's lips, the complete stillness of his victim's desiccated corpse. In that moment, Rose no longer saw the girl lying on the floor, but Leslie, her headless body abandoned in a nameless tower.

"Rose Carver." Clemente straightened up, his face gone slack. "Why are you here?"

"What have you done?" Rose asked.

Clemente's dark eyes tracked slowly down to the girl as if someone had pointed out a minor stain on his floor. "She was the daughter of a maid. I would not normally take the child of a servant, but your *Americano* soldiers are coming. I need my strength."

"You killed her." Rose's heart thrummed so hard she shook with its efforts.

Clemente tilted his head, the wattles at his neck forming a grotesque set of double chins on one side of his throat. "*Claro*, woman. That is what vampires do in times of need. If you're concerned for her mother, don't be. I'll see she's compensated."

Something burst inside Rose. Could a succubus draw anger from her votaries? It certainly felt that way, though Rose doubted it. No, this blistering torrent was all hers. It scoured away thought, restraint, even sanity, setting fire to her mind.

Rose covered the distance between them in one spastic leap, clearing the oversized table and narrowly missing a crystal chandelier. Her fist caught Clemente on the right eye with the force of a two-ton sledgehammer and a sound like a gunshot.

He reeled away, gasping, one side of his face visibly caved in.

Good. Rose could hurt a vampire.

Careful of the girl's corpse, Rose set her feet and barreled into Clemente, planting one shoulder into his ample belly while simultaneously sweeping both legs in a classic wrestling takedown she had learned at Camp Den. The back of his head smacked the floor, and she fell atop him. She tried to spin into a side mount, even managed to get one forearm under his chin to control his bite, but the fat vamp had finally begun to resist. And he was strong.

Clemente sat up. Somehow, he managed to get a boot beneath him and stood, holding Rose tight when she tried to scramble down. With a powerful roar, he flung her across the suite. She collided with a stucco-over-brick wall. Something in her left arm cracked. She cried out as pain shot through that side but managed to rebound off the floor to gain her feet. Drawing healing, she mended her broken bones almost instantly.

Clemente put on a good show of appearing unfazed by Rose's attack. His face, the part that wasn't dented into his skull, remained slack, but he was panting, and a faint sheen of pinkish sweat glistened on his cheeks and forehead. He felt pain no matter how aloof he tried to appear. That realization gave Rose no end of satisfaction. How many other little girls had this monster killed in his undoubtedly long life? A hundred? A thousand? Whatever pain she dealt him could never make up for even one.

Unfortunately, Rose's satisfaction at causing Clemente pain vanished in the next instant when the vampire's sunken eye righted itself and his cheek lifted back into place with a wet pop. A series of multi-colored bruises blossomed and healed across his injured flesh before it finally settled on its unnatural pale hue. The wound was gone.

The vampire could heal faster than her. Good to know.

"Have you lost your mind, woman?" Clemente spat a wad of bloody phlegm on the floor. "You come here seeking my help, and then you attack me over some little whore? You're insane."

Rose balled her fists. "You haven't seen insane yet."

She rushed him, this time feinting a jab at his face. He tried to block, and she smashed her opposite elbow into his nose. Blood sprayed, and Clemente grunted. He grabbed at her, but she evaded him. He might heal faster, but she had an edge on physical speed. She sidestepped, caught him with a wicked snap kick to the knee followed by an overhand right that reapplied some of the damage he had managed to mend.

Clemente staggered back. He wiped at his injured nose, and his fingers came away bloody, a sight that finally broke his stoic façade. He snarled, baring his teeth, and charged.

Rose weaved under Clemente's next punch with time to spare. Her new depth and breadth of votaries amazed her. She drew all she could, and still more power remained, a seemingly bottomless reserve she could never empty. Relying on that surplus, she closed the distance between them. She set her feet just as her combat trainers had taught her at Camp Den and unleashed a furious hail of blows that pummeled Clemente's ribs and sternum like cannonballs.

Clemente dropped to one knee. Blood and sweat dribbled from his damaged face onto the hardwood floor. Rose seized his upraised arm, cocked her fist, and drew in all the strength and speed at her command.

"Never again," she whispered.

"STOP!" The voice shook the room.

Seven vampires rushed through the broken doors, Rubio in the lead. They held submachine guns and were decked out in black body armor.

Behind them came Matt with several of the Dog Ears, including Watts and Satterfield.

"Don't shoot," Matt screamed, his face so pale he could have been one of the vampires.

Clemente threw off Rose's grip and stood. "Kill this ungrateful bitch!"

"No!" Matt shouted.

And that was when the room blew up.

The near wall behind the vampires blasted into a chunky gale filled with stucco, plywood, and brick shards the size of Rose's clenched fist, all of it heralded by a monstrous explosion. Sunlight poured into the opening.

For the second time in five minutes, Rose flew through the air. This time she collided with Clemente's dining table, which flipped, sending heavy chairs in every direction like bowling pins. Heart thudding in her chest, she desperately clung to consciousness, drawing healing and awareness, her hearing gone to an incessant buzz. She stood, coughing, trying to get her bearings in the smoke and sudden daylight. She had thought it still dark outside.

Her hearing returned in a rush as her draw of healing took hold. Someone screamed in pain, but she couldn't see who through the pall of smoke and dust in the air.

"Matt?" she called.

"Here."

Rose followed the sound. She was shaking, disoriented, and her eyes watered so much her vision looked like a kaleidoscope. Rubio darted past her, both hands pressed over his eyes. Black, green, and purple splotches decorated his exposed skin.

A second vampire, a tall woman, followed him. She too covered her face, especially her eyes. Together, they tripped and stumbled across the debris-strewn suite toward the exit, both wailing in pain.

Gunfire resumed outside, or perhaps Rose simply became aware of it again. It sounded far louder than before, owing to the now missing northern wall.

Clemente and two other vampires lay on the floor unmoving. Putrid green, purple, and even black splotches covered their exposed skin, and a stench like sour milk wafted up from their corpses. Rose covered her mouth and nose and hurried on.

Matt emerged from the murk, his expression raw with panic and worry. He spotted Rose and seized her hand to drag her from in front of the gaping hole into the adjoining hallway. "Oh, God, I thought you were dead for sure." Matt threw his arms around Rose, his cheek pressed against the side of her neck.

"I'm okay," Rose lied. She couldn't stop shaking. She couldn't get the image of that poor girl out of her head. She pushed Matt away, not roughly, but firmly. Part of her wanted to melt into his embrace and never let him go. But was that a genuine feeling or something borne of charm?

"Sorry." Matt released her, a flash of hurt passing across his visage, there and gone in less than a second.

"We need to leave," Watts said as he and Satterfield materialized from the smoke behind Matt. "Those were hellfire rockets. Probably came from drones. Either they're softening us up for another round of the same, or their regulars are coming. Either way, we don't want to be here when the Army arrives."

Another explosion rocked the *hacienda*.

"Agreed," Matt said. "We're evacuating now. Is everyone together?"

"Should be," Satterfield said. "I told them to meet up in the game room. Most of the vamps and all of the human guards disappeared around three a.m., so they weren't there to keep us separated."

They descended the *hacienda*'s parquet stairs two at a time. The physical activity, just having something to do with her body, helped Rose fight her shock. It gave her somewhere to put her mind besides her grief.

They reached the second-floor main hallway. Watts and Satterfield dashed into an adjoining corridor. Rose made to follow, but Matt took her by the wrist to stop her.

"What is it?" Rose asked.

Watts pointed. "Game room's this way."

"You two go," Matt said. "If we don't catch up, get everyone back to the States. Meet at Cause Point Beta, got it?"

Satterfield looked between Rose and Matt, her eyes wide with worry. "Sir, we should stay together."

"Not this time."

"Where are you going?" Watts asked.

"Rose's sister is in the basement. We're not leaving without her."

22

———

CHOICE

"Thank you," Rose said, as she and Matt ran for the basement door. "You didn't have to do this."

"Yes. I did. I owe you that much."

Matt kicked open the door leading to the *hacienda*'s basement, bounded through, and hit the stairs with draw-enhanced speed. Though his injured leg slowed him, he was still faster and more adroit than any human athlete. Rose had to hold herself back very little to keep from tripping over him.

She drew discernment. "Someone's down there."

Matt skipped the last five steps to land in a crouch, holding up a hand to forestall Rose. She stopped just above him, her heart in her throat.

A mass of wights huddled around the door to Clemente's comic book vault. Rose counted at least thirty, probably more. A gaggle of lesser vampires stood amongst them, affecting cold indifference, but Rose saw through their façade. They yearned to attack.

The wights growled like feral cats. Several of them slunk forward, their pale skin unnaturally bright even in the basement's dark confines.

Matt tensed, setting his feet for a confrontation. Which, while brave and maybe even a little endearing, was beyond idiotic.

Rose put a hand on Matt's shoulder, staying him, as she descended the last couple of steps. She drew charm. "We're here for my sister. That's all. We don't want trouble."

The wights froze. Silence held for a long moment while the two sides watched one another. Rose couldn't tell if she had ensnared the creatures with her charm—the things were impossible to read. But they hadn't thrown themselves into a killing frenzy, so there was that.

A thump and click followed by the sound of sliding bolts echoed from the vault door behind the vampires and wights. It opened with a hiss, and the group made way for Rubio and several of the older vampires accompanied by seven human guards armed with automatic rifles.

Rubio held his face, now healed of sun damage, perfectly still, devoid of emotion. He stopped five paces from Matt and Rose, human and vampire cronies flanking him. They too affected looks of stoic nonchalance.

Rose swallowed. All at once, she wanted another chance to speak with Matt. She was still pissed at him for withholding the truth of his past, but that didn't matter now. She had fallen for him. That was why his dishonesty hurt so much. And at this moment, when death seemed imminent, love made everything else trivial. She wanted to say so much, to let him say so much more—explain himself so that she could think of him without rancor, without hurt. But she could see that chance slipping through their fingers.

"You killed Clemente," Rubio said, his voice low and full of malice.

"Sunlight killed him." Matt took a step forward as if he might take on the entire horde on his own.

Rose stepped forward, taking her place at Matt's side. For better or death, she refused to let him fight alone. She matched Rubio's flinty gaze without flinching. "I would have killed him myself if that rocket hadn't done it for me."

The wights growled, as did the weaker vampires. They adjusted their stances, leaning forward. Several of them sniffed the air as if scenting blood.

Rubio and the older vamps remained unnervingly still. "He was helping you. Why attack him?"

Rose considered the vampire for a long moment. Surely, he knew his father's appetites. Would he even understand if Rose tried to describe her horror at what Clemente had done in killing the girl? She had to try. She spoke quickly, detailing the gruesome scene, her outrage, and the ensuing fight. She didn't stint in showing her fury or letting challenge enter her voice. If these creatures valued a human life at nothing, then she would gladly die fighting them.

Slowly, Rubio nodded, once like a bidder at an upscale auction. "My father was stupid sometimes. He indulged himself too freely."

A flicker of surprise passed over the face of the female vampire at Rubio's side, there and gone before Rose could credit it. A couple of the younger vamps shifted uneasily, but no one contradicted Rubio.

Faintly, Rose heard gunfire and screaming voices echoing down the stairs. The Army was nearing the *hacienda*. Several of the wights turned their gazes that direction.

"With *Papi* gone, I am leader here," Rubio said. "My human thralls are fighting your American Army, but they will not win. I ordered them to dynamite the *hacienda*, bring it down on this vault so the *gringos* won't find us. We'll wait out your soldiers here."

Matt stiffened beside Rose. He too glanced up the stairs as if he could see the explosives. He had to be thinking the same thing as Rose. Were the vamps planning to keep them as bomb shelter rations?

"We came here for my sister," Rose said.

"*Papa* wanted to be in your comic book. It was his dying wish, I think."

"I'll see to it. Let me get my sister and go. I'll make certain Clemente is part of *Drawn*."

No one moved for a long time. It felt like hours but was less than a minute. Then Rubio gave them that disturbing slow nod of his.

Matt opened the interrogation room door while Rubio and his companions filed back into the comics vault, leaving the wights and six of the lower status vampires in the hall. They eyed Rose with unveiled hatred, or else hunger, but did nothing to stop her as she slipped into Melody's room.

Matt made room for Rose but remained in the doorway keeping an eye on the vampires. "Hurry."

Melody lay asleep on the interrogation chair, her wrists and ankles strapped in place. Fresh bite marks stood out on her neck, her jaw, even her wrists. She opened bloodshot eyes at Rose's approach and gave her sister a wan smile. "I knew you would come."

"What did they do to you?" Rose unfastened the leather straps, sudden anger making her tremble. At that moment, filled with all the drawn abilities of her many fans, she felt confident she could run through the gathered wights and vampires in the hall like grease through a duck. Her heart thumped in her chest, her thoughts whirling through tactics and killing moves. She didn't care that the vampires possessed powers of their own— their blood ties. Those monsters had to die.

Melody sat up as if she meant to stand but froze when she saw Matt standing in the doorway. "What's he doing here?"

"Helping save you." Rose hooked an arm around her sister's shoulders, intent on assisting her to stand, but Melody refused to rise.

"You said it would just be us. I'm not going anywhere with him."

Rose had no time for her little sister's stupid vendetta against the Order. "Listen, there's a hallway full of wights and vampires out there, not to mention the U.S. Army on its way. If you don't get your ass up and follow us, and I mean both of us, right now, you're gonna end up dead. Can you walk?"

Melody shrugged off Rose's arm like an obstinate child and got to her feet. Without warning, the entire *hacienda* shook, a deep, concussive boom thrumming through its ancient foundations, making the walls groan as if in pain. Melody stumbled but recovered.

"We've gotta move." Matt waved at the dust sifting down from the ceiling. "I, for one, don't plan on getting buried with Rubio and his crew."

"Come on." Rose reached for her sister's hand.

Melody twisted away. "I said no. Not with him. Not with any of them. It's you and me or no one. If you abandon me now, I'm going to save our family without you."

"Don't be stupid. We can't go it alone, Mel. We're not strong enough to take on Society without help. The Order's got its problems, I'll admit that, but it's getting better, more reasonable. It's like-minded succubi in the Order who have the best chance at changing Society—making it something worth serving."

Melody stared at Rose, her brown eyes unwavering. "Do you have your phone with you?"

Rose lifted an eyebrow. Had the vampire venom rattled her sister's brain? "Why?"

"Give me your phone. I know you're buddy-buddy with the vamps. They wouldn't have taken it from you."

"Rose," Matt said, "we don't have time for this."

Melody held out a hand.

Slowly, Rose pulled her cell from her jeans pocket and opened the lock screen. "It doesn't work here. The vampires have it jammed, probably the Army too."

Melody typed away for a moment then handed the phone back. She had added a number to Rose's contacts list. "You can reach me there. We'll talk once you figure out these guys are using you."

"I'm not leaving you here," Rose said.

Melody strode to the door, not even bothering to look back. "No. This is where I leave you."

Though she still wasn't perfectly steady on her feet, certainly not the smooth killing machine she had been the night Leslie died, Melody slipped past Matt with draw-borne grace. Her footfalls echoed down the hall and up the stairs, gone in seconds.

Matt looked at Rose, his mouth a flat line, his eyes full of concern. "Should we try to stop her?"

"No. She's made her decision. We both have."

23
____

WE ALL FALL DOWN

Tears stained Rose's cheeks by the time she finished the call with Leslie's mother. She slid her phone into the drink holder next to her seat and stared out at the scrub brush spooling past her window. The land between Lerado and San Antonio looked the same as that in Mexico: patchy green, empty, and forlorn in some way she couldn't pinpoint.

"You okay?" Matt pulled out his earphones, which he had used to give her privacy for the call.

"I told her the military would handle the transport from Mexico." Which meant the Order would foot the bill.

Matt nodded. He had offered to make the call himself, arguing that he was Leslie's commanding officer, but Rose had demurred. It wouldn't have felt right letting him take that burden.

"She'll be back with her family in a couple of days. They'll have the funeral this weekend."

They drove alone, the rest of the Dog Ears scattered amongst the remaining van and four SUVs they had brought to Mexico. Rose got the feeling Matt had arranged things this way, but in their mad scramble to abandon the *hacienda* she hadn't noticed.

They rode in silence for a time before Matt said quietly, "We need to talk about wrangling."

Wrung out emotionally and physically, Rose wanted to say no. But one look at Matt's face changed her mind. He needed this.

"Okay," she said.

He bit his lip, something Rose had never seen him do, as if he might taste the words before he spoke them. "My parents divorced when I was three. My dad raised me. That's a lie. A bevy of *au pairs*, babysitters, and butlers raised me until I was twelve. Till then, my father hardly noticed me. Robin," Matt pursed his lips. "Mom, had lost me in the custody battle. Dad had money and political ties she lacked, so she got no visitation rights."

"That's horrible," Rose said. "You didn't know your mom?"

"Sometimes my dad was generous, especially when he was away on extended business, and he'd let her visit. But never when he was around. She was like some fabulous aunt who blew into town at whim between globetrotting and jet-setting to every amazing place on Earth. I didn't know her. I didn't know either of them."

"What changed when you turned twelve?"

"I became a polydraw."

"And suddenly your dad was interested."

Matt tapped his nose. "Dad's a sine. He has many gifts, but he can draw only one at a time. When he discovered I was not only a polydraw, but that I was a sime to boot, I suddenly became his pride and joy. Granted, he was still a senator, and head of the Indrawn Breath, but now he was taking me to work, showing me off to his friends."

"And you loved it," Rose said.

"And I loved it." Matt gave her a self-deprecating smile. "He hired instructors. I worked with some of the most powerful succubi and incubi in American Society. I soaked it up, and my dad, the great Senator Jason Craft, was proud of me for the first time in my life."

"When did David Lord come into the picture?" Rose could see the question weighed on Matt. He heaved a sigh before answering.

"I first shook hands with David Lord on my fifteenth birthday. Dad said he had a special surprise for me. Since I had expressed interest in maybe becoming an FBI agent—there's an entire secret division of the Bureau devoted to succubi affairs—he had arranged to have me shadow one of their top operatives.

"I followed Lord on a pickup that very night. We captured three rogue incubi, men who were using charm to run a drug operation. Not only were they dealing cocaine and molly, but they were also building a vast votary base off all their marks."

"And you liked it," Rose said, no bitterness in her voice, no recriminations, just pure interest. She pictured a fifteen-year-old Matthew Snow following the charismatic David Lord like a hungry puppy.

"I had the time of my life."

"Then what?" Rose asked. "Your mother found out?"

Matt shook his head. "Dad told me not to tell her. She wouldn't understand. So, I didn't. She'd visit, we'd hang out, and I'd say nothing about hunting rogue succubi. By the time I was eighteen, I was running my own team. We crisscrossed the nation, putting down what we considered enemies of the state. Whether that state was the U.S. or Society, I don't know. Both, I guess."

"You were arresting slinkers."

"Yes. Mostly. Not that they were all innocent. There were bad actors, like those drug runners, who legitimately broke the law, both Society and U.S. But, over time, I noticed a lot of the so-called malefactors we arrested turned out to be people with families. Often, my orders didn't specify crimes committed, just gave me an address, a name, a basic description. I started to wonder just who these people were."

"You didn't ask?"

"Of course I did. Lord assured me they were homegrown militants bent on harming our way of life. I trusted that answer. It was the same one my father gave when I put the question to him."

"But eventually you stopped wrangling and joined the Order," Rose said. "How'd that happen?"

"It was three months before my nineteenth birthday when Robin came to visit. I was feeling disillusioned, confused. I was questioning everything about our way of life—my way of protecting our people."

"So, you told her."

"She cried. It wasn't what I expected. I thought maybe she would just blow it off. She had always seemed so flighty to me, so devil-may-care. I didn't even know if she realized Dad was effectively running Society."

"What about the fear factory? Had Lord told you about it?"

"Not precisely, but he had made—I don't know what you would call them—overtures maybe? Hints? He had alluded to someplace that held the people we arrested, and that some were now votaries for him and a few others. I got the feeling he wasn't supposed to talk about it. Like maybe my dad had ordered against it. I don't know."

"So, is this when Robin decided to fight? Did she come up with the idea of Camp Den after you told her what was happening to you?"

Matt shook his head. "Nope. She had that idea years and years before this. She had been building and planning a way to counteract the Indrawn Breath, to counteract Dad, most of my life."

Rose tilted her head. "Does that mean she knew about the fear factory for years?"

"I don't know. She's never told me how long she knew about it. She's a much more secretive woman than you'd guess on first meeting her. Back then, all she told me about was the Order."

"And she made you a part of it," Rose said.

"I didn't join her right away. I should have, but I was a teenager, and I had heard all my life that what I was doing was right. I was important. I was powerful. I was better than any human and most succubi. Nothing Robin said could convince me otherwise."

"Did you tell your father what she was up to?"

"No. I was torn between them. I couldn't be disloyal to either one."

Rose stared at Matt. He watched the road, but she could tell he noticed. All his life he had believed he was elite, a man evolved to be greater than ninety-nine percent of humankind. It was the counter to her own story, believing her powers a curse, one she must hide in shame and fear. Both stories were fraught with lies and half-truths. Both were equally insidious and toxic to a young mind. "What made you finally change?"

"Walter Green Middlebrook," Matt said the name with reverence. "He was a slinker. A man with almost no identity. He had been arrested a few times for vagrancy in North Carolina and Virginia. From what I've ferreted out, I don't think he ever hurt anyone in his life. He certainly wasn't an incubus bent on becoming the next Mussolini."

Matt fell silent, and Rose gave him time to gather his thoughts. His jaw tightened before he spoke again. "Lord primed him."

"For the fear factory?"

"He tortured Walter in an abandoned mill where no one would hear him scream. But I heard. I was obliged to watch. To—" Matt broke off.

"To participate?"

"It wasn't like my hands were clean even then. I had roughed up my share of men and women. It was how we instilled fear."

Rose covered her mouth. "You were drawing courage by then? But I thought you said you had never been to the fear factory."

"No. But Lord taught me the fear draw early on. We used it like pepper spray or a Taser. It's the one draw a succubus can focus on an individual, which makes it powerful in its own way. How can someone run or fight when fear overwhelms them?"

"Like the night you took me."

Matt glanced her way and nodded.

"And you drew fear from this Walter guy?"

"Until the moment he died." Matt trembled, his muscles standing out in his forearms. "Lord acted like it was nothing. Like Walter's death was as meaningless as roadkill. We left his body strapped to an old office chair where animals could get at it, where time would take its toll.

"Afterward, Lord saw how that affected me. He tried to talk it away. He explained that terrorists weren't worth mourning. But it was too late. My eyes were open. I had finally realized that I was the monster I was supposed to be fighting."

Rose put a hand on Matt's taut arm. "You don't have to tell me this."

"Yes, I do. I'm not looking for absolution, Rose. No one can give me that. But I'm falling in love with you. And that means I must tell. I should have done it before, but I was afraid."

"Afraid I wouldn't be able to handle it?" Rose's heart was racing.

He nodded.

"Stop underestimating me, Snow."

A ghost of his half grin curved his lips. "Yes, ma'am."

"What's it like?" Rose asked, tentatively. "The fear draw."

"It's like winning the Super Bowl, the World Series, and the Indianapolis 500 all rolled into one. It drowns out everything else."

"How?"

"It snuffs your other emotions, especially compassion. You cease caring about anything besides getting more of the fear draw. And you can steal it from pretty much anyone, even the weakest human."

"That sounds horrible." Rose tried to picture Matt priming votaries to fear him but couldn't. How could anyone with a conscience do that? It defied human, and succubus, decency.

"It doesn't feel horrible. It feels…perfect. I guess it's like any drug. You get addicted, and you want more. Pretty soon, it doesn't matter what you have to do to get it. You'll do things you never imagined just to feel that elation."

"You had a hard time giving it up." Now that she had them, Rose couldn't imagine denying herself access to her votaries. But Matt had done just that, and with the added enticement of insatiable craving.

"That night I took your courage—" Matt hesitated, his gaze fixed on the road ahead as if he couldn't look at her.

"It was the first time you had done it since kicking the habit?"

He nodded, a pained grin turning up one corner of his mouth. "You gave me no choice. I couldn't keep up with you."

"I'm sorry I made you do that." Lovely. Just what Rose needed, more guilt, more regret. She had nearly sent her lover back into the throes of addiction psychopathy.

"Hey." Matt put a reassuring hand on her knee. "I'm okay. No harm done. If my time as a taker for the Breathers taught me anything, it was control. Speaking of which, there's something else we should discuss about drawing."

"What's that?"

"It's called spillover." Matt sounded like an actor in one of those cheesy STD commercials. *Talk to your doctor about herpes today.*

Rose lifted an eyebrow at him.

"I don't suppose the Pruett twins ever mentioned it?"

"No."

"And we don't cover it at Camp Den because it doesn't affect most trainees. It's a side effect of having a huge votary count. Most succubi never experience it, only stars and athletes, maybe some politicians. It's like a feedback loop of emotions you get when your votaries all think a certain way. Like I said, it's rare, but you might feel what they feel, especially when they're mostly all of one mind like yours are."

Rose frowned, trying to suss out his meaning. "But how are my votaries all thinking the same way? That makes no sense. Are you saying I'm somehow controlling their thoughts? Like I'm charming them from afar?"

"No. It's not a matter of them thinking the same thoughts at the same time. It's about expectation. You're a superhero to them, so they expect you to act a certain way. I think maybe that's why you got so upset with Clemente even before you found him with that poor girl he killed. You hated the vampires almost from the start because your fans would expect Rose Carver—Superhero!—to hate them."

Rose thought about that. She didn't feel her dislike of the vampires had come from outside herself. Catching Clemente in the act of murdering a helpless girl had ignited her blistering anger, no one else's. But maybe she had gained something of a heroic cast from her votaries—a sort of craving to save others rather than slink away from trouble. She hadn't felt like running in a long time.

She started to ask another question, but Matt's phone chirped. He slipped his left earphone into place.

"Hello?"

Rose couldn't hear the voice piped into Matt's ear, but she saw his brow furrow, his lips crease at the corners.

"Mont Stivens is Kosher," Matt said. It was a key phrase indicating that all was clear on Matt's end. He listened for a long time, his expression going from grave to shocked.

"What channel?" Matt asked after a moment, his face pale. "Okay. What about rendezvous? Yeah, that's good." He remained silent a long time, then said, "And about the other, you're certain?" He winced at the answer.

Matt ended the call. "That was Gunny Lipe. Camp Den's gone."

"What?" Rose bolted upright, her heart in her throat.

"FBI raid. Grab your laptop. He said it's on all the newscasts. There was a fire. Some folks escaped, Lipe among them." Matt looked at Rose, expression sober. "Most didn't."

The top headline on CNN.com read, "Suspected Terrorist Cell Raided, Burned." She clicked the live video link.

The screen filled with an aerial view of Camp Den. Links burned merrily, smoke billowing from its many windows, its bricks black with soot. Both the training barracks and teams housing were also ablaze.

Men and women dressed in body armor with the letters FBI emblazoned in yellow on their backs stood conferring or talking into radios while firefighters doused the buildings. It was obvious whatever had happened was over. No one seemed overly concerned with getting shot.

"According to sources within the FBI, agents this morning raided a terrorist compound disguised as a fitness boot camp," said a bland male reporter as the images played. "Sources say that Camp Den, Total Body Takeover, was a front for a domestic terror group known as the Order. The Order's stated intentions were to overthrow the U.S. government and establish a new one in its place. Although the FBI attempted to surprise the group, members resisted arrest, opting to launch an offensive using small arms fire and explosives. A three-hour standoff ensued, after which FBI agents, bolstered by local S.W.A.T. forces, infiltrated the compound. A fire broke out in the camp's main building shortly after they entered. It's unclear whether the terrorists intentionally set the fire or it was the result of an ammunition explosion.

"Though sources with the FBI report arresting eighty-five Order members during the raid, David Lord, the agent in charge on the scene, stated this morning that as many as thirty to fifty members might have escaped during the firefight."

Rose clicked the pause button. Her stomach felt sour, her throat tight. "Oh, God."

"Robin's dead," Matt said.

"What?" Rose jerked as if slapped. "Lipe told you?"

"Said they were fleeing, trying to get as many people into as many cars as they could. A bullet got her as they were driving away. She died instantly."

"Oh, Matt, I'm so sorry."

Matt's eyes glistened, but no tears fell. Some of the color came back into his cheeks, his ears reddening. "It's not going to end here. Not like this."

"Do you think…" Rose searched for the right words. "Do you think the Breathers found Den by reading *Drawn*?"

Matt first shook his head, sighed, then shrugged. "I don't know. It doesn't matter."

"I don't want what we did to be the reason this happened."

"It's not your fault," Matt said. "It's not anyone's fault, except my father's and David Lord's."

Rose nodded, little mollified, but unwilling to belabor the point. "What now?"

Matt ground his teeth. "I have to tell the team. Lipe only managed to get eighteen people out with him. That gives us a total of thirty-one ops."

Rose sat back in her seat, the enormity of their loss hitting her for the first time. She hadn't been privy to the number of Order recruits before the raid, but just counting the ones she had seen in training, that number had been in the hundreds. Now the Breathers had most of them.

"What about all the slinkers who didn't join teams?" she asked. "How many of them are there?"

"Five or six hundred maybe, but most of them are monodraws, and weak ones at that. I'll put out a call for them, but how many do you think will answer? They're back to their slinker ways."

"We can find them," Rose said. "The microchips—"

"They don't stay chipped," Matt said. "It's easy to remove those things."

"They don't stay chipped," Rose repeated, disgusted by her short-lived excitement. Of course, they didn't. These were people like her. "What are we going to do?"

"Clemente paid me a visit when you were interviewing Melody," Matt said.

"What for?"

"He wasn't a very old vampire," Matt said. "Not compared to the ancient ones down in South America. He didn't have much sway with them. He was despondent over not being able to help you."

Rose wondered if she might feel some pity for the creature at hearing this.

Nope.

"So?" she said.

"So, he gave me a contact—an American one."

"Another goddamned vampire?"

Matt nodded.

"Hell no. We tried that already. I don't care if they're our cousins, they're monsters. We can find help someplace else."

"Where?"

"I don't know. Didn't Robin have any more contacts? Someone opposed to the Breathers?"

"Sure. But she didn't have fifty someones. Rose, we need help. Lots of it. We can't guarantee we're going to keep the people we've got. I want to find the fear factory and take down the Breathers. But we don't have the numbers for that. Not alone. We need help, or else we might as well disband the Order and hide."

Admitting he was right set Rose's teeth on edge. She thought of

Leslie, who had died fighting the Indrawn Breath, of Melody whom she found frustratingly gruesome and pitiable by turns. Whatever lives the two of them might have otherwise had, those paths were gone now, consumed by the machinations of power-hungry men inside the Indrawn Breath.

"How are you supposed to contact this vampire?" Rose asked.

"Clemente gave me a phone number."

24

THE ENVOY

Three days passed, during which eight of the Dog Ears fled. No one faulted them for it, least of all Rose.

The remaining team met up with a gaunt and haunted-looking Gunny Lipe at a Motel Eight in Arkansas a few miles west of Memphis. His crew had likewise dwindled from twenty down to just six people willing to continue the fight. Rose had looked for Moss among them, but he too had fled.

"Stayed with us the first two days." Gunny Lipe, sitting in a chintzy motel chair, sounded surprisingly sympathetic when Rose asked after Moss. "I thought he might stick it out. He wanted revenge that first day. But once the anger passed, the poor kid deflated. He took off last night without a word. I wasn't going to stop him."

The gunny's wife and daughter had gone missing. His son, away at college in Michigan, had called to say he was fine. Lipe ordered him to abandon school to hide with friends in Oregon.

"For all the good it will do," Lipe had said when he told Rose about it. "The boy's near as stubborn as you, Carver."

Lipe had no delusions about his wife and daughter. He knew Lord would take great pleasure in secreting them away in the fear factory. The old gunny's eyes burned with hatred whenever he spoke of the man. Given the situation, it was a foregone conclusion that he would favor enlisting whatever help they could get, even if it meant siding with vampires against their own.

Lacking a better plan, Rose resigned herself to the group's consensus, but she insisted on being the one to make the call. To her surprise, Lipe and Matt agreed. She didn't know what she would be able to discern over the phone. Perhaps the vampire's voice would give her some clue as to its motivations. But that hope turned to ash the instant someone picked up on the other end.

"Hello?" said a spritely female voice with a thick southern drawl.

"Umm, hi. I'm calling to speak with Piper Ross. Is she available?"

"Sorry, Mama's out getting her hair done. Who is this?"

Rose quirked an eyebrow. The girl on the other end sounded maybe seventeen. An innocent, happy seventeen. One completely unassociated with vampires.

"I think I may have dialed a wrong number," Rose said.

"Not if you were trying to reach Piper Ross. There's only one of her in Denver, South Carolina. Are you a vampire?"

Rose rocked back in her cheap hotel room chair.

Matt lifted his eyebrows.

"Ah, no, I'm a succubus."

"Oh! That's awesome. Mama's told us about you. What's your name? Are you coming to see us? I've always wanted to meet a succubus. Mama says we're pretty much the same thing. Of course, I'm probably not telling you anything you don't—"

Rose had started to speak three times during the girl's chatter, and finally settled on blurting, "My name's Rose Carver and—"

"Oh. My. God! You mean like from the graphic novel, Rose Carver?"

"Uh." Rose considered lying. She hadn't expected a *Drawn* fan to answer the phone; she didn't have time for this. But the girl's genuine enthusiasm dashed that idea. "Yes. I'm that Rose Carver."

Gunny Lipe and Matt gave her knowing smiles. Rose shrugged helplessly.

"My name's Grace. It's so cool to meet you! I mean, not meet you, 'cause we're just on the phone, but I've read every issue of *Drawn!* I'm even on the top tier Patreon, the one the Pruett twins call Drawn Cron—I had to look up what cron meant, it's like some programming term for making things happen on a schedule, I—"

"We need Piper's help!" Rose felt bad for interrupting, but Grace's verbal onslaught showed no signs of slowing.

"Oh! You should have led with that. Buried the lead there. Well, I'm Piper's youngest daughter. I can't speak for her, but I think she's going to say yes. You sound nice. And Mama's always going on about how our kind have got to stick together, and I think that includes a succubus. What sort of help do you need?"

Rose had to laugh. This girl—could Grace be a vampire? If so, she certainly didn't act like the sort Rose had met in Mexico—exuded hyperactivity. It was infectious.

Whatever discernment Rose had tried to garner wasn't coming, not the drawn variety anyway. But her natural discernment told her Grace was genuine.

"I'd rather discuss that with Piper if that's okay."

"Sure, that's fine. Should I have her call you back at this number?"

"That'd be great," Rose said, smiling.

"Okay. I'll call her right now. She'll probably get back to you quick, I bet. It was nice talking to you, Rose. I think we're going to be friends!"

***

Gravel crunched under the van's tires. The sun had lately dropped below the horizon, leaving behind a bruised swirl of purple clouds and the barest twinkling of stars. The blue LCD clock on the dash read 8:35.

"How much farther, you think?" Rose asked. They had turned off South Carolina Highway 76 to follow a long, winding country road several miles into the falling darkness, only to leave even that small paved road behind for dirt.

Matt shrugged. "GPS doesn't even show this road on the map."

"Why can't vampires live in nice, cozy suburbs like regular folks?" Watts asked from the backseat.

No one laughed.

Rose sat rigidly, one hand gripping the door handle. "If we don't find something in the next minute or so, I say turn around,"

"You think we're being set up?" Matt asked.

Rose shook her head. "I don't know. I feel—"

"—wigged out," Satterfield supplied. She sat beside Watts on the center bench, watching the unkempt weeds and fallow fields slide by with avid, roaming eyes.

Rose gave her a nod. Though the two of them might never be friends, Rose appreciated her former squad leader's loyalty. In the days since the fall of Camp Den, many of the Order's most stalwart supporters had slipped away from their ranks. Not Satterfield. She was a fighter. She was loyal. She knew a good cause when she saw it.

The track curved right, meandering away from gray farmland and into a thicket of oaks and pines that closed over the van like greedy fingers.

"I don't like this." Rose wished they had brought Hanks along. But Matt had argued against that idea. She and Lipe were needed for protection back at the hotel with the rest of the Order. If Society somehow found the team, the only option would be to run. Lipe and Hanks represented their best chance at escape.

"I'm turning around." Matt pulled the van to one side of the dirt track and had just begun a K-turn when headlights burst to life ahead of them. Rose let out a little yelp despite herself.

Figures moved in the twin beams. Even with drawn sight, Rose had a hard time numbering them. Twenty? More maybe. They milled about, never standing still.

"Wights," Matt said.

"Do we run?" Satterfield asked, leaning forward for a better view.

"No point," Rose said. "You saw what these things did in Mexico. They're too fast, and there's too many of them."

A man-shaped shadow detached itself from the wights. Rose could see nothing of his face with the headlights behind him. He made a beckoning motion. "It's okay, y'all. We won't hurt ya. Come out and say hi."

Rose looked at Matt.

He shrugged. "Let's see what he has to say."

Shielding her eyes, Rose drew speed and strength, dexterity and discernment, hearing and sight as she climbed from the van. A cloud of vampire stink assaulted her nose, cloying with its odd sweetness and undertone of fetid animal odor.

The vampire who had spoken glanced over one shoulder. "Stevie, shut the lights off, we're blinding 'em."

One of the wights, a gaunt man dressed in a faded Guns N Roses t-shirt and jeans with no shoes, stuck his head inside an old U-Haul truck, fumbled for a second, and switched the lights off.

"Sorry 'bout that." The vampire looked maybe twenty in the darkness. Tall and lean, his pale skin contrasted sharply with the shock of unruly black hair on his head. "Name's Triston Presley, but everybody just calls me Press." He stuck out his hand to Watts, who had put himself between the vampires and the succubi.

The wights went still. All at once their shuffling ceased, and twenty-two pairs of red eyes zeroed in on Press's raised hand.

Watts, who had been about to shake, froze, hand half raised.

"Will y'all stop that?" Press said, looking back at the wights. "I'm fine." To Watts, he said, "Don't mind them, they think there's gonna be trouble, but there ain't, is there?"

Watts threw a glance at Matt, who shook his head, then took Press's hand. "Nope. No trouble at all."

Press smiled with such pure, little boy earnest that Rose nearly forgot the young man before her was a vampire. For all she knew, he was a thousand years old. But looking at his wide-eyed enthusiasm, his seemingly genuine need to gain Watts's approval, softened her resolve.

The vampire pumped Watts's hand vigorously, then did the same with Matt and Rose. "So glad to meet y'all. Really," he said. When he reached Satterfield, he paused and sucked in a breath before proffering his hand. "Really," he said again, "it's a pleasure. You must be Ms. Carver?"

"No. My name's Valerie."

"Oh, well, it's still a pleasure," Press said again, raising Satterfield's hand as if he meant to kiss it.

One of the wights, a tall female, her silver hair spilling down her back like a mane, grunted a word that might have been Press's name or merely a belch. Either way, Press stopped, gave a little shake, and released Satterfield's hand. "Shoot, y'all ain't here to see me," he said.

Was he blushing? Even in the weak starlight, she thought she saw a telltale flush creeping up his pallid neck.

Press backed away a few steps. He suddenly didn't seem to know what to do with his hands, so he jammed them into his pockets. Still backpedaling, he said, "Climb back in your van and follow us. I'll take y'all up to the house."

"Hold up," Matt said. "Where exactly are you taking us? Where's Piper Ross?"

"Mama's up at the house. That's where I'm taking you. No need to be suspicious. I ain't lying, I promise."

Press said this with such earnestness Rose nearly laughed. She knew vampires shared the ability to charm with their succubus cousins. They might even be better at it overall. But she felt no mind-bending delusions coming off the slim vamp—just nervousness.

Matt made no move toward the van. "This feels like a trap."

Press nodded. "I can see how you might think that. Mama said as much. She said if you needed some convincing that I should tell you that she's the vampire queen of South Carolina. If she wanted you dead, you would have been the minute you crossed the state line. But she ain't got no hard feelings toward you. In fact, she wants to help you if she can. So, she's betting y'all are gonna come up and speak to her, and she guarantees nobody will get hurt when you do. She said that'll probably get you guys moving."

Matt stood silent for a long minute. He shared a look with Rose and the others. Then he turned back to Press, quirked his half grin, and said, "Mama's right."

25

THE JAILED QUEEN

The house turned out to be an antebellum mansion situated atop a low hill surrounded by forest. Perfectly groomed hedgerows bracketed a meandering path up from the home's gravel drive to its enormous wraparound porch. The wights, who hadn't bothered to ride with Press in his U-Haul, opting instead to run alongside it on the road or else through the darkling wood, gathered close as the vampire led Rose and her companions to the house.

Discernment told Rose little about the situation. She got nothing from the wights, with their roving red eyes and slack faces. They were just too alien. Press's posture, his facial expressions, even the way he walked screamed *genuine but nervous*. He kept looking over his shoulder, his gaze drawn to Satterfield, only to jerk back as if slapped every time.

"This is home," he said as they mounted the whitewashed wooden steps, which appeared newly refurbished. He entered without knocking. The wights remained outside, crowding the yard.

The house's front entrance opened onto a large vestibule, its walls hung with headshots of lovely smiling women. Press led them into a sitting room outfitted with a four-cushion leather couch, several matching recliners, and a ninety-inch flat screen affixed to one wall, blaring *The Voice.*

Four women sat on the couch with a fifth ensconced on one of the recliners. When Press and the others entered, the woman on the recliner stood, smiling. She glanced back at the ladies on the couch. "Grace, sugar, pause it. We got guests."

The speaker was petite. She stood probably 5'5", her figure slim though feminine. She smiled and said, "You're Rose, right?"

Rose nodded. Was this vivacious little woman in her low-cut pink top and tight jeans the self-proclaimed Vampire Queen of South Carolina? Impossible.

"Pleasure to meet you. I'm Piper." She held out her hand, and Rose shook it. "And I know you, too," Piper said, turning. "Matt Snow. Those Pruitt twins got you down perfect. You're just as handsome as your picture."

Matt smiled as he shook the vampire's dainty hand. "Nice to meet you, Ms. Ross."

"So that means the supermodel here is Valerie Satterfield, and the hunk is Tanner Watts." Piper shook each of their hands in turn then asked, "Y'all hungry?"

Rose stared at Piper for a moment, nonplussed. "Yes?" she finally ventured.

"Good. Follow me." To the ladies on the couch, she said, "C'mon girls, we'll finish the show later."

Piper threw open a set of intricately carved double doors with a flourish, to reveal a brightly lit dining room. At its center stood a table long enough to seat at least a dozen. Silver serving dishes heaped with green beans, black-eyed peas, and heavily buttered ears of corn stood ready to eat. These lesser dishes, along with two full-sized cakes and an assortment of pies, ringed a whole pig cooked to perfection.

It must have been her nerves or the vamp stink that had masked the sweet scents now wafting over Rose. Her mouth watered at the sudden influx, and her traitorous stomach growled audibly.

Piper laughed. "I'll tell the cook your tummy approves."

Rose blushed but didn't hesitate to sit when Matt pulled out her chair. He took the one next to her with Watts and Satterfield seated across from them.

Piper and the youngest of the women, a cute blonde with golden hair to her waist and sparkling blue eyes, filled large platters with a sampling of every dish for Rose and the others.

"I'm Grace. We spoke on the phone," said the blond girl when she handed Rose her platter. "It's awesome to meet you. I have all your comics from the Kickstarter. Maybe later you'll sign a couple of them?"

Rose nodded, accepting the food. "Sure."

Grace beamed. "Awesome!"

"Gracie, sit down," Piper said with an indulgent smile for the girl. "You can badger our guests later. Sorry about that, Rose. She ain't been fit to live with since the day you called. Can't talk about anything but *Drawn*, and Rose Carver, and getting to meet a real live succubus."

"It's okay," Rose said. Was she the only one finding all this domestic tranquility strange? One look at Matt told her the answer was no. He sat rigidly, staring at the cadre of beautiful women seated around them. They smiled and chatted like, well, like real people. Satterfield and Watts looked as bewildered as Rose felt.

"Dig in, y'all," Piper said. "We don't stand on ceremony here. And if this ain't enough, we got plenty more." She threw Watts a good-natured nod.

Rose took a bite of pork. It tasted heavenly. She mooed in delight, forgetting herself for the barest of an instant. When her ecstasy abated, and she could finally open her eyes, she found Piper staring at her, a pleased grin creasing her red lips.

"I'm glad you like it. Our cook doesn't get to make these sorts of things too often."

Rose swallowed, embarrassed that she had forgotten where she was and just who—what—she was dining with. "You're not eating?"

"We will, but I wanted to make sure it's okay with you first."

Rose's back stiffened. An image of the girl tumbling from Clemente's lap to the cold floor flashed through her mind. She held her breath. "You're not going to…kill someone, are you?"

Piper's pretty black eyelashes rose so high they threatened to merge with her bangs. She sat up straight, one hand on her breast, her mouth agape. "Oh, God," she said. "You think I would kill someone? And right here in my dining room?"

"I—I'm sorry," Rose said. Could this be real? She drew discernment and felt nothing but genuine astonishment and disgust from the vamp.

"It's fine, dear," Piper said. "I don't know what you saw in Mexico, but that ain't the way we do things in South Carolina."

"But you're not going to eat regular food, are you?" Matt asked.

Piper favored him with a winsome smile Rose didn't like one bit. "No, sugar, we don't eat that sort of thing. But, so long as none of you object, we have this." She lifted the top from a heretofore untouched serving bowl.

"Is that spaghetti sauce?" Rose asked but knew an instant later it wasn't when the scent of raw meat reached her nose.

Piper shook her head. "This is Carpaccio: thin-sliced beef with lemon juice, a sprinkling of olive oil, and just enough Parmesan cheese that we can taste it without getting sick."

"I got too much cheese on mine one time." The young woman Piper had called Olivia wrenched her face into a pained grimace. "Thought I was going to die."

"It put her into a coma, poor thing." Piper doled slices of meat and sauce out to each of the ladies.

Rose watched all this in quiet alarm. She couldn't wrap her brains around the image of a sexpot southern belle playing the matronly hostess while slathering raw meat onto silver plates. When she could stand it no longer, she said, "Could I ask you a question?"

"Sure, hun," Piper said. "I mean, that's sorta why we invited y'all out here, ain't it?"

"Are you a vampire or not?"

Piper chuckled. "I am."

"But you don't act like a vampire."

"How many vampires have you met?"

Rose shrugged one shoulder. The vampires at the table had

quieted. They watched her with curious gazes. "I don't know, ten or twelve, I guess."

Piper nodded. "All Mexican vampires—Clemente's people?"

"I guess so."

"And we don't act the same as them?"

"Not even a little bit," Satterfield said. "They were all creepy and mysterious."

"Let me guess, they stood real still sometimes, and then would suddenly whoosh into motion when you least expected it?"

Rose nodded.

"That's just them putting on airs," Piper said. "Some of the older vamps way down south do that. I don't know if it's because they're old and they can't help it, or if they do it for kicks, but all the would-be drug kings in Mexico copy them."

"Oh," Rose said.

"I hope those guys didn't give you a bad first impression of our kind."

Rose pursed her lips.

"What did that bastard do?" Piper set her fork down with a clink.

Rose related the story of the girl Clemente had killed. Though the memories never left her long either waking or sleeping, she found that speaking them came hard. By the end, she was in tears. Matt gripped her hand under the table.

"Oh, you poor thing." Piper came around the table, pulled Rose to her feet, and gave her a tight hug. The little vampire wasn't cold at all. On the contrary, her skin felt almost hot to Rose's touch. They stood that way for nearly a minute, Piper's ear pressed against Rose's collarbone, while Rose hiccupped like a stupid little kid.

"I can't believe I'm crying." Rose broke the embrace to swipe her napkin from the table, which she used to dab at her eyes. Thank God she hadn't bothered with makeup tonight.

Piper tut-tutted her back into her seat, smoothed down her hair one time, and then gave her a glowing smile. "Honey, this here is a house full of women. These walls have heard their share of crying, and they ain't nearly cried out. What you saw, it was disgusting.

Nobody should ever see that kind of thing. But if they do, and they don't cry, they got no soul. He deserved what he got. I just hope you understand that not all my kind are like what you saw down south. Me and my girls—"

Press cleared his throat.

"Me and my family," Piper amended, giving him a grin, "don't live that way. We'll prove it if you give us a chance. Can you do that?"

"I can try."

Piper returned to her seat at the head of the table. "You've hardly touched your food. Eat up, girl, and we'll talk about something happier, like destroying the fear factory."

"You know about that?" Rose asked.

"Enough. Grace is our funny book expert."

"Graphic novels, Mama," Grace said.

"Then you know we've got nothing," Rose said. Matt gave her a grimace, as if she had just tipped her hand in poker, but she ignored it. "We have no idea how to find the fear factory. And even if we did, it'll be heavily guarded."

"Do you have any leads? Any idea at all where it might be?"

"No," Rose said.

"Yes," Matt said at the same time.

All eyes turned his way. "I'm sure you've seen the latest online issue of *Drawn*—you're aware the Indrawn Breath instigated the raid on Camp Den?"

The *Drawn* twins had made short work of transforming Rose's combined body cam and drone footage in Mexico into a double-sized online issue of *Drawn* less than a day after the Dog Ears returned to the States. They did the same a day later with footage from inside Camp Den. Rose had cried over their depiction of Robin Ambrose's tragic death. Rabid fans, millions of them, bought the downloads. Judging by the reviews, they shared Rose's sentiments, and they wanted more.

Rose hadn't been able to contact the twins since she got back. She chalked that up to their busy schedules, but it concerned her. Nevertheless, she continued to wear the assortment of cleverly concealed cameras they had given her. Even if Luke and Brendan didn't return her calls, their constant *Drawn* updates proved they were receiving her audio and video uploads, as did her ever-increasing votary count.

"Yes!" Grace moaned. She sounded genuinely distraught.

Piper nodded. "We did. And we're sorry for your loss. I met your mother once, years and years ago. Brilliant woman—so passionate about her cause. It's a colder world without her."

"Thank you," Matt said. "Before she died, my mother told me she knew the fear factory was somewhere in the South, probably on a military base. She said it was likely in Georgia or South Carolina."

"That's a lot of real estate," Piper said.

"Maybe not." Matt had finished his meal. Placing his napkin on the table, he met Piper's eyes. "We've been discussing a plan to find the place. It's a big risk, but we think it'll work."

Piper lifted an eyebrow. "Do tell."

"Let's leave it there for now. We have a plan," Matt said, giving Rose a pointed look she ignored.

"One you're not sharing?" Piper's gaze flitted between them as if one might divulge a secret.

"Not yet." Rose put down her fork. "We still have some particulars to work out before we can move forward, but we're certain it's doable."

The idea was simple enough. According to everything the Order knew, though the Breathers could and would place regular humans in the fear factory, they much preferred succubi since the latter could draw. That made them far more valuable as votaries. Given this preference, it made sense that, should one of the Order succubi get captured, that person would end up in the fear factory. The Breathers were wise to the Order's tracking chips. They removed them from those they caught. But if one of their captives carried a second chip, one far better concealed than the Order's usual device, that person could lead the Order straight to the fear factory.

Matt thought he should be that volunteer. He argued that Lord would relish the idea of imprisoning his traitorous former protégé as a personal votary.

Rose found that argument ludicrous. Matt's father was head of the Indrawn Breath and an early frontrunner to become the nation's next president. Jason Kraft might be callous enough to give Lord his wayward son. Matt certainly thought so. And from her experiences with Lord and even her own sister, Rose judged their boss to be a wicked man indeed. But would Kraft, clearly a shrewd Washington insider who knew how to guard his secrets, risk the sort of scandal his son's illegal imprisonment would entail should it leak to the press? Rose doubted that. He would save Matt if for no other reason than to protect himself. That alone made Rose the better choice.

They had butted heads over the matter for the two days leading up to this meeting without an agreement. Gunny Lipe, Satterfield, and Watts were no help. They all immediately volunteered for the duty upon hearing the plan. Therefore, Rose had come up with a strategy to get the job done, but that could wait. First, she needed Piper's help.

Silence had fallen at the table, everyone sensing the tension between Rose and Matt. Watts broke it.

"Before we talk location, maybe we should talk price," he said. "I'm sorry, but I doubt you're doing this out of the goodness of your heart. What will we owe you once the fear factory is gone?"

"Brawny and smart." Piper slipped him a sideways glance. "And you're right; our cooperation comes with a price."

"Which is?" Rose asked, foreboding tightening her stomach.

"Simple. We help you with your kind, and you help us with ours."

"Does that mean you want us to fight for you?" Matt asked. "Because we're sort of in the fight of our lives at the moment."

"It may come to fighting—it may not. But either way, I'm willing to make the first investment."

"Meaning?" Rose asked.

"Meaning, I'll commit to helping you win back the Society if you promise to help me leave South Carolina."

Rose cocked her head to one side. "You can't leave?"

"Vampires aren't usually the social type," Piper said. "We tend to go it alone. Even those who can and do make children eventually part ways with them. Now I've only been a vampire for about forty-five years. And in that time, I've made all these children. We, collectively, have made this family. They are loyal to me, just as I am to them. The old guard vamps don't like that. They say it's unnatural. That it could cause attention—the thing they loathe most in this world. So, they do the one thing they wouldn't do for any other cause."

"They band together against you," Rose said.

"Exactly."

"No offense," Watts said, "but then how are you still alive?"

"Oh, they've tried to kill me. Twenty years ago, a whole mess of 'em came at us—thought they could pick us off one by one. We set 'em straight. Nobody messes with my kids."

"You killed them?" Rose asked.

Piper gave her a cold grin. "Every single one I could catch. The rest hightailed it out of my territory. Since then, it's understood that South Carolina belongs to us. They don't come in; we don't go out."

"Which means you're a prisoner," Matt said.

Piper nodded. "Granted it's a big prison, and one I love, but who likes being told to stay in one place? It's not in my nature to take that sort of thing lying down. And it gets worse. Just last November one of the ancient vamps from Europe, this old fossil named Octavius, had the gall to send me a letter saying I couldn't have any more children. That's why I need you all."

"But what do you expect us to do about it?" Rose barely managed to keep the incredulity out of her voice. The Order had just suffered a major loss, and Piper was talking about pissing off every vampire on Earth. "We're not exactly an army here."

"Not yet, but if there's one thing I envy in you succubi, it's your gift for organization. Vampires could never weasel our way into government, religion, sports, and all that other stuff like y'all. We can't hide like that. I figure, we win back Society for you, and then you help us beat our enemies into submission."

"That could work," Rose said, her mind whirling. She had to admit she liked the idea of hammering vampires whenever she got the chance. Of course, going through with Piper's plan meant siding with a vampire, something she wasn't sure she could stomach, no matter how nice Piper seemed.

"Hold on," Matt said. "I see two flaws here." He turned cold eyes on Piper. "First, who says we're going to become the leaders in Society just because we expose the Breathers? It doesn't work that way."

"You'd be surprised," Piper said. "People, and that includes vampires and succubi, flock to power. Besides, me and mine will make certain you get the reins. With our mixed strength, no one could stop us. What's your second objection?"

"You've already told us you have more children than any vampire in the world. If we help you take out your competition, what's to stop you from growing a real army of your own? How do we know you're not looking to destroy us—maybe take over the planet once you've got enough children?"

"And saying, 'I promise I won't,' ain't gonna cover it?"

"No."

"Taking over the world would be stupid." Grace rolled her eyes. "We're not aiming to create a vampire dystopia."

"But we don't know that for certain, do we?" Matt gazed around the table with a frank expression. "We'll need a sign of good faith."

"What do you suggest?" If eyes could cut, Piper's would have sliced Matt in two. She must have sensed what would follow.

"A hostage exchange," Matt said without hesitation. "Two or three would be best."

Rose nearly choked. Had he gone insane? He certainly hadn't mentioned this before now. But maybe that had been his plan all along. He knew she would balk at this idea. Rose stilled her tongue only because she, Satterfield, and Watts had promised to keep quiet during negotiations.

Matt ignored Rose, his gaze riveted on Piper.

"Hell no." Piper gestured around the table, taking in the women and Press. "Maybe you don't understand how it is with us, but these aren't people I bit. These are my children. We're every bit as blood bound to one another as you are to your parents. I don't care how those South American vamps do it; this is my family."

"Hostage is too strong a word," Matt said. "I should have said 'guest.' When the time is right, you'll send us a guest, and we'll offer our help."

Piper leaned back in her chair, eyes cast down, staring at nothing for a long, silent moment. "Okay," she said slowly, "but I choose."

"No wights," Matt said.

"Of course not."

"And Press has to be one of them."

For the first time since meeting her, Rose saw anger flash across Piper's face, there and gone like a fleeting shadow. "No."

"Oh, yes."

"He's my only son." Piper's voice had grown subtly deeper, more intense.

"Mama, it's okay," Press said. His gaze darted to Satterfield and back to Piper. "I'll be happy to go."

"Press, honey, it ain't safe."

"I'll be okay."

"We aren't going to harm him," Matt said.

Piper crossed her arms. "It ain't him I'm worried about."

"Come again?"

"Didn't y'all wonder why I sent all my wights out to meet you with Press?"

"To protect him," Rose said.

Piper shook her head. "Honey, Press is just a year and a half a vampire. But maybe you don't know what that means."

Rose shook her head.

"It means he has the self-control of a one-and-a-half-year-old most of the time."

"Hey—" Press began, sounding offended, but Piper raised a finger and spoke over him.

"Especially when it comes to the sight and smell of human or, and sometimes especially, succubi blood. Those wights weren't there to protect Press. They were there to protect you."

"She's making a big deal out of nothing," Press said. "I'm in control."

Piper grunted. "Point is, I'm willing to let a couple of my girls go with you when the time comes—though it ain't necessary—but not Press. He's too dangerous yet."

Rose looked at Matt and the others. "What do you say?"

Satterfield nodded her agreement. Watts too gave a tacit nod.

Matt remained silent for a long minute, seemingly oblivious to every eye in the room watching him. Then he said to Piper, "I mean no offense by what I'm about to say."

"Fire away."

"We don't know you. You've been kind to us tonight, treating us like guests, but we've been through hell this past week. I can't simply trust you."

"I understand that," Piper said.

"Good. Then you'll understand that we can't make this sort of promise on a whim. You help us break the Breather's hold on Society, then we'll talk."

Piper worked at one of her teeth with her tongue for a moment. "In other words, we serve you with no guarantee you'll return the favor when the time comes, and I still have to turn some of my daughters over to you as hostages?"

"Take it or leave it."

Rose somehow managed to keep from scowling at Matt. What was he doing? Didn't he realize they needed Piper and her children? How else would they ever come close to measuring up to the Breathers?

"What's to keep you from double-crossing us once you're in power?" Piper asked.

"The same thing that will keep you from seeking power once your enemies are gone. Guests."

Rose peered into the van's side mirror, searching for signs of pursuit. She saw none, but that only made her stare all the harder. For all she knew, an army of Piper's wights ran alongside them, hidden in the black woods lining the road.

"You're quiet," Matt said without glancing Rose's way. He swerved the van to one side of the dirt lane, avoiding a particularly large chuckhole.

A couple of Piper's daughters, who had set a bumping, suspension-creaking pace, zoomed ahead of them in a black SUV. They were leading the succubi to one of Piper's many properties, a house situated on the banks of Hartwell Lake in the neighboring town of Anderson, South Carolina. Piper had insisted her girls drive their own car to emphasize their freedom.

"You weren't serious about giving them hostages, were you?" Rose tried to spear Matt with her gaze, but he likely didn't notice in the dark.

"Why not?" Satterfield asked from the backseat. "It makes strategic sense."

"You'd actually hand members of our team over to vampires?" Rose twisted around to glare at her former squad leader.

"If it meant ensuring their cooperation? Yes. I'd go myself."

They turned onto a lineless, narrow blacktop that would eventually lead them to a four-lane highway marked SC28/US76 on Matt's phone. It was blissfully smooth after the dirt track.

"I don't trust them," Rose said.

"Good," Matt said. "No matter how Southern sweet Piper acts, she doesn't control an entire state's worth of territory without some form of ruthlessness to back it. What we saw tonight might have been real or a complete act. Either way, we can't forget we're dealing with a powerful being here. We don't want Piper Ross for an enemy."

"You're making my point for me," Rose said, throwing her hands up. "Why give that sort of person anything, let alone some of our people? We have no idea what she'll do to them."

"I'm not worried about the hostages," Matt said. "She won't harm them."

"How can you possibly know that?"

"Because she loves her children. That much I'm sure of. As long as we have some of them, she's vulnerable. My concern is what happens once we remove Piper's fetters? What happens if we destroy, or at least severely diminish, those vampires who have been keeping her prisoner? Will she grow so powerful she'll rival or even overthrow the Order? We could be arming our personal Taliban the way the U.S. did back in the eighties and nineties."

"I've got no draw on discernment," Watts said, "but I didn't get that vibe from her. I think she just wants the other vampires to leave her alone."

"Maybe." Matt dragged the word out as if considering the possibilities. "But what if she changes her mind in the future? Vampires live a long time after all."

"What kept them in check before now?" Rose asked. "Not just Piper, but vampires in general?" She wasn't done discussing the hostage situation but found her curiosity piqued by this notion.

"Society," Matt said. "Well, that and the fact that vampires are so rarely fertile. They've never had our numbers, which made us a threat. With six children and all those wights—" Matt whistled. "That makes her an anomaly. It's why the other vamps keep her cordoned off like this. It's one of the few things they can all agree on."

"Want to hear something even scarier?" Satterfield asked, her voice quiet in the darkened van.

"No," Rose drew the word out. "But tell me anyway so I can stay up all night."

"Piper could have more than six children. We only saw the ones she allowed us to see."

Rose groaned.

"What makes her so special anyway?" Satterfield scooched forward on her seat. "How come she can have more children than other vamps?"

Matt shrugged. "Maybe her venom is less lethal than average. Just biting a victim rarely does them much harm. Mostly, it just wipes out a few hours of their memories, maybe makes them feel like they're catching a cold. That's how vampires create votaries. But turning someone's a different story. The vamp must dose the victim with a lot of venom. I have no idea how much, but I know most people die from the attempt and the majority who survive turn into wights. Six full vampire children is extraordinary. Before Piper, the most I had ever seen was two."

"So, you're saying we've sided with a vampire who could potentially birth an army given enough time." Watts sounded awed and not a little fearful.

"Yep."

Ahead, the vampires hung a left, following a well-kempt street that fronted Lake Hartwell. Docks and jetties lined the waterway, over-topped by palatial homes with sprawling yards. Just the sorts of places Rose-the-slinker had never visited in her meager life.

"I can't help thinking we've made a big mistake," Rose said.

"Maybe," Satterfield said, "but what's the alternative? It's not like we can take on the Breathers alone. I don't even know if we can do it with Piper's help, but we're certainly better off."

The vampires' SUV rolled to a stop. A large, wrought-iron gate covered in green ivy swung outward, its hinges groaning.

"That's not ominous," Watts said, grinning in the dark.

26

DRAWN TOGETHER

Piper Ross's lake house was huge. Only the top level, a sprawling, many-gabled edifice festooned with dormers and faux castle turrets, rose above the driveway. The rest occupied the side of a large, lawn-covered hill that gentled its way toward the lake.

Olivia who, so far as Rose could tell, served as Piper's most-favored daughter, unlocked the front door and ushered the succubi inside. "Welcome to the lake house. It might be a little stuffy—hasn't been aired in forever. Mama doesn't care much for the water. I have no idea why not; I love it. But we don't get out this way too often. Mostly we just lend it to friends whenever someone needs a place."

The other vampire, a thin girl called Sabrina, said little but went about turning on every light in the place so Olivia could give them a tour.

After showing her guests the house's seven bedrooms and four baths, Olivia led them onto a massive back deck lit by a series of pewter lamps. There was a pool below them, an inferior yet preferable twin to the lake's black water some hundred yards away. The moon shone on it, a rippling silver crescent ensconced in filmy gray clouds.

"Pool should be clean—we have a service—the lake not so much, but it's more fun for skinny dipping." She gave Watts a sensual grin with those words, which he flatly ignored.

"How are the neighbors about parties?" Matt asked.

"They shouldn't give you much trouble long as things don't get rowdy. How many people are coming?"

"About a hundred."

Rose thought Olivia might blanch at that number, but she merely nodded.

"We had a wedding here back a few years ago, at night of course. Probably had two hundred and fifty all told. Nobody called the cops."

"Good," Matt said.

"But they can't sleep here. This neighborhood wouldn't go for tents full of partygoers crowding the lawn."

"We meet here—make it look like a summer barbeque—then have everybody camp out in the woods near your place. How about that?"

Olivia nodded slowly. "I think Mama would be okay with that."

Matt turned to the others. "Let's have everyone gather here two days from now. We'll meet with the team leaders. The rest can relax a little. That'll give us some time to get our plan straight."

They started making calls.

Three days later, Rose sat on a supremely comfortable lawn chair in shorts and a swim top at the end of the mansion's brick drive. She had early elected herself to the position of front door greeter, waving in the straggling succubi who arrived in ones and twos by vehicle or, more often, on foot. This task helped her avoid Matt, who busied himself barbequing steaks, ribs, and vegetables out back with Watts.

They were going to have more words about Matt's hostage plan, but Rose saw no sense in pressing the matter just now. None of that mattered if they failed to take the fear factory.

One highly dubious accomplishment at a time, thank you. Besides, Rose had her own plans.

A gold Lexus streaked with mud splatter pulled into the drive. A deep dent creased the left front fender, though the headlight remained intact, and a long, slender crack ran nearly the length of the windshield.

Rose stood, drawing calm and focus. Few of their people could afford a Lexus, even such an abused model. This might well be one of the neighbors come to complain about the noise or simply to assuage their curiosity. Or it could be Breathers come to slaughter them all.

Rose tried to peer inside as the car drew to a stop in front of her but saw nothing through its tinted windows. She drew strength, speed, and resilience as she casually placed her bare feet in a basic boxing stance.

All her preparations fell to pieces, however, when both car doors opened, and the Pruett twins climbed out.

"Oh my God!" Rose's delight at seeing the twins surprised her no less than it did them. She rushed to Brendan, who had been driving, nearly tackling the small incubus against his car, and hugged him hard enough to split a rib.

Luke rounded the car, and he, too, got the hugging of his life. "Missed you, Rose," he said, his voice hoarse.

"My God, you two, stop it. You're making me emotional." Brendan fanned himself in comic exasperation.

Rose ushered them inside. Two dozen succubi and incubi mingled in the massive living room, looking for all the world like a Paris after-party at some high-brow modeling agency. They spoiled that illusion, however, by drinking everything from mid-expensive champagne to dollar store beer. It was a risk, letting them drink. They wouldn't be able to draw if something happened. But Matt figured, and Rose agreed, that anyone brave enough to join this insane mission deserved a real party with real booze. A few waved, beckoning Rose and the twins to join them, but she shook her head, leading the boys along a quiet, darkened hall to an empty bedroom.

"I smell vampires," Luke said once Rose had shut the door.

"Two are sleeping in the room next door."

"My brother doesn't like their kind ever since one jilted him," Brendan said.

"She did not jilt me. She ripped my heart into confetti."

"Potato-patato."

"Where have you brats been?" Rose whirled on them. "I must have left you a hundred messages since Den fell."

"We know, sweetie," Luke said. "We got them. We couldn't reply."

"We've been incognito," Brendan said. "Look at these coarse fibers? Do you think either of us would dress like this if we weren't in hiding?"

He was right. The twins wore denim jeans, t-shirts—Luke's said *Talk Nerdy to Me* in bold letters—and running shoes. Rose had never seen them so dressed down.

"I take it you didn't hear what happened to us?" Luke asked.

Rose shook her head.

"The IRS, baby," Brendan said. "They raided the house in Tampa, seized nearly all our stuff."

"Assets and memorabilia alike," Luke added.

"Froze our bank accounts, everything. You can't imagine what it's like to have your American Express Black Card declined at Neiman Marcus."

"Luckily, we had plenty of cash laid by."

"Smelly stuff." Brendan wrinkled his nose. "So last century. But handy as a nineteen-year-old pool boy."

"Are they still after you?" Rose asked. "I mean, you don't think you led any Breathers here, do you?"

Brendan chuckled. "Not a chance, darling."

"If there's one thing we know how to do, it's hide." Luke sounded far more morose about the idea than his brother.

Brendan cupped his cheeks, staring up at the ceiling in mock dismay. "Oh, woe is us! Who cares? Everybody has troubles, am I right? But that sort of thing can't stop good art. You know what we've been up to?"

"What?" Rose asked, grinning. It was good to be with the boys again.

"The next installment of *Drawn!*" He fished a newly minted comic from the backpack he wore and handed it to her. "That's just the mock-up, but it came out great. We probably won't change much."

The cover showed Melody strapped to a chair defiantly glaring at Rose who stood over her, hands on hips, screaming words not detailed on the page. A pale face stared through a barred window in the door behind them. It looked a little like Clemente.

"There was no window in the door," Rose said.

Brendan rolled his eyes. "Artistic license, baby doll. Don't get hung up on details. We got everything in this one: the creepy comic collection, your sister's accusations against Matt, that girl Clemente..." He trailed off at the look that crossed Rose's face. "Oh, sweetie, I'm so stupid. I—"

"It's okay," Rose said. "Really. Is this already on the shelves? Or are you having trouble getting it out since you're on the run?"

"Soon. No one's touched our distributors," Luke said. "We think the Breathers are afraid to attack anyone except us since it might show the public that what we're drawing is real."

"Plus, we've got a little something else to show you, something big." Brendan gave his backpack a significant shake. "We've been working like crazy to get it all done as quickly as possible."

"There's more? I can't believe you made anything while running from the Breathers."

Brendan shrugged. "Computers are wondrous things. We uploaded this entire installment to our editor while swilling bourgeoisie slop at a McDonald's in Dahlonega."

"Too bad it isn't on sale already. I need every votary I can get right now." Rose flopped onto the bed still staring at the comic.

Brendan and Luke shared a look.

"You found the fear factory?" Luke asked.

Rose leaned forward, dropped her voice. "Not exactly, but we've got a plan."

"Why do I get the feeling this isn't the type of plan that sees you safe and warm on the other side of it?" Brendan asked.

"Are you two still in contact with that succubus doctor from Palm

Beach? The one who implanted all the newbies with tracking chips? What was her name?"

"Rebekah Stanislaw." Luke looked to Brendan, then back to Rose, his eyes narrowed. "Yes. Why?"

"Do you know if she's coming here?"

"I think so," Brendan said. "What's this about?"

Rose fished the tiny transmitter she had taken from Matt's stash, the one he had so cunningly hidden in his shaving kit behind the towels in the master bath. It was thin as a straightened paperclip and about the length of her little finger.

"Matt has a plan on how to find the fear factory. But mine's better."

They sat mesmerized, nearly fifty succubi crowded into a slightly less than full-size theater at the heart of a vampire's mansion. Though the large room's gently inclined floor and plush, red stadium seats could accommodate an audience of two dozen, it came nowhere near hosting every succubus and incubus in the house. People lined the side and back walls, with more spilling out into the main hallway. Even so, Rose had forced most of the latecomers out, promising them a second showing of whatever the geek twins had brought.

And what they had brought was…interesting.

It was a cartoon—

"Anime, darling," Brendan corrected when he heard Rose call it that.

—version of the *Drawn* graphic novel. Though she would never say as much to the twins, the idea disappointed Rose. What was the point? Her adventures were already well known to her fans. What she needed now was a vehicle to solidify her current votaries while simultaneously gaining new ones. How could rehashing old material accomplish that?

So Rose thought right through the opening credits and up to the first line of dialogue, delivered by a woman who sounded so much like Rose she at first wondered if the twins had somehow recorded her voice and cobbled it together for the part. From that point until the end, she sat, like all her peers, engrossed in the tale. She had lived it, and yet the story absorbed her. Was that crass? Narcissistic? Maybe. But then again, the twins' movie was just that good. Better than good. Witnessing their strange magic, their way of coaxing what had been an already compelling storyline up from the pages of a comic book onto the big screen, felt tantamount to watching a musical genius score a new symphony.

The end credits appeared, and the crowd burst into a standing ovation. Suddenly, every succubus within reach was patting the geek twins' backs, congratulating Rose, and generally treating them like celebrities. Rose, Matt, Satterfield, and Watts had to push their way through the press as team leaders took charge calming everyone down.

Rose led their group into a plush office across from the theater room. The twins sat on an overstuffed couch while the others commandeered office chairs.

"How did you do that?" Rose asked the instant she had barred the office door.

"You liked it?" Luke sounded genuinely worried.

"Are you kidding?" Watts asked. "I don't even watch cartoons—"

"Anime," said Luke, Brendan, and Rose in unison.

"—yeah, those, and I loved it!"

"Is that the only episode you've completed?" Matt asked. "We can give you space here if you need it. I can't promise you much in the way of equipment, our budget is nil, but I think we'd all love to see more."

Luke shook his head. "Thanks, but we've finished the entire first season."

"Fourteen episodes," Brendan said.

"What? How?" Rose felt her eyes bulging.

"It's what we do, darling. We draw, and we draw. Didn't hurt that we cut a deal with Netflix before all this IRS badness started either. We wanted that shit done."

"Or that we've been working on this little bombshell pretty much since the day we met you." Luke lifted his chin, putting on a haughty expression that would have put Colin Firth's rendition of Mr. Darcy to shame.

"By the time MegaCon rolled around, we already had eight episodes in the can," Brendan said.

"When does the first episode release?" Satterfield asked. Rose could see the gears turning in her head.

"We'll need to do some adverts on comics sites and podcasts—drum up some enthusiasm," Luke said.

"We don't have time for that," Rose said. "And forget one episode. How soon can they get the entire first season up for streaming?"

"Now, wait a second." Brendan leaned back and folded his arms. "You can't just dump it like that. You dole it out—whet the fans' appetites for it."

"Well…" Luke rubbed his stubbled chin. "There is the binge factor. Look what they did with *Stranger Things*. Most of our fans will watch the entire season in a day or two and then probably recommend it to friends. We might be able to convince Netflix to release early. Maybe, get it up in a couple of days? That'll make it downloadable by the weekend, which means more people can watch it uninterrupted."

"No good." Matt shook his head like a man warding off a car sales-man. "We've gathered a lot of slinkers here—Order-trained, but still slinkers. They've come because we've promised to take out the fear factory. But the longer we wait, the more we'll lose. We've already made ourselves a juicy target with this many succubi in one place. Sooner or later, the Indrawn Breath is bound to find us, and everyone here knows it. They're not going to stick around long no matter what we promise them. Tomorrow night would be best. One or two days at most. Which means we need every votary you can muster, and we need them now."

Brendan's eyes widened. He stared at the others as if one of them had just suggested he swallow a Volkswagen. "A couple of days? Are you insane?"

"No," Rose said. "Not insane, out of time. And look what you did with *Drawn*. It's a blockbuster all on its own. Your fans, our fans, will eat this anime up."

The twins shared two ends of a look—Luke's thoughtful, Brendan's incredulous.

"We could—" Luke began.

"We can't—" Brendan said at the same time.

Rose, who stood next to the office door, paced over to them and squatted so that she could put a hand on each of their knees. "I haven't asked much of you two. I've gone your way since we first met, and you never let me down. But now I'm telling you, we've got to do this thing, and I can't do it without your help. Please make this happen. I need you."

"We can release it ourselves," Luke said at once. "Leak it."

"That'll blow the contract with Netflix," Brendan said, though without much fire.

Luke shrugged. "Rose needs us, Bren."

Brendan met Rose's gaze with his striking blue eyes. A slow smile curved his lips, and though it looked a little tremulous, it held. "Oh, to hell with the contract. It's just money, right?"

27

FEAR BAITING

Less than twenty-four hours later, Rose stood on the sidewalk in front of an Avis car rental office about a mile from the Greenville/Spartanburg airport in South Carolina. Despite the heat and humidity, she floated in a void of peace drawn from her swelling legion of votaries.

Well, near-peace. Nothing could fully quench her anxiety.

The back of Rose's right thigh itched. She had healed the tiny incision where Dr. Stanislaw had inserted a second tracking device, but Rose still felt the thing like a long splinter under her skin. She desperately wanted to scratch it, but discernment stayed her hand.

A subcompact car pulled into the lot, Melody at the wheel. Rose put on a smile she couldn't feel and raised a hand to wave at her little sister. Even drawing calm, Rose's pulse quickened.

Melody pulled in next to the curb. Rose shoved her overnight bag into the car's rear seat and climbed in on the passenger side.

"Thanks for coming." She leaned over to hug Melody.

Melody accepted the embrace, though she held herself rigid, face forward. She did manage to pat Rose on the back once and roused a semblance of a smile. "Ready to go?"

Rose nodded.

Melody got the little car headed east on Highway 85.

"Are you staying in a hotel near here?" Rose asked.

Melody chuckled.

"What?" Rose asked.

"Drop it, Anna. We both know why you're in this car with me, and it ain't to make small talk."

Rose sat stunned for a moment. She had expected some pretense, even if just for the length of the car ride. Hell, she had been entertaining the notion that Melody might have turned against the Breathers after all—sort of a take this cup from me kind of hope. But the mocking tone in Mel's voice shattered that thought. Matt had been right all along. Melody had allowed herself to be captured by Clemente back in Mexico to bait Rose into escaping with her.

Rose drew more calm, folding it around herself like a shell, quieting her mind. "Why do you think I'm here?"

Melody's lips turned up in a genuine grin. "To lead your friends to the fear factory. Why else?"

"Mel, I—"

"Save it, Anna. If you had ever been on my side, it would have been in Mexico. You made your decision then."

"It's Rose."

"What?" Melody glanced over, brows knit.

"My name is Rose now."

"What has that got to do with anything?"

Rose didn't answer. She stared out the window at the verdant trees whipping past. Her heart felt like a stone. "You killed Leslie, didn't you, Mel?"

"That sharpshooter girl in the tower? Yeah, I killed her."

Rose's calm fluttered like a moth's wing. She tightened her grip on it, forcing her mind to still. "I don't know what's been done to you. I don't know how you became what you are—"

"But you're going to save me, right? You think I'm being charmed into doing the things I do, but you're wrong. I make my own choices. I do what I want." She looked over at her sister, her lips worked into a sneer. "But you still think you can help me become the innocent little girl I was before, don't you? That you can reform me."

Rose shook her head. "No. I can never forgive what you've done. You're a monster. A beast. You're not my sister."

"Fuck you."

Rose turned to stare at Melody. She could see the arteries pulsing in her sister's neck, hear the rhythmic beat of her heart. "After this car ride, if I ever see you again, I will kill you."

Perhaps it was Rose's lack of vehemence or her uninflected tone that caught Melody's attention. She glanced at Rose. "Shut up."

They drove in silence for several minutes. Rose stared at her sister the entire way, never saying a word. For her part, Melody refused to look over.

Melody pulled off the highway onto a rural road surrounded by farms, small homes, and rundown businesses. The scent of livestock peppered the air.

"Stop staring at me," Melody said.

Rose went right on staring. She felt no anger. She was too calm for that. And yet she knew, somewhere buried beneath her borrowed tranquility, lay a vast ocean of hatred for the stranger sitting beside her. The gulf between them spanned far more than their five-year age difference. Never would she have credited the idea of so loathing any member of her own family. With a jolt that she managed to keep inside, Rose realized her feelings toward Melody matched what she felt for Clemente and his ilk. The heat of it surprised and frightened her.

Melody turned onto a one-lane dirt road. Trees grew thick on both sides. The little car sped along the dry track, Melody pushing it to unsafe speeds.

Rose remained quiet. If Mel was trying to frighten her, it wouldn't work. Rose wondered which of them would fare better in a wreck.

Melody drifted the car through a tight curve, the back wheels scraping across red clay, and then slammed on the brakes. Rose finally turned her gaze from Melody to peer out the front windshield. A black SUV, parked sideways, spanned the road. David Lord leaned against it, grinning.

"Scared yet?" Melody asked.

Rose climbed out of the car.

"Hello, Rose," Lord said. "You don't look surprised to see me."

Melody skipped into the man's embrace. She kissed his neck, his jaw, and then hugged him, pressing her face against his chest.

All the while, Lord kept his gaze on Rose. "Get the kit."

Melody threw a smile over her shoulder at Rose. It looked manic. She giggled as she pulled open the SUV's rear door. She climbed half inside and returned carrying a white medical box with a large red cross on the lid. She opened it on the hood of her car.

Though she heard no telltale sounds, nor saw any unnatural movement, Rose became aware of watchers in the woods. Discernment told her there were at least ten of them, probably more. The pungent odor of gun oil told her they were near.

"You came alone," Lord said.

Rose nodded.

He eyed her for a long moment while Melody fished inside the med kit. Rose returned Lord's gaze. If he wanted her fear, he would have to earn it.

"Where are the others?" Lord asked. "Where's Matt Snow? This meeting has his stink on it."

"Sleeping," Rose said. "I drugged him."

"Sly girl. How about the rest of your people? Where are they?"

Rose said nothing.

"We'll get it out of you eventually," Lord said with a shrug. He glided forward, his movements predatory. "We know about the transmitter."

Rose nodded. She continued to draw calm while forcing her face to remain still. She steadfastly put all thoughts of the new transmitter out of her head, focusing instead on the old one in her shoulder. This was the dicey part of the plan. Any hint at her deception and it would crumble.

Melody stood from the open med kit, a scalpel in hand. "Give me your arm."

"No," Lord said.

Melody whirled on him, her brows lifted, her lips wrinkled with a frown. "But you said I could do it."

"You're too angry with your sister. I don't trust your hand not to slip."

"David, I can do this."

"Give me the scalpel." Lord held out a hand.

Reluctantly, like a child caught with a dangerous weapon, Melody dropped the blade into his palm.

"I get time with her later, right?" she asked in a wheedling voice. "You promised."

Lord nodded, though his gaze never left Rose. "You know I keep my promises."

Melody grinned.

"Will you let me take the transmitter?" Lord asked Rose. "Things will go easier if you don't struggle."

"Struggle," Melody said. "Please, struggle."

Rose had known this moment would come. Though she had never imagined someone removing her tracking chip on a deserted dirt road in South Carolina, she had expected the Breathers to take it eventually. She had even worn a tank top to make things easier. She considered protesting. A little playacting might help convince Lord that she was reluctant—maybe keep him from looking for the second transmitter. But that wasn't her style and acting out of character at this point would only make him or Melody suspicious.

Rose heaved a sigh. "Fine. Take it. It's not like I can stop you in the long run."

A slow smile spread across Lord's lips. "You saw one of my people in the trees?"

Rose shook her head. "Didn't have to. I smell them."

Lord withdrew a bottle of iodine from the med kit. "Sorry, we have no analgesic. But then, I hear you've got quite the votary count these days. A little cut shouldn't hurt you."

He took Rose by the arm, his hands surprisingly gentle as he turned her so that her shoulder more fully faced the sun. He brushed the spot above her old chip with iodine then made a short, precise cut with the scalpel.

Rose hardly felt the incision. The factory-sharp blade combined with Lord's deft hands made it practically painless. With dexterity unseen in humans, Lord withdrew the square transmitter from Rose's shoulder using a set of tweezers. He dropped the device into a plastic baggy, then proceeded to clean Rose's cut with gauze and alcohol.

It was the work of a second for Rose to close the wound as Lord whisked away the blood.

"Now what?" she asked.

Lord grinned. "Now the other one."

For the first time since leaving the airport, Rose felt a breach in her perfect wall of calm.

Lord tilted his head to one side. "You thought we didn't know?"

Melody guffawed. She leaned toward her sister, her mouth open like a donkey braying. "The look on your face, Anna! It's priceless."

"Where is it?" Lord asked.

Drawing charm, Rose pursed her lips, trying to look confused. "I don't have another chip."

"Yes, you do." Lord turned to the trees. "Jim. A hand please."

A short, rawboned man with a dark beard and square glasses stepped from behind cover. He moved to stand in front of Rose with the surety of one cloaked in discernment. He stared at her for a moment, watching her eyes with interest.

She held her body still, determined to give nothing away.

"It's in the back of her right thigh."

Rose cursed. What had she done to give it away? Had she glanced at Lord's or Melody's legs? Had she moved in some way that telegraphed what she was striving to hide? She would never know.

"I'm afraid I'm going to have to ask you to drop your pants, Rose," Lord said. "This is completely professional, I assure you."

"No."

"We insist." Melody stepped around Lord to menace Rose.

Discernment told Rose her chances of escaping this mess hovered somewhere near zero. But if she let Lord disable her second transmitter, the Order would have no way to track her—no way to find the fear factory.

Jim was a problem. No matter how Rose planned to make her escape, even attacking Jim first, her imagined scenarios ended with him outguessing her. She could see in his body movement, the way his eyes stutter-stepped over her in rapid saccades, that his draw on discernment outstripped her own by orders of magnitude. Trying to strategize against him was tantamount to playing chess against a supercomputer. Alone, she might escape him. Her discernment told her he was likely a monodraw. All she would have to do is run. But teamed up with Lord and her sister, Jim formed a considerable stumbling block. He could predict her choices, her attacks, before she launched them, and warn the others.

Jim gave Rose a grin. "It really is too late, ma'am," he said in a thick southern drawl. "I'd just do what Mr. Lord says."

"Yeah, Anna," Melody said. "Do what Mr. Lord says."

"It will go better for you in the long run." Lord wasn't looking at Rose. He swabbed the scalpel clean with alcohol then held it up to gleam in the sunlight as if inspecting it for microscopic imperfections. He didn't charm her. Why bother? He had her trapped.

Rose ground her teeth. She could not escape. That much was obvious. And yet, she knew herself. The Order had at least taught her that much. She might be facing singular outcome odds, but so the hell what? She wasn't about to lay down and take this shit. If she had even a glimmer of a chance at aborting this now-failed mission, she had to take it.

Rose drew speed. Her fist sounded like a shotgun blast as it split the air, rocketing toward Jim's chin. In the instant before impact, Rose had time to consider whether Myra Hanks, the Order's near-precog, could have evaded this blow. Despite Myra's enormous draw on discernment, Rose doubted it. Some things were unavoidable.

Or, maybe not. Jim was already moving before Rose had even decided to throw the punch. She tried pulling back, redirecting the blow to catch Jim on the downstroke as he spun to his left. But the thin incubus predicted her reversal as clearly as the original blow. He bobbed under her fist, rolled right, and ended up behind Rose.

She found herself unexpectedly facing a scalpel-wielding David Lord.

The blade flashed.

Rose might have dodged it except Jim, anticipating her move, shoved her in precisely the right spot to throw off her balance, thereby keeping her within Lord's range.

The scalpel sank into Rose's upper arm. She grunted at the pain as blood spurted from the wound. This wasn't the finessed stroke of a roadside surgeon, but the deft slash of a professional killer. Rose knew her peril. She tried to spin, both to get Jim from behind her and to put Lord between her and Melody.

Jim placed a hand to her lower back, applying no more pressure than a gentleman might when leading his beloved in a turn on the dancefloor. And yet that slight touch wrecked Rose's plans. She staggered sideways, and Lord kicked her feet out from under her.

Rose crashed to the dirt with a painful "Oof!" She tried to roll back to her feet, but Lord pinned her down. He put a knee on her throat while Jim secured her free arm.

Melody handed Lord a syringe, its ampule filled with a clear liquid.

"No!" Rose struggled to rise, drawing enough strength that she felt her bones creak under the pressure.

Lord grunted, struggling to match her strength, even with Melody and Jim's help. For a brief, hopeful moment, Rose thought she might win free. She kicked and shoved and wiggled her body in the dust, giving her assailants a game fight.

But then the others arrived. Suddenly, a squad of Breathers surrounded Rose. Strong hands seized her, shoving her down, stymying her efforts to slip away.

Lord sank the needle into Rose's neck. Something hot and prickly cold by turns raced into her head and down into her chest. Within seconds her vision turned gray and fuzzy at the edges. Whatever this stuff was, it worked fast.

Rose tried to draw wakefulness, but it was no use. No draw could keep her conscious against the tide of fatigue drowning her mind.

Her sister's face was the last thing Rose saw before the darkness took her. Melody grinned.

"Sweet dreams, Sis."

28

RESISTANCE

The fear came in waves. Rose tried to fight it. She knew she had no reason to fear David Lord. He wasn't even in the room. But no amount of telling herself that could break the fear draw. He had her courage, and through it, he robbed her votaries.

She lay on a hospital bed, strapped down at the waist. Had she the wherewithal, she could have broken the leather strap cinched across her lower abdomen. She knew that. But she wasn't able to touch it.

Merely thinking about the strap made her cringe. She turned her gaze away from it to silence such thoughts. She had a sneaking suspicion David Lord could read her mind. Ludicrous of course…but still.

The woman in the bed next to Rose was insane. Though Mary had been paranoid to the point of near incoherence when Rose first arrived— three days ago?—the woman had been speaking then. She had managed to tell Rose she was from Culver City, California. She owned a small laundromat and dry-cleaning business there. That part, what Rose figured was real, had been stuffed between Mary's ranting conspiracy theories about who was talking behind her back and who had told Society she charmed her customers. Not much charm, of course. Just enough to keep them coming back.

But that had been three days ago. Lord said some votaries in the fear factory lasted far longer than others. Some withstood the fear for months. Others, Mary among them, cracked within days.

Mary jabbered something. There might have been a word in there, but if so, Rose couldn't make it out. Mary's brown hair clung to her sweaty forehead. She rolled her eyes this way and that like a bewildered animal, the whites glistening in the harsh hospital light.

Rose had ceased telling her everything would be okay. Rose didn't believe that, and saying it did no good.

Mary wailed and thrashed, sometimes laughing, sometimes crying, throughout her every waking hour. The same went for the other patients—votaries—blubbering, screaming, and crying in adjacent rooms. Their sounds of fear never ceased. They echoed along the corridors, a discordant melody of madness Rose couldn't shut out.

Thomas, the Army nurse who brought them meals and checked their vitals, had said Mary would probably receive a feeding tube in the next day or so if she didn't start eating again.

Thinking of Thomas made Rose look again at her strap, which in turn sent a claxon of fear screaming through her mind. No thinking about the strap! The strap was fine. It needed nothing from her. She could not improve it in any way. Rose looked away from it, turned her mind elsewhere.

Thomas was nice. He had been an Army nurse for four years now. Someone, Rose figured David Lord for the culprit, had charmed Thomas into seeing his patients as insane domestic terrorists. The details were a little fuzzy, but that was another thing Rose wasn't supposed to think about. It didn't matter what Thomas thought of her and Mary and however many others were locked away in this facility, he was a good nurse. He saw to their needs. He treated them well despite his charmed delusions.

Sudden fatigue washed over Rose. Her hands shook under their own weight. She tried to lift them but couldn't. Lord was drawing strength and speed from her, inducing her to, in turn, draw those attributes from her votaries.

Mary made a gurgling sound, a refutation. She too must have sensed Lord's draw.

Rose grimaced. With a defiant growl, she resisted drawing from her votaries. She tried with every part of her self-control to deny Lord his demands.

But with that denial, her fear of him grew. Was he so aware of her that he could direct her fear? Surely not. She was just one in his legion of votaries. He couldn't know that she fought him.

Could he?

The fear increased. Rose began to sweat. She heard voices. These weren't the inarticulate screams and wails of the mad in surrounding rooms, or even Mary's yammering. These voices emanated from behind her, beneath her bed, in the closed and locked cabinet next to the sink.

"Anna! Anna, help me!"

Desperately, Rose scanned the room, wide-eyed and frightened. She could never find the child who screamed for her no matter how she searched. She looked and looked but found only crazy Mary gibbering at her.

A whisper brushed Rose's cheek, making the skin on her neck pucker with gooseflesh. It was the worn and raspy sound of an aged woman pleading for water. She was so thirsty. With the whisper came the scent of fetid breath, like that of a person sick with something catching. Rose flattened herself against her sweat-soaked sheets, unable to escape, shivering in fear.

A nail scratched at the underside of Rose's mattress. The sound went on and on, running the length of her body from heel to crown and back again. The vibrations sent a greasy tickle racing up her back that made her squirm.

"It's my mind!" Rose shouted at the sounds—at the empty room. "It's not real! You're not real!"

"It's dark," said the child in the cabinet.

"I'm thirsty, so thirsty," said the old woman.

The finger began anew its long traversal of the bed.

Rose drew voice from her votaries and screamed. The titanic sound shook the room, rattling its door in the frame. For a moment, nothing existed outside Rose's tormented howl. She filled it with all her fear, doubt, and worry. When it finally died, Rose's lungs felt deflated, and her ears rang. She lay back on the bed, panting, becoming slowly aware of Mary's panicked wails.

Guilt put a knot in Rose's stomach. She had added to Mary's crippling fear. That hadn't been her intention. "I'm sorry, Mary."

The other woman ignored Rose. She writhed on her bed, insensate to the world outside her tortured thoughts, a mad invalid of no more use than a battery for her succubus masters.

A battery provided power; it never drew it. But Rose had drawn just now when she screamed. Without thought, and in desperation, she had borrowed voice from her votaries, which meant she could access her powers. That realization sent a blade of shame slicing through her guts. Her votaries were off limits! They no longer belonged to her. They were Lord's.

And yet.

Rose focused on the strap across her belly. Defying her revulsion, she took it in both hands, her knuckles white with strain. Without much hope, she reached out to her votaries' strength and speed, beckoning to them like lost pets too long astray. To her surprise, they came readily, filling her limbs with vibrant energy. Though every fiber of her mind told Rose that escape was wrong, to even contemplate it could mean her death, she committed to tearing the strap from its moorings. And she would have done it—she would have!—but no sooner had she drawn than Lord drew in turn, sucking away her power as fast as she could call it. Her strength and speed evaporated. Somewhere, Lord must have been doing battle, perhaps with Matt, perhaps with other friends Rose loved. And though she yearned to cut off the flow, Rose could not help but aid Lord in that fight.

Terror wracked her mind and body. It left her shaking and sweating, her muscles cramped from warring against one another. Despite her best efforts, Rose could not fight it. The fear consumed her.

Time passed. A minute or a year, she didn't know. Rose knew only the shuddering, jittering horror of Lord's draw. Somewhere far off, the hospital room door clicked open. Thomas entered. He wore digital camo scrubs with his rank, specialist, embroidered over his name tape and the Army star beneath.

Rose writhed against the strap. Some part of her, a sort of backseat driver in her head, whispered that she had no reason to fear Thomas. He posed no threat. He wasn't even an incubus. By the look on his face, he had nothing but concern for his patients.

But that rational part of Rose held no sway over the stark terror suffusing her mind. She screamed and tried to scramble back from him but went nowhere.

"It's okay!" Thomas held up his clipboard and free hand. "It's just me. You're both fine."

"Don't hurt me!" Rose shouted. She clawed at the bed with feeble hands. She knew—KNEW—Thomas would strangle her, beat her, give her drugs to make her blood sizzle like meat on a grill. He meant to kill her. Violate her. She lay defenseless before him.

Thomas moved to the upright cabinet in the far corner. He stood before it for a moment, his brow furrowed as if in thought.

"The doctor says I can't give you a sedative. But I don't know why. He never explained..." Thomas trailed off, peering at the clipboard in his hands.

"Don't touch me!" Rose shouted.

"You deserve some sleep." Thomas fumbled a key from his pocket and tried it on the cabinet's oversized lock, but his hands were trembling too much to slide it home.

"NO!" Rose shouted. "The little girl's in there."

"What little girl?" Thomas asked.

"The one who calls my name. She's angry with me. She wants to hurt me."

Mary wailed an incoherent string of syllables filled with fear and regret.

"There's no one in this cabinet," Thomas said, but his hands had stopped working the lock. "I'm not supposed to give you anything."

Rose focused on him. Thomas's face kept changing. One moment he was a thin twenty-something Army nurse, one whose job increasingly made no sense to him, and the next he was a demon. His skin grew pale, clotting up like oatmeal. His eyes elongated to stretch around the sides of his head, even as the whites turned a brilliant yellow, bright as the noonday sun. Tusks extruded from beneath his upper lip, gleaming white and dripping with greenish poison. His body arched, his back bent, his fingers morphed into claws long as butcher knives.

"No!" Rose shouted, and Thomas flinched. She had to fight the fear. There was no escape—nowhere she could hide from it. She could cower and give in, or she could fight.

But fighting was futile. Hadn't she learned that already? Was she so stupid she couldn't take the lesson? She had fought Lord that first day when he had brought her here. She had railed against him and Melody—

Rose jolted as if someone had slapped her.

Melody.

She, too, had infused fear in Rose. She wasn't the prime figure, she didn't loom so large as Lord in Rose's mind, but Melody had her own fear draw on Rose.

A flash of something besides terror hammered through Rose's distressed mind.

Anger.

It was fleeting, squashed by fear, and yet it had been there. Rose thought again of Melody, of her little sister's glee at watching Lord break Rose's spirit. She pictured Melody's intense stare as Lord drew out Rose's courage, siphoning it off like gasoline from a wrecked car.

"No!" Rose hurled the word like a grenade, her anger spiking once again.

Thomas bumped into the cabinet behind him. Items rattled inside.

Something joined the anger growing inside Rose's head: a seed of courage to combat the fear. She seized upon it, drawing more.

Thomas flattened against the cabinet, his face gone bloodless, his eyes wide and rolling. The clipboard slid from his hand to clatter on the floor. "What's happening? What are you doing to me?"

The phantom sounds that had so terrorized Rose ceased. She heard now only the muted wails of votaries mingled with Thomas's exhalations and Mary's incoherent muttering. Strength of will pervaded Rose's mind, drowning out the fear. For the first time in days, she felt her thoughts coalesce into a sane stream of consciousness. Suddenly, she knew where she was. She knew what she was doing.

"I'm sorry," Rose said.

Thomas jerked as if she had slapped him. He tried to sidle away but seemed incapable of tearing his gaze from Rose. Sweat beaded his forehead and upper lip. He looked like a rodent pinned by sudden, brilliant light.

Rose drew still more courage from Thomas. It enveloped her like a blanket straight from the dryer—delicious, intoxicating, protective. Her fear of Lord and Melody evaporated under its enveloping heat.

Calm now, in control, Rose drew strength. Her votaries were vast and deep. Lord and Melody hadn't begun to siphon off even the barest amount of talents from Rose's fans. With a calm she would not have believed possible seconds before, Rose slid her fingers beneath the strap pinning her to the bed and ripped it in two.

Thomas screamed and fell backward to sprawl on the floor. He searched Rose's face, eyes skittering about like a couple of brown beetles. His mouth hung open and his brows lifted so high they might have been part of his hairline.

Rose bounded from the bed, barefoot and dressed in a hospital gown. Not that it mattered. She crouched next to Thomas, watching him, her head tilted to one side.

He was a pathetic little thing, shuddering beneath her gaze. She seized his collar, and Thomas's bladder let loose. The weakling. He screeched but dared not pull away from Rose's grasp. Smart. If he so much as looked away from her, Rose would crush him like an insect. He disgusted her.

Rose halted.

Aghast, she released Thomas's collar and scooted back from him till she bumped the railing on her bed. Had she been about to kill a defenseless man? Yes. Worse, she had relished the idea.

Rose swallowed. A stream of fear threatened to seep back into her mind. Lord would be livid if he found her out of bed—if he saw she had broken the precious strap. He would do terrible things to her. So would Melody. They'd—

No.

Rose shook her head, gritted her teeth. No more fear. No more quivering at the mere thought of Lord and Melody. She had spent her life slinking from one town to another because of fear. She had forgone love and friendship because of fear. She had denied herself a real existence because fear had ruled her every decision in life. No more. She needed courage, and she knew where to find it.

Having opened the flow once already, Rose found the courage came more easily a second time. She drew from it—from Thomas— obliterating her fears with a torrent of boldness, bravery, and audacity that spared no room for dread or timidity or much of anything at all.

Rose watched Thomas cower and call for his mother. She should feel something for him, but she didn't. Or, rather, she did, but no more than she felt for the lamp next to her bed or the floor beneath her feet. A cold, dispassionate sort of calculus clicked along inside her head.

She took stock.

She was drawing Thomas's courage, something new to her, but not altogether surprising. His courage had led her to that of her votaries like Hansel and Gretel's bread trail. Now she drew the courage of millions, which more than sufficed to protect her from the fear links placed on her by Lord and Melody.

Good. Right? It certainly seemed so, but at what cost? Rose could feel—not feel?—her loss of empathy for things outside herself just as Matt had described it. Dispassionate realism filled her mind to the exclusion of all else. It felt pure and clean, especially after suffering so many days of terror, but also cold. Even without compassion or empathy, Rose could see that. She cared nothing for Thomas. Breaking his spine would mean no more to her than plucking an apple from a branch or cracking a lobster's shell for dinner.

But it should.

Rose spared Thomas another look. He writhed and groaned when he saw her focusing on him.

"I'm a psychopath," she whispered.

"Please don't," Thomas cried. "Please, please don't."

Were all her votaries acting this way right now? Millions of *Drawn* fans driven to the brink of fear-induced insanity?

Doubtful. Hopefully, Thomas was either particularly susceptible to the draw or acutely affected due to proximity. If they felt anything, the average *Drawn* fan likely suffered only the mildest discomfort, just as they would feel the tiniest bit sick or weak when she drew healing or strength from them *en masse*.

It didn't much matter either way. Rose wasn't about to relinquish her draw on Thomas, or her legion of fans. She needed them if she had any hope of destroying this fear factory.

Part of her thought she should simply set the building on fire. An inferno would kill the Breathers' votaries. Many of those votaries were insane like Mary, or at least well on the way to insanity. Fire looked like the quickest way to victory.

"No," Rose said. She had to think like Rose without the fear draw. Her dispassion wouldn't last. Eventually, she would relinquish all this courage, leaving some future incarnation of herself to deal with whatever choices she made now. That future emotional self might be traumatized by wanton killing, especially of innocent votaries, some of them likely her family. By protecting them, she protected her future self. And self-preservation seemed logical.

Rose headed for the door. She purposefully did not cave in Thomas's skull as she passed him. She felt certain future Rose would approve.

With no more fear than a woman entering her home, Rose tried the door but found it locked.

She drew a breath, and with it, strength, speed, and resilience.

Time to do her duty.

29

END TIMES

An alarm blared to life the instant Rose burst through the doorway. She glanced left and right, braced for attack.

None came.

The hall, lit by bright overhead fluorescents, stood empty. She was in a hospital: wooden doors with plastic file holders affixed to the wall next to them, white Formica floors, beige paint, the sterile scent of industrial cleaners. Strobe lights near the ceiling flashed in time with the alarm. Rose considered ripping the speakers from the wall but dismissed the idea. She had more important things to do.

She headed for the elevator at the far end of the hallway. She could hear ranting, screaming voices behind the windowless doors she passed. These too, she ignored. She could do nothing for the Indrawn Breath's other votaries. If she wanted to help them, and normal Rose likely would, she needed to find Lord.

Where was everyone? She had expected Breather succubi guarding the votary rooms, or at least charmed human soldiers. She peeked over a nurses' station as she passed, but no one hid under the desk. A long envelope opener shaped like a Musketeer's saber lay atop an inbox next to the computer. She took it—better a weak weapon than no weapon.

She started to press the down button on the elevator but paused, her finger hovering over it. The fear draw made her courageous, but it didn't have to make her stupid. Climbing into a steel box controlled by the Breathers was probably ill-advised, even if this place appeared empty aside from the insane.

Rose turned in a slow circle, looking first for surveillance cameras —she spotted one mounted on the ceiling just past the nurses' station —and then for stairs. The door leading down stood next to the elevator.

She could do nothing about the camera. If security had seen her leave her room, then so be it. The alarm was already tripped, but she had a feeling that wasn't for her. Otherwise, there would be guards. No, something else was happening here.

Rose cracked the stairwell door, ready should someone attack, but the landing before her stood empty. Distant gunfire echoed from below, a sound she hadn't heard over the blaring alarm. The acrid scent of gun smoke and burning plastic wafted into the hallway like old friends.

Rose bounded down three flights before a new thought struck her. She froze midstride, one fist gripping the handrail, mind racing.

"I'm not thinking straight."

She had a goal—destroy the fear factory—and it seemed sound. But was that the fear draw talking? Sure, it stole her votaries' courage, but it likewise stole Rose's caution. She felt no compunctions about taking on the Indrawn Breath. But shouldn't she? This wasn't like checking items off a grocery list. She stood on the verge of walking into a firefight dressed in a hospital gown, barefoot, and armed with nothing more than a letter opener. And that seemed perfectly reasonable to her.

Rose had stopped on the second-floor landing. The sounds of fighting echoed just below her. Muffled voices screamed orders and battle cries that reverberated up the stairwell. She stood still, listening for a count of thirty while she got her priorities straight. Then she descended the remaining steps at a walk, drawing hearing and discernment to complement her outrageous courage. Perhaps discernment could curb some of this fearlessness. She wasn't indestructible, and if she walked into someone's line of fire, her corpse would prove it.

The stairwell doors had no windows. Rose crept close to the one marked 1st. Crouched low, she flung it open, propping it with her foot so she could ease her head around the doorjamb for a quick look. She expected bullets to come whizzing her way and tensed to move, but none did.

The stairwell fed into a sprawling entranceway—a large open space bereft of chairs, couches, or tables but fronted by a wall of cracked and broken glass. Eighteen soldiers dressed in camouflage combat gear stood with their backs to her, facing the entrance. Rose saw at a glance these were regular humans, but they were laying down suppression fire for a wave of draw-enhanced succubi in black, who converged on the building's front doors, guns blazing.

Shadowy figures moved in the night just beyond the doors, lit now and again by bursts of muzzle fire. Discernment told Rose this had to be the Order on the attack.

She scanned the Breathers' line three times as they exited the building to face the Order advance. No David Lord. No Melody. Nonetheless, at least five of their number were polydraws, and likely fear-drawn.

The Order needed Rose.

Now.

She charged from her hiding spot, footfalls landing so fast they blended with the sound of machine gun fire. She took the closest human soldier from behind. He never sensed her. She plunged the letter opener into the gap below his helmet and above his flak jacket. She had his sidearm before he hit the floor.

The remaining human soldiers, advancing in a line now that the succubi had cleared the way, didn't notice the enemy in their midst until Rose had already dropped three of them. Body armor was only as good as its gaps, and the space between neck and ear was a major flaw.

One of the faster men had time to squeeze off five rounds in Rose's direction. Unfortunately for him, she had already covered the space between them before his finger tightened on the trigger, discernment having given him away. She barreled into him like a loaded barge, got her muzzle under his chin, and ended his lackluster attempt at taking her life.

With votary-borne speed, Rose slipped a combat knife from that soldier's belt, cut his tactical harness, and had his AR-556 pressed to her shoulder inside three seconds.

Twelve more seconds saw Rose eliminate the rest. She stood now in the fear factory's empty waiting area surrounded by dead men.

Dead at her hands. She knew that should mean something to her. Perhaps, when she dropped the fear draw, it would. Right now, for this version of Rose Carver, it meant victory.

A shift in sound from outside caught her attention. Though they were busy contending with Order ops—the remnants of the Dog Ears combined with whatever former Camp Den graduates had agreed to join them—the Breathers had finally noticed Rose's rear guard assault.

One, a woman, called for support, and two others joined her. They dashed back into the building, glass crunching under their churning boots.

Rose observed their approach longer than was probably safe, examining both the situation and her reaction to it. Her heart persisted in its steady rhythm, as did her breathing. Neither increased as fear-drawn enemies raced to kill her. She felt as calm as if she were watching a movie. Interested, but unconcerned.

Then she moved.

She bounded into the air, bullets ricocheting from the spot where she had stood only seconds before. One of the Breather women matched Rose's leap, trying to meet her in the air, but Rose had anticipated the move. Did the fear draw enhance her discernment? Or was the application of immense courage a panacea to distractions that would otherwise dull Rose's senses? She considered this as she flung a knife over her enemy's head.

The blade passed harmlessly above the Breather, who lifted her gaze to watch it sail past, a gloating smirk on her full lips.

Rose put three bullets in the woman's now-exposed throat.

As she had planned, Rose landed beside the fear factory's glass doors. Broken shards bit into her bare feet, but she healed them instantly. Good thing too, since one of the two remaining Breathers who had come after her had already reversed direction to confront her.

He lunged at Rose, wielding a combat knife with air-cracking speed. She barely had time to spin away, and even then, the blade bit into her shoulder high up near her throat. She grasped the man's wrist and was on the verge of crushing one of his kneecaps when the third Breather brought his rifle butt down on Rose's head.

She crashed into one of the building's doors with a sound like an exercise ball bouncing off a steel floor. Rose's vision darkened at the edges, and she found herself momentarily staring down a gray tunnel. She drew healing as she spun away from her enemies. She still felt no fear, only impatience.

The man with the knife stabbed at her again. Rose juked sideways, keeping her body at an angle to him. The strike meant to spear her heart instead jabbed her opposite shoulder. The pain was immediate, white-hot, and ultimately inconsequential.

Rose shoved her rifle into the man's side where his body armor split to allow for torso movement. She squeezed the trigger, and he jerked, his cry of pain and surprise cut short by the immediate collapse of both lungs.

Rose gave him a supercharged shove. He slammed into her remaining attacker who stumbled under the sudden dead weight, and the two fell in a heap. Rose trained her rifle on them and squeezed the trigger.

The firefight outside seemed to have gone as well for her comrades as the battle inside had for Rose. The sporadic gunfire of moments before ceased, and figures advanced on the building out of the dark. Rose backed away, careful to hold her rifle up and stand in the light. She didn't want to inadvertently get herself shot by her own.

The first person through the entranceway wasn't who Rose

expected, though with her fear draw she felt no real disappointment, only curiosity.

Piper Ross crunched into the fear factory, a wave of succubi, vampires, and wights at her back. Her auburn hair shone in the light, windblown and perfect. She wore a black t-shirt, what looked like yoga pants, and a pair of black running shoes. She smiled when she saw Rose.

"Hey there. We in time for the party?"

"It's a trap," Rose said.

The grin slid from Piper's lips. Her eyes became suddenly predatory as she swept her gaze around the massive entranceway. Others had joined her now, many of the succubi calling out greetings to Rose.

Piper motioned them to silence.

"How do you know it's a trap? Are there Breather soldiers massing nearby?"

Rose ignored the vampire's question. She didn't have time for it. "Where's Matt? For that matter, where's Hanks? She could confirm the trap."

"Hanks is back at our strongpoint. Matt didn't want her exposed to attack. As for him, I don't know where he is."

A brief chink opened in Rose's perfect calm. A hint of fear sizzled through her brain, down her back.

"What do you mean?" she asked.

"He volunteered to let the Breathers capture him so we could find this place—so we could find you. He was desperate."

"That didn't work for me. They found my extra tracking chip."

Piper nodded. "We know. That's why Matt had Stanislaw put one in that ruined knee of his. He hoped the bullets lodged in there would mask it. Far as we can tell, it did. That's how we found this place."

"Where are we?"

"Eisenhower Hospital, Fort Gordon, Georgia."

That made sense. Though Rose had been delirious with fear the last several days, she had noticed that her nurse, Thomas, and her other caretakers had all been uniformed soldiers. Then another thought hit her.

"You left South Carolina?"

"Yeppers," Piper said, grinning. "So, your boyfriend's plan had better work or me and mine are roadkill."

An explosion outside cut off whatever Rose might have said in response. Several of the wights still outside shrieked, blown apart by the sudden concussion.

"No!" Piper screamed. She started that way, but Rose caught her wrist.

"You can't help them. The best you'll do is get yourself killed. We have to move everyone further inside."

Piper hesitated, looking conflicted, but then nodded.

Rose and Piper fell back, urging the rest of their people to follow as the front of the building lit up with tracer fire. Someone was strafing the entire area with high caliber rounds and rocket-propelled grenades. The sound was deafening; the stench acrid. Flashes of white and orange light flooded the entrance, though the rounds never strayed inside the building. Anyone who hadn't managed to crowd inside during the first five seconds was dead.

Then the gunfire and explosions ceased. Silence fell.

Piper, her lips compressed into a line, looked at Rose. "We're right where they want us, aren't we?"

Rose nodded. She drew more courage, shrouding herself in it like armor. "It's what Lord wanted from the start: all of us in the fear factory."

30

FACES OF FEAR

Someone put a hand on Rose's shoulder in the press of Order ops, wights, and vampires. She spun, drawing speed and strength, ready to fight.

"Rose," Satterfield said, embracing her. "I can't believe you're on your feet."

Rose pushed her former squad leader back. "I'm fine. Have you seen Lord? Or my sister?"

Satterfield frowned momentarily at the rebuff but shook her head. She unslung her backpack and pulled from it a pair of Rose's jeans, one of her favorite t-shirts, a sports bra, and a set of running shoes with socks. "I figured you'd be wanting your own clothes, but I had no idea I'd be handing them to you in the middle of a siege. Otherwise, I would have brought Kevlar."

"These are fine." Without the fear draw, she would have been self-conscious dressed in a flimsy hospital gown tied over nothing but her panties. With it, she didn't care.

Satterfield gasped when Rose let the gown drop.

What was the big deal? Sure, a few of the guys stared, but so what? Trying to hide her nakedness wasn't practical. Case closed.

"Quit staring, you bunch of creepers," Satterfield said. "I swear, we're in a warzone, and you're interested in checking out a girl's boobs? Who raised you people?"

"Who's in charge here?" Rose asked as she finished pulling on her shoes.

"Watts!" Satterfield called.

The large incubus, who had been conferring with a couple of the original Dog Ears, trotted over. He looked haggard. Blood from a deep gash above his left eye had dried on his forehead. "Good to see you alive, Carver. How are you feeling?"

"Sane, if that's what you're asking," Rose said. "What's the plan?"

"Our original plan died five minutes ago. The Breathers knew we were coming. We figured they would react quick, but we'd have surprise on our side. We didn't. They surrounded us and, well, you saw the rest. I think more of us would have died if you hadn't taken out their rear guard."

"Is this all we've got?" Rose asked. She counted about three dozen Order ops, five vampires, and maybe fifteen wights.

"No," Piper said.

Sudden, brilliant light flooded the front entrance, cutting off Rose's reply. Hundreds of men and women dressed in combat gear and armed with M16s stood in rank upon rank on the sloping hospital lawn, cutting off the parking lot.

David Lord led the way, marching as if on parade. Melody, and Lord's supercharged master of discernment, Jim, flanked their commander, shoving Gunny Lipe and Myra Hanks, bound and gagged, ahead of them. Strunk brought up the rear, carrying an unconscious Matt over one shoulder.

Lord's group crunched their way into the building, the soldiers having halted about ten feet from the hospital's ruined entrance, weapons at the ready.

A wave of fear mingled with colossal charm boiled over Rose. She staggered under its weight. Fists trembling at her sides, she drew more courage, fortifying herself against the onslaught.

"Clench!" Rose screamed, drawing voice to amplify the sound. The word reverberated around the ruined entranceway. Unfortunately, it was already too late.

Order ops dropped to the floor, their weapons left to dangle uselessly on their tactical harnesses as they succumbed to the onslaught. Some wailed and cried, tears and snot glistening on their cheeks, while others groveled in the broken glass, cutting themselves and seeming not to care.

The vampires, however, including the wights, had no such reaction. The five daughters Piper had brought with her alternately watched Lord and his party while stealing glances at their mother. The wights stood like killer robots awaiting instructions.

"You're immune to fear and charm?" Rose asked.

"I knew succubus charm couldn't touch us, but I had my doubts about the fear. I've never run across it before." Piper smiled prettily as she spoke. "To tell the truth, it surprises the hell out of me. I thought for sure we'd feel something. Not that you'll hear me complaining."

Satterfield, who must have had the presence of mind to clench before Rose's ill-timed warning, looked grave. She placed herself between Rose and Lord, rifle shouldered.

"I won't lie," Lord said, "I'm surprised to see you up and about, Rose. Pleased, of course, but surprised. There's only one way that's possible. You're fear-drawn."

Satterfield's eyes skittered Rose's way. A look of doubt crossed her strained features.

Rose felt a thousand miles removed from everything happening around her. She saw no reason to answer Lord. He was right, but saying the words would upset her friends and allies. Why do that?

She turned her mind instead to the problem at hand. Logic insisted she sacrifice Lipe, Hanks, and even Matt. They meant little compared to the hundreds, possibly thousands, of people the Indrawn Breath had socked away in this hospital. Their deaths now might save millions in years to come.

If Rose attacked, given her depth and breadth of votaries, especially since the twins had released the *Drawn* anime a few days ago, she could kill Lord and Melody inside ten seconds. Even if the battalion at Lord's back engaged, they'd be too late. They were human.

Myra Hanks shook her head. Though gagged, her eyes implored Rose not to fight. Almost imperceptibly, she twitched her head at Jim.

Jim was a concern. Lord's prognosticator would foresee Rose's attack and likely thwart it. He had done so easily enough before. But the odds were different now. Rose's goals had changed. She would die to stop Lord and her sister.

A slow smile turned up the corners of Lord's mouth. "Oh, aren't we a piece of work, Rose Carver? I may not have the sort of discernment my pal Jim wields, but I can see the gears turning in your braincase. Woman, you're in ice-cold killer mode. You're ready to sacrifice us all."

Rose drew speed, stamina, strength, and dexterity. She didn't bother with discernment. Things would be as may be once the shooting started. She tensed to move.

David Lord drew the Ruger 9mm auto at his hip so fast, it seemed to materialize in his hand. It coughed once, and Gunny Lipe's head exploded. Blood and other matter sprayed across the glass-strewn floor.

The Order ops screamed en masse, writhing in abject horror.

"No!" Satterfield staggered back, her rifle forgotten in her hands, her face a rictus of terror and pain.

Rose's draw on courage snapped like a winter-dry twig. She sagged, and her knees nearly buckled. She only kept her feet because Piper caught her around the waist.

"Clench," Piper hissed in Rose's ear.

She did so, blocking the external fear and charm, but nothing could shield her from the horror bubbling up inside her. Witnessing Gunny Lipe's execution acted as a catalyst to ignite her fear, her shame, her stultifying realization.

Until a moment ago, Rose had been a fear-drawn monster perfectly content to sacrifice herself and everyone she loved to achieve her goals. That included every friend she had made in the Order, the man she loved, and even her own family.

"Quiet!" Lord shouted, and the Order ops fell silent. He turned to Rose. "I want you to understand. I mean business tonight." He pointed the 9mm at Hanks.

He's priming us.

The thought shattered through Rose's shock and horror. This had all been a ruse. All of it. Rose had walked into a trap, and she had led the Order in after her. The ones Lord hadn't captured when he took Camp Den now huddled inside his fear factory being primed to serve as votaries.

Her gaze fell on Jim. The slim incubus's draw on discernment must have been vaster than Rose could imagine. He had known this would happen all along. The bullet fragments in Matt's knee hadn't concealed his second tracking chip. Jim knew all about it and, therefore, so did Lord.

Myra Hanks, reading Rose's face at a level Rose would never experience, nodded.

"I could kill you, Rose," Lord said. "You and pretty Valerie and all your vampire bitch friends."

Piper tensed but said nothing.

"But Jim tells me you'll be more valuable to me alive. He says you're key to a quick victory over the world's Societies. You've already tasted the fear draw. Jim says, given time, you'll make an unparalleled general for our side."

"You knew I'd draw fear," Rose whispered.

"Sorry, darling," Jim said. "It was a foregone conclusion."

"Come without a fight, and I promise what's left of your people can go free," Lord said. "At this point, we don't need them."

Rose shook her head. Her brain burned—a million thoughts of escape blowing through it like sizzling leaves. None would work.

"Told you she wouldn't go for it." Melody grinned at Rose, obviously relishing the thought of a fight.

"You'll let them go?" Rose asked. "No fear factory. No torture."

"None," Lord said.

"Even Matt?"

"What are you doing?" Piper asked.

Lord's grin broadened into a smile. "Even Matt."

He motioned, and Strunk unceremoniously dumped Matt's inert form on the floor with a jarring thump. Strunk drew a pistol from his shoulder harness and pointed it at Matt's head.

Rose started to nod.

"No," Piper said. "I'm not letting you give up. I can't. If we lose here, the old guard vampires will kill my children. And if they can't, these bastards will."

"You were dead the moment you struck a deal with these traitors," Lord said. "Run home and be thankful I'm too busy to exterminate you now."

"We had a deal," Piper said to Rose.

"I can't let him put my people in the fear factory," Rose said. "We've lost. I've lost." She felt ashamed at hearing her own words, but she saw no other recourse. Wasn't it enough that she should give herself up to the Indrawn Breath? Did she have to get everyone she loved killed in the bargain?

Piper bore her teeth—her real teeth—a second row of fangs that unsheathed from her gums like tiger claws in her mouth. "You haven't lost. You've given up. What you need is a kick in the ass!"

Piper threw back her head and shrieked. The sound rent the air, shattering what glass remained in the building's front entrance.

Rose clapped her hands over her ears, though that did little to assuage the stinging pain in her overtaxed eardrums. And nothing whatsoever to stop the lance of fear that followed.

Wonderful. Vampiric fear on top of everything else. How come vampires got to be immune to succubus fear while Rose had to endure both? Sometimes, life really sucked.

The vampires and wights inside the building joined their voices with Piper's, emitting ear-piercing screeches of their own.

"What are you doing? You won't stop them this way. You're only delaying them." Even using a draw of voice, Rose could hardly hear herself speak over the cacophony.

And yet, somehow, Piper heard her. Without interrupting her wail, she nodded toward the soldiers outside.

Rose turned that direction just as a wave of wights and vampires crashed into the soldiers lined up outside. She blanched in horror. It was like staring into a meat grinder.

Guns fired. Men and women shouted. Blood flew. Hundreds of wights boiled into view from either side. They slammed into the humans, all fangs and claws, biting and rending, moving from victim to victim, seemingly unfazed by bullets, knives, or fists.

Vampires, all female, flowed amongst the wights like lithe shadows dealing a more refined form of death than their beastly siblings. They, too, threshed the battalion like wheat, but with a kind of grace and poise that transformed murder into something more akin to art.

Meanwhile, Piper continued screaming even as she launched herself at Jim. She moved with blinding speed and fetched the lean incubus a glancing swipe with her nails despite his attempt to evade.

He spun half around, one hand rising to touch the four bloody scratches on his throat. He stared at his blood-slicked fingers, his mouth agape, eyes wide.

Were vampires immune to succubus discernment too? Or was Piper just that fast?

Rose dismissed the thought. There was no time. In the havoc caused by the vampires, Myra Hanks had dropped to the floor, depriving Lord of his main hostage. Distracted, he hadn't noticed.

Rose shouldered her pilfered AR-556 and squeezed the trigger.

Melody kicked Lord an instant before Rose fired, pushing them apart, saving his worthless life. She rolled and came up firing her own automatic.

Satterfield dove into Rose, bowling her over, and cried out as bullets strafed her back.

Heart racing, Rose pulled Satterfield into a quick roll. She expected to feel hot blood pouring from her friend's wounds, but her Kevlar vest had done its job.

They scrambled to their feet. By unconscious agreement, Rose launched herself at Lord even as Satterfield squeezed off a half dozen rounds at Melody.

From the corner of one eye, Rose saw Piper attempting to get her hands on Jim, who successfully evaded her. Rose wondered if the discerning incubus could feel the half dozen vampires and wights scrambling his direction to aid their mother, or Myra Hanks now poised to kick at his knees.

Perhaps not, or perhaps they presented too many variables for the monodraw to overcome. Either way, Piper had her teeth in his throat inside five seconds.

At some point during her tumble with Satterfield, Rose had dropped her rifle. No matter. She had her votaries. She drew from them a vast ocean of strength, speed, and stamina.

Lord, who had likewise gained his feet, tried to raise his Ruger, but he wasn't fast enough. His eyes widened in shock when Rose knocked it away then chopped him across the throat with the knife edge of one hand.

She followed him as he staggered back, choking, and smashed his temple with an elbow.

He moved fast, trying to duck away, but his fear-drawn speed couldn't match Rose's legion of fans. She kicked him in the ribs and socked his jaw with a vicious uppercut.

Lord spun, pulling a knife from his jacket, intent on ramming it between Rose's ribs.

She saw it coming.

With a sound like a rifle shot, Rose crushed Lord's kneecap. He screamed, his momentum throwing him off balance. Rose twisted the knife from his hand, performed a spin, and sank the blade into his throat.

Lord's voice cut off in a strangled, gurgling gasp.

"NO!" Melody screamed.

Satterfield had her pinned on the floor, Melody's arms twisted painfully behind her back. Melody screamed again, incoherent this time, and wrenched her arms downward. Bones and joints snapped inside her arms and she grunted at the pain, but the move paid off. She spun at an impossible angle, her shoulder dislocated from her body, and kicked a surprised Satterfield in the face.

Melody kipped to her feet and raced toward Lord, her left side a deformed ruin. She seemed not to notice but dropped to her knees beside him, her expression devastated.

Lord was dead.

Melody lifted her gaze to Rose, and for just an instant, Rose saw her sister inside. Melody's draw on fear must have broken at the sight of her lover's demise.

"Mel." Rose lifted a hesitant hand toward her sister.

But as fast as it had come, the moment died. Melody's face grew still, the lines of shock and anguish drained away, replaced by cold, calculating malice. A rending, popping sound came from within Melody as she jerked her misshapen shoulder back into place, her wounds healing. She stood.

"I'm going to kill you."

"Melody," Rose said again, drawing charm without much hope. "Listen to me. I can help you overcome the fear draw. You can be yourself again. Come with me."

Without warning, Melody drew Lord's knife from his throat in a spray of blood and flung herself at Rose, the air cracking before it.

Myra Hanks, still bound and gagged, kicked Melody's shins, catching her at an angle. Melody lost her balance but managed to turn her trip into a roll that brought her up next to a bloody-faced Piper Ross. The vampire queen of South Carolina caught Melody's wrist and relieved her of the knife. Melody cuffed Piper with a left hook to the jaw. It sounded like someone hitting a steak with a baseball bat.

Piper reeled back, but smiled, displaying her two rows of pearly white teeth tinged with blood. A crowd of her children, wights and vampires alike, hissed behind her, their feral eyes marking Melody for death.

Rose saw the instant Melody realized she could not win. Though her sister's fear-drawn calm was absolute, a flicker of irritation crossed her face. No doubt, clear discernment told her she could not win this fight alone. Her lips drew down, twisted into a sneer. She met Rose's eyes for the barest of a second before bolting away from the vampires, just avoiding their outstretched claws. Her way clear, she dashed for the exit with the speed of a bullet.

Satterfield and Piper started after her, but Rose stopped them.

"Don't bother. You'll never catch her."

Rose bent over Matt. Despite the sound of gunfire and raucous battle, he still lay inert on the glass-strewn floor, his face pallid, his eyes swollen and dark. Rose pressed two fingers to the side of his neck.

"Oh, thank God," she breathed when she felt a steady pulse.

"Will he be okay?" Satterfield knelt near them, removing Myra's handcuffs and gag.

"I don't know. He won't wake up."

Sporadic gunfire and the sounds of men and women screaming caught Rose's attention. She wanted to stay with Matt, but the battle outside the hospital still raged. Flashes of muzzle fire periodically cut through the night, followed by the crack of high-velocity rounds.

Except, it was no longer a battle. It was a slaughter. Though the soldiers put up a game effort, focusing their fire against single targets at the command of their sergeants, their adversaries were too fast and too resilient to succumb to such tactics. A handful of Piper's wights lay broken and bloodied on the hospital lawn, having sustained too much damage even for their impressive healing abilities, but far more soldiers littered the ground. This was a battle of attrition, one the soldiers could not win.

"Stop them," Rose said. "It's over."

Piper, who stood watching her children in frank astonishment, made no move to comply.

"They've never fed like this," she said. "I've never unleashed them. Not even my daughters."

Rose stood to face the petite vampire. "Stop them! Those soldiers aren't part of this. You're murdering them!"

Piper focused on Rose, though turning her attention from the carnage seemed to require real effort on her part. The screams and gunfire continued for the space of ten seconds while the two stared at one another. At last, Piper nodded.

She stepped around Rose to stand in the hospital's ruined entrance. And though she said nothing, the vampires and wights ceased their attack. Those who were feeding, and there were many, released their victims to assemble before their mother.

"If you want to live, stand down!" shouted Rose to the soldiers, a handful of whom had gathered the nerve to pursue the vamps.

The order echoed across the lawn and was repeated again and again by those still alive. The soldiers threw down their rifles and huddled in groups, their wary eyes never leaving the vampires and wights gathered before them.

"What now?" Piper asked.

"You need to leave."

The voice caught Rose by surprise. She spun, her heart leaping in her chest, to find Matt leaning heavily on Tanner Watts, unsteady on his feet, but alert.

Rose kissed him, wiping tears from her cheeks. "When you didn't wake up, I thought…"

"I'm okay," Matt said, though they both knew he lied. His hands shook, and sweat beaded his forehead. He was fighting the last vestiges of whatever drugs Lord had dosed him with. Even with his powerful draw on healing, he would be some time overcoming that. "I need you to gather everyone who can walk and get out of here. Post security is charmed to ignore everything happening here, but that won't last. Sooner or later, this place will be swarming with Army MPs."

"Isn't that what we want?" Rose took his free hand and held it tight. "The more people who see the fear factory and what the government was up to here, the better, right?"

Matt nodded. "Up to a point, yes." He leaned close to Rose, his lips brushing her ear. "We need our people to think this is a major victory, but we don't know that yet. My father's still in charge of Society. He's powerful enough to sweep this under the rug. I don't want you here if that happens. We need some of our number to survive."

Rose jerked back from him, her eyes wide. What was he saying? They had won. It was over. Wasn't it? "But—"

"Please don't argue about this," Matt said. "The Order needs you."

"We can't stay either," Piper said. "Dawn is coming. We'll help you escape."

A siren echoed far off in the distance, growing closer. Rose continued to stare at Matt, her mind awash in conflicting feelings.

"It's the right thing," Matt said. "You know it is."

"My family is in here somewhere," Rose whispered.

"I'll see to them."

"I was supposed to do that." Rose couldn't fight the quaver in her voice.

"Yes, you were. But it won't matter if Society captures you. Take the ones who can run and go. I'll do my best to make so much noise, my father won't be able to cover this up. If that works, I'll see you in a day or two, and I'll bring your folks with me."

"And if it doesn't?"

"If it doesn't, you go on fighting. You and Piper bring Society to its knees. Break it before it can break the world."

Rose stared around at the succubi, most of whom only now rising to their feet. They turned forlorn and worried expressions on Matt and her, and though no one voiced a question, Rose could feel their expectancy. They wondered what they should do next.

She wanted to run like hell and tell them to do the same. But that sort of thinking had gotten her—gotten them all—into this predicament in the first place. They needed leadership, and they were looking at Rose to find it.

Could she abandon them after they had fought so hard to rescue her from the fear factory? No. She had led them here; she would lead them out.

Rose firmed her jaw and nodded, gratified to see many of them do likewise. Heart heavy, she gave Matt one last swift kiss. "You've got two days, Snow. After that, I'm coming to find you."

He smiled and squeezed her hand. "I'll be there."

Rose crunched across the glass and out the front doors, Piper at her side. Her people followed close behind, intermingled with Piper's many daughters. As one, they loped off into the darkness.

Rose didn't look back.

ABOUT THE AUTHOR

David Alan Jones is a veteran of the United States Air Force where he served as an Arabic linguist. A 2016 Writers of the Future silver honorable mention recipient, David's work spans the science fiction, military sci-fi, fantasy, and urban fantasy genres. He is a martial artist, a husband, and a father of three.

An eclectic reader, David counts Anne Tyler, Stephen King, Lois McMaster Bujold, Robert J. Sawyer, J.K. Rowling, and many others among his favorite, and most influential, authors.

You can find out more about David's writing, including his current projects, at his website: davidalanjones.net.

Want to know what's new

And coming soon from

Falstaff Books?

Try This Free Ebook Sampler

https://www.instafreebie.com/free/bsZnl

Follow the link.

Download the file.

Transfer to your e-reader, phone, tablet, watch, computer, whatever.

Enjoy.

www.ingramcontent.com/pod-product-compliance
Lightning Source LLC
Chambersburg PA
CBHW051650180726
48284CB00006B/1941